TRITON EXPERIMENT

ALSO BY PIPER J. DRAKE

London Shifters series

Bite Me, Sing for the Dead, Survive to Dawn

True Heroes series

Extreme Honor, Ultimate Courage, Absolute Trust

Total Bravery, Fierce Justice, Forever Strong

Safeguard series

Hidden Impact, Deadly Testimony, Contracted Defense

Stand alone titles...

Siren's Calling; Red's Wolf; Finding His Mark; Gaming Grace;
Evie's Gift; Keeping Cadence

TRITON EXPERIMENT

TRILOGY

PIPER J. DRAKE

For

those of us who continued to grow after the 932nd

CONTENTS

HUNTING KAT

BOOK 1

CHAPTER 1

"GIVE ME BACK MY BRA, you little tube rat, or I'll rip out your spine and steal your soul."

Scampering for the open door, he assumed he'd be fast, too fast for anyone to catch. And he would have been—if Kaitlyn had been human.

Lightning quick, she pounced, nabbing him by the scruff and bringing him to eye level. She bared her teeth in a silent snarl.

"You found him!"

The scrawny ferret squeaked, probably relieved at the sweet sound of salvation, as Skuld breezed in from the corridor.

The ship's engineer whisked him out of Kaitlyn's hand, and her bra fluttered free. The tiny marauder had dropped his loot. After catching the lingerie, she looked it over carefully. If those sharp teeth had done any damage to the lace . . .

"Sorry, Katy." Skuld tucked her pet into the front of her rumpled ship suit, raising the seal until only his furry face peeked out from her cleavage. "I was, um, working with one of the station engineers and Chester slipped out of his cage when we bumped into it."

Uh-huh. Skuld practically glowed, her cheeks flushed and hair tousled. She always wore her ship suit loose over her slight frame, the sleeves rolled up at the elbows, but this time the baggy legs had been hastily tucked into magnet-soled boots. Mingled with her usual scent of lavender soap and engine oil was a man's musk.

Considering the ferret's cage had been built of solid plasteel and doubled as Skuld's desk, they had to have bumped it hard. For the cage door to have opened, they would've been going at one heck of an angle. And Kaitlyn stopped considering any further because she *really* didn't want to know.

"He's lucky he didn't damage anything," she growled, letting the sound rumble from deep in her chest in a way no human could.

The perpetrator trembled in his bosom of safety.

"Aw, c'mon Katy. Chester wouldn't do anything intentionally. He thinks your stuff is neat." Skuld fluffed her soft, golden-brown waves. "Besides, why have fantastic lingerie when you never show it to anyone?"

Kaitlyn turned away and stowed the garment in the appropriate cubby. "I like the way it feels to wear it."

"You'd like the way it feels to let a lover take it off too." Skuld took up the familiar argument. "Slide the straps down your shoulders, unhook the back and let the cups fall away. Or maybe they could play with it on for a while, bite at you through the lace. You've got a great rack."

"Skuld!" For the love of klepto-weasels and big ships' engines, the woman needed to shut her mouth.

"You need to get boinked, Katy. Tumbled, screwed, whatever you want to call it." She tugged an oil-stained rag from a hidden pocket and slapped it against Kaitlyn's thigh. And damn but she made it sound easy—but then, Skuld had always been admirably comfortable with her sexual desires. "Okay, fine, when you first came aboard you had some issues to work through. And it took a while to ease into working with the guys."

"I had my reasons." The kind that gave Kaitlyn nightmares—waking and sleeping. Evils she could never forget because they were burned into her genetic code.

"It's been three years." Each word dropped like a stone. In her own way, Skuld had no mercy. "You can work with our people now and merc teams from other ships. You don't even flinch when strangers come aboard anymore." Skuld paused. When she spoke again, her voice turned gentle. "You've come a long way. You can hold your own and you deserve more than mission after mission, scouting and doing those impossible search and rescues." Skuld slapped the rag against her thigh again. "Now go out and get some."

"What makes you think I want some . . . whatever?" Kaitlyn folded her arms.

Raising her eyebrows, Skuld marched past Kaitlyn to the cubby and yanked out the black bra, then turned to wave it under her nose. "No one owns an entire collection like this unless they're thinking about sex or at least want to feel sexy." She swept her arm out to indicate the small medical bay and alcove serving as Kaitlyn's personal quarters. "You're effectively solitary unless someone is bleeding, burned, or full of holes. The rest of us get some interaction, get off ship and socialize. It's not healthy for you to be alone, and regardless of what you want the rest of the crew to believe, *I* know you don't want to be." Skuld pursed her full lips. "C'mon, give up the specs. What revs you up?"

"No—"

"Ah." Skuld cut her off, staring Kaitlyn straight in the eyes, heedless of how it engaged the predator in her. Probably because of it. "This is me, Katy."

Kaitlyn set her jaw and took a deep breath, reaching for patience or forbearance or whatever it would take to not rip her very clever, way too insightful shipmate to shreds. Only Skuld could harass her with immunity, constantly prick her temper and walk away unscathed.

"Okay, okay, I think about sex." There, an admission.

"With who?"

No one alive and kicking. Nobody since Katzer. "Haven't met a guy who interests me that way yet."

"I kinda thought you might be omnisexual since you react to just about everyone with the same level of intensity. But are you solely into men?" Skuld asked.

"Yes."

"Well, what kind of guy?" Skuld folded her arms across her breasts, making Chester squeak again. "You don't even notice the science personnel, so academic types must not be your thing."

"It's more about the lack of balance between intellectual and physical." Kaitlyn figured emotional development was a factor too, but she wasn't in a position to criticize anyone in that regard. "Brains or brawn, too much of either one and not enough of the other just isn't my thing. Pass."

"It's not like anyone would know how strong you are to look at you. You're just about my height and only a little bit curvier. And you don't talk enough for anyone to be intimidated by how much smart is packed into your head." Skuld wrinkled her nose. "You scare more people off with your 'come near me and I'll rip your face off' attitude than either of those things."

"Didn't keep *you* away. From day one you've popped right into my medical bay and stomped all over my personal space." Kaitlyn nodded to indicate the current situation.

"Well, I did pause for a picosec or two." Her brows drew together at the memory. "You stepped on board the first day, looking all dark and broody with all your long black hair and those deep brown eyes staring right through every one of us."

"Uh-huh."

Back then, Kaitlyn struggled to control her cat instincts, still new to the changes. Walking on board Dev's ship for the first time, without bolting or attacking his crew, took every ounce of control she'd had left.

"Then those others came aboard loading cargo and got nasty. When you dropped that spacer on the deck because he grabbed my hair, I figured you were badass." Skuld said, giving Kaitlyn a melting smile. "But badass with a protective edge. Call it instinct."

Kaitlyn grunted. "More like lack of survival skills."

Seeing the spacer try to hurt Skuld had flipped a switch inside Kaitlyn, giving her an outlet and a path of action. It still amazed Kaitlyn how little Skuld knew in the way of self-defense, but Skuld's position as engineer rarely placed her in combat or even off ship during missions.

Skuld shrugged. "We're talking about you here. Start simple, Katy. I know this is a stretch of verbal skills for you. What kind of man do you sweat for?"

"Fine." The image of Katzer's lopsided grin and rakish expression floated across her memory. No. He was gone. "I like a guy who looks good in uniform."

"Now we're talking. What kind of uniform?"

Kaitlyn shook her head. "It's not about the kind of uniform, it's about what it takes to wear it and make it something real. There's a difference between a person who looks good because they've got a uniform on and a soldier who makes the uniform look good."

And the thought of that kind of soldier made her blood heat.

Skuld looked ready to pull out a comp tablet and take notes. "It's pretty obvious you're not even going to notice a guy unless he's smart enough and strong enough to take you."

"I can respect a man who can hold his own."

"You don't need to say 'against you'—it's a given." Skuld grinned. "The other merc teams we coordinate with come and go. There's always at least one tough guy in the bunch, trying to make a conquest out of you or prove he's the better merc. You always shut him down. And then once he's beat, it's like he's ceased to exist on your radar."

Because he no longer represented a threat. "So?"

"You get along with every permanent member of this team because we've each got a talent you respect."

Truth. "And this applies to a guy for me how?"

"If it takes respect for you to live with us on ship, it'd take at least that for you to let a man into your bed. He's got to earn it." She paused, pursing her lips as if considering. "And no alpha asshole, either. You're moody enough for the both of you."

"Alpha asshole?" They turned to see Dev leaning in the doorway.

Kaitlyn had fallen silent at the sound of his approach. She absolutely refused to admit participation in this conversation to her captain.

"Kaitlyn gave up her specs on men."

Of course, Skuld would spill every detail anyway.

"And this unique condition enters in this how?" A grin

hovered around Dev's lips, just waiting to make an appearance. He stood there, dying to laugh right in her face.

"Can you imagine an overbearing, domineering jerk of a guy in combination with Katy? So not good for her. He'd have to be assertive and straightforward, but not an alpha-hole." Skuld rolled her eyes. "Has there ever been a guy who could make her smile?"

"Yes." He said it slowly, watching her. "At least one."

Too much history hung in the air between them. He'd been there, held her, as she stood at the comm the final time Katzer's voice crackled across the link.

Smile, Kitten.

Katzer had even made her smile through her tears before he'd gone offline in a soundless explosion in space.

First kiss, first love, first loss. There hadn't been anyone to call her Kitten since.

"Is it time, Kat?" Dev's voice brought her back to the present. He was using the personal nickname he'd given her as she grew into her place as one of his crew. He'd bled for her back then—earned the right to use it. "You ready to go looking for a smile?"

The deceptively light question had a world of comprehension behind it. He'd seen what she'd survived, knew how she'd been broken.

She lifted her lip in a snarl. "I'd sooner take a hole to the head."

"Well now, maybe you don't need a smile so much as a tad less aggression toward those of us of the male persuasion." Her captain held up his hands in a harmless gesture. He knew how to handle her, how not to antagonize the predator.

She dropped the snarl but lifted her chin in a sharp motion. "You getting too tired to handle it?"

Dev didn't move, but suddenly he filled the whole doorway. "I can handle you just fine, Kat. We both know it." She might be faster, stronger, but he was more experienced. He'd taken her down when she'd lost control, contained her before she hurt innocents. If she ever went feral, he'd be the one to help her back to human, again.

Satisfied, she subsided.

He relaxed into the doorframe once more. "A little work on your social skills wouldn't be out of place."

Kaitlyn watched him, wary. She didn't just owe him. He'd also proven over time he had a lot to teach her, and his comment clued her in to a pending attempt to add to her knowledge base. Shit.

Dev pushed away from the doorway, stepped into the room, and presented a data stick the size of Kaitlyn's pinky finger. "I've got a messenger run for you. It's for a person on Dysnomia Station who likes his privacy. Easy hand off, just be sweet and don't maim the nice man."

"You talk as if it's a given I'll want to." It might be, but she didn't like Dev making assumptions.

Dev only grinned. "Now, Kat, you got a true talent for violence anyone can appreciate—from a distance. In fact, you make it into the sort of thing they set to music on occasion." He *would* bring up the time she'd fought at his back in the middle of a formal ball. There'd been music, all right. A touch of steel threaded through his voice. "As your captain, I'm looking to expand your skill set into the negotiation and diplomacy areas. I know it's outside your comfort zone, but I do like to give you a challenge every now and again."

Also true. And okay, maybe she'd been more antagonistic towards men than necessary. She was wary around strangers in general, but her bias was obvious. It couldn't hurt to do a single messenger run and try not to scare the bejeebers out of the contact guy.

"Fine," she sighed, taking the data stick. "I'll play sweet and nice."

"Why not check in to one of the station hotels and spend a night or two off ship?" Skuld perked up as she made the suggestion and followed her words with action by grabbing one of Kaitlyn's duffels from under her sleep pallet and tossing lingerie into it.

"Oh no." Kaitlyn slapped the cubby closed before Skuld trotted out the whole collection for Dev to see. "I can do the messenger run and be right back aboard ship within a couple of hours max. That'll do me just fine."

"You do have a mighty backlog of R and R time you need to be taking, Kat." Dev peered over Skuld's shoulder to see into the duffel bag. "Those runs you take on the jungle planets after missions don't count as either rest or relaxation."

"Running through jungles and woods *is* relaxing." Absolute truth. Sometimes the wildness took hold and the only outlet Kaitlyn had was to shift to her panther form, burn off the energy in the kind of motion humans couldn't achieve.

Her beast rose up at the thought of shifting. Her paws driving into soft soil, muscles gathering, surging—

"You have relief for the clawed-and-fanged you." Dev conceded her point with a nod. He waited, watching, as she swallowed and got her composure back. "But you need to unwind for the human aspect. You need to be thinking about taking some real time away."

Whatever. She and her animal aspect preferred to run, hunt. "I'll think about taking leave after the next mission, maybe visit one of those resorts or something for quiet time." Kaitlyn shrugged.

She hadn't fooled Dev, but he let it go. "Messenger run goes at fourteen hundred hours station time." After turning to go, he tossed a parting comment over his shoulder. "In the meantime, I'm going to try to scrub the images of lacy bits out of my memory like a good captain."

CHAPTER 2

"LET'S go to Dissention Bar and hit up Syn for a few beers, maybe something stronger. I need to scrub the sight of your sorry ass out of my memory."

Lieutenant Christopher Rygard grunted in reply. DeSarto's grumbling tended to be mostly hot air anyway. With regret, Rygard changed into his only remaining uniform. The other set would take at least another full day cycle to get back from the cleaners, if salvageable at all. He'd have to make do. Regulations required his team stay in gear on Dysnomia Station, even off duty. Until he made the decision of whether to re-up, he wouldn't requisition another set.

A quick look in the mirror confirmed he'd pass cursory inspection. His dark hair, cut close around the sides and back, remained a touch long on top. His face had been cleaned up, the claw marks across one temple healing quickly under clear medical sealant. He'd have to shave in the next day or two, but the shadow across his jaw was still short enough to look well-kept. He didn't need a perfectly smooth jaw unless he was in formal dress uniform.

"C'mon, man, you planning on creating a crime scene tonight, or you trying to look pretty for the hell of it?" DeSarto threw a towel in his direction.

Rygard grinned and a line of white teeth flashed in the mirror. "Not looking, my friend, but I'll keep my options open."

In truth, he rarely fished for the kind of temporary companionship most soldiers indulged in off duty. Oh, he could have it easily enough, but those encounters left him feeling empty. Aside from the professionals and cybers, the Dear John communication he'd received before this past mission had soured him on trusting anyone enough for intimacy.

"Good. You need to move on and get your system running again. Find happy again."

Rygard chuckled. "Yeah, you pegged me. Mr. Happy."

He fell silent as he looked in the mirror and saw the other man's expression in the reflection. Compassion looked out from a dark, battle-scarred face, not soft but knowing. DeSarto had been present when the Dear John communication came in. The entire team had been there. Plenty of them had received similar messages of their own, all beginning with "Dear" and ending with "I kicked your boots to the curb." Centuries old, the messages had become a recurring bit of history in the service.

He'd met her between tours on a long stay home. She became the light in his life, made him happy. Her friends told him they'd never seen so much joy in her and all because of him. But reality kicked in when he'd returned to duty. Suddenly, she didn't think it so great to be a soldier's girl if he wasn't there to flaunt to her friends. Truth came out: she'd landed richer game long before she caught Rygard —a different mark located inside the solar system, sitting at a desk job. Rygard had only been a meaty side piece for the greedy leech.

She never returned the engagement ring he'd spent a year's pay on.

He sure as hell didn't want it back.

His team, they all knew what it did to a person. Shit, their unit specialized in the extremely dangerous and ridiculously impossible. They never knew their destination until they arrived or if they would return until they made it back. Each soldier went out on the next mission to purge the hate and leave behind the drama of civilian life. A mission had a specific objective and clear set of orders, letting them focus on the reason they enlisted in the first place—to protect and serve their planet and their race. Happiness would come and go with potential partners who loved the idea of a soldier but probably not the reality of loving one. The only sure thing for any of them? They never waited long for the next mission.

"I need a drink." DeSarto made the statement an imperative. "You need several. Let's get going."

Rygard stared into the mirror for another moment, noting the circles under his eyes and the pallor of his skin, then turned away. Funny how he'd left on the last mission looking to forget her. Instead, he'd piled on a mess of other issues. He looked like hell, and he thought he might deserve to be there.

"It doesn't bother you, man? What we did this last time out?"

DeSarto halted and a muscle jumped in his jaw. "We followed orders."

"There's orders, and then there were the direct orders. They had nothing to do with our original objective—"

"You going to question our CO?" DeSarto looked him

directly in the eyes. "In the field? Not me, man. I'm not going to call him on the extra cargo."

It wasn't the first time the missions had twisted, that side trips were added, commands given in the field that had less to do with strategy and tactics and more to do with monetary gain. What they'd done, under orders or not, had left a bad taste in all of them. None of the soldiers looked each other in the eye on the jaunt back to Dysnomia Station, and every man immediately hit the showers to wash the blood of innocents from their hands.

Rygard slammed his fist down on the dresser. Too much greed in the damned universe. A person couldn't trust anyone or anything, not even his own gut.

What he needed to do was hit the bar and find oblivion at the bottom of a glass. Maybe then there'd be room in his head to make the one immediate decision looming in the next day.

"Rygard, man, you think too hard."

True fact.

THE LOWER LEVELS of Dysnomia Station were only well lit if the denizens were willing to spend the cred. None of them were. Corridors curved and crossed, then curved again, creating an elaborate labyrinth of gloom and flickering auxiliary glow strips.

A human might have been intimidated—the shadows an effective deterrent to those who didn't belong. Kaitlyn knew better.

A controlled shift had taken her years to learn, but it proved a useful trick to change only her eyes to cat physiology. She knew from experience they remained brown while the shape of her irises morphed into slits. She even formed the nictitating membrane in each eye, helping her protect her eyes from dryness or damage. Most importantly, she gained much better visibility in low light conditions.

Darkness provided cover. It made prey easy to stalk. The corridors held no secrets from the panther side of her. In fact, they remained suspiciously clean. The random piece of trash or crumpled beverage can lay on the floor, but there was none of the disgusting refuse indicative of a true slum. She smelled rancid sugar, carbonated beverages that had spilled and been allowed to spoil, and the unpleasantly ripe odor of unwashed bodies. Yet the circulating air flowed clear of the scents of fear, violence, and death or sickness. These halls held no threat, and the denizens weren't likely to be one either.

She stalked toward unit 141-I, confident she was the top predator in the territory.

Kaitlyn came to a stop, pausing to flick a thoughtful look around the doorway. The danger wasn't of the simple, direct, stab-you-in-the-back nature. It had more technological savvy, elegance. She stepped into the blind spot of the micro surveillance camera and presumably the safety zone from the laser threads installed around the entryway.

"State your name, purpose, and ship of origin." A tiny hologram of some sort of nematode floated where a normal person would have stood.

Kaitlyn couldn't help a faint grin. The little squirmy had a shock of red hair and was wearing a blue ascot. For an invertebrate, he was kind of cute. She wanted to bat at him with a paw to see if the hologram responded. "Kaitlyn Darah. Messenger run for Captain Devron Rishkillian."

Their ship had no name. They flew a mercenary vessel, after all. Sometimes it benefited them to come and go without everyone taking note of their conveyance.

"Security passed." The itty-bitty worm tilted his head to the side. "Come inside, have a cup of brew."

The door slid open with a *whoosh*, and her nose flooded with the richly sensuous smell of coffee—not the mud they usually served in station commissaries. Her nostrils flared. She tasted the air a second time. No, not the cheap stuff. The scent of properly roasted beans, freshly ground, greeted her.

Whatever wack message run this turned out to be was worth it to find a source of good coffee.

"Whoa . . ." A heavyset man rotated on a motorized chair to face her, pushing magnification goggles away from beady, close-set eyes. He blinked twice while awkwardly leaning forward to study her. "You don't look like a merc. Dev's team is supposed to be leet."

Uh-huh. And a nerd on servos would know what it took to be elite?

Kaitlyn crossed the room.

Nerd boy watched her approach. Not in fear, but shrewd assessment. "Speed, plus two. Agility, plus two. Appearance, definitely plus five. Intimidation, minus two— even with the visible boot knives and combat knife." He pulled the goggles off his broad forehead and began to clean them with the hem of his shirt. "Ever consider laser- or sonic-based firearms? Maybe ballistics?"

Her temper flared. "You want intimidation?" She shot a hand out, caught his throat, and lifted him by the jaw until he hung a few inches above his seat. Glaring, she let a growl rumble up from her chest, then bared her teeth, the canines elongated to sharp fangs. "How's this?"

Eyelids blinked over dilated pupils, and calloused fingertips scrabbled against her grip. "K-kick-ass factor, plus five. Overall hawtness, plus ten."

Kaitlyn let him down with a thump. The motorized chair creaked with the sudden return of his body weight. She had partially let him go because he gave off no scent of fear—only excitement and a touch of arousal. He made no flailing or sudden movements to incite violence from her predator side, no threatening gestures or attempts to pull a weapon. He wasn't making any attempt to hurt her. Okay, maybe a little creepy, but he meant no harm.

Also, he was technically her client.

"I'm Kaitlyn," she offered, feeling awkward. Dev had wanted her to practice her people skills. It might be a tad belated but hell, better late than never.

"Kaitlyn Darah, I know." Nerd boy massaged his throat with a rueful scowl. "I'm Boggle. Dev said you'd be impressive. I'm so rarely impressed anymore."

He turned his chair to a counter and grabbed two steaming beakers. One sloshed when he shoved it in her direction. She hesitated, looking at the dark liquid. By smell, it was the source of the lovely coffee aroma, but why the hell serve good stuff in a freaking beaker?

"Go on." Boggle sloshed it a bit more as he waved the beaker back and forth. "It's just coffee."

"Thank you." Gingerly, Kaitlyn took it, specifically not allowing a touch, so there wasn't a chance of misinterpretation with even accidental contact. "Sorry if I hurt you."

She wasn't sure why he was in need of mobility assistance. Medical science and technology could repair most damage humanoids encountered, so whatever kept him in a chair was serious. A twinge of guilt hit her as she thought about how she'd dropped him right back down into his seat.

Boggle waved a hand. "Degenerative issue in my spine. By the time I made enough credits to afford treatment, it was only enough to stop progression of the condition, not reverse it. I've made my peace with it. How's the coffee?"

Another deep whiff almost had her eyes rolling into the back of her head, and she couldn't wait any longer. She took a slow sip.

Heaven.

"Oh yeah." She came back to herself to see Boggle watching her. His grin transformed his face into boyish glee. "You're the perfect anthropomorphic. Everything about you screams cat."

She'd been purring. So long aboard ship, surrounded by shipmates who knew what she was, she'd lost her caution. The coffee turned bitter on the back of her tongue. Dev proved right again—she needed to get out more, keep her guard up and her attention sharp. She placed the beaker on the counter. "Glad you enjoyed the freak show." She took the data stick out of the pouch attached to her thigh. "Here, message delivered. I've got an experiment to get back to."

She turned, but Boggle zipped forward. "Wait!"

In a flash, Kaitlyn leaped on top of the chair and balanced the balls of her feet on the armrests. Her face stopped a breath away from his, and her hand gripped his throat again, a fraction of a second away from maiming him. She didn't lift him this time.

A rush of arousal filled the air. Gross. She hadn't scared the piss out of him, she'd pushed him into a money shot. *Oh, ewww.*

Dev was a dead man. Improve her social skills, her ass.

She jumped back, landing lightly, with a strong urge to wash her hands.

"S-sorry," Boggle breathlessly apologized, his voice turned earnest as he rushed to continue. "I wanted to meet you. I'm sorry. But you're magnificent, a perfect blend of visceral instinct and cold efficiency. I know everything there is to know about your history. The Triton Moon Base incident, your capture. I have the details on your virus and genetic code—I even pulled all of your old school records. I have analytics on every mission you've been on."

Jeezus, if this represented Dev and Skuld's idea of a matchmaking attempt, they were both dead.

Boggle held up both hands. "I'm definitely not your type, too much invested in my cerebral stats as opposed to well-rounded, and that's fine with me. I just . . . I wanted you to meet me."

Kaitlyn paused. Just meet? She shifted her weight from one foot to the other, poised to move, but undecided.

He looked around frantically, then reached over to a console and pulled up data. His fingers flew across the terminal with a speed and delicacy that rivaled a Terran hummingbird.

"I'm an information specialist—a hacker, of sorts. I retrieve intel on every mission for Dev and conduct client assessments," Boggle babbled, sweat beading at his forehead. "I wanted you to have direct access to me if you needed any help along those lines. You need connections independent of Dev. You need to develop a network of informants and contacts for the future. I wanted to be the first. I can support you better than anyone else out there and I'm not afraid of what you are."

Obviously not. Prey rarely went out of its way to come

face-to-face with her. Strangely, the more he spoke, the less inclined she felt to leave.

She knew through a hundred unconscious tells if a person lied. Body language, eye movement, heart rate and breath. Scent provided another tell to her panther's nose.

Boggle told the truth. Not many people did.

"I'm creeped out by you." Her tone was flat, harsh. She suffered another flash of guilt. Probably not a normal thing to say, or nice, but she would be honest too.

His entire bulk shrank in on itself, but a smile trembled above his double chin. "Look. I know how people look at me. And I've come across badly with all the wrong signals. You're the first flesh-and-blood person I've risked meeting face-to-face in years." He swallowed loudly, his tongue slipping out to lick his lips. "I know you have trouble with the social skills too. I figure we're even there. You deal with me, I'll deal with you. No pressure."

Kaitlyn paused, holding perfectly still as she considered. He had a point. Several actually. They did have common ground between them, sort of. If she looked past the perverted tendencies, he had been up-front and was fundamentally a good person. Her gut told her so.

Besides, people usually made her wary or tempted her to hunt them. Boggle was just Boggle. Neither threat nor prey.

Yeah, no, that line of thought wasn't what a mainstream person would follow either. *Oy.*

Decision made, she stepped back into touching range and held out a hand.

His grin returned—a look of pure delight. He wiped his hand on his pants and shook hers, the touch only slightly sticky.

"So." He looked over to his console. "I've got your first bit of intel."

She waited. He sweated.

"And?" she finally prompted.

"Don't hit me."

She chuckled, the unaccustomed sound clumsy in her throat. He apparently *did* know her. "I won't."

She decided she should make an effort not to act out in violence toward him anymore. She hadn't exactly treated him with consideration in her initial interaction either. She'd try to better moving forward.

"Dev's ship undocked and left the station the minute you cleared the air locks. They're gone."

CHAPTER 3

"CAPTAIN MUST THINK HE'S HILARIOUS," Kaitlyn fumed, striding into the hotel lobby. Boggle played the message on the data stick for her once he broke the intel. Dysnomia Station had several establishments to choose from, and the communication from Dev indicated a two-night reservation for her here. A higher-level place, catering to those who could afford luxury.

The young man behind the counter didn't look capable of handling an enraged customer barging into the foyer. His eyes widened and darted to the right and left without meeting her glare. His scent carried the acrid tang of fear. "M-may I help you, Miss?"

His hand probably hovered over the security alarm.

She took a steadying breath. This aggression toward males in general had been part of the reason Dev and Skuld set her up. Social skills—she needed to remember those, even if she didn't need to worry about them with Boggle. Besides, she had a heart. Taking her temper out on an innocent bystander held no appeal, not when she could shred the two culprits once the ship came back into port.

Forcing her brows to relax and her lips to smooth out of a snarl, Kaitlyn slid her wrist ident under the scanner. It beeped softly, likely inaudible to human ears.

"Ah yes." The young man's face cleared in relief. "Miss Darah."

He tapped a few icons on his display. "Your wrist ident is programmed with the access code. Please proceed down the hall to the elevators. You're on the nineteenth level, room thirty-six."

She gave him points for recovering. Modulating her voice, she managed a moderately pleasant, "Thanks."

Entering the room, she took a quick survey of the sumptuous king-size bed and full bathroom. Dev and Skuld had gone all-out. A message notification blinked from the console in the sitting area.

"Now Kat, we know you're mad." Dev's image materialized on the holoprojector, his expression stone-cold blank except for the slightest twitch at the corner of his mouth. He wasn't even trying to look repentant, the jerk. She wondered what the penalty would be for killing her captain. It might be worth it. "But consider this a deception for the greater good."

"I'll keep up the training sessions with Chester in your place so your communications experiment won't fall behind schedule." Skuld's image popped up over Dev's shoulder. "Find yourself some smart, fit specimen in uniform and take him for a tumble!"

Dev made a shooing gesture, the holo flickering in response. He must have decided to wrap up the message before Kaitlyn got well and truly worked up into a rage. "Back in two days. Your message is delivered, so take some R and R. That's an order."

The holoprojector darkened. The sneaky bastard.

What in hell was she supposed to do for two days? And no. She refused to follow Skuld's directions.

And how was Skuld going to simulate the communications training Kaitlyn had wrestled into the tube rat's tiny head? Visions of borked terminals and spontaneously combusting circuit boards flashed before her eyes. The ferret's havoc would give Skuld repair work for weeks. Course, considering this bit of misguided scheming, she had it coming to her.

Kaitlyn turned to study the duffel bag sitting at the foot of the bed. Sighing, she unsealed the seam and peered inside.

Yup. Nothing but lingerie, a sleep shirt, and one change of clothing, for two more days. She cursed and sent the bag flying into the far wall.

Damn it. She needed a drink.

PUT ENOUGH Terran military in a bar full of mercenaries and someone was going to have an issue. Rygard sat off to the side, nursing his latest drink while keeping an eye on the casual insults being traded around the room. Except for a small herd of technogeeks in a private corner, the entire establishment bustled with a sea of servicemen and mercs.

A few honest working people and cybers wove through the tables, offering what wasn't on tap. There was a flavor for every taste—pretty boys, sensual ladies, alluring androgynes, the rough and rugged, and more. The professionals, at least, could be trusted about what they wanted in exchange for the services they offered; they weren't out to tie a person up into a lifetime of one-sided commitments.

Several other civilians flitted from soldier to merc like butterflies, offering equal distraction without the associated price tag. Those were the ones for whom sex wasn't a career. Instead, they used their appeal to lure soldiers and mercenaries alike, latching on in search of a long-term standard of living. When Rygard brushed off yet another inviting hand, DeSarto shook his head.

"You're like a magnet, man. Why deny your charm?" He knocked back the last of his drink and signaled for another while craning his neck to eye up a passing lady. DeSarto was popular too, with his ebony skin and good-natured laugh. He had a way of putting others at ease with his presence. "Enjoy the good life."

Rygard grunted, not ready to have his spirits lifted.

Beautiful people—those butterflies—floated around the bar with expensive silks and sparkling accents, every word they whispered as artfully intended to ensnare a person as their painted eyelids and crimson-stained lips. What those butterflies took from a person like him cut deeper than creds from his account and left behind scars on his soul, not just his skin.

Rygard shook his head. "Maybe I don't see what I'm looking for yet."

"Well, you keep looking, my man. Maybe try someone different from your past type, get out of your comfort zone. Maybe have a threesome, or a foursome. Hell, five if you can find that many people you've got chemistry with here tonight." DeSarto shoved away from the bar with a stumble. He took a second to right himself, then staggered after the woman who had snagged his attention. "I'm going to go get some. I'll let you know how it goes. Ha!"

Hard to cut a man if he anesthetized his heart with copious amounts of alcohol.

The woman would trigger an issue. Rygard knew it right away. That particular butterfly had flitted from a pack of mercs, where she'd been leaning against the shoulder of the largest muscle-for-hire, and now stood at the bar to order a drink. Yet the smile she gave DeSarto as he came sniffing around definitely communicated a come-hither.

Butterflies and dogs. Regardless of gender or orientation, people did the damndest things to each other.

Rygard signaled for another drink when the fight broke out. The bulldog merc from the table had finally noticed his missing butterfly. DeSarto moved in, fondling the goods with irreverent hands while she did the same in return. A couple of words, some grunts, and an angry bellow sparked the conflict. When several mercs from the table joined in, a couple of servicemen came to DeSarto's aid on principle. His friend held his own without issue, even seemed to dive in with enthusiasm, so Rygard continued to enjoy his drink.

"This gets much bigger and I'm calling security." The bartender kept a practiced eye on the brawl as it escalated. More servicemen and mercs jumped into the fray. The bar had been built sturdy, the furniture fused into the floor. Firearms were locked away in storage at the entryway, limiting fights to hand-to-hand combat.

"Give it another minute, Syn." Rygard lifted a chin toward DeSarto. "He's about to take down the main opposition."

A new commotion started at the entryway. Even the technogeeks in the corner stirred from their holo-game to peek over the booth and get a good look.

Mercs and servicemen alike fell like downed logs. It took a minute for Rygard to see what cleared a path through the minefield of fighters, and when he did, he wondered if he'd had one drink too many.

Lightning quick, a little package of curves dodged a drunken punch, grabbed a merc's arm, and used her momentum to send her over a table. The newcomer brushed dark waves of hair out of her eyes before planting a hand in a serviceman's back, helping him into a pile of his friends. Two other servicemen focused enough to rush her, but crouching low, she delivered a powerful leg sweep. A sharp elbow to the sternum rendered each of them out of commission. Straightening, she continued her course, heading directly for Syn and the bar. By the time she made it, unconscious and groaning people lay in her wake. Her left hook was a thing of beauty, and she had a wicked right slant kick.

The intensity of her feral glare seared through Rygard as she passed, moving on when he didn't offer any threat. Had he ever seen such fiery brown eyes before? Carnelian, almost. She chose the very last stool and sat with her back to the wall. When she ordered a Scotch, he thought whatever gods of chance were out there had given him the perfect common ground with her. Same drink of choice.

Syn placed a glass of amber in front of her. "On the house. You saved me the trouble of calling security."

Rygard chuckled. People picked themselves up off the floor, and it seemed they'd forgotten the whirlwind who had passed through them. A wonderfully mind-numbing thing, alcohol. They probably wouldn't want to remember they'd gotten their asses handed to them by a pint-size explosion of sexy anyway.

Well, maybe they would.

He watched her swirl her Scotch, inhaling slowly before taking a long sip. When she set the glass down, it became obvious she would need a refill in short order.

Without lifting her face, she glanced up, her fierce gaze

locking on him through a dark veil of thick, long lashes. He realized he'd better say something or she might take offense at his regard.

Lifting his drink, he nodded. "Mind if I buy you another?"

KAITLYN STUDIED the man for a beat before the question popped out. "Why?"

He blinked, caught without a response. Not what he'd been expecting, probably. The light from the bar top caught the gold highlights in the man's hazel eyes. Not a pretty boy, which she actually preferred, his features too strong for the beautiful-boy-toy look and his build too massive. His white complexion was ruddy from time spent planetside. Terran military, by uniform. Skuld would call him ruggedly handsome, with the stubble across his jaw and his barely regulation haircut.

He shrugged. "You look like you could use one, or more."

True. Before she could answer, he left his stool and walked toward her. A fighter, and a fast one, despite the bulk suggested by his expansive chest and shoulders. She didn't mistake the potential in the way he moved. Unlike the rest of the people in the room, he wasn't inebriated to the point of slowed reaction time.

He also seemed aware of her assessment, holding his

hands out to his sides in a sign of "no threat" as he sat on the stool next to her. His gaze never left hers. The challenge he offered had nothing to do with a fight and everything to do with her.

"Maybe." She couldn't think of anything else to say.

He smiled, the flash of white almost predatory. "Maybe usually means yes."

"Maybe means maybe," she snapped. She didn't like word games.

Dark eyebrows shot up, and those hands opened wide again. "Okay, maybe." He shifted to lean on the bar, not closer to her but not farther away either. "Let me know when maybe turns into a yes or a no."

Despite her ire, she felt a smile tugging at the corners of her mouth. The soldier exuded a familiar charisma, an attitude she hadn't encountered in a long time. Not since Katzer.

And wasn't that a funny kind of ironic?

She drew in a long breath.

Anger, fear, joy, arousal—all the strong emotions diffused through the air. The scents gave hints her panther aspect could read. They told a story. He carried them all, faint and faded with the passage of time, but enough to catch her attention. And over it all, a pleasantly masculine musk blended with the smooth aroma of Scotch.

Well, Dev and Skuld *had* effectively marooned her on the station for two freaking days. No use chewing on useless thoughts and wasted experiments. She could spare the time for a second drink. Besides, a long-forgotten part of her wanted to see what the soldier would do next, was curious about him.

In the days before the attack on Triton Moon Base, she'd never made time to flirt. Only Katzer had caught her up, made her curious enough to pay attention. And their time together had been a stolen kiss and a promise that ended with his death.

They'd been young and he'd died before his time. So had a lot of others.

She finished her drink in a smooth pull. Too many ghosts haunting her lately. Carefully setting the glass down, she looked over to see the soldier watching with appreciation and approval.

"I guess . . ." What the hell did normal women say? "Yes?"

"Sorry, can you repeat that?" He turned completely toward her, leaving himself open as he leaned in closer. "I didn't quite hear you."

For the first time in years, a male's proximity didn't set off her temper or cause a spike of fear. Instead, her pulse quickened in a few uneven skips and heat rushed to her face. Kaitlyn turned to look at her empty glass. Damn it. People did this all the time. She could speak, really, she could. "Yes, you can buy me another."

Silence. She peeked up. He grinned, a twinkle in his eye. Without taking his gaze off her, he jerked his head at the bartender and tapped her glass. "The lady will have another, on me, and I'll have the same."

She took the reprieve to focus on the bartender as she thanked him for the drink. The bartender looked from her to the soldier and then back at her. A slow smile pulled on one side of his face, and he simply said, "You let me know if you need anything else."

Great. Even the bartender found her amusing. Skuld and Dev would probably have paid to see what transpired. In fact—Kaitlyn shot a careful glance around the bar area—

she wouldn't put it past them to pay for the surveillance feed. Fantastic.

"You going to drink it, or warm it up in your hands?"

Heat rushed across her cheeks again. His voice sounded pleasingly smooth and a touch light, considering his heavy build. He must have been younger than most soldiers she'd encountered on the edge of the solar system. Like the Scotch, his voice hadn't yet taken on the smokier tone that came with age. After lifting her glass, Kaitlyn took another sip, letting the mellow hint of toffee spread across her tongue. She liked the flavor better without the extra years.

His smile flashed readily, and the spark in his eyes turned from amused to wicked in a picosec. "Mind if I have a sip while I'm waiting for mine?"

He caught Kaitlyn without words again. She started to slide it over, sure he noticed the flush of her heated cheeks or some other tell betraying her interest in him. He met her halfway. Warm and strong, his hand closed over hers, then he lifted the rim to his lips as her skin tingled under his light grip. She could have snatched her hand back, but she would've dropped the glass.

She turned her head away again, sure he'd laugh at her awkwardness.

Instead, he leaned a touch closer after he'd had his sip. His proximity burned all along her side, the heat of him seeping right through her uniform. One arm on the bar and the other along the back of her chair, he effectively bracketed her, and every nerve vibrated with anticipation, not fear or aggression. What was he doing to her?

"Normally, people suffer bodily damage for getting this close to me." The words popped out before she could filter them. She cringed inwardly. Definitely not something a normal person would say, especially if she wanted him to hang around.

He choked out a laugh. "I can believe that."

She looked up, surprised when he didn't move away. The intensity of his gaze met hers with enough force to steal her breath.

He leaned in until he hovered a whisper away from her cheek. "Am I going to suffer bodily damage?"

His voice did naughty things to her. Kaitlyn swallowed past the catch in her throat. She needed to find some of the metal usually strapped to her spine and reinforce it or she might melt right there, in the curve of his arms. Tilting her head to one side, she let her hair fall in a curtain between them. "Maybe."

She felt his smile against her hair. Just when she thought the tension would kill her, he backed away—not far enough to open up the bracket he'd formed, but he'd given her space.

She sucked in air as if she'd been held underwater. Then she took another long sip from her glass. Things fuzzed into a pleasant blur after another minute or two. Good Scotch took the edge off a girl.

"Before I risk excruciating pain, do I get a name? I'll want to tell my medic where the damage came from." His words came out light but held a stronger note than curiosity.

"K-kaitlyn . . ." she stuttered as he gently brushed her hair away from her face, his fingertip running along her cheek. She kept her eyes fastened on her glass of Scotch. "Kaitlyn Darah."

"Kaitlyn." He more than said her name—it was as if he tasted it, savoring the way the word formed in his mouth. "I'm Chris Rygard. Or just Rygard."

Now there was something she could focus on.

"Lieutenant Rygard." She jerked her chin towards the epaulets on his shoulders. "Commissioned officer."

He didn't get arrogant the way most officers did, only nodded. A fact, nothing more and nothing less. She liked him better for it.

As if she needed more reasons to like him.

"I'd rather you leave off the rank." He raised one eyebrow as he held out his drink to her.

Hers proved empty again. Fancy that.

She risked lifting her head and instantly regretted it, her face passing too close to his mouth. Needing fortification, maybe to restart her pulse, she reached for the proffered glass. Instead of passing it to her, he held it closer until the complex aroma of the Scotch filled her nose. Hesitantly, Kaitlyn rested her fingertips over the back of his hand as she took a sip. Electricity zinged all the way up her arm.

She wanted more, wanted to rub against him and feel skin against skin, purring the whole time. Confused, she took a hefty gulp, the Scotch burning down her throat and into her lungs. Better the burn than the mistake of purring again.

"How long have you been a merc?"

She blinked at the question, absently running the tip of her tongue over her bottom lip as her mind tried to catch up.

Rygard chuckled. "Do it again, sweetness, and I can think of a lot of things I could do to your lower lip."

"Only the lower one?" Now where had those words come from? Didn't matter; she'd finally delivered a good comeback.

He only grinned, his focus on her mouth.

Kaitlyn cleared her throat, biting the lip in question. Suddenly, her mind filled with thoughts of what it would be like if he kissed her. Which would be a train wreck. It'd been a long time since she'd kissed, and she probably sucked at it, abysmally.

And wasn't that a buzzkill? Still, she rallied, squaring her shoulders and lifting her chin. She didn't take the opportunity to widen the space between them.

"A few years." There, she'd finally managed to answer one of his questions with something other than a maybe or a stuttering mess.

"A few years is a long time for a merc." He said it as if it were fact.

She shook her head. "My captain's been a merc a couple of decades. I've got plenty of time to be me."

"That so?" He tilted his head to one side. Damn, even if she ducked, he would see her blushing now. "And what are you?"

Loaded question, and he didn't even know it.

"A lot of things." She should have gotten defensive. Normally, she shut down, usually walked away. Instead, she sat there feeling giddy, a smile tugging at her lips and a suspiciously bubbly sensation forming in her gut. Like she'd turned eighteen all over again.

She was enjoying herself.

Skuld would never let her forget it.

FASCINATED, Rygard continued to watch her. Beautiful Kaitlyn Darah presented so many contrasting shades, he didn't know where to begin. He only knew he wasn't going to leave the bar without her if he could help it.

Sleek and black, her merc's uniform fit her luscious curves like a second skin, her movement not impaired in any way. He'd seen the fluid speed she possessed when she'd plowed her way through the bar brawl. The harnesses she wore across her shoulders and thigh were high quality. The combat knives he could see matched the kind his unit used. He bet she had boot knives too, and maybe a couple of hidden blades. Gear of such quality spoke of a successful mercenary.

Seasoned, profitable mercenaries capable of wreaking the kind of damage he'd seen, just to get to a glass of Scotch, did not sit tucked up on barstools blushing like schoolgirls. But here she perched, sleek as a cat and cute as a kitten.

"Where are you staying?" He wanted to be able to find her, needed to know if she wanted him to.

Her cheeks flamed and her chin dropped at the question, a few locks of dark hair falling across her face. She stuttered again over the name of the hotel, an expensive place, and a damned sight better than the tight quarters he shared with DeSarto.

"And you don't have any place to be after this?" Hard to fathom someone like her not having plenty of options for her evening, but then, hard to believe she was even real. So different from the brisk and efficient professionals or the garish butterflies floating around the bar.

She really was a lost soul, having wandered in for a drink.

She shrugged, and her lips twisted into a wry grin, reminding him she was a down-to-earth mercenary despite the sweet face. "I piled up too much unused R and R. My captain left me here with direct orders to have a little fun."

She might not have realized she'd given him the opening, but he seized it. "I think I can help you with that fun."

Those big brown eyes blinked at him. Her lips parted, but no words came out as he caught her speechless, again.

He almost groaned. His cock had been straining in his pants for what seemed like forever. Damn but he wanted her, and he didn't want lightly—not with the scars he had in his memory.

"Last call." Syn cleared their empty glasses. "You two want another round before I close up?"

Little Kaitlyn nodded, and the bartender poured her another Scotch. Rygard had to give it to her. She'd drunk enough to put a body twice her size under the table, and yet her hands remained steady. The only impediment she suffered was in reaction to his teasing. And hell but he could entertain himself with that all night.

As Syn poured him his glass, Rygard held out his wristband to settle the tab. The bartender leaned over the counter and spoke in a low voice for Rygard's ears only. "You hurt this lady, I will kill you."

Rygard didn't laugh at the other man. As was patently obvious from her earlier performance, Kaitlyn could handle herself. But when she smiled . . . like Syn, he would have ripped any person to shreds who took that light away.

If he lucked out, he'd see a different kind of pleasure take over those delicate features. Soon.

Please, for the love of gods old and new, soon.

He might not survive being this turned on otherwise.

CHAPTER 5

KAITLYN FIGURED she might not survive the next five minutes.

Her heart wasn't going to make it. It had kicked into overdrive at the bar, stopped a couple of times in the elevator when Rygard leaned in even closer, and currently threatened to pound through her chest.

Rygard. In her room.

Alone.

Well, not alone. She stood there, trying to pull her courage together. Not a panic attack, not the debilitating memories of her capture and torture. No. This felt more like being caught in a swarm of fluttering birds scattering in every direction and tugging her with them.

And damn it, a hard-core merc like her didn't flutter. She'd been through hell and back again the past three years. With her enhanced reflexes and strength, she could probably take him if she felt threatened. Probably.

The soldier in question sat on the corner of the bed and gave her a lazy, confident smile. "Come here, Kaitlyn."

He held out his hand.

She melted, drawn toward him without the slightest clue of what to do next. Threatened was the last thing she felt. Anticipation sang through every nerve in her body. His scent spiced the air with arousal, but he sat relaxed and gentle as he took her hand. He tugged her closer until she stood between his knees.

"Hi." Stupid thing to say. She bit her lip to keep from blurting any more inane commentary.

He chuckled, but it didn't feel like he laughed at her. "Hi there."

Relaxing, she explored the chest harness fitted over his uniform. He wore it in a configuration she'd never seen before, and the distraction helped steady her. After a moment of letting her play, he ran his hands lightly over the backs of her thighs.

His touch seared through her uniform and across her skin. She trembled, nightmares hovering at the edge of her memory. Hands could abruptly turn cruel, inflicting pain and . . . damage.

She sucked in air and looked up from his chest to his face, his mouth and brows relaxed in an expression so clear and different from that of her torturer. Desire crashed through her and she froze, caught between the now and then. Gentle pressure on her lower back coaxed her closer until their lips hesitated, only a breath apart.

And he waited for her to come to him.

Her heart expanded until she couldn't breathe, thought she'd suffocate if he didn't kiss her. This was her chance to erase those memories, replace them with what should be. She made her decision and closed the distance.

His lips pressed warmly and firmly against hers. The kiss started soft, until he opened his mouth and she opened to match him. He explored, tasted, with sweeping strokes of his tongue. When he released her, she almost whimpered, then she nipped at his lower lip and licked the little bites. He growled, sucking at her lower lip before claiming another deep kiss.

Could the man get any sexier?

Her cat rose to the forefront, growling in return as she slid her hands along his shoulders, feeling his muscles ripple under the service uniform. Letting her cat out to play, she reveled in his touch, stretching and arching into his embrace. And damn but he could do things with those hands. He massaged and stroked, finding erogenous zones she didn't even know about along the backs of her legs, her sides, the curve of her back. She drowned, moments from surrendering all coherent thought.

A solid click echoed in the silence. Gasping, she jerked in his arms.

"Easy," Rygard soothed her, his hands slow as they slipped the thigh harness down her leg. He kept her anchored with his gaze while he undid her torso strap and slipped it over her shoulders.

Her mouth went dry. She'd never undressed in front of a man—not voluntarily. The remembered sound of cloth ripping filled her ears, of chains rattling moments before they dug, cold, into her fevered flesh. If he undid her uniform, she wasn't sure she could keep from clawing him, defending herself from the rapist who'd died already.

But Rygard waited for her.

Hands trembling, she reached out and unfastened his harness. He helped her slide it off. Burying one hand in her hair, he cradled her head and coaxed another kiss, and then another. His hands roamed over her as before, easing her back into a comfort zone and teasing her through the fabric until she pressed into him again.

"Please." She didn't know how to ask for what she wanted next, had never tried. This had already gone light-years further than the single kiss she'd shared with Katzer.

"What do you want, sweetness?" He nuzzled her shoulder and cupped her breast with a hand.

She couldn't give him her neck—not yet. She ducked to one side and nipped at the corner of his mouth, teasing until his lips returned to hers. Instead of struggling for words, she growled and tugged at his uniform.

His fingers pressed against the front seal to hers, slowly unfastening it to expose her throat and the rise of her chest. Her pulse raced as she waited for his touch on her skin.

The door chimed loudly in the silence of the room, accompanied by an obnoxious round of knocking.

She leaped back, muttering a string of curses.

Still seated on the corner of the bed, Rygard raised his eyebrows in amused surprise. She gave it even odds as to whether his amusement came from her sudden position a yard away or because most of her threats were anatomically impossible, unless one was a heavily modified hermaphrodite.

"Identification," she snarled to activate the room's comm link as she strode toward the entrance.

"Messenger. Requires retinal scan for delivery."

"What the fuck?" She palmed the door open, aware of Rygard behind her. He stayed out of sight, ready to provide her with backup, however casual his posture. Warmth spread through her chest and a smile tickled the corners of her mouth. A companion strong enough to cover her six— how hot was that? Very.

A messenger stood there, scrawny and skittish. The scent of rancid soda, body odor, and good coffee clung to their jumper. Well, she knew where they'd picked up the package and who had sent it to her. It wouldn't have a sender ident.

She took the retinal scanner from him and underwent the required imprint. Once it beeped an affirmative, the kid handed over the parcel and scuttled off down the hallway. She closed the door and hit the privacy indicator. It'd have to be a station-wide emergency to get the door open again. She turned to put the box on the little counter by the entryway.

"What's the delivery?" Resting one hand on her hip, Rygard used the other to brush her hair off one shoulder. She held still, giving him the opening. He pressed a kiss against her neck, sending shivers across her skin.

"Not worried about it." She leaned into him, very aware of how comfortably she fit against him.

The hand at her hip squeezed. "It's marked for immediate attention. Whoever sent it spent the cred."

He made a good point.

She started to open the package, but he began trailing a string of kisses down her neck, alternating nibbles and light suction. Okay, giving him her neck felt good. He had eased his grip on her hip and massaged it instead. His groin pressed into her ass, the hard ridge of his erection settling against her.

"I thought I was supposed to open this." Her voice sounded husky.

"Mmm. And I'll focus on the package I want to unwrap."

"Oh." And she melted, right there, under the heat of his hands and lips.

Abruptly, he stopped, swatting her behind as he stepped away. "Open your package, sweetness."

She bit back a snarl, rubbing the mild sting. No one had

ever spanked her and come away unmarked. But his lazy grin returned as he waited for her again, and her temper faded into a different kind of heat. Well, maybe she'd mark him, in a way he'd enjoy.

She narrowed her eyes in a mock glare before turning her attention to the delivery. Removing the wrapping revealed a puzzle box. Fantastic. She planned to fill Boggle's hideaway with dry ice to chill the ever-clever technogeek off. It took two tries, and some muttered cursing, before she figured out the barely discernable icons.

Inside, she found a sleek little jamming unit and a palm-sized comp. At her touch, the screen of the comp came alive with scrolling text and images. The data represented a background check on one Lieutenant Christopher Rygard and a single line message: *He's clean. Turn on the jamming unit for the rest of the night.*

Not okay.

She would need to have a serious talk with Boggle. His intentions were good, and a part of her softened at this proof of his concern, but this was an invasion of her privacy and Rygard's. It would be one thing to gather intel on a person of interest for a job. She didn't ever want to commit this kind of breach of privacy, even by proxy, for personal reasons.

Then another realization sank in. Shit. He'd been tapped into surveillance on the station, confirming that sensors were installed inside her room. Privacy must not exist, even in a luxury establishment like this one. Although Boggle provided the means to gain some, it meant he'd been watching earlier . . . and she'd taken a shower.

He wouldn't. Would he? Better for his health if she didn't ask. She'd still follow up and have that talk with him.

"Whatcha got there?" Rygard returned, his fingertips tickling along her side.

She deactivated the comp and waved the jamming unit. "Present from a new friend. He knows I like my privacy."

Giving a low whistle, he took the jamming unit from her and turned the sophisticated device over for inspection before handing it back. "Sweet piece of tech."

She looked upward and said to the ceiling, "Thanks."

Then she activated the jammer.

She walked into the bedroom, placed it on the nightstand, and turned to face Rygard. He'd followed her, and was up close and extremely personal.

He brushed her cheek with his knuckles, his voice gruff as he said, "Now where were we?"

"Somewhere"—she whispered against his lips when he leaned in close—"over there."

She felt his smile against hers more than saw it. "Okay. Why don't we go back over there, then?"

But he didn't turn. In a smooth move, he bent and wrapped his arms around her thighs, then hoisted her effortlessly. She let out a yelp and clutched at those broad shoulders, struggling to keep her claws retracted. He caught her mouth again in a long, fantastic kiss tasting of Scotch and toffee. And he kept kissing her, as if he could stand there forever.

She came up for air, focusing enough to gasp, "I'm . . . I'm too heavy for you to keep holding me like this."

And she was. After the change to her genetic code, she tended toward more lean muscle mass than normal human females. She had to be close to twenty pounds heavier than another human of the same height.

He only chuckled again, the sound rich with sensuality.

He turned and tossed her onto the bed as if she weighed nothing.

New experience, and incredibly hot.

She rose onto her knees to meet him as he stepped to the side of the bed. When he kissed her, one hand curved around the nape of her neck, she drank from him. His other hand ran the length of her torso and back, leaving a trail of fire along her side until she desperately wanted the feel of his touch on her skin. She barely noticed when he unsealed the seam to her uniform.

He cupped one breast, uttering a sound of appreciation at the sight of the ruby-red silk of her bra while he pulled the fabric aside. She called out as the wet heat of his mouth closed over her nipple, as excited by the sight of his mouth on her as the feel. He sucked, and it was as if he'd scorched a line from her nipple to the dampness between her thighs, tugging her closer and closer to something just out of reach.

She wove her fingers into his hair, encouraging him as best she could. She nibbled at his ear and kissed the strong cords of his neck. When his teeth grazed her, she jerked, then set her own teeth into his flesh.

Not enough to break skin, but he gasped. "Don't stop."

She didn't. She licked the spot and then set her teeth into his shoulder, feeling every muscle in his chest flex against her in response. His hands grasped her upper arms then and shoved her hard enough to put her on her back but not enough to scare her. He buried his face in her breasts, licking and sucking until she squirmed under the delicious weight of him.

He kissed his way down her belly, and panic returned. Her head cleared as his hands grasped her bare ass, and she reached down to clasp both sides of his head before he passed below her waist.

"What?" When he looked up, it was with gentle concern rather than the impatience or irritation she expected.

Gritting her teeth, she forced the words. "I . . . I have scars."

Four parallel marks ran raggedly across a black panther tattoo on the outside of her left thigh. It had been her futile attempt to slow the virus from traveling through her bloodstream and remapping her genetic code from human to a blend of human and feline. Because she'd inflicted the marks to tissue before the virus mutated the cells, they remained. Any damage she'd taken after the mutation always healed without scarring.

But the scars and the tattoo represented tangible evidence of the past—reality rather than some nightmare. She trembled under Rygard's fingertips, her soul bleeding at the compassion in his gaze.

He stood, and she thought he would leave. Instead, he shrugged out of the top half of his uniform, exposing an expanse of skin. "C'mere."

He pulled her to stand with him and dropping a gentle kiss on her forehead. He took one of her hands and pressed it against his chest. Beneath her fingertips, she felt the smooth ridges of scar tissue.

"You're the first to see these up close." His voice was rough with emotion. "I have scars too."

She bit her lip. She ought to tell him about her past, about the virus. Not contagious, but he should know he wasn't sleeping with a human. "I'm not—"

"Shh." He silenced her with a kiss.

When he set her free, she hesitated, caught between the need to tell him and the caution she'd practiced for years. He sighed and pressed her shoulders until she sat down.

"Where are your pajamas? You should put those on."

She blinked. What had she done wrong? Of course she'd done something . . .

"You didn't do anything wrong." He bent to kiss her again, and she could smell his arousal. He still wanted her but was apparently trying to give her an out.

But she didn't want out.

When he ended the kiss, she pressed her lips against his jaw, then trailed them down his neck. As she reached the juncture between his neck and shoulder, she set her teeth against his skin hard enough to draw another gasp. He took her hands in his and pressed them to the bare skin along his sides. All of this was new—nothing like the innocent experiments of her school days and nothing like the nightmare of her torture.

She let her kisses fall along his collarbone and across his chest, pausing to dart her tongue against his nipple before continuing down the V of his abs. When she reached his waistband, she fumbled with his belt.

Almost reluctantly, he helped her, indecision warring with heat as he stared down at her.

She appreciated his concern, but she wanted this. As his pants slid past his waist, she nuzzled his briefs. The musk of his arousal became so strong, the cat part of her stretched. When she pulled at his briefs, freeing his cock, droplets glistened at the tip. Curious, she licked at the tip, the taste salty-sweet.

He groaned.

Fascinated, she licked again, reaching out with hesitant fingertips to steady his cock. His shaft felt silken soft in her hands—softer than she ever thought a man's skin could be. She turned her hand to cup his balls and took the tip of him into her mouth.

He made a sound—half groan, half encouragement. Sucking gently, she opened wider and took in as much of him as she could. He swelled and hardened when she used her tongue tip to explore the rim at the head of his penis. He shuddered, leaning over her. It felt wonderful—him filling her mouth, the taste of his skin and the softness against her tongue. When she withdrew and looked up, every hint of resistance had left his face.

"You've still got your boots on." Not sexy, and sure as hell not something a normal person would probably say. She didn't care anymore. It was a fact, and he probably needed them off if he planned to do what she wanted him to do.

He bent and freed his legs from the rest of his uniform and boots. As he rose, he loomed over her, one arm hooking her around the waist and tossing her back on the bed. He reached for the nightstand, swiped open the hospitality panel, and drew out a small canister. A hiss sounded through the room as he applied the spray-on condom to his erection.

When he settled between her legs, fear shivered in a far corner of her mind, and tremors started again as she fought the urge to clench her knees closed. Reaching for now and not a nightmare, she wrapped her arms around his neck.

"I've got you," he murmured. "We can stop anytime."

She buried her face into his shoulder and breathed in the scent of him, overriding the remembered stench of her past. Desperately, she lifted her head and gulped air, etching his face into memory. "Don't stop."

Those intense eyes locked on hers. She felt the tip of him nudging against her entrance. For a split second, panic froze every thought, but he waited, watching her.

Hazel, not silver. Warmth and passion, not cold cruelty. Gentle patience.

"Please." She hadn't realized she'd whispered the word. She wanted this, wanted to know what it was like to do this and enjoy it. Above all, she wanted him.

He pressed into her, entering and stretching. It had been a long time, and her first experience was anything but gentle. He withdrew a bit and slid in again, deeper, until she gasped. Muscles she didn't know she had clenched around the length of him. Dizzy with the feel of him inside her, she looked into his face again, saw a maelstrom of emotions there in his gaze, gone dark, and in the turn of his mouth.

And then he began to move. She moaned, arching to meet him, to give him better access. It felt so good, so right. Pure sensation had never taken over so completely. Her world narrowed to the rhythm he set as he pushed into her, sending her wave after wave of pleasure.

SWEET, sweet, Kaitlyn. She was like a drug, and he couldn't get enough. Her response made it clear to him how little experience she had. He'd bet no partner had taken the time to bring her over the edge, make her come. Her previous experiences might even have hurt her. He'd meant to let her go when he'd seen the fear in her eyes, meant to get her into sleepwear and tucked safely in bed.

But she'd surprised him again, making the choice on her own, and when hot lips closed over his cock, no doubt remained in his mind about what she'd decided.

He pressed into her as her inner muscles clenched around the length of him, so tight, so wet. Her hands fluttered against his sides, his back, teasing him into a frenzy. He released her mouth long enough to flip her legs over his arms, giving him deeper access as he picked up the tempo and pushed farther into her. Her head fell back, and she called out in pleasure. Her hands grasped at his sides, his ass, urging him.

He couldn't help himself—he rode her harder. But innocent Kaitlyn had surprising strength. She could take every bit of what he gave, her hands encouraging him and pulling him into her. Her full, generous breasts bounced with the force of his thrusts, the sight so erotic he struggled to last.

He pulled out, fighting for control. She blinked in surprise, but he didn't give her time to say anything. Instead, he kissed her breathless, sucking hard on her plump lower lip as he toyed with her breasts and teased her without mercy.

Control back, he entered her again, hard and fast.

"Ah!"

He froze and waited for her ragged breathing to steady, ready to stop if she asked. But she wrapped her legs around him and ran her heel along the back of his thigh in an unspoken request.

Gods, it felt so good to be inside her. He found a rhythm in time with the tiny mews of pleasure escaping her throat. He reared up over her, grasping a full breast with one hand and using the other to pull her hips to him in an even closer fit. She tightened around him in response, and he almost lost it again.

Slowly, he pulled out again, then kissed his way down her body, determined to bring her with him when he came. He wanted to give her every pleasure he knew how to give, one right after the other, to show her how good it could be. When he looked down at her, her expression remained clear, composed.

He wanted her wild.

He pressed his fingers against her clit, stimulating her with firm, circular strokes. She threw back her head in response and arched her back, hands fisting the bedcovers. "I want you to come for me, sweetness."

She didn't answer, not with words, but the sounds she made were enough. He increased the pressure, the friction, until she whimpered. He couldn't stay away any longer—not after watching her writhe under his touch. She was close. Climbing between her legs, he entered her so fast they both called out.

He stroked in and out of her once, twice, and then flipped her legs over his arms again. This time, he didn't wait for her to coax him. He thrust into her fast and hard, feeling her convulse under him, rising to her orgasm. Her hands grasped at his sweat-slicked back, fingers curling.

"Yeah . . ." Close, so close.

"Yes! Please!" she answered, her face buried in his shoulder. Her fingers dug into him, her entire body convulsing with her orgasm.

Her inner muscles milked him, pushing him over the edge. One more thrust, and he came inside her in a hot rush of pleasure.

CHAPTER 6

"HOW LONG HAS it been since you've been held?"

Nestled in the curve of his arms, her head pillowed against his biceps, Kaitlyn looked up into Rygard's sleepy face. Relaxed and sated, his gaze still simmered with desire. Had she ever felt so wanted before?

"Years." Simple answer. Even then, she didn't dare tell him she'd never been held like this. That no one had ever lain with her wrapped in a cocoon of intimacy. Not Katzer, not anyone. She could stay right there, snuggled against Rygard's chest, listening to his strong, steady heartbeat until she fell asleep.

And she'd never trusted anyone to watch over her asleep. Not even her captain.

He sighed against her hair, one hand gently brushing a strand away from her cheek. "Why so long, so alone?" His expression shifted, suddenly vulnerable. She saw it in the twist of his lips and the set of his jaw. It seemed as if the next words she spoke would shatter him.

He was a soldier, had to be hardened to have made officer. Too old to be commissioned straight out of the academy, he would have worked his way up through the enlisted ranks instead. He'd have seen his share of what combat could do to a person.

A discreet alarm chimed somewhere in the direction of his discarded uniform.

He heaved another sigh. "I have to report back in."

She sat up, the sheet clutched to her chest. She didn't know what to say.

Still naked, he stood, a wicked grin playing across his lips. "Going to remember what you see?"

An answering smile pulled at her mouth. Unable to do anything else, she watched him, all sculpted and deliciously built. Definitely worth remembering, and she had a photographic memory.

His cock began to swell as she continued her heated study. He shook his head and stepped into his uniform, then jerked it up his legs to his waist, careful to tuck himself into his pants. "I have to go."

She nodded.

He seemed to be fighting some inner temper as he shoved his arms into the sleeves and yanked the uniform around his sculpted chest. Looking at her, his eyes softened. "I don't do this."

"This?" She whispered the question. She knew but didn't at the same time.

"This." He stepped toward her, leaned forward, and took a soft kiss. When he drew back, he rubbed his thumb over her bottom lip, his forefinger under her chin. "This is temporary."

It sucked to hear, but she wasn't stupid. Without words again, she focused on fastening his uniform into place, hiding all of his fantastically scrumptious physique.

He laughed softly. "No woman has ever dressed me

before." A pause, then his voice changed, saturated with emotion. "Are you trying to keep me?"

She risked a quick glance up through her lashes to his face, then dragged her gaze back to his uniform. She wanted what she saw there far too much, and neither of them could afford it. "I didn't know that was even allowed."

He stepped away, awkward silence hanging in the air. His attention fell on the small comp from Boggle. Idly, probably for something to do with his hands, he picked it up and activated it. She moved to take it from him, but then held back. She didn't have anything to hide.

"More tech." His voice returned to a light, airy tone. Then he started to read the display.

Brows drew together, and his mouth thinned to a strained line. The muscles across his shoulders and in his neck tensed, hardened. He didn't simply pull away, he opened up light-years of distance between them.

He waved the comp at her. "You had a background check run on me?"

She shook her head, her hair tumbling loose around her shoulders. "A friend sent it to me with the jammer. He must have thought I should know."

"Doubt it. You must have had a great time bagging this stud."

"Look." Not sure the background check rated this much anger, she watched him warily. "I don't do this either."

"Oh, c'mon. A merc, looking the way you do? A 'friend' sends you packages by personal messenger with a background check on your guy for the night? You've obviously got your choice of 'friends.' Maybe I'm just the new flavor."

She almost laughed in his face. "What is your malfunction?"

Suspicious because Boggle sent her a package. Seriously?

That look crossed Rygard's face again, open and bleeding. "A sweet face like yours, too innocent to believe." Then the expression hardened. "I got news for you, I don't have the cred or the political influence to make me worth attaching yourself to. I've got no secrets worth blackmailing me. You wasted your time, and mine."

The bolt of pain that pierced her chest caught her by surprise. He made her feel cheap—something less. The memory of a collar sat around her neck, a phantom weight. She dropped her gaze to the bedsheets, giving way to another being's dominance for the first time since her mutation. His words broke her in a completely different way than her rape had, in a way more intimate and vulnerable because she had chosen him. She fumbled for her duffel at the side of the bed, then yanked a silken sleep shirt over her head, unable to bear the exposure any longer.

"Maybe I should send one of the other guys from the bar to keep you company for the rest of the night."

Jackass.

She opened her mouth to retort.

The entryway exploded. Literally.

She blanked on anything she would have said as she dove for her weapons harness. Rygard beat her to it, tossing it to her as he grabbed his own. Not bothering to put his on, he freed his gun and crouched, ready to fire, his body firmly between her and whatever would come through the door.

"Murderer." A deep voice, not human, snarled through the smoke. A tail lashed into view and withdrew, the owner using the wall as cover. The scent of felines billowed into the room.

A heartbeat passed, then two.

"I haven't killed anybody in at least three months." Kaitlyn freed every blade she had and laid them within easy reach on the bed and floor, keeping her big combat knife closest to her. "You?"

Rygard's silence was eloquent.

"So we're guessing they're all here for you, then." Fantastic. She'd have to remember to look over Boggle's intel a little closer.

"All?" Rygard grunted as he used one hand to yank down the dresser unit for cover. He couldn't pick apart the different scents entering the room, obviously.

As far as she was concerned, he'd have to take her word for it because there wasn't time to explain. "Three, incoming."

A strange huffing cough issued from around the corner. It wasn't because of the clearing smoke. Only jaguars made the sound, confirming her read of what headed toward them. This wouldn't be a conventional fight.

She grabbed her combat knife and took the handle in her teeth. She'd need it.

"Down." The word came clear through her clenched teeth, her voice dropping deep, already changing. Rygard responded, turning to put his back to the dresser. His eyes widened.

She shifted.

One second stretched into an eternity as every nerve in her body blazed. Her body reabsorbed bones and reformed them, muscle tissue twisted and reshaped, tendons detached and reattached in new configurations. Her face stretched forward, forming a muzzle, jaw dislocating and lengthening to make room for fangs. Her hands curled in agony, becoming paws with razor-sharp claws. What had taken weeks of excruciating pain the first time the virus mutated her now lasted a mere second as she forced her shift from human to panther—the pain concentrated into undiluted hell.

She panted.

In this form, thought processes tended to be simpler, more focused, as she let the cat instincts move to the fore.

Time jumped forward again. Her opponent came leaping through smoke, over the dresser and Rygard. She met him head-on. Midair, she planted her forelegs against the inside of his shoulders. The jaguar was bigger than her. He had broader shoulders, a heavier head, and stronger jaws. She had speed and a combat knife clenched in her teeth. When they parted from the first clash, she left the jaguar's shoulder laid open to the bone.

The big cat hesitated.

Kaitlyn didn't.

She slashed the jaguar again. Then she dropped the knife as she slammed into him, shoulder to shoulder. Twisting to avoid his slashing hind paws, she went for the hold. She had him, a kill grip directly behind the skull.

Her favorite hold. She could crush a human's skull from that angle with her jaws. She might not be able to crush the jaguar's, but he'd still be dead.

"Arteq, *ganna kei al!*"

Kaitlyn guessed the shout included a name. Rygard turned his back on them, pointing his gun at the entryway and the speaker. To give the man credit, he hadn't frozen at seeing the woman he recently bedded turn into a big black cat. She'd have been inclined to give him credit for his combat reactions too, but he'd been an ass earlier and they weren't out of this yet.

Forget it. His cred was in the red. He'd brought the damned predators to her door.

"Who are you?" Okay. She'd give Rygard points for making the question very, *very* intimidating.

"We come on Blood Hunt." The voice spoke Standard but didn't sound human. She twitched an ear. The taste of the jaguar's blood was in her mouth. Blood tasted good.

"Explain." Rygard still managed scary just fine.

A feline growled, and a tail lashed into view again. "Murderer. You and your men came into our pride lands, shot our kindred, stole their young. You will all pay."

Shit.

Blood on her tongue and skin under her teeth, she slid closer to cat.

They came here for a reason. She wasn't a part of it. Her opponent was no longer a danger—not dead, but not conscious. She would give him back. They should go away.

Dragging the jaguar between her forelegs, she moved past Rygard, around the dresser, and into the open. After dropping her burden short of the entryway, she backed away cautiously.

Rygard knelt at her back.

"Arteq!" A humanoid crouched over the jaguar. The musk identified it as male. Feline, but not. Snarling, the strange male pointed a weapon at her.

She bared her teeth and hissed.

"Don't!" Rygard snapped. He issued a warning shot from his gun, short of the jaguar and humanoid.

An answering shot came from the entryway, hitting the dresser directly between Kaitlyn and Rygard.

Kaitlyn streaked around the dresser for cover and curled next to Rygard. Growling, she forced her shift back.

"Hold." A new voice spoke, with a quality Kaitlyn recognized even as she panted through the changes. So dominant, every word held power.

Alpha.

She gritted her teeth, every muscle ripping and tearing, melding back into the human her. It took effort to finish her change instead of halting midshift in response to the command.

"L'akesha, ah shu deya. We bear no ill toward the female."

Wasn't that just dandy?

"They might let you go," Rygard murmured, his weapon trained on the intruders.

She wouldn't leave Rygard. Outnumbered, by the person and the species, he didn't have a chance. Besides, how slow could station security be? No way a hotel like this didn't have alarms.

Gods damn it! The jammer.

It was her fault the cavalry wasn't going to arrive in time to save either of them.

"The female, have her come to us. We will question her and let her pass unharmed."

"Why question her?" Rygard called out.

"She is not what she seems."

She snagged her uniform and struggled into it as they talked. She glared at Rygard. "What is it with all of you deciding I'm some sort of deceptive tramp?"

He winced.

"She bested Arteq, kindred."

Temper boiled up inside her. "Hell, I gave him back."

"Shut up, sweetness." Rygard said it quietly, for her.

"She is called Sweetness?" Obviously, they had hearing on par with hers.

Silence. She shrugged at Rygard. Collecting her knives, she began plotting the best way to get to the nightstand and deactivate the jammer.

"We hold fire. You hold fire. We will face each other and speak."

Not a request, but better than a shoot-out in the close quarters of the room again. After exchanging looks with Rygard, she nodded. They stood, slowly, ready to take cover and strike back if it turned out to be a ruse.

Two alien males stood at the entryway, in the open. They were large. The first stood taller than Rygard but rangier. The second, the dominant, was every bit as heavily built and loomed even taller. He filled the space around him with the sheer force of his presence.

Behind them, the jaguar lay still, its chest rising and falling as it panted.

The dominant inhaled slowly, scenting the air.

When he spoke, he directed his words to Rygard. "Your scent is one of the trails we hunt. Blood hunt."

Rygard didn't answer.

The alien's topaz stare fastened on her, the force of it slamming into her as tangibly as any physical blow. Still, her gaze didn't falter under the weight. "You are . . . new."

"Yes." She didn't bother to hide the real growl in her voice. The sound couldn't come from a human woman.

"He is your mate?" The question hung in the air.

"No."

A pause. She smelled the embarrassment off Rygard, which meant they could too. Served him right.

But damn, she wouldn't leave him hanging on his own.

"He is my companion, for tonight." It killed her to say it —made her feel even more like a slut. And this all made her feel like that was somehow wrong. "And he was about to leave."

Rygard's jaw clenched.

The smaller one sneered. "A female chooses?"

A clawed hand lashed out, and the lesser male bled from his nose.

"A dominant female is cherished among our kind." The alpha's focus shifted to Rygard. "A male, dominant enough to match her, is respected."

Well now, wasn't that interesting?

"Why? Out of respect for the female, we will not kill you without understanding. I will ask you *why*, human."

More questions, and thankfully, not in regard to bedding her. She changed weight to the other foot, intent on the secondary male. He stood with hunched shoulders, spine slumped. She could take him. He bared his teeth at her, but his scent, acrid and pungent, gave him away. He feared her.

Rygard surprised her by answering, rolling his shoulders. "We didn't know. Me and my men, we didn't know." He looked to her, then to the alien. He had no trouble meeting the other male's gaze. "We were on a reconnaissance mission on your planet. Commanding officer issued new orders to pick up a package on the return to the landing shuttle. It's happened the last couple of missions in the sector. Anyone disobeying orders ended up with shit assignments, the kind that get you killed. The adult cats were already dead when I arrived. I only collected the package."

"Cubs," the secondary male screeched. "You stole kindred cubs!"

The air sharpened with the bitterness of Rygard's shame, his guilt.

He teetered on the edge of action, clearly a step away from doing something stupid.

"We'll get them back for you." All eyes turned to her. She looked at Rygard. "We can. They're alive."

They'd taken the cubs alive for a reason. A huge gray market existed for pets. She should know—she'd been one. There must be one on station. Her lip curled at the thought, red haze edging her vision.

She turned to the dominant male. "If we return the cubs, he and his go free. They were following orders."

"And this commanding officer?" The male sounded intrigued, but Kaitlyn wasn't fooled. Raging fury waited, banked in those eyes, his scent sharp with anger. The strength of his personality pushed at her—invisible, intangible, but very real.

Kaitlyn shrugged. "I don't know him."

And it would be the commanding officer's death proclamation.

The alien's gaze bored into her. Stubborn, she met him, fighting the urge to look down. She'd done it once today. She wouldn't give another overbearing male the advantage.

She'd feel guilty about the CO's death, probably. But saving Rygard's ass, and his men, had a more generous helping of her concern. She understood the trials of obligation in following the orders of a rotten commander.

"The word of a murderer has no value." She couldn't argue—opinion formed in the eye of the beholder. "We will take your word, female, and see how much value it has."

"SERIOUSLY?"

He didn't answer. For the first time in his three decades, Rygard was at a loss for what to do. Kaitlyn paced the length of the hotel room and back again, fully dressed and lethal. The felids had left, taking their big cat with them. No damage to the actual door—they'd used a slim lock hack and smoke bombs when they'd attacked. The only evidence remaining of their visit continued in the form of her tirade.

And she was magnificent in a rage. More importantly, she hadn't left him to die.

"It's a freaking mistake repeated throughout history." She didn't shout, but her words shot out sharp as knives. "Following orders, my ass. You're an officer. You, at least, have permission to think."

He didn't try to defend himself. He'd gone over the same reprisals on his own. Besides, she'd stepped up for him a few minutes ago, even after he'd started to make a solar-class asshat of himself.

Suddenly, violence incarnate filled his vision. Before he could blink, she stood toe-to-toe with him, pinning down every thought in his head.

"Why?" She asked the same question the felids had, needed a different kind of understanding.

He owed her at least an explanation, probably more. After all, she'd jumped neck-deep into this for his sake. "My tour ended with the last mission."

She didn't blink. Apparently, she knew what it meant. She proved it with her next words. "You weren't going to re-up for another."

He sighed. "I was searching for a yes or no at the bottom of my glass when you came into the bar."

One gracefully curved eyebrow arched high. "I'm guessing you haven't reached a decision in the time since."

Despite the insanity of the attack, or maybe because of the adrenaline still coursing through him in response, Rygard's blood heated. "Well, sweetness, I got a little distracted." He risked settling his hands on her waist, then tugging her closer when she didn't draw blood. "Maybe more than a little."

A smile hovered, but her countenance remained somber. "It doesn't bother you?"

He had an idea of what she asked, but he found the body in his hands beautiful, and those eyes shone all human. "I get the impression it isn't the way you came into this life." There, he saw it. Her gaze lowered, not to deceive, no, but to hide the flash of pain. "Tell me about it. Tell me why you spent so long alone."

Her lips parted, and a faint tremor passed through her entire body. He tightened his hands on her waist, trying to provide an anchor, but she shook her head.

"We've got a mission," she said quietly. "You need to report in and then come back to take care of this." A pause, then she flicked his hands away from her. The space she put between them left him cold. "You said this was temporary. I get that. But we'll see this through. And don't worry about what it'll cost you in rep or cred. I'm not that girl."

CHAPTER 7

"STATE YOUR NAME, purpose, and ship of origin."

"It's damned cold out here and there's a panther at your door." Her snarl carried down the corridor.

The little holographic worm with the shock of red hair immediately responded. "Come inside and have a nice cup of brew."

She shot through the door even before it slid open completely, Rygard a half step behind her.

"Boggle, please tell me why the corridor is freaking subzero." Her voice pitched to be pleasant, but Boggle was a smart little technogeek. He had the grace to look nervous and wisely handed her a steaming beaker of richly fragrant coffee.

"We had some intruders prowling." Boggle turned and sloshed another serving of coffee into a fresh beaker before swiveling his servo-driven chair to face them, then held it out to Rygard. "The usual precautions weren't a sufficient deterrent, so we adjusted the environmental controls until they responded as desired and took themselves out."

"Were they humanoid?"

Boggle shoved a handful of snack crisps in his mouth and crunched loudly. "Remotely."

She held her breath to avoid the combination of masticated carbs as his words sent crumbs toward her. She wondered if he'd had the same visitors she and Rygard entertained earlier. "Feline characteristics?"

He gulped down coffee in a loud chug and wiped his mouth with the back of his hand before shaking his head. "Reptilian."

"Sket'zes." Rygard didn't bother to hide his distaste. "If they're on base, the gray market auction will be held soon."

"You looking to buy something?" Boggle belched and turned to his console.

"More like reclaim some merchandise before it goes off station," she clarified.

Fingers froze on the console, then a few screens cleared and new ones came up as Boggle reset his parameters. "Specs on the merchandise?"

"Live." She wasn't sure what sort of specifications to provide but figured she'd give it a try and he'd let her know what else he needed. They were still working out this whole friends-with-information thing. "Small feline cubs, probably to be sold as exotic pets."

She gave Boggle a quick recap on the situation, sticking to the pertinent details regarding the felid intruders and the deal they had made.

Staccato taps beat out a speedy rhythm on the console as he entered the search parameters and began hacking through various databases. Boggle talked while he worked, his attention fastened to the display. "Very unusual merchandise, exotic animals for pets. Only wealthy buyers for those, with the means to put the animals through decontam and bypass customs procedures on their home planet. Means the merchants are specialized too, with characteristic systems set up for maintenance and care of the animals while they're on station. They'll have sophisticated security and private guards."

"Find them." Kaitlyn didn't worry. Anything on station, she could handle alone. "Any intel you can give me to locate them is key, additional support for planning to get them out is bonus."

"You just going to walk in, take them, and walk out again?" The incredulous tone of Rygard's voice pushed an internal button . . . or three. "I know these types. Shady isn't the word for them."

She turned, slowly, to look at him for the first time since they'd left the hotel room. The entire journey—and she'd made sure to take the long and confusing route to Boggle's safe house—had provided her time to find her center again.

"You might have intimate knowledge of me, but you don't know me. You've made that abundantly clear." She held up the comp holding Rygard's background data. "I'm about to study up on you and make a few communications. While I'm gone, I suggest you decide whether you're going to open your mind to learning anything new about me or if you're going to hang on to what you've already assumed. In the meantime, I trust Boggle to make sure you don't go off on your own and get yourself killed."

Anger twisted with hurt inside her chest, and she needed distance to breathe, maybe clear her head again. She and Rygard had reached an uneasy truce for now, but Rygard was still wary of her, and she hated the feeling of being unjustly labeled things she was not. She shouldn't care. But here she was.

Besides, she'd promised those felids she would retrieve their kindred cubs.

"Boggle." She made his name a request. Her new friend didn't disappoint her. His focus still on the display, he nodded and made a shooing motion with one hand.

She turned on her heel and left.

Hell. To be honest, she retreated.

RYGARD REMAINED SILENT FOR A MOMENT, watching her leave. The previous night, he'd been fascinated by the contradictions she presented. Now, he didn't trust a single thing about them. Another pretty face, out to play him. Wasn't she? A couple of those contradictions made him wonder how stupid he might be. Probably a little. Maybe a lot.

"I take it that things aren't exactly smooth between the two of you." The sweaty technogeek turned away from the scrolling data displays to look at him. "She didn't ask for the data I sent on you. I realized she planned to go with you and wanted her to know who she chose, but I guess my gift didn't go over well."

The stab of guilt hit hard.

There was a long moment of scrutiny. The kid perceived too much. The servo-chair spun again, and Boggle brought another console to life at the end of the counter. "You can try running a search on her background information, if you want to even things out a little. Good luck. It's buried under so much security, even I would practically have to hack to the earth's core to get to it."

Why so much security? "Because she's a mutation modification? How did she get her hands on the procedure?"

Boggle shook his head. "You soldier types absorb better

in a briefing than you do reading up on reports, don't you?" He turned away from the display, leaving data searches running on the screens behind him. "She didn't go looking for the procedure. But that's her story. Let me tell you mine instead, to make up for prying into your business."

Rygard wasn't sure he cared. Then again, Kaitlyn had come here, and it seemed this person had access to a lot of information most wouldn't know. It made her story about being a well-paid mercenary a lot more plausible than the image he'd had in his mind of her just being a con and a user.

Boggle didn't wait to hear whether Rygard wanted to listen or not. "Three years ago, Triton Moon Base was occupied in a hostile attack. It was intended to be used as a forward position to launch attacks on Earth. Only, it wasn't just a military base. It was half-scientific in nature, so there were as many civilians on that station as there were military personnel, including families of both."

Rygard knew of it, even if he hadn't been in the solar system when it happened. "We were briefed on the incident. A small group of student cadets got a distress call out to Earth and provided valuable intel to Terran rescue forces. Impressive."

Wait. Realization trickled through Rygard as he got the sense that a puzzle was coming together in front of him.

Boggle swiped one of the smaller screens and quickly brought up a set of data, including an image of a much-younger him. He'd had a much less sophisticated moto-chair back then. "I was a student, on station during the attack."

Well, damn.

"It took weeks for Terran forces to mount a rescue and retake Triton Moon Base." Boggle's face was pale under already-white skin. "The cadets they talk about so much?

When the attack first happened, they led all the civilian students into hiding in the BioDome. The invaders couldn't find any minors to hold them hostage against the adults on base."

"Gutsy." Rygard would have loved to meet a bunch of young people with such potential. He didn't know where they'd all dispersed to after the incident.

"Yeah, well, the cadets were brave. All I did was hide." Boggle gripped the arms of his chair. "Courage doesn't make anyone invincible. Some of those cadets—most of them—were taken captive at some point or another during the occupation."

Rygard stilled. Being a kid wouldn't have necessarily made being taken prisoner easier. It could have made things worse. Anyone taken in that occupation would've faced a lot of things, every one bound to be a nightmare. Anyone who hadn't fallen victim might carry a whole lot of survivor's guilt too.

"There's no shame in surviving an impossible situation," Rygard said gruffly.

"Almost all of those cadets died, the ones who were captured. All but one." Boggle's voice was strained. "After it all, I volunteered to gather their student records and achievements for a memorial service. I know everything there was on file for every one of those cadets, the dead and the living. And I accessed the restricted information on how they died."

Rygard remained silent, waiting. He had an idea of what happened—starvation was likely, torture, probable—but there was a reason Boggle was sharing. It wasn't just to make up for having breached Rygard's personal privacy.

"The invaders were conducting experiments on prisoners," Boggle said, finally. "A virus from their home planet had been isolated and weaponized. They were testing the efficacy on the captured cadets. It was like the old Terran legends about lycanthropy, people who were part human and part animal. The new mutation modifications you're talking about? Based on that."

No.

Rygard's gut twisted as he thought about Boggle and how he might be linked to Kaitlyn. He connected the data points. "You and her. You're about the same age."

Boggle nodded.

"She was there."

"Yes," Boggle said simply. "She was a cadet lieutenant colonel, about to graduate and go to university. The attack on Triton Moon Base changed it all and when everything went to hell, she was one of the natural leaders."

Not surprising. The woman Rygard had just met wouldn't have hidden and hoped for rescue. She had stayed with him earlier when she could have left on her own, fended off attackers side by side with him, and even promised to right a wrong he'd committed. And she had changed from human to cat.

She'd been there, on Triton Moon Base. Been captured. Survived.

"You'll want to ask her the rest. Anything you want to ask right now, I'll only answer if it's about me." Boggle waited, his expression earnest.

"Why do you do this stuff for her?" Rygard asked, wanting to find out what he could, even if it was only tangential to her.

"Back then, Kaitlyn existed as a bright, vivacious girl—beautiful, larger than life. She didn't know me. Since then, she's built a new life for herself, different from the goals and dreams she'd had before, but I think who she is now is better." Boggle's hand reached out for a beaker of coffee, and he took another noisy gulp. "That sounds like it's about her, but we need to establish that to get to why I want to help her."

Rygard struggled to reconcile all the new impressions he was getting about this woman he'd just met. It felt like there was no solid footing under him and every time he breathed, there was some new facet of her to face.

Boggle continued, his voice becoming breathless. "The data never lies. It's there if you know how to see it, in her history and psych profiles. She has an integrity you don't find in people anymore, not real ones. Once she makes you one of hers, she'll do anything for you. But no one from school looked for her after it all. Everyone just assumed she'd take care of herself and didn't need them. But they were wrong. She needs friends." He paused, then resumed tapping at the terminal. "When she met me yesterday, she didn't remember me, but she also didn't let outer appearances stop her from taking a chance."

Looking at the sloppy habits, the social awkwardness, and the gamer stats on comp tablets stacked in the corners, Rygard would have left. But he could guess what friendship meant to Boggle.

"And you're obviously one of hers." Boggle jerked his head at Rygard. "Look at what she's doing for you."

"She knows this is temporary. It can't go anywhere." Even to him it sounded flimsy, a weak statement with nothing to support it.

A wave of dismissal answered him. "Doesn't matter. Once you're one of hers, she'll move planets for you. The data doesn't lie. It's why I want to help her and it's why you should patch up the fight you two had. Whatever is between you two now, no matter how short-lived, when she gives friendship, it's forever."

"ALL RIGHT." Kaitlyn entered Boggle's domain with a sigh. "I have a better idea of what resources we've got to work with."

Boggle reached for his coffee setup, but she shook her head. She'd already had enough for the time being. "Water's good."

A bag of water came flying her way, and she snagged it out of the air mid-arc, then pressed it against her temple. The cool temperature eased away the beginnings of a headache. After a moment, she pulled up the built-in mouthpiece and sipped.

Rygard was still standing, shifting his weight uncomfortably from one foot to the other. She raised an eyebrow as she studied him. She'd been away long enough for him and Boggle to have had any number of conversations, but she didn't think it'd been so much time that Rygard would be experiencing physical discomfort standing. People who went out on missions the way he did tended to be on their feet, a lot. So if it wasn't physical, it was mental or emotional.

"You have questions for me? Or maybe something you want to say?" She wasn't in the mood to carry anyone's baggage. Best to get this aired out before they really got into the detailed planning for what they were about to do.

Boggle cleared his throat. "I could leave."

"This is your space. If we don't want to do this around you, we're the ones who should leave. If we make you uncomfortable, it's still us who should leave." She said it to Boggle, but she kept her gaze on Rygard.

"No. Anything I have to say can be around him, if you're both okay with it." Rygard's voice was quiet, serious.

"You both can stay," Boggle said quietly. She didn't detect any scent of fear, any lie in his body posture.

She moved farther into the room and leaned against a table edge, careful not to disturb the clutter on its surface.

"I'm . . ." Rygard seemed unsure of exactly how he wanted to word his thoughts, and he dragged one hand through his hair. "I'm realizing I jumped to a lot of conclusions and I don't know much about you. But you showed me something to save me, back in that hotel room, and that's a dangerous secret. How did you become . . . modified?"

Kaitlyn huffed out a laugh. "Modified. That's one way to put it."

"I gave him some background on Triton Moon Base," Boggle added helpfully.

Oh, she didn't want to do this. But she'd basically challenged Rygard to open his mind, and now he was asking her to fill it. To let him know about her. She couldn't expect him to change his assumptions about her if she wasn't willing to give him new context with which to form his impressions.

"Fine. I'm guessing you know about the group of cadets, so let's skip all that and go straight to the fact that I was captured." She'd gone through all of this before, didn't want to talk through all of it again. She turned to Boggle. "You have my files from back then, don't you? The confidential interviews they conducted with me after?

Boggle nodded.

"Pull them up, please." She started to feel more and more distanced from herself.

Boggle did as she asked, bringing up a list of files on a larger screen. She was familiar with the file names. She and Dev reviewed them, made sure they had copies of them all before she had left Triton Moon Base to become one of his crew.

She pointed. "Play this one on-screen, please. Audio and visual."

Inside her, everything tightened and twisted. It took effort to force her lungs to expand and take in air. Sharing sucked.

A voice issued from sound projectors all around the room—hers. Her tone was cold, her words flat and dead. "The virus took days to spread through my body. Fevers, acute muscle cramps, possibly a seizure, but I'm not sure. Halfway through the change, he came to my cell." A pause. Kaitlyn closed her hands into fists and fought the desire to walk away, let the file play without her there. On-screen, past-her was slumped in the chair and still, too exhausted to even try to move anymore. "He wrapped my hair around my neck, saying it would do for a collar until he could have a proper one made. Then he . . ." Her voice in the recording hitched, and she cringed in present time, knowing what was coming. "He raped me. It took another couple of days for the change to complete."

The clip ended. She breathed. It was behind her now. She'd built a new life, and—she looked up at Rygard—she'd created new memories. Even with how terrible he'd been after, she didn't regret being with him in the moment. The moment had been . . . really nice.

Boggle cleared his throat before he spoke again. "There

are later briefs going into more detail. They made her tell every detail eventually."

He stopped to chug more coffee, grimacing as if he had a bad taste in his mouth.

Kaitlyn continued. "The rest of the captives didn't survive the virus or the genetic mutation it forced on us at the cellular level. It was bioengineered to create true therianthropes, shapeshifters. It succeeded, but obviously it had a low rate of success."

Her. Just her. And she carried enough rage for all of them. She was trying to learn to live with enough joy for them all too.

"Is there more I should know?" Rygard sounded like he was struggling to keep his voice steady.

Her temper flared. She was angry he'd pushed her to reveal her trauma and frustrated that he'd assumed she had chosen to be the way she was.

"Rape turned out to be only one aspect of the torture. Beatings occurred repeatedly, and humiliation—chained to the lead invader's chair and displayed as a trophy." The information kept flowing. She didn't know if she cared enough to stop it, even as Boggle winced. "The mutation is permanent and irreversible. According to my psych profiles, I was never suicidal, but I've spent the last three years trying to overcome trauma enough to interact normally with males of any humanoid species."

She lifted her chin in Rygard's direction pointedly.

There was regret in his eyes, but he didn't look away from her gaze. At least he wasn't trying to dodge accountability.

Mollified, she continued. "I lost friends. Some of them died in the final battle when the Terran forces arrived. A Cadet Lieutenant Katzer was an ace pilot, as young as he was. His name is in the history archives. He died opening up a clear line of attack for the rescue forces."

She'd been on the comm with him when he'd died. But his voice wasn't coming to her now, when she was sharing her story with someone else. Even if she never heard it again, she'd remember him.

"I—" She could keep going. Finish giving the big picture of what had led her to the person she was today. She could. "I wouldn't talk for days to anybody but Captain Devron Rishkillian, a merc captain we rescued from the brig in the early days of the enemy occupation. He was the one who helped us figure out the enemy weren't aliens at all. They were human colonists, evolved from generations in a different solar system and returned to take over our planet of origin."

Boggle helpfully swiped a display and images slid across a few screens as a visual aid.

Kaitlyn looked away after a glance. She didn't need any visual reminders. The faces of her captors were burned into her memory. "After it all, Dev used some deep connections in the Terran upper command chains to allow me to sign on with his crew instead of being hidden away in some laboratory to be studied like a scientific specimen."

Almost there. She was almost up-to-date. Three years distilled down to just a couple more sentences.

"I've been working on how to control who and what I am after the virus changed me. Communicating and building relationships with the people around me are still works in progress." Her next words would cut deeper and maybe would make Rygard bleed guilt. She didn't care, because it was a truth he should take into consideration. "You're the first man I've been with intimately since the incident."

"Can't be." The words burst from Rygard on a note of anguish.

She kept her gaze steady on his, still feeling separated from herself.

Boggle's voice interjected, bitter. "Kaitlyn's been conducting her own research on Captain Rishkillian's ship, between missions. She completed her biology degrees remotely in record time. Almost all of the data available on the virus is either from her or built on the foundation of her findings. You can track her recovery and acclimation to the changes in her physiology by reading the body of her research, if you have the academic chops for it. The confirmation for what she's telling you is all there."

She hadn't needed the backup. She was used to fighting her own battles. But like Dev and Skuld, it was . . . nice . . . to have Boggle there, supporting her.

There was silence, then Rygard finally spoke. "Kaitlyn, I'm—"

She shook her head. "Don't. Not yet. Don't say words when you haven't had the chance to process everything you just found out."

He closed his mouth and clenched his jaw. She didn't scent anger coming from him. He was distressed, yes, but he was listening now and respecting her wishes.

"Now you know who I am. Give it all time to sink in, then figure out how you feel," she whispered, too tired to be assertive about it. "Then, if you really are sorry, give me a sincere apology."

Finished, she gave herself a shake. Weight had lifted off her, and even if she still felt raw, she thought maybe she'd shaken off enough figurative salt to heal and grow now.

"What's the intel you've gathered so far, Boggle? We've got planning to do."

CHAPTER 8

"FOR THE RECORD, I am not happy," Rygard muttered.

Kaitlyn answered with a low growl and butted her head against his thigh. Then she turned, powerful muscles bunched under sleek fur, and she launched herself onto the hovering grav platform. Her tail lashed from side to side, betraying nerves, before she touched the controls with a single claw and yanked her paw back quickly. The containment field rose, enclosing her on the platform.

She did it for him, putting herself at risk and facing captivity again. She'd stepped back into a cage and locked herself into her nightmare. And all without actually speaking to him about what it meant to her.

"The only reason I'm playing along with this is because I can't think of a better plan." Of course, the plan she'd come up with bordered on the ridiculous. Success relied completely on several things furry. Rygard would take solid weaponry and standard tactics any other day.

He put his hands on the steering grips and started through the maze of corridors, headed for the holding areas Boggle had located for them. It was in a different portion of the station, on lower levels where the poverty and squalor coated every surface. Rygard kept his weapons obvious and close at hand to discourage the silhouettes lingering in shadowed alcoves and doorways.

Her plan turned out to be elegant and simple. As a soldier, he knew it had the best chance of success. And beyond saving his own ass, he needed to do this to make things right.

They traveled together in silence. The sounds of his boots echoed in the corridors as he deliberately made his presence known. He knew they were close when Kaitlyn started pacing. A few more steps and even he could smell the stench, hear the strange cacophony of animal calls mingled with human misery.

"What's this?" The guard on duty seemed rough around the edges, bleary-eyed and slurring. His uniform hung on his frame sloppily, stained and thrown on like an afterthought. One hand was buried in the tangled hair of a collared slave at his feet, her eyes dull and her lips wet.

Rygard could take the bastard if things went south. Hell, he wanted to bash the other man's face in now. Reining in his temper, he gave a simple answer. "Last minute entry for the auction."

The guard's gaze narrowed in suspicion. "Thought all of the shipments were in."

Rygard tensed when the man kicked the slave girl to one side and reached for a comp tablet, then typed with clumsy fingers. Glyphs and images flashed across the screen in a sluggish progression. Finally, the listing came up for the panther. Boggle had done his thing.

"It's late." The guard checked the listing as received.

Rygard shrugged, not relaxed but not ready to take out the guard and go to plan B either.

"I'll take it in." The guard reached for the platform and Kaitlyn turned, letting loose a bloodcurdling scream. Her lips drew back to reveal an impressive set of teeth accented by a pair of fangs capable of ripping into a man and doing serious damage. Despite the containment field, the man backed away. Pale and wide-eyed, he waved Rygard in, calling out, "Felines are toward the left back corner. Park it and get back out here."

Walking through aisles of cages, Rygard went where he was told, trying to ignore the misery around him. Merchandise had been arranged on shelves all along the aisles, tagged and ready for auction. Some of it was live and not all sounded animal. Some called out to him, wailing for mercy. Others huddled, cringing when his gaze swept over them. The room stank of desolation and despair.

The ones who didn't respond at all frightened him the most, sitting in their cages with the glazed eyes of the lost. Dead already, their bodies simply hadn't caught up yet. He couldn't save them all, not there and then. And even if he could, they'd have no place to go.

Finally, he had a visual on the cubs—the ones he'd personally collected. Kaitlyn saw them too: her ears perked forward, and her mouth dropped open as she panted. Rygard halted the platform near the cubs, in the shadow of a stack of cages, and set it to remain stationary. With luck, sensors wouldn't register movement until Kaitlyn broke cover.

Pausing, he stared into her carnelian eyes.

"Thank you for helping me make things right." No guarantee he'd have the chance to say it later. "If anything goes wrong, I will come after you, sweetness. I promise."

Those eyes didn't blink, but he couldn't read them either.

He turned on his heel and headed back out.

KAITLYN CONSIDERED his words when he left, using them as a lifeline as she struggled with old trauma and instinct. Even in cat form, she needed human thinking to succeed.

She could have left him to the alien felids. They seemed willing to let her go free. She'd had nothing to do with the situation.

She could go the high road and claim an angelic desire to help Rygard redeem himself and save his life. The man was probably an excellent fighter, but he'd been outnumbered and wouldn't have been able to fight off the jaguar to boot. And there were the cubs to think of too.

But no, that wasn't all of it. She'd hated the way his lips twisted in disgust as his opinion of her disintegrated in less than a microsecond. He'd accused her of conning him, as if everything about the way they'd met and the time spent together had been calculated, a symphony of lies. She could only show him who she was because more words weren't going to change his perception. Even if he seemed okay after the deal they'd made with the felids and the background she shared with him, he didn't have enough to know the truth of her now.

And somehow, that mattered far more than it should.

"Lights out," the guard called, his voice harsh. She heard him rattle the cages of a few of the captives still moaning or begging for freedom. "Shut up!"

The memory came back to her of the slave girl's dull stare, the stink of sex in the air. She crouched down within her cage, suppressing the need to claw at the containment field. Rage filled her, her heart picking up speed, sending blood coursing through her body. She'd been there. She'd been that girl.

Light blinked out, leaving them all in oppressive darkness. The acrid stink of fear intensified as if the dark made the hopelessness of captivity worse. With no sense of day or night, time stretched out endlessly. In the past, she'd listen for any sound, half–needing some sign of life and half–terrified of what new torture it would bring. She remembered the despair.

But now, darkness was exactly what she needed. This was a night of action. She shoved the echoes of terror far back in her mind and gathered her legs underneath her, ready and waiting. She ignored the ghostly weight of a collar and chains—refused to let them hold her.

A few emergency units here and there on the ceiling and walls gave off light. Faint, but more than enough for her to see by.

Chattering came from the near wall. The cover of the ventilation shaft shuddered as the corners were compromised from the inside and a tiny head squeezed out one side. Chester squeaked a greeting, then worked the rest of his long furry body free and dropped to a stacked crate below. A harness had been strapped to him with a rolled-up bundle attached.

In moments, the ferret stood on his haunches, examining the grav platform. Giving him a hint, Kaitlyn tapped one side with her paw, drawing his attention to the controls. A brief pause and Chester pressed the button to deactivate the containment field.

She leaped off the pad, shaking off the phantom chains from her past and climbing quickly up the crates to the ventilation shaft. It took two carefully quiet jumps to nab the cover and pull it completely free. After setting it to the side, she turned and leaped back to the floor, then glided on silent paws to the cage holding the jaguar cubs. Kindred, the felids had called them. Sensing her approach, the male stood his ground, hissing a challenge. His fur stood up across his arched back as the little female huddled behind him.

She figured they wouldn't trust her—not with the trauma they'd suffered thus far. She turned to Chester, gently nipped the plas-wrapped bundle off his back, and tore it open to reveal a piece of fabric. It carried the scent of the felid aliens and the jaguar. She'd requested it earlier while her plan came together.

Her ferret sidekick hopped his way to the side of the cage, working his magic on the containment field as Kaitlyn presented the cloth to the cubs.

She prayed the male was intelligent enough to catch the scent quickly and calm before the guard came.

"I said, shut up!" Too late for quiet. "Fucking beasts."

A beam of light shot through the darkness toward the front of the holding area. Chester managed to deactivate the containment field at the same time the cubs hushed, sniffing at the cloth warily.

No time left.

Kaitlyn lightly butted the little male with her head, bowling him over, then very carefully closed her jaws over his scruff and hoisted him. Instinctively, he relaxed in her hold, and she turned and darted up the crates. She leaped the last three meters directly into the ventilation shaft. This part of the rescue had completely nixed Rygard from the plan. No way could a person of his bulk squeeze into the shaft, much less maneuver.

After placing the cub carefully at the juncture for a

connecting shaft, she nudged him once with her nose to force him on his belly. The command was clear—stay. Seconds later, she had the female cub and placed her with her brother. The final trip was for Chester. There was no way the tube rat could make it up the crates again, much less jump the three meters to the ventilation shaft itself.

Their luck ran out.

"Hey!" The beam of light landed on them as she bent to pick up Chester. The guard's hand reached for his gun. Stupid. He should have reached for his communicator and sounded an alert.

Either way, it wouldn't save him.

All panther now—a silent shadow, Kaitlyn dodged out of his pitiful ray of light and streaked across the distance between them. She overshot the guard and pivoted to take him from behind. She leaped onto his back, then grabbed him at the juncture between his neck and his skull. Her jaws crushed his skull before he could cry out again. His body fell forward, but the man died before he hit the floor. Couldn't risk him sounding an alarm. Human or cat, she had no remorse for killing his kind.

Captor. Rapist. Torturer.

Growling at memories, Kaitlyn quickly moved Chester into the ventilation shaft.

She turned back for her kill. Two tries to get the carcass into the ventilation shaft. Dead man was annoying, even now. She returned to the cages a final time to snap up the plas-wrap and scented fabric so she wouldn't be leaving behind any odd evidence to trigger investigation.

She needed to hurry before another guard came to check on the noise. The other felines in containment paced and roared in response to her movement. Like her, they didn't belong in cages. No time to free them.

Killing the first guard wasn't enough to make up for leaving them behind.

She hesitated a moment longer. She didn't want to abandon the captives but couldn't free them now. Boggle would make sure they were found. Nothing left for her to do but to get back. She turned and leaped up the crates. She gathered her legs under her, then made the final jump for the ventilation shaft.

Pain pierced her left haunch, knocking her out of the air.

Kaitlyn yowled, crashing down on the crates. Her rear leg numbed, useless. Unable to stop herself, she tumbled down the stack. The ground caught her, hard and unyielding. A nerve dart broke off, the needle still in her flesh.

The new guard crept toward her. Smarter, this one. Quiet. In his hand . . .

Her snarl cut the air, silencing the beasts around her.

The sight of the collar, the attached chain hanging in loops, enraged her. Fear and remembered hate froze her.

How long had she sat before Master's feet? Collared. At his mercy. So many creative ways to inflict pain with a simple length of chain.

Never again.

The numbing spread from her left haunch. A normal cat would have been paralyzed. Her genetics were better. She could resist the drug, deal with the guard. But she needed to think like the human. Dev had taught her control, had showed her the way back to human thinking.

The guard stepped closer, the chains rattling.

But not quite a human. Humans spent too much time being squeamish.

She lay on her side, panting hard. He nudged her with a foot. Her temper spiked.

Still, lie still.

She needed him closer.

This one was sober. But his breath smelled of rot and ketones. Too much meat. It wouldn't matter anymore. As he leaned in, she waited. The chains clinked against the floor by her head.

Now.

She struck out with a forepaw. Lightning quick, at the perfect angle. His jaw didn't just break. It ripped away from his face.

"ALL CLEAR." Boggle's hands skimmed across the consoles as he watched the displays. One set of feeds showed the actual activity in the holding area while the other displayed the false images he projected to the security systems.

They watched the black shadow haul the second body up to the ventilation shaft. Kaitlyn's rear leg clearly dragged with the effort.

"She's going to be in a crappy mood." Boggle stated the obvious as he set a fresh batch of coffee to brew. He also started setting out medical supplies.

"We'll have to deal with the bodies."

Boggle turned to him. "Upset she killed them?"

Rygard shook his head. "Not at all. The first scum had it coming to him, and the second hit her first." He paused. "She was quick about it. No hesitation."

"I know." Boggle grinned. "She has excellent speed and efficiency in both cat and human forms. You should see the stats on her previous missions."

Several images of Kaitlyn in action flashed up on the far display, accompanied by streaming data. Rygard stepped closer, but he wasn't focused on the information. Instead, he reached out to touch one static image of her face.

"You wouldn't think it to look at her," he murmured.

For a few seconds, only the sound of Boggle munching on his snacks filled the room. Then the technogeek commented quietly, "She's not that girl."

"What?" Rygard's focus remained on her image.

"Your former intended. Your ex." Boggle shrugged. "Kaitlyn is Kaitlyn."

Before Rygard could answer, a scratching noise came at the vent. Chester's face squeezed out from one corner, then they heard a solid *thunk*. The cover popped off the ventilation shaft to expose Kaitlyn's dark form, crouched, a shadow in the darkness. Twin carnelian eyes glowed for a long moment before she blinked slowly and turned in the tight space.

One cub and then another gently dropped to the counter below, followed by the squirming ferret. Rygard took a step toward them, but a low growl warned him back. One of the cubs struggled to its feet, arching its back and letting out a hiss.

They remembered him, and not in a good way.

Kaitlyn descended with liquid grace despite her injured haunch, then stood over the cubs. Her black muzzle nuzzled them tenderly until the disgruntled cub's anger subsided. Chester squeaked and whined, rearing up on his hind legs for attention. One large black paw descended on the ferret, gently squashing him.

Rygard's chest tightened. He could almost visualize the ghost of her human form comforting them. He knew the softness of her touch, remembered how she'd helped dress him. It wasn't in her to be a user. Somehow, he could see her more clearly without the distraction of feminine curves.

Clearing his throat, he jerked his chin toward the private corner he'd set up for her. "Your uniform and gear are over there when you're ready to change."

Baby furries settled for the moment, Kaitlyn padded over to the table and grasped the medical supplies in her mouth, then continued behind the screen he'd erected for her. In minutes, her silhouette stood straight and human and devastatingly curvy.

"Thank you." Boggle whispered the reverent words.

"I can smell arousal." Kaitlyn's warning came through clear. "You both are pervs."

Boggle swiveled in his chair. "Right. Eyes on the monitors."

"Copy that," Rygard muttered and followed suit, turning away from the privacy screen.

At the edge of his periphery, the ferret scampered across the counter and stood on hind feet. He, at least, had a clear view as she dressed.

Rygard didn't want to be jealous of a weasel; he really didn't.

It took several minutes and some creative cursing for her to extract the broken needle from her hip.

"You need help?" Rygard offered, despite Boggle's warning cough.

"Got it covered," her voice growled out, more cat than human.

"She doubles as med officer for the crew, does her own field triage." Well, the geek could have given him *that* intel a little sooner.

"And the tranq will wear off faster in my system than most." She stepped out from behind the screen, fully dressed. Her gaze settled on Rygard, and one eyebrow arched. "It's not like you haven't seen all there is to see."

He let the grin stretch wide across his face. "Never gonna get tired of it, sweetness."

No return smile. His chest constricted. He might not get the chance again.

Gods he had messed up, in so many ways.

"Uh-huh." She shrugged into her harness and secured it in place. "Are we good to go, Boggle?"

"Triggered the fire sensors in the illegal market as soon as you got back. Suppressants engaged, washing away the blood from your kill. No damage to any of the captives." Boggle pointed at the nearby display screen. "The alarms brought station security on-site and officials are taking custody of all beings in the holding area. An investigation has already been launched. No signs of our involvement discovered so far—that includes the two bodies you left in the shaft, but too much time goes by and they'll find those."

"I'll have to go on a corpse run later, when things have died down." Kaitlyn stepped over to the cubs and ran a hand over the brave one. He accepted her touch without hesitation despite the difference in her shape.

For the cub, trust was a simple thing. She'd earned it. To Rygard, trust existed as a twisted-up mess inside his head. After all this, he'd trust her in combat to watch his back, probably even follow her lead into any hellhole out there and believe she'd bring him through alive. He'd missed that feeling, leached out of his unit over the last few missions.

But the part of him beating inside his chest shrank away at the thought of letting her past his defenses. Something told him he might not survive the hole she'd leave behind.

"Let's move to the rendezvous point and get these two home." Kaitlyn coaxed the cubs into a black pack and gently shouldered it, rearranging her knives on her harness to accommodate the bulk but still provide easy access.

"Ever think about adding a gun to your gear, sweetness?" As soon as the question left Rygard's mouth, Boggle choked up soda.

She spun slowly, burning Boggle first with a look, then turning the stare to Rygard. "Hard to pull a trigger with paws."

Well, she had a point. "Easier to shoot a man from a distance than rip his guts out."

There it was—Rygard knew the twitch at the corner of her mouth betrayed a smile. He only had to coax it out. His stomach flipped, and he admitted to himself that he got a kick out of living dangerously. She didn't answer. Instead, she turned and headed for the door.

"I told you, you should consider firearms." The technogeek slipped in the parting shot to her as she passed.

Rygard hid a grin. He had to admit, the geek had balls after all.

IT WAS a quiet trip back up to the mainstream levels of the station. After arriving at the docking area, Kaitlyn let Chester loose to return to their ship. When she'd made the call to Skuld, her friend hadn't asked questions, only sent Chester to Kaitlyn as soon as the ship docked and broke seal.

The questions would hit as soon as she stepped aboard.

How much detail would she give Skuld?

"You think too hard, sweetness." Rygard was walking in an easy spacer's stride alongside her, intent on the ship in the docking slip ahead of them. He seemed relaxed, but the tightness around his mouth and eyes betrayed his wariness.

She was wary too. Even if they brought the cubs back, the felids might still want his life, despite their agreement.

She shrugged. "Got a lot to think about."

"If we get through this, there's still shit to deal with." His jaw was working, and she could hear his teeth grind.

She studied him for a minute. "Share."

He sighed. "There's a standing order to report encounters with people like you, humans with adaptations. Brass wants to keep an eye on any citizens playing with enhancements."

Kaitlyn digested his revelation. It made sense. The attack on Triton hadn't been aliens. The invaders had been human colonists, mutated beyond recognition. The military would be wise to keep an eye out for other colonies developing similar science.

She was safe on Dev's ship as part of his team. "Military knows about me."

"I still have to report it and my CO won't wait to check before coming after you."

"Charming." She'd have to get back to the ship as soon as possible to avoid killing an asshole.

As they walked the ramp to the felid ship, the air lock cycled open. The two felids stood inside, waiting for them with lashing tails. Her friend, the jaguar, was crouched to one side and not looking warm or fuzzy. Offhandedly, she wondered what they'd been up to in the intervening time and whether Rygard even had a commanding officer to worry about anymore.

Once the air lock closed behind them, effectively caging them inside the ship, the alpha male stepped up to Kaitlyn.

"You have them."

Moving slowly, Kaitlyn slid the pack off her back and opened it. The male cub emerged first, bursting out in a tawny streak and clinging to her shoulder. He yowled his general displeasure as he looked around him. The little female poked her head out of the pack but stayed inside the perceived safety.

She nudged the male cub with her chin. "What are you doing?" Her answer was a sandpaper tongue licking the line of her jaw and pinpricks where his claws dug deeper for a better hold. Fantastic. She looked up at the alpha male. "You want him, come detach him."

There was a strained silence, and she felt Rygard tense beside her—ready in case things got violent. Kaitlyn wasn't worried—the only anger she scented in the air was coming from the other male, the less dominant, and he didn't bother her. Even the jaguar was calmer.

She looked into the alpha male's face and saw a glint of humor. Her lip curled in challenge. She was not for any being's amusement, not ever again.

"You." Kaitlyn pegged the male cub with a look. "Let go and get off."

Needle claws retracted, and he slid down into her arms until he was almost sitting on his sister's head. Kaitlyn sighed. His tiny ears were laid back and he scrunched up in a sad fluffy ball. She scooped him up in one hand and gave him a consolation nuzzle before placing him on the ground. She lifted his sister out of the bag and placed her beside him. Then Kaitlyn gave them each a pat on the rump to get them headed toward the alpha.

"They are returned, safe and whole." Despite his acknowledgement, the big male didn't move to take them. Instead, the jaguar came forward to stand over the cubs.

"Obviously." Her patience thinned.

When he stepped forward, she stood her ground, and so

did Rygard. If anything, the man managed to loom over her without moving closer.

"You have our thanks." The alpha reached out to touch her hair and caught a dark lock on a clawed fingertip. She grabbed Rygard's forearm, signaling for him to stay still even as she held steady under the alien's scrutiny. "I am known as Nahkrir."

She nodded, not trusting her voice. His will was tangible, pressing the air around her. Humans didn't affect her nearly so much. Then again, she hadn't encountered many humans willing to go toe-to-toe with her. She was guessing Nahkrir hadn't either.

"A gift, for the service you have done our people." He held up a necklace of shining platinum links so fine, they flowed over his fingers. Hanging from the necklace was a small pendant of blue amber. "Wear it."

It was not a request.

She was also guessing the necklace held a whole lot of meaning because he put it around her neck himself and fastened it into place. Resisting the urge to bow her head, she kept her chin up and her eyes locked on Nahkrir's. Alpha he might be, but she could stand up to his presence just fine. The less dominant male had his ears back in displeasure and Rygard vibrated with contained anger.

After another moment, Nahkrir stepped away. Rygard relaxed a fraction. She had to give the man respect. Not too many would have stood their ground, and if they had, they would have lost control.

Nahkrir finally looked at Rygard. "Blood Hunt is appeased, human. You may go." He paused. "You are fortunate to have her company. Good things are never finished."

Well, she had said Rygard would be leaving. Apparently, Nahkrir pitched in his own opinion.

The air lock door cycled open behind them. She realized there must have been an audience watching via sensors. And they'd given an eloquent dismissal.

Kaitlyn nodded and backed away. They might have behaved peacefully, gift and all, but she still wouldn't give them her back. The spark in Nahkrir's eye told her he knew it too. His nod acknowledged her and reassured her that he took no insult.

When their feet were planted safely on the station deck, Rygard wrapped an arm around her waist. She let him keep his arm there since he controlled his temper long enough to clear the alien ship's surveillance. "I'm escorting you back to your room to get your stuff and seeing you to your ship before they decide to take you back home as a souvenir."

CHAPTER 10

"EVERYWHERE WE GO, you're surrounded by men." Restless, Rygard paced the length of her room as she packed, seemingly unaware of his frustration.

"Everywhere we've been, I've been fighting males. Totally different situation." She tossed her duffel bag onto the bed and gathered what few belongings she had, not looking at him. "In fact, I still need to collect two corpses. I doubt that's what you're freaking about."

No. He wasn't exactly sure what had him wrestling with the mess of feelings and anxiety inside him. He knew he shouldn't, but he wanted her, and he didn't deserve all she'd done for him, much less what he desired from her now. Very little of it made sense, and none of it was wise.

He quit his pacing and braced one arm on the wall next to her. "I'll take care of the bodies before the station security finds them."

"No." Kaitlyn stuck her tongue out at him.

The sudden mischief caught him off guard, and he focused on her lips. Abruptly, he only wanted to do naughty things to her mouth and tongue. Wanted her to do things with them.

Focus.

"I said . . ."

Shaking her head, she cut him off, then gave him a pointed look that started at his feet and traveled the length of his body. Rygard bit back a groan as his cock swelled under her gaze. With effort, he tried to process her next words.

"There's no way you'll fit in those ventilation shafts to retrieve it. There's too much of you."

Damn it. She'd given him too much of an opening. To hell with focusing.

"Too much, huh?" He dipped his chin, giving her an evil grin, and watched color rise in her cheeks as she tried to hold up under the heat of his stare. Finally, she ducked her head, the way she had when they'd first met.

She was getting bolder, his Kaitlyn, but still shy for him. Gods, how could he ever think she could be anything but genuine?

"You're too much in a whole lot of ways."

She was wary, and he deserved it. He reached out and tapped the pendant that rested below the hollow of her neck. "You make interesting connections."

"Contrary to popular belief, it's not premeditated." She lifted her face, her eyes narrowed and jaw set.

Something tightened in his chest. "I know, sweetness, I'm getting that. It just hasn't been my experience with other women."

"I'm not whoever you keep thinking of."

True. He'd known it from the minute she'd plowed her way through a bar brawl to get to a glass of Scotch. But he'd let the past turn the taste of her bitter.

Struggling to figure out how to fix what was between them before she left, he glanced at her packing.

"Lace?"

As he craned his neck to get a better look, she darted in and set her teeth against his neck.

His cock was rock-hard in an instant, and he dragged in a gasp for air. "Do that again."

She licked the spot and then slowly bit him again, not hard, but enough to scorch his skin and send his pulse skyrocketing. Groaning, he buried one hand in her hair, loving the silken feel in his grip. Okay, maybe she wasn't completely shy anymore.

But it was a good thing.

The heat of each kiss seeped through him as she placed them along the line of his neck. He tightened his fingers in her hair, then pulled her head back just enough to capture her mouth in a hungry kiss. She was so sweet—honey and cinnamon—her tongue dancing with his and her lower lip perfect for sucking. Her hands gripped his sides, pulling at his uniform, demanding skin.

Releasing her, he let Kaitlyn sit back on the bed, her expression glazed, her kiss-bruised mouth slightly parted. Tearing at the fastenings, he was out of his uniform in a second. He took her hands and pressed them against his torso, every nerve and fiber of his being focused on her touch. And she ran her hands over him, caressing and petting, stroking his desire hotter and higher.

He cupped her face—looked deep into those fiery brown eyes, seeing the vulnerable woman inside the predator—and hesitated. "I'm sorry."

She nodded, her gaze holding steady.

Gods, he didn't want to hurt her again.

She must have sensed his withdrawal. Her hands

tightened on his sides. Her lids lowered, thick lashes falling in a veil and then rising again as she looked right through him.

"Come inside me, please?"

KAITLYN WANTED IT, needed him. Suddenly, she couldn't stand the thought of parting ways without one more memory to take with her.

A good memory.

She watched the war of emotions cross his face as he struggled to decide. For a moment, she thought he'd leave, and her heart stopped. His hands, still on either side of her face, had frozen. When she tried to look down, his palms stopped her. His thumb stroked across her cheek, and she let loose the breath she hadn't realized she'd been holding.

And then his mouth closed over hers, and she gasped against his lips. He pressed her back onto the bed, shoving her duffel out of the way with a powerful sweep of one arm. He drank her in, licked at her lips, and then swept into her mouth. When her tongue met his, he encouraged her, deepening the kiss as he pressed his thigh between her legs. She writhed under his weight, frustrated, her uniform preventing her from feeling his skin all along her body.

"I need this off." She was growling, she realized, and he laughed at her, a deep, masculine chuckle.

He levered himself off, stripped her of her uniform and lingerie, and turned his attention to her exposed form. Holding her at the hip with one hand, he ran the other down her side and then up over her belly and gripped one breast in a firm hold. When he closed his mouth over her nipple, Kaitlyn let her head fall back as she focused on the feel of the moist heat of his tongue teasing and licking. His other hand came up to massage her neglected breast, lightly pinching at her other nipple until she squeaked. His hands froze.

"Too hard?" His voice was husky, his eyes half-hooded.

Swallowing hard, Kaitlyn nodded a fraction. "Just a little."

"I'll kiss it better." And he did.

Oh, what the man could do with his mouth.

Kaitlyn was wet, embarrassingly ready and wanting him. But he held her down under his weight, licking and suckling at her breasts as he used one hand to stroke up and down her torso. Gripping his shoulders, she pricked his skin. She arched her back from the pleasure of his attention and ached for more at the same time. He grinned at her and grazed her nipple with his teeth on purpose, making her jerk in surprise.

She cursed. He laughed.

He paused again briefly to retrieve the canister from behind the hospitality panel again and apply a spray-on condom. Then he climbed over her, claiming another kiss and gripping her waist. In a smooth roll, he flipped onto his back and lifted her to straddle him. Instead of entering her, he held her by the hips and ground against her wetness. Kaitlyn panted, dizzy with need. She ran her hands over the hard planes of his abs and chest, loving the feel of all those muscles. And Rygard watched her while rolling his pelvis against her—the pace driving her further to distraction. She tried to match his rhythm, but he had her so sensitized. And then he shifted a hand so he could press his thumb against her clitoris and rubbed hard and fast until she clutched at his chest for balance.

"Please." She was almost feral with need. "If you don't fill me now, I . . ."

She didn't know what.

Rygard didn't make her finish the sentence. Lifting her by the waist, he slid her off him, then paused for a long kiss. And then he turned her, coaxing her onto her hands and knees. His hands caressed her hip and lightly stroked her inner thighs.

Kaitlyn bit her lip. She'd been in this position before. It hadn't been a good thing. She shivered, fear running down her spine and along her skin. But Rygard kneeled low behind her, urging her thighs wider with his shoulder and blowing a soft puff of heat against her outer lips. She sucked in air. *That* was different . . . in a really good way. When he began to lick her in strong, sure strokes, the ghost of memory was driven from her mind.

Every touch of his clever tongue made her tighten. She mewed deep in her throat as he nibbled at her.

"Are you going to come for me, baby?"

Words were not an option. She was too close to . . . something. He slid one finger into her as he set his teeth against the inside of her thigh. She cried out with the pleasure of it. Her body tightened even more as he pumped her with his finger, and Kaitlyn couldn't think, could only focus on the feel of him stroking her until she slid over the edge into orgasm. The ecstasy burst through her in short, jagged waves.

"That's it, sweetness." He continued to touch her, helping her ride through the pleasure of it, extending it.

As her pulse slowed, she became aware that he'd placed his hands on her hips and was pulling her back to the edge of the bed still on her hands and knees. Rygard bent over her back and dropped kisses across her shoulder and down her spine. Standing behind her, he nudged at her entrance, gripping her backside to steady her. When he slid into her, filling her, it felt so good she rocked her hips back to meet him.

His hands dug into her. "Careful. I don't want to hurt you."

But she liked the feel of him, touching places inside her in a different way from before. Looking over her shoulder, she rolled her bottom back against him again. He groaned and his chest expanded as he took a ragged breath.

"Kaitlyn. *Fuck.*"

His hands shifted, took a better grip. He withdrew from her slowly, holding her in place so she couldn't take initiative this time. When he thrust into her, it was controlled and deep, forcing a cry of pleasure from her.

"Again?" His voice was dark, caressing her.

Panting, Kaitlyn felt herself tightening around his shaft, preparing for a wild ride. "Please."

He rocked into her, and then again, picking up tempo until he was thrusting into her hard enough that they both called out. His hands shifted to her shoulders, giving him better leverage, letting him penetrate deeper. He was so hard, so perfect a fit, stimulating every pleasure point as he slid in and out.

"Do you want me to come?" His hands left her shoulders; one buried itself in her hair, gently tugging her head and encouraging her to arch back. She didn't think it possible, but her excitement jacked up another notch. His other hand reached under, fingers finding her clitoris and rubbing in firm circles as he continued to pump into her.

Ecstasy zinged, her sensitized nerve endings firing out of control. "Yes!"

She could feel the orgasm cresting, starting low in her

belly and rippling through her entire body. He was drawing her higher and tighter, out of control, until her world exploded. As Kaitlyn convulsed, caught in the throes of pleasure, Rygard drove into her again and once more, coming with her at the final moment with a ragged cry.

CHAPTER 11

"HAD A BUSY COUPLE OF DAYS, KAT."

It wasn't a question. Kaitlyn didn't bother to turn at Dev's words. He'd listened to her summary of her time on station and the impromptu mission she'd soloed. Even if she didn't have to explain why she'd needed Chester, she would have told him. He was her captain. Of course, she'd skimmed over a couple of details, but there was no way in hell she was telling him *those*, even if he asked her directly. His face had been carefully blank as he'd left, claiming he needed to do some pondering.

Right. He'd gone off to laugh himself silly.

At least Dev had been kind enough to take himself somewhere else while he did it.

"Package came for you."

She did turn then and cocked her head to one side as she studied the black case in Dev's outstretched hand. Puzzled, she took it and placed it on her desk, then thumbed open the catches. Nestled in protective plasfoam was a sleek magnum handgun.

Dev let out a whistle. "A nice firearm you've got there, Kat. Somebody knows how to pick out a gift."

"I don't use guns." And her captain knew it. Still, she could guess who it was from, and she bit her lip to fight off the smile trying to take over her mouth.

There was a small message disk in the case. She activated it and the text laser-projected in the air above the disk.

Rygard picked it for you. Enjoy. Boggle.

Below someone had scrawled another message.

Pick up another skill set. Rygard.

"I'm thinking you found the smile we sent you looking for." Dev was grinning like an idiot.

Oh no, she was not going to admit it . . . even if the corners of her mouth were already turning upward. Before she betrayed herself with a full-blown smile, she bared her teeth. "Maybe."

"Not maybe, Kat. The man is standing in the air lock now, waiting for you."

"What?"

He held up his hands with the familiar oh-so-innocent look on his face. "Could be I'm wrong, but he fit the specs you were giving Skuld not too long ago. Not the uniform I expected, but he's built solid and looks to know his way around a fight if it comes to it."

Kaitlyn didn't wait around to let Dev tease her more. She was out of her cabin and down the hall, headed for the air lock.

"LIKE THE GIFT?" Rygard smiled as she turned the corner and stepped across the threshold of the open lock.

It hadn't been that long. Still, she drank in the sight of his strong, sculpted features, his muscled physique barely contained by his fresh uniform.

As if he would have changed over the last twelve hours or so.

"Thank you." Suddenly, Kaitlyn fell back to feeling awkward. She hadn't expected him to return. He'd gone to report in and make his decision. Either way, she figured he'd move on. She stood just short of him, unsure.

Rygard reached out for her hand and tugged her closer. "I made my report. Kept details to a minimum. Met you, escorted you back to your ship. CO wouldn't have wanted the other stuff in the report anyway, considering how shady it all was." He chuckled. "The minute he tried to head out to collect you from your team, high-level orders came through. He's not in command of our unit anymore. Your captain is an interesting man."

Kaitlyn huffed, blowing a lock of hair off her forehead. "Don't go thinking whatever it is you're thinking. He's my captain and that's it."

"You trust him."

Well, true. "It's not like . . ."

"No," Rygard agreed. "But you do trust him and that's a good thing. He'll watch your back."

Relaxing, she risked leaning into him. His arms slid around her waist in an easy embrace. She turned her face into his neck and breathed the clean, spiced scent of him. "Mmm."

"I wonder if those felids really left the station yet," he murmured.

She didn't know and didn't care. Nahkrir had told Rygard Blood Hunt was appeased, but whether that had been specifically regarding Rygard or whether it applied to everyone involved wasn't clear. She didn't think the felids would go after Rygard or anyone else who'd been following orders, at least. That had been the whole point of her helping him make things right.

Giving in to her feline urges, she rubbed her face against his skin, transferring her own scent to him and picking up as much of his as she could.

"I decided to re-up for another tour." He said it quietly, but layers of emotion hid there.

She nodded against his shoulder. "You don't need to deal with him anymore."

"Gotta hope the next-in-command will be a better man." A pause. "I'm good at being a soldier. The service is the only thing I know. My unit is specialized, sweetness, the missions we complete make a difference where no one else can. I joined because I had the edge, and violence is what I do best."

"Neither of us is exactly made for domestic living."

He rested his chin on top of her head and held her close, wrapping her in his strength. "No. We're not. And watching you make the wrong things right, seeing the way you had my back when I didn't deserve it, I can't leave my unit yet. I need to know the new commander is the right man to lead the team. I need to see my unit get back to being the strike force we were meant to be, not some band of poachers in uniform. Once I'm sure of all that, maybe I could be a merc, but I'm not there yet."

No. The service was his family. She got it.

"But I'm not going to forget you, sweetness." He stepped back, hooking a finger under her chin and tilting her head until her gaze met his. "First leave I've got, I'm coming back for you."

No need to let on how happy he'd made her. She fought

the urge to glomp onto him and instead let the purr vibrating in her chest loose. "If you can find me."

He grinned at the challenge. "Don't say goodbye."

So she didn't say anything.

He kissed her then, long and unhurried. Their tongues danced, tasting and exploring. She nipped at his mouth and he sucked on her lower lip, his hands tightening around her waist until she pressed against him.

They parted breathless.

And then he was gone.

AFTER RETURNING TO HER CABIN, Kaitlyn collapsed on her bunk and stared up at the ceiling. She felt a little hollow, but it wasn't a bad thing. It was in a place that had been too broken before to be anything but a shattered mess of pain. Rygard might not have made her whole again—she was too damaged. But he'd been good for her. And, she hoped, she'd been good for him too.

She would meet up with him again, as friends at least— and definitely something more.

TRACKING KAT

BOOK 2

"UNLESS YOU ARE BURNT, broken, or bleeding, take yourself out of my medical bay." Kaitlyn didn't bother to turn as the footsteps paused in her doorway.

"No follow-up threat?" Dev's voice surprised her. The footsteps hadn't matched her captain's usual swagger, and the air circulation carried scent up and away too quickly for it to reach her. Considering the multitude of aromas her enhanced sense of smell forced upon her when someone appeared in her doorway, usually shot and bleeding or in some stage of infection, the powerful circulation could be a blessing. Even if it did allow her captain to surprise her.

She didn't turn away from the observation window. "The only people on board are crew. They all know I won't hesitate to tear a person apart, even if I do have to put them back together again."

They'd seen her do it. Course, it hadn't been a crew member, and that particular fugitive had tried to kill her. The bounty on the man required him alive so she'd still had to stitch him up afterward.

"Convenient, you being ship's medic and all." Dev

stepped into her space anyway. "Course, this is my ship and I am captain, so I could make the point that it's my medical bay and you are one of my crew."

"You could." But it'd be for a reason. Her captain didn't play territory games without one. With her, territory meant a lot more than the average humanoid. Still, she had human logic, she could use it. "In response to your hypothetical point, I'd say you gave me this position when I became part of your crew and thus ceded this territory. Still my facility and personal space. Besides, you put in this window specifically for me."

"We had a particularly good haul from before I got that installed, made a fair chunk of cred from almost dying. Made sense to invest it in the ship."

She raised an eyebrow and watched his reflection in the window. "Modification to the hull of a spaceship never comes cheap and a window isn't an upgrade to the ship's structural integrity unless you invested in extremely high-quality materials."

"Which I did."

"It's got a perch perfect for sitting and staring out into whatever." She turned from the window and let her legs dangle over the edge as she faced him. "Too high for any normal human to get up here and enjoy."

And she needed this space, needed this window. The view into infinity eased the pent-up frustration of the beast within. Lately, she needed peace however she could find it. The panther aspect of her lurked, restless and irritable, beneath her skin. Ready to break loose.

She planted her hands on the ledge, then hopped off for a drop of several meters and landed on her feet with ease. The distance was farther than a human would willingly jump too. She hadn't had to worry about that for years now.

She straightened, then looked her captain up and down before locking her gaze with his. Her predator aspect rose in a wave as the force of her personality crashed into his. Confidence, charisma, command presence—people defined it in their own way. It wasn't something limited by words or descriptions. It was something a person experienced, a gut reaction, in any interaction with anyone else.

Her captain had won her respect and her trust years ago, but she still tended to . . . no, *enjoyed* butting heads with him on occasion.

"I've also invested a decent amount of cred." She waved her hand toward the cozy alcove containing her bunk and a neatly organized set of storage cubbies. "None of this was here before, and the separator with adjustable opacity settings wasn't cheap either."

"Skuld has the engine room, but the engine and the room are still mine. You and your medical bay are still mine." He believed in what he was saying as truth. No dissembling there. Her captain never bothered since she could identify a lie. Heartbeat and scent were easy giveaways. "This is my ship and my crew is safe on it, every one of you."

Also truth. But why? Why was he pushing her buttons? Especially when he couldn't stand toe-to-toe with her in a physical fight anymore.

"Sit down before you fall down." She snapped the words out, aware that her movement toward him took her in a slow half circle. She couldn't help stalking him. "Please."

Okay. Walking in without challenging her would've been a bad idea. His tactic forced her to think in human terms, to confront him on a battlefield of words. Her territory was only hers because she was his. Because she'd made the decision to give him her loyalty almost four years ago.

And this was why he was her captain. He always did what it took to help her keep herself in check.

"Temper, temper, Kat." Dev shook his head. He took his time about it, but he still hooked a stool with his foot and pulled it over to have a seat. "You're running on a shorter fuse these past couple of days and I need you to put a leash on it."

"And I need you hale and whole to hold the leash." She shot back the truth as she took a scanning device from her worktable and began to run a diagnostic. Ever since her first mutation, he'd always been the one to talk her back to finding the human part of herself. He helped her control the beast her torturers had burned into her DNA. "This latest injury to your knee isn't healing as fast as it should. You're putting too much strain on it."

As mercenaries, their missions tended to be varied and challenging. Every one of the crew maintained a high level of physical performance no matter what their special skill sets might be.

"No time to be lounging with my feet up, twiddling my thumbs."

She snarled. "Do the right thing to heal properly."

More than half their missions came from high up in the Terran military chain of command, engaging confidential ops when official troops couldn't be assigned. Dev's team did well when going through the proper channels would have taken too much time. Without Dev and the trust those ranked officers had in him, the connection would be lost and they'd be just another merc team looking for a job.

Besides, she needed him to be a-hundred-percent. The entire crew needed him to keep her under control.

Memories surfaced of Triton Moon Base, of the invasion and her capture. Young faces contorted with fear as she'd raged, trapped inside the tiny room they'd put her in after her escape from their attackers. Her fellow cadets—the ones that hadn't been captured—hadn't recognized her at first, couldn't handle her. The stink of their terror only enraged her further, inciting the prey drive in the beast she'd become. It'd been Katzer who'd had the presence of mind to lock her in and stay at the door until Dev could arrive. Until Dev talked her back to coherency and human thought processes.

"You're my captain."

And the only person still alive who could call her back to herself when she went feral. Katzer was gone.

"I'm not the only man with a portion of your trust." Dev's voice might have been gentle, but the quirk at the corner of his mouth betrayed the mischief.

With an effort, she let go the darker worry riding her. "It's only been a few months and Rygard hasn't witnessed that side of me yet."

"He's fought beside you, seen you go furry, and come out of it still a rock-solid companion." Her captain ticked off the good points on each finger. "Those things aside, I do believe you've let him put a smile on your sweet face. I owe the man a debt for bringing a bit of light to one of mine."

His.

Okay, a part of her had shifted and settled into place when he'd claimed her as one of his. She recognized the need, but he'd recognized it before her. The need to belong, be accepted.

"I'm also assuming he helped you past a few other key obstacles in your social development." Dev raised an eyebrow at her. If he wiggled his eyebrows, she'd toss all respect to hell and rip him to shreds out of embarrassment.

Just no. No need to discuss any further details of her liaison with Rygard. She retreated to a safer course of discussion.

"He's seen me in cat form . . . when I was in control."

"Ah." He nodded. Singular knowledge lived behind those eyes. He'd been there as the changes to her genetic code ripped through her body cell by cell, back when her shape-shifts hadn't been as smooth. They might be quicker and easier these days, but they still caused her seven hells worth of agony.

Silence.

Diagnostic scans complete, she went to her dispensing units and brought back a small bottle. Pills rattled inside it as she slapped it down on the table beside him.

Unruffled, Dev stood, his weight evenly distributed on both legs, as if the one knee wasn't a swelling mess. "As it happens, I'll have some time on ship to give this a bit of tender care."

She shot him a glance before fussing with her equipment on the table. As a predator, she could sense his weakness, wanted to take a swipe at him, test him. Part of her needed reassurance he could still handle her, wanted him to counter her attack—and another part of her crouched deathly still.

Prey.

Dev didn't step away. He stood taller, weight distributed over the balls of his feet. The air of authority around him crystallized and became unmistakable. "Put a leash on it." He looked her directly in the eyes, and his will stood up to hers through that direct gaze, driving out any misconceptions about his status as prey. Relief flooded through her as he continued with his informal briefing. "We're taking on passengers. Military. They're a special team put together to provide support to your soldier's unit for the next phase of Rygard's mission. From the intel packet I was sent, the orders are escalating from reconnaissance to decisive action. These won't be your average grunts. Each will have special skill sets and every one of them is trained to look and listen, observe and *think*. I want you in control, not a hiss or a snarl out of you. Not a single hint that you're anything but a merc unless I give my say-so."

"Understood." For now, she could give him that.

She would need more from him to keep her head clear and the predator locked down.

CHAPTER 2

KAITLYN ARRIVED in the cargo hold as the intercom announced confirmation of the ship-to-ship docking procedure. Dev's merc vessel was a decent size, built primarily for intergalactic and interplanetary runs. The hull had some aerodynamics taken into design consideration for the odd atmospheric landing, but mostly it was meant to remain in orbit with shuttles to take teams planetside when necessary. Enough room for her to roam most of the time, yet not so big, they wouldn't feel it as the significantly larger military cruiser extended its transfer tube and locked it into place over their cargo doors, hissing as the seals cycled and equalized air pressure.

Skuld caught sight of her as she stepped to one side, slightly behind the rest of the crew. Kaitlyn traded nods with a few, but for Skuld, she smiled. A little. The gorgeous brunette had changed into a clean ship suit, crisp with fresh starch. Normally, her gear was splotched with random oil splatter and grease from working with the ship's engines. Skuld moved to join her and gave her a nudge with an elbow. "You think any of them will be cute?"

Kaitlyn shrugged. "Not too worried about it."

"Well, you have a rugged officer and a gentleman by the name of Rygard." Skuld bobbed her head, soft golden-brown waves bouncing. "But it's been a while since we've gone into port at a decent space station, and I've got an itch to scratch. At least hope a couple of them will be cute, for me."

A snort escaped before Kaitlyn arranged her features into a properly blank expression. Skuld managed to crack her mood every time. Dev might keep her in control, but it was Skuld who reminded her what it was like to enjoy random things. "I do focus on one partner at a time." And she missed Rygard, a lot more than she'd admit out loud. "But I will hope at least one of them meets your . . . needs."

The smile Skuld gave her dazzled. Then it was suddenly replaced by an uncharacteristically somber expression as delicate eyebrows drew together. "My last couple of choices haven't been stellar. You'll tell me if my hormones overlook jackass warning flags in favor of muscular prowess, won't you?"

It took a minute to sink in. "Seriously? You're going to rely on my opinion of the male side of the species?"

Did they somehow hop through a wormhole without her noticing?

"I'm always willing to give a guy the benefit of the doubt. You tend to assume all men are assholes, with very few exceptions." Ah well, it was her Skuld after all. "The way I figure it, between the two of us we should be able to identify a candidate who might be worth more than a one and done for me."

Kaitlyn pinched the bridge of her nose as she worked

through Skuld's logic. "I'm almost afraid to ask, but I will anyway. Why are we looking for a candidate?"

"You came back aboard after the mission on Dysnomia all soft and glowing. Didn't yell at us much at all for leaving you there without warning. I figure Rygard had a lot to do with your good mood. Hell, it lasted for a solid week. That's a lot of unwinding he did for you."

Kaitlyn tipped her head to one side. "It was not all rest and hot sex."

Skuld grinned. "I bet there was a lot of that though. Only other activity that relieves stress so well for you is beating people up and you don't do that to crew. The courier run you did on station didn't include an anticipated body count either. Besides, Cap'n said you made friends with his contact."

Kaitlyn didn't look away as Skuld glanced at her sideways. Wouldn't hurt Skuld to wonder a while longer as to whether there actually had been casualties. Healthier to always assume there might be, actually. As close as they'd grown, Skuld shouldn't ever forget what Kaitlyn could do, did do, on some of their more serious missions.

There'd been a bar brawl—and a body count, to be honest—from the little adventure on Dysnomia Station. None of it had fallen within the parameters of her original assignment. Still, Dev hadn't had to cover her tracks with the on-station officials, and she'd saved more lives than she'd snuffed out. She'd lose no sleep over it. In fact, she'd not only managed to refrain from seriously damaging her contact for the delivery, she'd even made friends with Boggle. Bonus. And then there was Rygard.

"Let's just, see who comes aboard, okay?" Kaitlyn tried for the cautious route. "I'm pretty sure the captain wants me to hang back and stay unobtrusive."

Eyes widening, Skuld nodded. "Gotcha. We're going to keep the warm fuzzy off the radar for now."

Of course, her panther form wouldn't be what Kaitlyn considered warm and fuzzy. If Skuld tried to call her fluffy next, there might be an issue.

Kaitlyn relaxed, letting her shoulders drop a touch and her hands fall loose at her sides. Skuld might be cheerful and bubbly, and there was a sharp mind behind those pretty blue eyes. She could be trusted not to let important things slip despite her tendency to babble in ways Kaitlyn never would.

"If at all possible, let's keep it quiet." Kaitlyn met the gaze of several of the crew standing nearby. They weren't eavesdropping. Still, couldn't blame a person for overhearing a conversation held right next to them. Might as well make the message clear. "Somebody might have the security clearance to know about our crew and why I'm allowed to be part of it, but Dev would've mentioned it. Better to save him the fuss and keep it to ourselves."

Over the last couple of years, there'd been plenty of attempts to restrain her for immediate transport back to a military lab by people who didn't wait to find out she was aboard with approval from someplace high up in the command structure. Since the events on Triton Moon Base, the Terran military had a standing set of orders to take any encountered shape-shifters into custody.

Dev's security clearance wasn't obvious until he needed to wave it in the officious faces of the overly zealous. That sort of clout tended to be better used with the least frequency possible. Anything Kaitlyn could do to avoid the nonsense was all to the better, plus saved her endless hours of anger management.

"It's kind of amazing how you're not bitter about the

situation." Skuld twisted a lock of hair around her finger. "I mean, with your temper and all. We've had to get tricksy to avoid you being taken into custody in the last couple of short missions."

"Dev says it spices up all our lives." And yes, she winced at the dry tone of her own voice.

Skuld only smiled more. "We've got your back, Katy. Always."

How could she not smile in return? "Appreciated."

And that was why she wasn't bitter. Life could have been so much worse.

She'd been on Triton Moon Base when the virus had been used for the first time against Terran personnel. That virus, and what it did to her genetic code, was the reason shape-shifters were sought out in the first place. It wasn't sanctioned, and any indication of its presence could indicate a spy from the very hostile force that attacked Triton Moon Base four years ago.

"Seems we've got our welcome party assembled." Dev strode into the cargo area from the main corridor. "Did our impending guests knock yet?"

Kaitlyn crossed her arms over her chest. "No. I'm guessing they're waiting for us to open the cargo bay doors."

Dev raised his eyebrows. "Whatever happened to the pleasantries?"

She lifted one shoulder in a half shrug. "We could wait for them to give the blast shields a kiss with whatever ordnance they've got on hand."

"Nah, we're all on the same side for this mission. None of that sort of fun is going to happen this time . . . most likely." Dev waved a hand as he walked over to the control panel next to the cargo bay doors and keyed in a sequence to give him visuals on the group waiting on the other side.

"Besides, this is a special detail. Ought to be full of all sorts of unique individuals to interest us."

"So each of them carries a different type of ammo?" Skuld continued the banter. "I call dibs on the one packing the largest gun."

"They would likely be compensating." Kaitlyn gave a small smile but wiped it off her face as the doors began to cycle open. For Skuld, she smiled occasionally, and for Dev, once in a great while. These soldiers, though, they were strangers.

The first man stumbled back a half step as the doors opened outward. He wasn't in danger of being hit, but he hadn't gauged the distance right either. He didn't wear the officer's uniform well; it looked so new, she was guessing it still carried the original starch and creases. Rather, the uniform marked him. It reminded her of tourists wearing big plastic badges with bright letters spelling out, "Hello! My name is . . ." Without the starched fabric and shiny officer insignia on his shoulders, no one would ever think him military, much less an officer. Two bars, connected. Captain.

Having spent her childhood on the military-and-science installation of Triton Moon Base, Kaitlyn had encountered her share of commissioned officers. If this man had ever seen combat, she'd give Chester a bath for Skuld, with lavender-scented bubbles. The little tube rat would love that.

The officer in question finally stepped on through. He waited a long moment, looking around the cargo bay before resting his gaze on Dev. "Captain Devron Rishkillian, I presume. I am Captain Percival Harold Petrico-Calin IV." Another pause, to which her captain did not respond. Good. If the officer was such a stickler for formality, he should give her captain the called-for respect. Finally, the visiting officer tagged on the courtesy due. "Permission to come aboard, Captain?"

Defensive. The man brandished etiquette as if he were waving a big stick.

"Permission granted to you and your team, Captain Petrico-Calin . . . the Fourth." Dev's response carried no inflection whatsoever.

She dragged her thoughts out of the past and focused on the present.

A woman stepped in after Petrico-Calin. No uniform, and she had less starch in her suit, but she stood like her clothing chafed in uncomfortable places.

Petrico-Calin inclined his head with respect. "And may I introduce Theodora Amelia Turner III, esteemed representative of the Terran senate?"

"Miz Turner." Dev's expression didn't change—not even a quirk at the corner of his mouth. Still, Kaitlyn caught the stiffening between her captain's shoulder blades. A minute move, one she was privy to because he trusted his crew and because she watched his back fairly often, literally and figuratively.

Turner's gaze swept the area, and unlike Petrico-Calin, her visual inventory took in every person in the room and cataloged them. "I would have thought you would have your entire crew mustered for this first meeting, Captain Rishkillian."

Interesting. Turner knew more about Dev's crew than she'd like. About two-thirds of the crew were present, mostly the ground teams who had few on-board duties aside from general maintenance. They were on hand to help stow any equipment their guests brought aboard. Tails, Hassle,

Durn, and the rest of the permanent crew that made up the core team were busy at their stations.

Dev shrugged. "Well now, we're a small crew, comparatively. They've got their duties to be attending to. I'd rather have my pilot at the helm, for example, instead of down here in the cargo bay watching me welcome you aboard. Kaitlyn, here, serves as my first mate and ship's medic. Skuld keeps us in the air and spaceworthy." Her captain kept the introductions short and sweet, holding the attention of the two on him. "If you gentlepeople will come with me, I'll show you to your quarters and Kaitlyn will see to showing your team to general bunks with the rest of our crew."

Petrico-Calin and Turner allowed themselves to be led away, another thing her captain wouldn't ever do. He had always seen to his crew before himself if he wasn't bunking directly with them anyway.

Skuld waited until Dev and the others had gotten halfway down the main corridor before nudging Kaitlyn. "So how many other soldiers are we taking aboard?"

"Beats me." Kaitlyn could hear them coming, her heightened senses picking up interesting, and very unusual, footsteps. "We'll find out in the next second or so."

The first to appear was a squat, solid wall of a man. A grizzled veteran, he didn't need the white blaze of hair that cut through his dark grays to indicate his age. Years of combat had weathered the brown skin of his face and crisscrossed his hands with scars. He stopped an exact inch from the threshold before settling his eyes on Kaitlyn and Skuld.

Kaitlyn pushed away from the crate she'd been leaning against to stand where her captain had been a moment before.

"Ma'am." The old soldier nodded first to her, then to Skuld. "Gunnery Sergeant, requesting permission to come aboard."

Ah, a soldier with actual manners. He'd said the words with real sincerity..

"My captain granted permission, Gunnery Sergeant, to you and yours." She considered, and then added to that. "You are welcome aboard."

"Thank you, ma'am. The team calls me Badger. I'd be obliged if you did the same."

"Kaitlyn." She nodded and then tipped her head toward her friend. "And this is our ship's engineer, Skuld."

Badger raised his fingers to tip an imaginary hat. "Ma'am."

He stepped over the threshold then and turned to gesture to the soldiers behind him.

Skuld burst out with a delighted clap of her hands. "A dog!"

Fantastic.

Chester chose that moment to pop his head out from the front of Skuld's ship suit. He'd been napping earlier, but the little ferret couldn't possibly sleep through his mistress's current excitement.

Chester might be an annoying tube rat, but he was crew and not just any weasel. Smarter than he looked, he was a key subject in behavioral and training experiments Kaitlyn conducted. He also helped Skuld retrieve tools when she dropped them in hard-to-reach places within the ship's engine. All the training aside, he was one of hers and had helped her in several tight situations, as much as his tiny brain could. He'd gone above and beyond in his loyalty. Besides, Skuld would be devastated if something happened to him. So Kaitlyn kept her attention on the dog.

The dog's ears snapped forward, dark eyes on the ferret. He didn't so much as tug on his leash or quicken his pace as he stepped into the cargo bay at his handler's side. But every muscle under his thick coat bunched, and he practically vibrated with tension. Black and tan, with the sharp features of a classic German shepherd dog from the Old World, he was a handsome specimen. Big too, with broad shoulders and a deep chest. She would bet he outweighed her in cat form.

She switched her weight over to one side, deliberately redirecting the dog's attention. Those big triangular ears swiveled her way, and the dog tilted his head to one side as he caught sight of her. Real intelligence met her gaze; a powerful personality lived behind those deep brown puppy eyes. Sure that she had his attention, she lifted her lip in a hint of a snarl. A faint whine, inaudible to human ears, was the only hint that the dog caught what the humans didn't. His gaze dropped to the floor for a brief second before rising back up to meet hers again.

He was not the top predator on this ship, and they both knew it.

"Staff Sergeant Taylor, ma'am. You can call me Tracer." The handler spoke to Skuld, his attention and his scent making it clear he had eyes only for her the minute he walked aboard. "This is Kx9-8775. We all call him Max."

"Can I pet him?" Skuld was still excited about the pooch and apparently heedless of the potential danger to Chester.

"Sure." Tracer rubbed the top of his partner's head. The dog easily stood at the man's hip, his big head at waist height. "Just keep your eyes on me as you step on over and don't look directly at him. He'll take it as an act of aggression if you look him in the eyes."

"Oh." Skuld had no problem following those directions. Kaitlyn decided to pretend she hadn't heard the giggle that followed.

When Kaitlyn was in panther form and in a particularly bad mood, Dev had given the same warning to Skuld about Kaitlyn.

Skuld stepped on over, and the big dog sat and offered a paw to shake.

Charming.

It was still a dog.

Chester apparently had less instinct for self-preservation than his mistress because he stretched his long body out to sniff noses. Kaitlyn tensed, her weight forward as she balanced on the balls of her feet, ready to intercede. The dog only craned his neck to meet the ferret—big black nose touching tiny ferret nose. Chester gave a pleased squeak.

"Look, they're going to be friends." The real delight in Skuld's voice had to be tugging at the heartstrings of every person in the cargo bay.

It'd be cute, if one snap of those jaws couldn't end Chester's existence.

"Max is a good boy, ma'am." Tracer said it with an assurance Kaitlyn almost believed.

Define *good*.

Chester was a good ferret in Skuld's eyes, but the little weasel regularly looted through Kaitlyn's belongings and stole anything that caught his fancy. At the moment, Kaitlyn wasn't sure if the ferret really wanted to make friends or if he was trying to figure out a way to get closer to the shiny tags on the pooch's collar. The canine might not care, but as close to Max's vulnerable neck as those tags were, he wasn't likely to let Chester get to them. Plus, if

Chester leaned over any farther, more than just the ferret was going to spill out the front of Skuld's outfit.

Wouldn't that be fun?

Kaitlyn didn't miss the way the handler kept his hand in his dog's fur, at the base of his skull. She also caught the way Tracer tightened his grip on the big dog's scruff as the ferret bobbed up and down under the dog's nose, sniffing and chattering in his continued efforts to make friends. It was a subtle signal and one the dog heeded. Chester was safe, at least while the handler was present.

She'd need to have a word with Skuld later to be sure she didn't leave Chester loose if the dog was anywhere without his handler.

"Ma'am, if you'd step behind me, please." Badger interrupted the meeting of tube rat and the beast. Skuld rose as asked, stuffing Chester back into the front of her jumpsuit when the ferret would have crawled out to climb all over the dog. Oh and wouldn't *that* have gone over well?

The next person to appear elicited a gasp from Skuld, but Kaitlyn had heard the telltale shuffle and ring of metal shackles. She wasn't startled by the sheer size of him, though the heavy-duty bindings didn't look to be nearly sufficient restraint. The two hulking military police flanking him did nothing to provide even the illusion of security. Black and gold scales stood out in contrast against his white skin, scattered in a diamond pattern at the sides of his thick neck and over his collar bones, disappearing beneath his shirt. He stood head and shoulders above the other men, which meant he towered over Kaitlyn and Skuld.

"Kaitlyn, you've taken out guys bigger than him, right?" Skuld whispered to her behind a trembling hand.

Kaitlyn had neutralized opponents much larger than

herself plenty of times without a moment's doubt in her ability to do so. Size wasn't the issue with this one.

She motioned Skuld to silence.

No. What gave her pause with this man was the confidence he carried across his broad shoulders, as if he wasn't being led bound, hands and feet in chains. He walked like a man who took each step because he wanted to, and Kaitlyn wondered if his guards realized it. They appeared too comfortable with the weapons in their hands and the shackles on their prisoner—too complacent. She wondered when the big man planned to leave them broken and bleeding in some dark corridor. Preferably not aboard Dev's ship.

He caught sight of her, and at that moment, the pooch rose to his feet, growling. Between the three of them, it was no longer certain which of them was the most dangerous or the deadliest. Oh, she'd give the prisoner size. The German shepherd dog would have to cede to either of them in terms of overall badass factor.

Kaitlyn watched the way the big man saw everything in the room without ever losing his focus on her, and she didn't dare break her gaze from his. The cat aspect of her crouched low inside her mind, watching and waiting for him to go away. One thing was certain: the man had the strongest prey drive of the three of them.

Plus, his scent told her he wasn't precisely human either, if the scales hadn't been enough of a clue. He didn't smell awful—no, not the normal human-trapped-on-a-ship-for-too-long-without-a-shower kind of issue. He carried musk around him the same way large predators did, as a part of his personality and an indicator of his mood. It might not stink, but humans definitely didn't produce it.

"No worries." Tracer was reassuring Skuld as he gave

the leash a sharp tug. Max came to a reluctant heel. "Those bindings are rated for much bigger humanoids. He's completely secured."

Kaitlyn doubted that, but then she'd recognized the issue as soon as the man made his appearance.

"Bharguest is with us on special consult." Tracer continued to give Skuld the information dump. "He's got firsthand knowledge of our destination and he's cooperating with us in return for his parole."

Interesting. As if the prisoner needed parole to gain his freedom. Nope. He had a different agenda, and if he was aboard Dev's ship, she'd want to be sure it didn't have anything to do with them.

"What did he do?" Skuld's words were spoken in a hush, the scary-badass factor affecting her bubbly personality.

Bharguest pulled back his thin lips in a silent hiss. As she'd done earlier with the Kx9, Kaitlyn changed her stance. Just like that, his attention snapped back to her.

Okay, she'd admit it. The man intimidated the hell out of her. If she'd been in panther form, every hair would be on end and her claws would be fully extended.

"Doesn't matter." Kaitlyn forced the words out and tossed them to the room in general, maybe to him. She truly didn't care what crime he'd committed to end up incarcerated. She did know where he wouldn't be allowed once he did get his parole. "There's a mission to complete. If done to satisfaction of the higher-ups, this person goes free."

And "freedom" was about as subjective a term as "good."

"Anywhere in the great big universe but the Terran solar system." Gravelly from disuse, the prisoner's voice still sent a shiver down her spine. Charisma: the man had it in spades—the kind to talk anybody into anything and lead people directly to their graves. "They've banned me from going there."

How fun. What a coincidence—she didn't plan to be anywhere inside the Terran solar system anytime soon either. But the why of it still left her wondering. And hell but Kaitlyn had never been one to curb her curiosity. She cocked her head to the side. "Do you care?"

The corners of his mouth turned up slowly in a wicked grin. Light sparked in his cold eyes. "Not at the moment."

Ah well, she'd never been a slow learner either. This situation had "proceed with caution" plastered all over it. She'd gone and done something interesting. Not the best move she'd ever made.

"Well then that's someone else's nightmare for another day." Shouldn't have called him a nightmare, but she figured he was somebody's. No sense in ignoring the fact.

Course, she gave several people in the Terran government ulcers and cold sweats at night. Yet she doubted anything she'd managed to date would be on scale with what this man was capable of. And that was as he stood now, in shackles. Set him loose and arm him? She wouldn't be sleeping either.

The prisoner inhaled deeply, the wide expanse of his chest stretching the fabric of his tunic. "It's been a while since I smelled so much danger bundled into such a tiny package."

"Can't underestimate the tube rat," Kaitlyn shot back without hesitation as both the Kx9 handler and Badger directed startled glances her way. "He might be tiny but he could rip your throat out in your sleep."

Chester gave a verifying squeak. Good boy.

"That's enough introductions for now," Badger growled

over the deep chuckle rumbling from the prisoner's chest. "With your permission, ma'am, we'll get him locked down in your ship's holding area and the rest of my people will come aboard and get settled in."

"Of course. I'll lead the way. Skuld can show the men to where they can bunk." Dev wouldn't mind the delegation of her initial task. This was more important. She never took her focus off Bharguest and wouldn't until he was safely off the ship and light-years away.

KAITLYN HARBORED no qualms about securing the entryway to the med bay when she turned in for the night.

Locks. Yup. Got 'em.

Skuld had been pretty absentminded in saying she'd set the ones on her quarters, distracted. She was already daydreaming about one of the newcomers, best bet was the dog handler, but Kaitlyn had given the verbal commands to lock up to Chester too. One of them would remember—most likely the tube rat.

At least he stuck to his training well. Kaitlyn noted that she should construct another study to determine how long his memory managed to hold on to certain commands without reinforcement. Might come in handy.

There hadn't been any issues getting their guests settled in their various locations despite her concerns regarding the one they called Bharguest. After she'd monitored the prisoner being secured in the holding facility, she'd doubled back to check on Skuld. The ship's engineer had no trouble with the other soldiers and had set them to bunking with Dev's grunts in the regular crew quarters. The cuteness, it was strong with Skuld, but luckily for them all, Skuld wielded it with a kind heart. Still, every one of them had been jumping to do as the sweet brunette asked, silly grins on each of their faces.

They all needed Skuld's kindness in their line of work, especially Kaitlyn. It helped her remember how to be human.

Maybe she ought to take a night walk to ensure everyone stayed where they were supposed to.

It wasn't that Kaitlyn thought something was going to happen. Life had taught her to double-check and triple-check. Murphy's Law was every bit as much of a reality as the laws of physics.

Finally alone though, she let loose a deep sigh. Every one of those new soldiers, with the exception of Badger, tweaked a nerve at one point or another. She could smell their interest in Dev's crew, especially her and Skuld. She had caught the speculative looks out of the corner of her eye. Skuld never let it bother her. Hell, the woman thrived on it and usually took her pick from the people who lined up. But Skuld wasn't aware of the constant stink of their pheromones. *Bleh.*

Kaitlyn had never handled the attention well, and that included before her life had been ended by the hiss of an injection gun.

Lighten up, Kitten. People are allowed to be interested in other people.

Even now, when she'd made a new friend in Boggle and had a thing going with Rygard, Katzer's voice came to her from memory. He'd had a lot of wisdom for a young man. Truthfully, they'd been kids. He'd have made an incredible soldier, military or merc, whatever he might have decided to be. He'd wanted her to go on living. Told her to.

And there were more voices in her life now to bring a smile to her face.

An alert chimed, different from the ship-wide notifications. This one was her own personal reminder, set to go off only in the medical facilities.

She strode over to her bunk and dialed up the opacity on the screen serving as a divider between her space and the rest of the med bay. Not that anyone could come through the locked door besides Dev—as ship's captain he did have an override access. Still, she felt better for the added barrier to ensure her privacy. She took one more minute to run her hands through her hair and wish for Skuld's ability to do the fairy-tale-princess transformation with cosmetics. Then her personal screen, set into the wall next to her bunk, lit up with an incoming vid call. The display blinked.

Holographic projection?

Obviously. She'd take the closest she could get to the real thing.

In moments, a high-definition hologram hovered over her bunk and Rygard gave her a wink.

There he was, life-size and breathing. His dark hair was trimmed close around the sides but looking a little longer on top. His square jaw was shaded with a day's worth of stubble. His skin was olive-toned, tanned from his time planetside. The hologram projected his full length, seated on a cot. He was built broad and solid, sturdy and rugged.

The definition was good enough that she could see the reflection of the light sources around him in his eyes—said a lot for his equipment. The lighting was dim and what she could see of his surroundings placed him in a heavy-duty utility tent. Of course, whatever mission he'd been deployed for rated high-security and the best the military could afford to ensure his team's success.

The only reason he could contact her was because the military crew they'd recently taken on board represented a supplement to his team. He'd sent her the encoded message only a short time after Dev had told her they were taking on passengers.

Still, no reason to question the why. For the moment, she embraced the good fortune.

"Hey, beautiful." He must have been studying her as she'd been lost in thought.

He had a holo unit with him too, and a three-dimensional likeness of her most likely floated cross-legged on a bunk right in front of him.

Just like that, her tongue twisted in her mouth and all she could get out was a single soft word. "Hey."

He grinned then, the creases of strain across his forehead disappearing. "Still not good with the compliments, huh?"

Her cheeks heated and damn but didn't he grin wider as he watched her.

"It's okay to get used to them. You deserve to feel good about yourself." He reached out and touched the holographic her. His holograph came just short of reaching her.

Suddenly, she ached for his touch—the feel of his hands running over her skin, rough and gentle at the same time.

She sucked in air. Holographic tech advanced every day, but the holo was still a holo. "I miss you."

His smile faded a little, no less warm, but a bit sad. "Miss you too, sweetness." A pause. "Won't be long now. The team should have boarded your merc ship. I'm waiting on a briefing from the commanding officer, but I got the impression from his last communication that he's going to be passing on information to me the old-fashioned way. Could take a while."

"Yeah." Traditional military types disseminated their information down through the chain of command. She'd learned procedure in her school days. Light speed communication wouldn't make that any faster. "As a commissioned officer, you should be hearing from the commanding officer as soon as possible."

"There are officers and then there are officers. 'As soon as possible' can be subjective." Rygard gave a noncommittal shrug. "Tell me about them."

Narrowing her eyes, she studied him. He'd drawn back from the camera, his eyes now in shadow and lids at half-mast, effectively hiding his expression. "You know who is supposed to be coming."

He tipped his head. "I know names, rank, position. I know skill sets on record. You met them."

"For a few minutes each at most."

"You read a person better in a few minutes than most can in days."

A warm flutter tickled her belly, and she smiled. Pleased, she nodded to concede his point and acknowledge the compliment. Scent, body language, the random wordless noises people made—they told a story, whether people were conscious of them or not. Being partly panther gave her an advantage in picking those up. She'd fine-tuned her perceptions over time with Dev's help.

"I don't like people who lean on their connections." Careful, careful. Even to Rygard, she wouldn't directly say she disliked a commanding officer. Too much chance the admission could come back to bite him, or her.

But Rygard seemed unconcerned. He chuckled instead.

"I figured when I saw the names. The attitudes match, huh?"

"If the two you're thinking of are the same two I'm thinking of, hell yes."

"What about the actual person leading the grunts?"

There was another point neither of them would spell out. Yes, a commanding officer led their team—hopefully they led them well. The CO was also the very visible part of the unit, handling incoming orders and commentary from higher-ups. If they did their job right, they stood as a shield for their people when shit rained down on them. Took up a lot of time and concentration—and that was if they were a good leader. If they sucked, well, an even greater need existed then. In every unit, a second person handled the details and knew each of the members of the team up close and personal. They monitored the morale and kept the soldiers in line. When they were all hip-deep in enemy fire, they gave the orders on the fly.

"Good man, solid." She paused. "A little on the grumpy side."

Rygard placed his hand over his mouth and rubbed his beard. Didn't manage to completely hide his smile or muffle the snort of laughter. "Anybody interesting?"

She raised an eyebrow. "Tell me why no one warned me there'd be a dog."

"We need the dog. See, this planet's electromagnetic field is a pain in the ass. It wreaks havoc with most of our equipment, scanners and communications especially." Rygard lifted a small squat device with a cable dangling out of each side. "We sacrificed a few of the worst scanners to mod the communications equipment enough to block out the effects and boost the signal. Otherwise, you wouldn't be seeing me as anything more than a static blob."

She huffed out a soft laugh and pressed the tip of her tongue against her upper teeth as the thought tickled her.

His eyes softened as he focused on her mouth. "And damn, sweetness, but I did want to see you. Really miss kissing that mouth of yours."

She bit her lower lip. Uncomfortable, she dodged back to steadier conversation. "The dog seems okay, for a canine."

"He's special. Those kay-ex-nines are all a step above the ones they used on Old Terra, way back when. They've been genetically tinkered with, and their training is intense. Without one-hundred-percent reliability from our scanners, we need the dog to do direct assessments. His paws will go where the scanners can't and he'll be able to do the scouting we need."

"I'm guessing the scouting is highly dangerous?" She could provide backup to the Kx9 unit and he knew it. In fact, her particular skills in scouting allowed her to go undetected. No one looking for human spies ever suspected a large feline in the trees. If they caught sight of her at all.

"Every aspect of this mission carries enough risk to require a healthy dose of caution." Guarded words. He watched her carefully.

They'd only spent a couple of days on Dysnomia Station together and a few brief hours here and there when their paths crossed over the last six months. It still surprised her how well he knew her. Of course, those first couple of days had started with a glass of Scotch and escalated to a close-range firefight, a covert rescue initiative, and some unexpected diplomatic relations with aliens. You really got to know the person at your back under pressure in that scale of chaos.

She shrugged. "The handler is okay, I guess. He's a little too boy-next-door for me. Got a bit of steel strapped to his backbone though or the dog wouldn't listen to him. That's one dominant canine."

"Noted." He sounded pleased. "Anyone else?"

"You mean the jackass meathead in charge of the heavy-armory units? Met him last night after the others. Man acted like he had X-ray vision and if he steps too close to Skuld he might not live to report in for duty planetside." The lecher in question had spent a good deal of time getting an eyeful of Kaitlyn too. She'd have taken time to impress on him how very sorry he'd be if he made any advances on Skuld or herself but she'd had bigger problems to worry about in the form of Bharguest.

"I don't like personalities like his. They're risk factors. You're a whole lot of sexy walking around on a ship where the only company they have is their hand or some other hairy backside. They learn not to press their advantage within the team, because those are the same people who have your back in combat." There was tension in Rygard's voice and he shook his head. "Whoever put this team together assembled the right skill sets, but wasn't concerned about diversifying the combat roster much."

Kaitlyn huffed, resisting the urge to cross her arms over her chest in reflection of what she thought of that. Even when technology and civilization advanced at light speed, some attitudes evolved slower than tectonic-plate movement.

"You hold your own and most of them will leave you alone. The grumpy soldier you sort of like will keep them in line and away from your friend." Rygard sighed. "I need reinforcements, and wish they were all good people. The intel we've been gathering here is enough to escalate to the next phase. We could be saving a lot of lives when we're ready to make our move, innocent lives, but I don't want you or your crew at risk because of them."

Saving even one innocent life would be worth putting up with a perv or two for a short space flight.

"It'll be fine." She crossed her arms over her chest. "No bloodshed until we hit planetside unless one of them draws blood on me first. Happy?"

Despite the shadows, she saw his brows draw together and his lips tighten into a flat line. When he spoke, it was through clenched jaws. "Anyone draws your blood and they will answer to me."

She hadn't expected to trigger such a strong protective reaction. Hadn't intended for him to get upset either.

"I didn't mean to—"

"It's fine, sweetness." He cut her off. He rolled his head, vertebrae popping audibly. "You're more than capable of defending yourself and your own. I've been proud to fight with you at my back and not too proud to admit you've saved my ass. But, remember this, Kaitlyn"—he leaned in until the light chased away the shadows and she could see his eyes—"you and me, we have something. For as long as you're mine and I'm yours, anyone touches you without your say so and they answer to me."

Wow.

Somehow, she'd always thought she'd have been annoyed if a man ever claimed her the way Rygard had. Instead, heat spread through her, and her chest tightened. "Back at you."

"Anyone else?" he prompted again.

At that, her temper did spike. "If you wanted to know about the prisoner, why didn't you ask about him?"

Thing about her, she tended to be a little too direct occasionally. Okay, most of the time. Still, he usually didn't mince words, and she appreciated it. Why was he dancing around now instead of going straight for the goal?

"I wanted to know your impressions on the entire team," he returned, his voice calm. "But I noticed you didn't mention him yet and from the information I've got, he's definitely one to catch anyone's attention."

"He's very interesting." She tugged on a lock of her hair and twisted it around her finger as she considered. "I'm actually not sure I could take him in a fair fight. Definitely not in closed quarters; I'd need room to maneuver."

Rygard's eyebrows shot up. "The night we met, you plowed through a bar brawl to get to a glass of Scotch. You sure this man is that dangerous?"

"Tweedle One and Tweedle Two definitely aren't the reason the man is still in custody." She dismissed the two military police with a wave of her hand. Usually, she had a modicum of respect for security forces, but these two were not the Terran military's finest by any stretch of the imagination. "He walked on board this ship because he wanted to. And the minute he got on board, he changed his mind about something."

"What?" Worry colored Rygard's voice, and his features froze in a scowl.

"Beats me." She shook her head. "He's good, very good, with body language. The only information I'm getting is what he tells me. He might as well be a couple of feet tall with big ears, shriveled, and green."

"Say again?"

"Never mind. Boggle had me watch some Old Terran movies." She considered for a moment, then got back on track. "The man is an alpha, more than just aggressive or assertive. He's not a normal human. Don't know what he is, but I sure as hell can tell you what he isn't. All I know is, I really, really want to know more about him."

"Stay away from him." Rygard didn't put any command behind the statement. He knew better. "I'm asking you to give him a wide berth. Not because you couldn't take him or because you're curious about him. I'm more worried about him getting curious about you."

Huh. Hadn't expected that.

She cocked her head to the side. "He hasn't said much yet. The couple of bits he's said though? Definitely does not play well with others. I don't like him aboard Dev's ship without knowing more. You mind if I ask Boggle to dig into his background since you want me to avoid him?"

"Wouldn't be a bad idea. But tell Boggle not to dig too far into this mission."

Technically, Rygard's team was on some sort of supersecret, need-to-know operation. Of course, operational security had layers, and Boggle excelled at peeling them back to get to information. Part of the reason she'd never made the decision to join the military after the injection had to do with those layers, the lack of transparency. She didn't like to go in blind, following orders from someone she didn't personally trust. Rygard's decision to re-up for another tour of service had less to do with that and more to do with loyalty to his unit. Tough choice.

When she didn't answer, Rygard tapped the mic. "You heard me. Don't go looking for anything that will draw attention to you. We got lucky the last time and from what I know of this incoming group, Dev might not be able to get things cleared before they bundle you up and send you back to Terra."

The threat had gotten old. She lived cautious, sure, but she didn't live in fear.

"We'll see." She never made a promise she didn't do her best to keep. Better to simply not make it.

He frowned at her yet kept his peace on the topic and moved on. "These soldiers all have special skill sets. From what I hear, they're the best at what they do. There should be an EOD specialist in the group."

"EOD?"

"Explosive Ordnance Disposal. Those guys are a special breed of crazy-but-controlled insanity, if you get what I mean."

Her confusion must have shown on her face.

"Things intended to go boom, this guy diffuses or contains them."

Damn. "So he voluntarily walks up to bombs and takes care of them?"

"Yah."

"Wait. You have bombs there?"

A pause. "There's land mines all around the area we're trying to scout. Diffusing a couple for an expedited path out would be useful."

"Duly noted." She paused. Would asking him to be careful be smothering? She didn't know, so she kept silent. Besides, they kept plenty of ordnance on board anyway. Hard to get all protective about someone when she put herself in similar situations all the time.

Rygard, however, couldn't sniff out explosives, whereas she'd taken the time to get as good as the canine they'd taken aboard. "You're not going to need to know the path, sweetness. Dev's team, including you, will only be needed to guard our home camp. We're covering the forward positions."

She shrugged. "Whatever you say. Work it out with Dev."

Any concern she let slip now might be interpreted as doubt in his abilities. At least, she'd take it that way. Better to show him how much she cared when she got there.

"We will." Rygard gave her a thumbs-up.

In her experience, the best plans always went south at the least opportune moment. Dev made contingency plans with backups plus more in case they were cursed with a particularly bad case of Murphy's Law. She'd be familiar with the area and the terrain, regardless of what the military men and Rygard had to say.

"There should also be another sniper with you, plus his observer."

"I saw the rifles. Nifty."

He chuckled. "You try the guns I gave you yet?"

Up until she'd met Rygard, she hadn't owned any guns. She hadn't gone unarmed; there wasn't a time waking or sleeping when she didn't have a few knives on her person. In panther form, she could hold a knife in her jaws, but she couldn't pull a trigger with paws. It was an old argument between her and Dev . . . and Boggle and Rygard. Rygard had finally circumvented the debate by gifting a few guns to her.

"I've gone through multiple virtual simulations, but I haven't been to an actual firing range, no." Why did she feel guilty? She'd studied firearm safety and trigger etiquette.

Rygard's expression softened, his lips forming a smile just for her. "I look forward to giving you your first hands-on lesson then."

Oh no, no melting right away. She lifted her chin. "If I decide to change my policy about carrying guns. I'd have to change up the way I carry my gear."

No lie there. Her pack had been specially designed for her to carry on her back in human form, but it could also be strapped to her back in panther form with a little help from somebody with thumbs. Otherwise, there were a few extra handles to make it easier for her to carry in her mouth and stash someplace until she could return and get it.

"You're a sensible person. I'll lay odds you'll learn just because you like to have extra skill sets at hand for any circumstance. You're too good a fighter not to."

He had her there. Plus, his confidence in her warmed her insides all gooey even if he hadn't managed to melt her. Yet.

"Maybe."

"That's a yes."

She snarled at him. "A maybe is a maybe."

He grinned.

It had become a game, the exchange. She couldn't help returning his smile.

"I miss you."

Her throat constricted when he said the words. The best she could do was whisper in return. "Miss you too."

She dropped her chin, her hair falling across her eyes. Even as a hologram, the intensity of his regard left her vulnerable. For him, she didn't feel the need to hide behind walls or defend herself. He'd gotten past those defenses.

CHAPTER 4

"GODS, YOU'RE BEAUTIFUL." Rygard watched her hologram, wishing he could reach out and touch the silk of her black hair.

He hadn't expected to miss her as much as he did. His girl. She'd gotten under his skin, and he'd found himself thinking of her at random times throughout his day. Little things, offhand comments he would have wanted to share with her if she'd been there with him.

Kaitlyn's dark brown eyes widened at his compliment, and color spread across her cheeks. In some ways, she was so guileless. He enjoyed that about her too.

"I'm kind of liking this chance to see you." He grinned as she fiddled with a lock of hair. It did his ego a lot of good to know he could unsettle her when life-threatening situations and high numbers of enemy soldiers couldn't. "It's late on the ship, isn't it? I get to tuck you in."

Her sweet lips formed a shy smile. "I wasn't planning to do anything else after talking to you besides go to sleep."

"Nothing at all?" Did he see a little shift in her eyes?

"Well, when you say 'nothing' like that, I feel like there

should be something." Her brows drew together in the cutest perplexed expression. "Skuld had this weird gift for me. It came to mind when you said that but there is no way in hell I'm using it."

From what little he knew about Skuld, he was guessing he was going to really like that present, or at least what it could do to Kaitlyn. "What'd she get you?"

His girl clamped her mouth shut and set her jaw at a stubborn angle.

Oh, this was good. He definitely wanted to know.

"C'mon, sweetness. Skuld's a good friend, you said so yourself."

She relaxed a fraction. "She is. But this . . . thing, yeah no. I'm not going to use it."

"I'm dying to know what she got you." And if it was what he thought it was, he hoped she'd consider using it while he was around to watch. His cock swelled in his pants at the thought, and he made sure she couldn't see, yet.

"Well, she figured I was going to be exploring . . . things, after you and I met, especially since we're not sure when we're going to meet up again."

"And exploring things is a good idea." He had a few suggestions, actually. He was going to drive himself to a serious case of blue balls if he didn't help his girl along a bit. "Why don't you bring it out now?"

The panic in those big brown eyes made him grin. Then her lids came down to half-mast as the tip of her tongue darted out and wetted her lower lip. "I don't think so."

"Why not? No one can see you. It's just me, in this lonely tent, with you." He let some of the desire he was feeling color his voice. "I'd enjoy watching you please yourself."

"I'm not . . . I don't . . . I've never done . . . that . . . for myself before." She sounded shy and uncertain.

"Are you against it?" He'd stop pushing her if she was. He was thankful she let him take care of her in person. "I'll stop."

"No, I just. . . don't know that I'd do it right." She blew out a breath with the admission.

"There's no wrong way to please yourself, sweetness. You don't have to show me if you don't want to, but I do hope you'll consider taking care of yourself. Even on your own." The thought of watching her was going to guarantee him a rough day if he didn't take care of himself too. "Do you have it nearby?"

"Yes." Quiet, curious, no fear in her tone, only hesitation.

"It won't hurt you."

"I know that!" A bit of tart in her reply there. Good.

"Then it can't hurt to give it a try." He winked at her.

The corner of her mouth pulled to one side in a dubious expression.

He sat up, letting her see how hard he was, despite the heavy fabric of his pants. "This is what you do to me. Just thinking of you feeling good does this to me. Won't you show me?"

Her gaze fastened on his groin and her breath quickened. He could see the rise and fall of her chest, wanted to see the smooth perfection of her skin instead.

"You're getting ready for bed, right?"

"Yes." She blinked.

"Get more comfortable then. What do you sleep in when I'm not there?"

Instead of protesting, she bit her lip, then unfastened her ship suit. She slipped out of it slowly, then let it fall to the side, outside the projection of the hologram. He feasted on the sight of her in a simple tank top and a pair of those lacey panties. Her necklace with the blue amber pendant drew his gaze to the center of her chest. Her skin glowed golden brown in the hologram, and he ached to touch her.

"You do like to wear those sexy little pieces of underwear, don't you?"

She shrugged, a long lock of hair falling across her eyes again. "They make me feel pretty, I guess."

"You are." He wanted to tell her again and again until she believed him when he said it. "You're beautiful."

She wrinkled her nose at him, and he would have argued with her, but she slid her hands up the back of her tank and undid the clasp of her bra so that a strap fell loose over her shoulder. He held his breath as her hands came back into view and she reached one hand across her chest to slide the loose strap down her arm. One arm free, she repeated the motion on the other side.

How was it possible for a woman to undress from the inside out? And how had he not known it could be this sexy?

His cock jumped as she slipped her fingers into the front of her cleavage and tugged her bra out from under the tank top.

Professional strippers hadn't teased him this badly.

"More comfortable now?" *He* wasn't. He was about to burst out of his pants.

She nodded. The silhouettes of her nipples stood out against the fabric of her tank top. It probably wasn't cold over there. Dev's ship was large enough to have a decent environmental-control system, complex enough to maintain room temperatures to the comfort of the occupants in each personal cabin space. His girl was definitely excited.

"Lay down then." He wanted to coax her, make her feel comfortable with herself.

Still hesitating, she cocked her head to the side for a moment, but instead of saying anything, she lay down.

He sighed happily. The curves of her breasts and hips were perfect. Her hair spread out around her in dark waves. Oh, he could capture the holo right there and store it to enjoy on many a lonely night to come. But he'd made a promise to his girl. His own personal memory would have to do. And he planned to burn the image into his brain.

She moved her hand, reaching for something. "You really want to see me play with this?"

Hells, yes!

Reaching within for control, he modulated his voice. "Will you?"

Watching her lie there, her brows drawn together and her mouth twisted in a perplexed frown as she studied the buttons, he couldn't help but smile. How did she manage to be adorable and sexy at the same time?

The vibrator in her hands suddenly came to life, and she messed with the buttons for another minute, turning the intensity up and down and adjusting the stimulation patterns. "I think I've got the controls figured out. They're fairly straightforward."

So clinical. Laughter rumbled in his belly. No. If he laughed, she'd stop.

"Try something simple this first time." He had no idea what she'd like; however, it sounded like good advice to him.

"I wish you were here instead."

His chest tightened. "Believe me, sweetness, I wish I were with you too."

He reached out to touch the hologram of her, wishing

he could brush a finger along her cheek, run his hands all over her body.

"Where do you wish I could touch you?" he asked her instead. "Show me."

She remained still for a long time. It was amazing how still she could be for so long, the way big cats could remain motionless.

"It's okay," he murmured. "I'm the only one here."

Hesitant, slow, she ran her fingertips along her jawline. With her eyes closed, head tilted up toward the camera, she drew a line down the side of her neck and across the swell of her cleavage.

"That's it." He couldn't take it anymore. He unbuttoned the front of his pants, then wrapped his fingers around his cock. "Where else do you want me to touch you? Use the toy and pretend it's me."

Her eyes still closed, she bit her lower lip and turned on the vibrator. Holding it in one hand, she hovered it between her legs, then touched the tip to her panties.

A delicate shudder ran through her body.

Oh yes.

He hadn't thought he could get any harder, yet he was rock-solid and aching for her.

She ran the tip of the toy over her panties until he thought the fabric was stained a little darker.

"Are you getting wet, sweetness?" He had to know for sure.

She froze, and without opening her eyes, she whispered, "Yes."

He groaned. "Good. I'm ready to be inside you. Do you want me inside you?"

There she went, biting her lip again. He wanted to kiss and suck at that lower lip, nibble, then suck again.

"Take off your panties. Let the toy touch you the way you want me to touch you."

Another hesitation, then she pressed her knees together and slid her panties off her rear and up and over her bent legs.

"Go on." He was already stroking himself, wishing she'd turn to show him the luscious folds at the apex of her thighs but not wanting to make her think too much.

The toy slipped between her legs again, and she teased herself with the tip, running it up and down her slit. After a moment, she gasped and squirmed.

"Does it feel good?" It felt damned good watching her.

No words. She only nodded.

"I want to be inside you so bad."

She opened her eyes then and blinked twice as her gaze focused on him. He didn't bother to hide his erection or that he was rubbing himself as he watched her.

"You are incredibly sexy." He gave her a smile and loved the one she gave him in return—a little shy, pleased, and definitely sensual. "Slide it inside you. Pretend I'm there, inside you."

"I want you inside me." It sounded like a plea, but she did as he told her. As she pressed the length of the vibrator inside, she arched her back and gasped.

He began to pump himself harder. The sight of her was almost enough to send him over the edge.

"Take it out and slide it in again. You know you like it." Words were almost beyond him, but he managed to give her the suggestion.

Watching her use one hand between her legs to work the toy, her other hand thrown over her head, tangled in her own hair, he pumped himself harder and faster. When she writhed, she breathed heavily, and her chest rose and fell, showing more and more of her cleavage.

She cried out, her hand working the toy faster. Her mouth remained open as she panted, inviting.

"Come for me, sweetness. I'm coming." His throat constricted and his balls tightened. Gods, he remembered those soft lips, her hot mouth.

Her hologram floated right in front of him, and as her entire body tensed, she cried out.

And he came in a shuddering release.

RYGARD STARED at the empty space over his sleeping roll for a long time after Kaitlyn signed off sleepy and sated.

The contrast of her had him so fascinated. Sharp and sweet, aggressive in a fight and shy in bed. He hadn't imagined the likes of her until he'd met her on Dysnomia Station.

When he'd re-upped for another tour of duty, he'd tried to keep expectations realistic. Long-distance, in his experience, never seemed to work out. Considering their occupations, either of them could have found someone else to catch their interest.

But Kaitlyn had gotten into his blood somehow, a spicy drug, and he'd never grown tired of the memory of her. Hell, a three-dimensional illusion of her had been more than enough to bring him to satisfaction.

Of a sort.

Didn't stop the hunger he had for the real her—didn't take the edge off.

Beyond how much she turned him on, he found himself worrying about her randomly throughout the day, especially when she was working with Terran military. Her captain might have connections high and deep in the chain of command, but a lot could happen out in space. One of these days an officer following orders too close to the letter was going to interpret those in the worst way possible for his girl.

But then again, she'd proven to him how very capable she was of taking care of herself. There was something wild about her, nothing to do with her mutated DNA, that gave her the strength and independence to leave her sheltered school days and fly out past the edge of the solar system. No telling where she'd go if she decided to go somewhere. There were the times, deep into the night, when he'd hear something out beyond the boundaries of camp and wonder if somehow she was out there.

Those moments unsettled him.

He'd seen her change, knew what she was, yet the longer he was away from her, the more he wanted to hold on to the memories of her in his arms. The panther part was just a hidden facet, an unfortunate side effect of the hell she'd survived to become an incredible woman.

And she'd been changing in the time since he'd met her. She didn't seem aware of it, but he'd seen it, even in the hologram. She'd long since grown into her delicious curves and her delicate face, but minute changes were still happening in the way her body moved. Sensuality whispered along every curve of her, temptation in motion, and whenever she came to rest, pausing for a moment with that perfect stillness of hers, she stole a person's breath away.

Watching her touch herself for him, stroke herself to climax, pretending he was there with her . . . she'd done it for him, been willing to step way across the line of her comfort zone for him.

He really was going to hell for instigating that bit of delicious yet excruciating torture.

He caught himself grinning like an idiot.

"You ready, man? Men are mustered, waiting for you."

Rygard snapped out of his thoughts to see DeSarto peering into the tent. "Yeah. I'll be out in less than five."

DeSarto nodded and started to let the tent flap down, then hesitated. "Your girl doing good?"

Surprised, Rygard nodded.

"She's on her way here?"

"Yeah." Rygard wasn't annoyed DeSarto was asking, but he wondered why.

"This merc crew has a good rep. Heard good things about Captain Rishkillian. It'll be interesting to see what she can do when they hit planetside. Looking forward to it."

"I'll bet you are." Rygard didn't say more. With DeSarto or any of the other men, it'd be more about actions than any words he could say on her behalf.

And Kaitlyn could definitely step into action.

Since Rygard didn't rise to the bait, DeSarto gave him a grin and left without further commentary.

Rygard quickly retrieved and disposed of the hidden wipes he'd used to clean up and pulled himself together. The moment he stepped out of his tent, any softness he had because of Kaitlyn melted away. The warmth she'd given him retreated to a tiny, sheltered place deep inside, and a cold, steady calm was left behind.

Hours remained until their next scouting excursion to the installation where they suspected human slaves were being held. From the number of vessels they'd counted landing and taking off, any captives on this planet were only there long enough to fill the holds of the larger Sketz'es spaceships.

In the meantime, he and DeSarto and had plans to take a preliminary look around, with an eye for a likely spot to move base camp once Captain Rishkillian's team arrived with their support detail. The current location succeeded in staying hidden from overflying aircraft and any of the foot patrols they'd seen, but lately there'd been odd noises in the night: the sounds of large predators prowling around the perimeters of the camp despite the repellents designed for biologics in this type of jungle terrain.

"Just swapped watch with the other detail and we're ready to head out." DeSarto tossed a small pack to him.

Shouldering the pack, Rygard nodded. "Say we take a sweep south to check out the location up on the plateau. It'd be a good overlook, what with the stand of trees and overgrowth."

DeSarto grimaced. "It'll be a bitch to cut out the interior to clear enough space to set up camp."

"Worth it, for higher ground and good cover."

His fellow soldier grunted and turned to head out. Rygard wasn't worried. Lack of argument from DeSarto pretty much amounted to agreement or at least indicated neutrality. Besides, this trip out doubled as a brief between him and his NCO. DeSarto would follow orders regardless. It was a measure of their friendship that they could make opinions known to each other without blurring the chain of command.

"We've got the intel we need to move on the outpost." DeSarto kept his voice low. No sentients around to hear, but caution was a habit. "The men are itching to take action, stop the next ship."

"We tag the next outgoing ship and track it to its destination, then take out this outpost and whatever incoming ship arrives next." Tough decision to make, especially with potentially human cargo on the slaver ship. Considering what DeSarto and the rest of their unit had observed, they were all developing a serious hate for the portion of the reptilian race known as Sketz'es involved in slave trade. He was too, but he wasn't going to let it cloud his judgment or theirs. "We need to infiltrate their galactic gray market. Get a better understanding of what other alien races are involved."

"Sketz'es run the show." DeSarto spit on the trail. "They send their info-casts out on broad bands of communication. Hard to find? Questionable? The Sketz'es can obtain it for you, for a fee. Damned lizards fly through space with no one to stop them."

Fierce fighters with heavy weaponry, the Sketz'es didn't bother with treaties or peace agreements. They bartered in things they perceived to be of value. If you had something they wanted, you were safe. If you were what they wanted, you better have more firepower than they did.

"There's no alliance out there, not yet. The Terran government is working on it. The other races? Hell, too many out there and not enough open communication to begin peace talks. Best we can do is gather as much information as we can and get it back home." The human captives weren't the top priority in his orders, though Rygard still planned to do his best for those poor souls. The more intel they could gather, the safer Terrans would be as a race.

Terran's home solar system, Sol, had layers of security, starting with the outermost moon stations like Dysnomia and Kerberos. The Terrans had learned from the invasion of Triton Moon Base and enhanced protections to ensure aggressors would never get as close to Old Earth again.

"Bastards are heavily armored. We capture one of their

ships, we can make sure our fleet is prepared to meet them." DeSarto hacked at undergrowth spreading across the trail as they moved.

"Yeah, but the colonies are still vulnerable." Rygard ground his teeth. "Too many of those are easy targets for slave traders like the Sketz'es."

DeSarto snorted. "Colonists are too excited about room to spread out. They don't really read the briefing on the dangers out there. Think the Sketz'es are boogeymen the Terran government made up."

"You're not saying they deserve it?" Rygard stared hard at DeSarto's back. His NCO could be an ass, but too far was too far.

"Hell no." DeSarto shot a look back over his shoulder. "Just sayin' a lot of them head out into the stars bright-eyed and full of dreamy propaganda shit instead of prepared the way they should be. They should be required to have a few retired veterans on their personnel rosters. Have some voice of preparation in their organizations."

Rygard snorted. Not a bad idea, but big problems were rarely completely solved by simple solutions.

One of the two suns shining down on this planet had set and the other was on its way down to meet the horizon. Double suns meant they enjoyed longer dawns and dusks, with extremely short nights in between. They never did their scouting during the brightness of day because they had plenty of time to gather intel before the pitch black of night descended.

Chitters sounded from somewhere off to his left. Something large moved in the underbrush.

Rygard drew his sidearm. He had a silencer unit on his weapon so if he had to shoot an indigenous life-form, he wouldn't give away their position. He'd rather not. Some biologist somewhere would be horrified at the idea for sure. His Kaitlyn would scowl but autopsy the corpse instead of questioning his judgment on the necessity. His girl was practical that way, and she believed in his decisions.

He shook his head. He needed to keep his thoughts on the situation at hand.

Rustling in the underbrush sounded again, closer and from the other side.

"What the fuck?" DeSarto kept the curse under his breath. He'd drawn his weapon as well and peered through the dense vegetation. More chittering came from all around them—even above. The two men stood back-to-back and edged toward the camp.

Enough daylight remained that the indigenous predators shouldn't be out yet. This sounded like a group, a pack of some sort. None of the biologics they'd identified in the region hunted in packs.

Rygard set his jaw and took a mental tally of the weaponry he had. DeSarto's gear included a couple of extra ammo clips strapped to his back where Rygard could easily reach them. His backpack was configured the same. Together, they had enough ammo to hold off a group of wild animals, especially if they could get some cover.

The strange chittering noise came again, closer, and they both whipped around in opposite directions, tracking the sound. He saw only rustling, moving shadows—nothing clear at which to take aim.

Shit.

And then the silence fell and all they could hear was their own breathing and accelerated heart rates. They were being hunted, and Rygard was beginning to wonder at the intelligence of their hunters. A random pack of wild things would have charged. They wouldn't have stalked him and

DeSarto this way. Would they? He stepped to one side, trying to head down the trail toward some sort of cover, DeSarto at his back.

An inhuman screech split the silence, quickly followed by a human cry in the distance—a man's shout cut short in a gurgling rush. It had to have been one of his men on sentry duty back at camp.

He and DeSarto broke into a shuffling run, careful to remain back-to-back and keeping their eyes on the shadows in the undergrowth, the both of them too experienced to rush at top speed. If they turned and ran toward their fallen man, they'd both be dead too.

A dark shape detached itself from a tree trunk high above their heads. It landed on the path between them and camp, then darted back into the plants before either of them could get off more than a shot. Another dark shape streaked past from a different direction.

Rygard had a fleeting impression of eyes—frighteningly human eyes.

The third rush came from the same direction as the second, swift and vicious with no pattern, no logic he could discern. DeSarto went down under a flurry of arms and legs and wild chittering.

Rygard swung around, ready to fire, but he couldn't get a shot in without risking shooting his partner. All he could make out was dark fur, a misshapen face. Humanoid but more primate than man. He tried to make sense of the mess of hairy limbs grappling with uniformed arms as DeSarto struggled. Abruptly, Rygard realized why DeSarto wasn't recovering as quickly as he should've. Ropes crisscrossed DeSarto, restricting his movement.

Wild things, nonsentients, didn't use nets. They didn't build traps.

The cool calm he normally kept in battle rippled. These weren't simple predators hunting in packs. This was a coordinated ambush.

He kicked out hard, taking the risk of hitting DeSarto, and experienced a momentary triumph when his boot made contact with soft fur instead of the armored vest of his friend. The attacker crumpled under the force of impact.

As the thing rolled away, more shadows streaked toward them. Rygard shot two more midcharge. Cold settled in Rygard's gut as he picked out more coming from the treetops. They'd be outnumbered in seconds. He unsheathed his belt knife and tossed it down so DeSarto could cut himself free while he covered them both.

The camp had come under full attack by now. The only giveaways were the chittering and occasional inhuman shriek or the strangled noise of a surprised man. Their unit had been seasoned in battle, and all of them fought as silently as possible, but against this many strange attackers, caught by surprise and on the defensive, they could only maintain their own silence.

As soon as DeSarto got to his feet, the two of them skirted the camp. They made their way to the communications tent and cut a new entrance in the side to gain access. DeSarto guarded his back as Rygard fired up the communications relay and coded in the message.

He cursed as he briefly fumbled with the keyboard, his reflexes too fired up. For a moment, he wished for Kaitlyn's friend Boggle and the way the man's fingers flew across the terminals. Taking a steadying breath, he got the message out on a secure transmission, setting it to loop.

"Hsst." DeSarto's warning had Rygard pivoting in a crouch to face the slit they'd cut in the tent.

Time was up. They'd been found.

He took one more second to throw a tarp over the terminals, hoping the beasts wouldn't break the equipment before the transmission got out.

Their attackers had taken the time to gather at both entrances and rushed in simultaneously. DeSarto let out a curse as clawed hands reached under the tent edge to grab at his boots as he fought off the things inside the tent. More nets, more furry bodies, and the two of them went down under the crush of numbers.

Rygard struggled wildly, a heavy weight on his chest, clawed hands scrabbling at his harness, disarming him. He cut several more before they got his knife away from him.

No room for fear—only primal instinct and the fight to get free. The things growled and chittered.

His last thought before he blacked out was a haunted worry. Kaitlyn was coming.

CHAPTER 6

HARD TO DECIDE which gave a person the better advantage, fear or ignorance.

When Kaitlyn walked into the holding area, the soldier guarding Bharguest had his back to the prisoner. From his stanceand tightly pressed lips, the soldier was more wary of her coming too close than of the death standing just behind him. He had no way of knowing what she was capable of, but he apparently assumed the containment field protected him from Bharguest.

Idiot.

Yes, the containment field would stun the hell out of a normal humanoid, or one as big as Bharguest. And yes, they'd put up the bars too as a secondary assurance. But hell, Kaitlyn wouldn't ever give Bharguest her back under these circumstances. Or any situation she could imagine, actually.

She dropped the tray carrying the guard's meal on a table along one wall with a clatter, keeping the second balanced in one hand. "Ready your weapon, soldier. I'm deactivating the containment field to slide this other tray in."

"The big bastard isn't going to reach through the bars and strangle you." The boy sounded amused at her precautions.

She just stared.

Any hint of laughter died, and the color drained out of the soldier's face. She could almost trace the blueish veins running under the thin skin of his temple. She crushed the urge to study the soft part of his neck, where the veins and arteries ran deeper.

As he raised his stun rifle, she paused to be sure he aimed it at the prisoner and not at her.

There was movement inside the cell. She snapped her attention to Bharguest. He'd been lying on his tiny bunk, mostly hanging off one end. Now he was standing, close but not too close to the containment field.

"Step back." She didn't put any force behind the command, but it wouldn't be mistaken for a request either.

He did as she asked, raising his arms slowly to show his hands were empty. Amusement lit his eyes, and one corner of his lip lifted in a part smirk, part snarl.

It took effort not to snarl back, but she knew when she was being baited. She took a step forward and slid the meal tray through the tiny slot at the bottom of the bars. The prisoner struck the tray, a portion of food suddenly in his hand as he leaned over the meal on one knee.

The soldier cursed, but Kaitlyn held up a hand, indicating he should hold his fire. Okay, so Bharguest had some impressive speed for a big humanoid. She'd barely managed to track his quicksilver motion. If it came down to him and her, she could move that fast. But she wasn't human, either, and she wondered again what the hell he was.

"There's a standing order to catch people like you and bring them in to Terran labs for study." She kept her tone nonchalant.

Donning a semblance of civility, Bharguest placed the food back in the tray. He took the tray in his hands and moved back to sit on the edge of his bunk. "That'd be how I got back into the middle of the Terran solar system. I hadn't been dirtside for a decade or more. When the soldiers offered an escort, I decided it could be interesting." He started eating, using the blunt spoon they'd given him to scoop peas into his mouth.

"And when they tried to make a lab rat of you?" She had trouble keeping her beast aspect under control on the best of days, but the way her control had been lately, a visit to the labs in person could have been catastrophic to her future.

Bharguest paused his shoveling and looked up at her. "Do I look like a rat, sweetheart?"

"Never seen someone quite like you." She'd be honest. After all, she could smell a lie, and she'd lay odds he could too.

He grinned, lifted a piece of simulated chicken protein in his fingers, and swallowed it whole. "No? I've seen a lot of things, although I have to admit you are a singular piece of art."

Now they were getting into too much information with too many people in the room.

"Put the containment field back up so I can eat." The soldier had lost his patience.

Timely interruption there.

But she wanted the conversation to continue.

"Why don't you take your dinner to the mess and eat with the rest of your team?" Making her voice sound as sweet and full of sunshine as Skuld hurt her throat. Still, she figured she managed to sound marginally pleasant. "I'll stand watch here for a bit to spell you."

No suspicion in the young soldier's face. Obviously, the enticement of better company, at least over his meal, outweighed whatever military rules and regulations had been ingrained in him. Still, to give him credit, he hesitated. "I ought to call for relief from my partner."

Kaitlyn nodded. "You could do that, but he's eating in the mess too. I'm here and I'm crew—first mate on this ship plus the ship's medic. Consider this a shared set of duties between our two teams."

He grinned. The compromise was good enough for him. "I'll be back in an hour."

Without waiting for more than a nod from her, he nabbed his tray and headed for the door, slinging his weapon over his back as he went. Pleased, she perched on the stool a good distance away from the bars and kept an eye on both the door and the prisoner. Bharguest had continued to demolish his meal during the exchange, still watching her.

They sat in silence for a few more minutes. She'd long since learned how to stalk her prey, waiting with an easy calm. Another part of her found amusement in the fact that her target was doing the exact same thing to her. They were waiting each other out. However, Bharguest had nowhere to go and plenty of time on his hands as they traveled through space. She had duties to attend to.

This round went to him.

"Tell me more about me." It wasn't about conceit or vanity. His impressions would be interesting, for one thing, and would also tell her quite a bit about him and how he was capable of gathering the knowledge he had.

He tapped the edge of his tray with his blunt spoon. "You didn't want to give me this spoon, did you girl?"

Not exactly the answer she'd been fishing for, but she understood that sometimes you had to let a person lead you to their answer. "No."

"Soldier boy over there wouldn't think twice about it." He tapped again, then again—some pattern. It wasn't the Old Terran Morse code. It was something else, strangely mesmerizing. "But you, you weren't surprised about my speed either. You knew how fast I could move already, knew what I could do to a man with this bitty tool."

Sure. She'd had to do some evil things with one of those in the past. Feeding time was when she'd managed to escape back on Triton Moon Base. And she'd left several dead bodies littering her passage out. They'd deserved it after what they'd done to her.

"Anything is a weapon, when the wielder has either the intelligence or the ability to use it."

Or the desperation.

"Ah, but you knew I had the ability. Someone taught you to observe and to learn and to understand what you've found." He sounded as if he was entertained, maybe entranced, by the concept. Maybe she was too. "You don't just watch, you listen. You use all your senses, don't you? Smell, taste, touch . . . I'd have expected you to be more tactile but someone beat that out of you, didn't they?"

Yes. Beatings had been the least of the methods used to terrorize her during her imprisonment. Torture could take many forms. Humans were capable of cruelty some aliens could never conceive of, and she'd been lucky she'd been human enough to survive it.

"Yes." He drew the word out, his tone taking on a hypnotic quality.

She allowed herself to float on the sound of it, trusting her other senses to keep her anchored to her own center. Let him think he had a power over her.

"You do use all your senses, but you still limit yourself," he continued, and she wondered how much he was talking to hear his own voice. "They struggled to make something as beautiful as you, as perfectly camouflaged. But you wouldn't survive the arenas, not as you are. They'd have to do more work on you to achieve the goal."

Her temper spiked.

"You survived these . . . arenas." Speaking the words took effort. She wondered if she should have been able to speak at all.

He chuckled. "Yes. I survived. More battles than they'd anticipated. I won a lot of creds for some of the idiots taking the bigger risks."

What sort of fighting had he done? Society had survived centuries, and the most popular form of entertainment for both the elite and the masses still involved putting a couple of life-forms in the same place to see which came out the stronger. The crowds cheered harder if one of them ended up dead.

"Why did you do it?"

He turned his head sideways, a full ninety degrees. "For the entertainment of the crowds? Maybe. They were amusing to watch while I fought. For rich investors? Yes. They'd come to see me, pretend to be brave. Then they'd piss themselves in my presence. Always good for a laugh. For beings fancying themselves masters? Not for long."

No anger there, only a finality cold enough to chill her to the bone.

"What sort of arenas were these?"

He chuckled, the sound creepy because he was genuinely amused. "Pit fighting, cage fights. Little girl, there were those and more. Battles held in huge arenas and we were slaves turned gladiators. From day to day, night to night, any form of combat you can imagine under any circumstances could be held for the pleasure of the crowds. The high rollers liked their private fights, their cage fights. If you were dropped in a pit it was because they didn't care if either of you made it out in one piece. They had good imaginations, the ones running the pits. Always provided new scenarios, new challenges. Took a long time to get bored with it all."

Kaitlyn didn't waste time doubting such a place existed. Someone else might question his claims or feign horror while secretly relishing every detail. Or worse, get righteous about the inhumanity of it all. Funny though, it wasn't such a stretch to believe the bloodthirsty trait wasn't limited to Terra or its natives. Plenty of the species she'd met had a craving for violence, and humans weren't the first to begin exploiting other planets besides their own. In fact, she'd bet the individuals in power weren't human.

Humans didn't have big enough colonies beyond the Terran sun's interstellar neighborhood to support such an organization on their own. These . . . arenas had to be interspecies, and anything outside the Milky Way was run by a species other than Terran.

But Bharguest was humanoid, had been human once. So there were humans involved. And that didn't surprise her either. Hypocrisy, sure, but humanity—that was a rarity among humankind.

She'd experienced this firsthand from Terran stock so far evolved, they'd claimed they weren't human anymore.

Evolution had been the excuse for superiority, and the justification for enslaving her.

It hadn't worked. She hadn't remained a slave. Looking at Bharguest behind the bars, she didn't see a slave either. "What did they do to equip you to come out of it alive?"

"You already know. Don't you?" He paused. "Tch. If you don't then you're not worth the story time."

She cocked her head to one side. "The ones who did this to me, I don't know if they owned the technology."

Truth. After close to four years of study, it had become clear that the human technology her captors had available to them when they'd colonized couldn't have advanced on its own to achieve the sophistication of the virus they'd infected her with back then. Hell, her equipment was cutting edge and she still had trouble analyzing her findings. They had to have taken the technology from another race, and if it was in use where this man had come from, she had to know more about it. They might have a cure.

"They only knew how to administer the virus, combine it with the creatures of their choosing." She offered him the information to see if it'd tempt him to give her more. "They claimed there was no way to reverse the effects."

And hadn't she been searching for one? All this time, and she barely understood the virus itself or why it had killed so many of her classmates.

"Why would you want to reverse the effects?"

She stared at him.

He narrowed his eyes, a smile hovering around his lips. "There isn't ever going back to what you were, girl. Even if they take the virus from every cell of your body, there's never a way back."

"I didn't choose this." Of course she knew there was no

way back to who she used to be, but damn if she wasn't looking for a way to the future she'd wanted for herself.

"Yes you did." Those eyes drilled into her, cold, steady.

She opened her mouth to deny him. A snarl came out instead.

Heat rushed to her face. Not anger. Embarrassment.

Bharguest threw his head back and laughed. The sound of his mirth echoed off the walls, making the room seem larger than it really was, emptier.

She waited for him to catch his breath.

"Oh, girl, been a long time since I found funny in a conversation outside my own skull."

"That's a shame. Conversation with one's own self can be kind of dull that way." She bit off the end of each word, hanging on to her temper to burn away her embarrassment.

"I'm going to have fun watching you pretend to be a little harmless girl alongside all these big, bad marines." He sat back on his bunk with a satisfied sigh, patting his belly as if the laughter had filled him more than the meal.

"Maybe."

"Definitely."

"Suit yourself."

Bharguest leaned forward and rested his elbows on his knees. "I answered your question. Now you play one of my games."

It was her turn to narrow her eyes. She tested the air, but there was no deceit in his scent, no telltale sweat or pheromones. The sound of his heart hadn't increased in tempo except during his little exercise in hilarity. It made her wary.

He didn't wait for her to agree. "You tell me about you."

What was there to tell? Too much and nothing

compared to what this man had likely seen. But it mattered to her.

"Not your history, girl. I don't give a shit about that." He cut into her thoughts before she realized the words had frozen in her throat. "I want to know what you are. Now. Here. And where do you think you're going?"

"Well, I can answer the last question." Dev leaned in the doorway, nonchalant.

She eyed her captain as Bharguest took Dev's measure. No anger—not in the way Dev held his body or scent. It was obvious he'd made an effort to come up on them unnoticed. She'd only heard him in the moment before Bharguest asked his last questions, and those had come out too fast.

Bharguest had heard him coming too, she thought.

"Captain. So good to meet you." Unruffled, Bharguest nodded toward the captain in some semblance of respect.

"The watch is about to change." Dev directed his words to Bharguest. "We're going to have to give you back to the stimulating company of the military police again for a bit."

"Things were just getting somewhere." Bharguest raised an eyebrow.

Dev shrugged. Kaitlyn buried a tiny nugget of satisfaction at the way her captain remained unperturbed by Bharguest. The prisoner seemed to make creeping people out an art form.

The soldier from earlier returned, nodding to her before resuming her post.

She paused a moment, giving the empty tray a long look, before heading out of the room and down the corridor.

Dev met her at the junction to the main corridor and walked with her a ways before stopping—far enough away from the holding area even she couldn't have listened down the hallway. Interesting.

"Kat, you with me?" Dev waited for her to meet his gaze.

"Aye, Captain."

"The good Captain Petrico-Calin the Fourth has demanded a briefing." Annoyance simmered beneath her captain's words, but then, he had little tolerance for idiots either.

Still, if Dev was having a word with her first, there must have been communication from Rygard's unit. New information, and it couldn't be good.

"So I'll ask you again, Kat. Are you with me? No slips."

Scratch that. It had to be bad news, very bad news.

Rygard.

"Kat." Her captain's voice demanded a response.

She reached deep and put an iron hold on the beast inside her. "Aye, Captain. Fit for duty."

THERE WAS no room on the ship large enough for a formal briefing of the full crew. Built for speed and mobility in and out of tight situations, many of their common spaces served dual or multiple purposes. With the need for a briefing to both Dev's crew and the military contingent on board, the only place to fit everyone was the mess hall.

Kaitlyn entered with Dev, then peeled off as he moved to the head of the main mess table. She hopped up to sit on a counter with Skuld and did her best to look inconsequential. Just one of the support crew.

Several more minutes passed before they had all of the military crew assembled, including, to her surprise, Bharguest and his military escort.

The CO stood and rapped his knuckles on the table to get everyone's attention. What little talk there was had been at a low volume, but it still took a few seconds for him to gather everyone's focus.

Kaitlyn frowned. All Dev ever had to do was stand up and all eyes immediately snapped toward him. Whether this CO was new to his team or not, there should have been a certain amount of respect given to his rank. Some judgment by the soldiers had been going on during whatever time the team had been assembled prior to boarding Dev's ship, and it hadn't been in Petrico-Calin's favor.

She wondered if this mass briefing was an attempt at team building or some other move to gain surer command of the men assembled. Information, especially on a mission of this level of secrecy, would normally be disseminated in smaller groups and filtered down through the chain of command.

"We don't entertain rumor in this unit." Captain Petrico-Calin could have chosen a better way to start his briefing. More frowns all around the room. Kaitlyn schooled her face back to a blank expression. If she noticed them, somebody was going to notice her. "Therefore, I am giving all of you the official news. Communications from our ground team ceased abruptly. All we have as evidence of what occurred is a distress message set on loop, sent out just prior to communication loss."

Fear for Rygard speared her gut. She quickly compartmentalized it and tucked it away for later. For now, she had to focus.

"Obviously, our mission has changed." Petrico-Calin turned his back to them all. She supposed it was meant to be a dramatic movement, but it only served to make it harder to hear him. "Rather than tagging the next outbound ship from the outpost and following it to its destination, we will go in to perform thorough reconnaissance on the site of attack and report back to HQ to await further orders."

A few men stirred. Tempers rose, and the scent of discontent soured the air.

Miz Turner, the suit who'd arrived with Petrico-Calin

stepped up. "I'm sure if evidence is found indicating the ground team is alive, orders will be to mount a rescue. But we must keep HQ abreast of the situation as any new information is gained to give them a clear picture of the state of matters planetside."

The reassurance might have mollified the soldiers present if it hadn't been delivered in such a simpering tone. Listening to the woman speak made Kaitlyn set her teeth, and she had to consciously loosen her jaw and keep her face relaxed. No need to let them know how dissatisfied she was personally. She wasn't under their direct command. No one would notice a lone panther in the jungle planetside, especially not at night.

Her captain knew her too well. "Correct me if I'm wrong, gentlemen, but I believe your intention is to send your very specialized Kx9 team out for the recon?"

Petrico-Calin's brows drew together. He must not have been accustomed to having another leader around in a position to point out the obvious in his carefully laid plans. "You are correct, Captain Rishkillian."

Dev grinned. "No need to send one team when we can send two. Kaitlyn Darah will coordinate with your Kx9 team to help with the scouting on the ground."

"I'm sure we have any number of men between the two teams equally as skilled in scouting, Captain."

Oh no, he was not about to make it a gender issue.

"Well, and that may be so in your opinion." Dev rubbed his chin. "But I can guarantee Kaitlyn is the best scout I've ever encountered in all my years in service or out, and every person on my crew would agree. She's got a given talent for scouting, goes right down to basic instinct."

Her captain could be a damned bastard about telling the truth even if the listener would completely ignore the panther sitting in the room; man was going to give her an ulcer.

"Permission to speak, Sir." Tracer spoke up from the other side of the mess hall. "Max is good. He's the best there is among the Ks. But there's going to be a lot of jungle to cover and if Captain Rishkillian says Miss Darah is as good as any he's encountered, we could cover twice as much ground and report to HQ that much faster. Speed is key if our boys are alive."

The pooch might be fast, but in terms of running speed, she had him. Of course, simple speed wasn't the point. The pooch would be searching for signs of any of the military team, working with what scents it encountered at the camp. She knew Rygard's scent already—had savored the lingering musk of him on her skin. She'd be able to find him faster, alive or dead.

An iron fist closed around her chest.

No. She'd deal with it if it became a reality and not before. She'd do him no favors by freaking over what-ifs when she could be covering ground to find out what had happened to him and his team.

The CO was watching her. Hell, everyone in the room had turned in her direction. One soldier had a particularly ugly sneer on his face. Meathead, as she tended to think about him. He leaned against one wall with his bulky arms crossed as if he was trying to make his biceps all bulging and veiny.

She decided to watch the dog. At least he didn't have anything but puppy curiosity in his big brown eyes.

"You have a point, Sergeant." The CO didn't seem pleased, but he didn't argue the logic either. "A coordinated scouting effort would be the most efficient use of resources.

We need to determine how the communications were disabled as well."

Discussion moved on to the communications personnel. Again, it would be a joint effort. Kaitlyn wondered if she should tag Boggle and get him to nab the original distress message. She wanted to know who'd gotten it out and what details it might contain. The military might have locked it down, but she had yet to give Boggle a data search he couldn't snag right out from under whatever layers of confidential encrypting any organization chose to try to hide it in.

There were few people in the universe she trusted, and Boggle had earned his place as one of them. He wouldn't try to soften it if the details told what she wanted to know before she got on the planet's surface to find out for herself.

When they were finally dismissed, she noticed Meathead leave behind Skuld, stepping up on her heels. Skuld didn't notice, but the marine gave her breathing room when Dev called her down the corridor to talk about something. Her captain was watching the man, and she would too.

"Looking forward to searching for that missing team, girl?" Bharguest passed her with his escort. "I'm thinking it's what the ground team found that you'll find more interesting."

CHAPTER 8

"PSST. KATY!"

There had to be some ingenious comment regarding the oxymoronic idea of whispering for attention, then shouting a person's name. At the moment, Kaitlyn was too tired to think of one. She'd had a lot to think about in the space of one waking cycle. Sleep would be necessary for her to be at her sharpest when they hit planetside. She needed to find Rygard.

Ignoring the summons at the door, she typed a quick message at her console and sent it off to Boggle. It was the wrong time on Dysnomia Station for him to be alert or anywhere near conscious, but he'd receive it when he got up, run a search, and be ready to talk to her the next ship day. She wouldn't be able to sleep otherwise.

Skuld wouldn't be ignored though. She tapped on the closed door to the med bay, paused, then popped up with ammunition Kaitlyn herself had provided. "I could always send Chester through the vents to deactivate the lock from your side of the door. You taught him how."

Damn. The ferret would do it too.

"I could eat him." It'd be gross in human form, but hell, she was alone in the med bay—who was to know if she shifted just for a few minutes.

"You wouldn't." The conviction in Skuld's voice squelched the faintest consideration of doing so from her beast-dominant mind. How did Skuld have so much faith in Kaitlyn when she herself didn't?

Besides, Kaitlyn owed the tube rat. He'd been key in letting her out of a cage back on Dysnomia Station. Plus, she had plans for future training. He'd be a pain to replace.

With a sigh, Kaitlyn walked to the door and disengaged the lock. It cycled open, and there stood Skuld with Chester in her hands. She'd been about to send him in, seriously.

"Ah, oh good." Skuld breezed right past Kaitlyn and motioned for her to shut the door behind them.

Kaitlyn hesitated. If it was shut, it'd take longer for Skuld to leave her to her nap.

"Katy. Hello?"

Rolling her eyes, Kaitlyn palmed the door closed and stalked past Skuld to sit on one of the stools by the examination area. Skuld skipped over and bounced onto one of the patient beds next to her.

"I need your help."

"Figured as much." Kaitlyn eyed Chester as the ferret nosed around the room, making his way toward her personal effects storage.

"I need you to help me find something."

"Chester can find things for you just as easy." In fact, it was part of his training.

"I'm pretty sure Chester's the one who hid it. So he could find it, but he doesn't want to."

Whatever it was, it had to be a private, lady-type object

then. The pervy weasel had a thing for them. And he had a tendency to steal what he took a liking to. Too many times, such things turned out to be Kaitlyn's underwear. It was an ongoing issue between them, coming up on epic proportions.

"Why do you think I could find it, then?" Stupid question. After all, she did know Skuld's scent, and an unmentionable item as personal as the one she suspected would definitely smell of Skuld, in very intimate ways.

Uh-uh. No way.

"Please, Katy." Skuld gave her the big sad blinky-eye look. Good grief, were those tears welling up?

Kaitlyn bared her teeth. Skuld had to be faking it, and crocodile tears wouldn't work. She wouldn't give in.

"Okay, too much, I know." Skuld wiped away the tears. "Still, I don't want one of those soldiers to stumble across it. I'd die, I know I would. He'd know it belonged to one of our crew and you wouldn't crack under the teasing but you know I couldn't stand it."

Funny, Skuld had no issue using her toys with her partners in her occasional trysts. Kaitlyn wouldn't have thought she'd be so freaked out by just the thought of a man stumbling across one.

"A couple of those guys creep me out." She was serious, quiet, and altogether sincere.

A snarl rolled through the room. When she realized it was her own voice, Kaitlyn stopped. "Which ones?"

"No Katy, let's just avoid giving any of them more of a reason to think of any of us, okay? You made it clear you're supposed to keep a low profile. It's only one."

The big meathead marine would take every opportunity to make Skuld uncomfortable. His particular type of testosterone poisoning would guarantee it. In the few moments she'd been around him, Kaitlyn had read enough of him to know.

"Please." Skuld reached out and touched Kaitlyn's hand. "Let's lay low and find my stuff. I don't want to cause you any trouble and I don't want to lose you."

Skuld protected Kaitlyn in her own way. And sometimes, Kaitlyn needed Skuld's gentle sort of leash for her wild side.

"How am I going to know which . . . toy it is?" Kaitlyn gave in. Somehow, there was going to be a whole lot of regret for agreeing to find the thing.

Skuld brightened, her smile lighting up the room. "Oh, it'll be super easy. It's the vibrator with the crazy batteries, you know, the ones that spontaneously combusted by accident that one time."

For the love of perverted tube rats and random karma, someone save her.

There'd been no hiding from the smell of the thing for days as the air cycled the stink of burnt batteries and feminine secretions all the way through the ship. Air fresheners solved the problem for the humans on board, and if any of the crew had a clue of what had caused the issue, Dev had made sure none of them dared say a single word. But Kaitlyn had been sneezing for at least a week.

Yeah, she remembered the scent.

"Fine. Let's get this over with." Kaitlyn rose and snagged Chester, shaking loose the brand-new pair of turquoise panties he'd managed to slip out of one of her cubbies.

"Pretty color."

"I thought so."

THEY STARTED NEAR ENGINEERING.

"Think it'll be easy to find?" Skuld wrung her fingers as she kept pace with Kaitlyn.

"If we're lucky, it'll be in an air duct." Kaitlyn paused, but no, no scent there.

"Why? Won't one of us have to climb in there to look for it?" Skuld walked over to the nearest vent and reached for the cover. She had to jump for it.

Kaitlyn pressed her lips together. No smiling. She had to jump for it, too, only Skuld looked so damned cute trying.

"We do not need someone stumbling across one of Chester's little caches of stolen stuff."

"Ooh, he does manage to jam things into the funniest nooks and crannies." Skuld joined her again as they continued down the corridor. "Good thing you trained him not to store anything in the engine."

"If he's going to hide stuff from you, it's not likely going to be in your room anyway."

"Remember when the Nibs found one of my other toys wedged in with their extra ammunition?" Skuld clucked her tongue. "That was crazy embarrassing, but they didn't say a single word. Just handed it over."

The specialist had been as embarrassed as Skuld, maybe more so.

"They are crew. Crew members all know to respect you." Kaitlyn didn't bother to add that everyone on Dev's ship knew not to breathe a single sound in regard to Kaitlyn's penchant for bits of silk and lace, no matter how many times Chester was seen scampering down the hallway with a stolen garment. They all had a healthy desire to live. Besides, there were a few other crew members with similar tastes in lingerie, just in recognizably different sizes.

While they searched, she kept an eye on Chester. The

ferret displayed signs of anxiety whenever they neared one of his precious hiding places.

"Ugh! All we're finding are purloined pens or shiny things!" Skuld tossed her hands up. "And why does he want a piece of random pressed fiber packaging? At least the sock seems like a little Chester-sized sleeping bag."

When they'd come across the pulled pin to a grenade, Kaitlyn had raised an eyebrow but figured they'd have discovered which grenade it came from in a fairly spectacular way if it had been on the ship. Since the ship's hull was still intact, she wasn't going to worry about it, or tell Skuld what it was.

They reached the weapons-storage room. Although every crew member had their personal armory kept in the foot lockers, extra ammunition and standard firearms were kept in this room. Also, any weapons picked up along the way from various missions were kept here if no one claimed them as personal loot. Not too many crew members came into the room besides Nibs as weapons specialist.

If there was a quiet, safe place in Chester's tiny head, this would be where he'd go. Never mind it'd be the first place to blow up.

Sure enough, Chester chattered and wriggled free of Skuld's ship suit. Skuld bent over and caught hold of him as he made a dive for the hard floor.

"What the . . . ?" Skuld released him in surprise.

Kaitlyn waved Skuld off from trying to pick him back up. Instead, she palmed the door shut behind them and started searching the room.

"It's here." Yay. Bounce, bounce.

"Yay!" Skuld clapped her hands together and, yup, bounced.

Amazing how she managed to *poing* in magnetized ship boots.

Kaitlyn had to climb one of the larger shelving racks and peer behind a storage crate to find Chester's hidey spot. His cache was a pile of small treasures. Heck, Skuld's missing sex toy was a tiny, hide-it-in-your-palm plaything. Otherwise, the ferret wouldn't have been able to lift it and scamper off with it. Chester sniffed her hand and gave her his sad face as she snagged the little battery-operated buddy.

She lifted her lip in a silent snarl. He slumped and got even sadder, dropping his head to the ground, then craning to look up at her from his submissive position.

"Anything else up there?" Skuld didn't join her up on the rack. It wasn't spec'd out to take the weight of both of them in addition to the crates already stacked there.

"Nothing in here belongs to him," Kaitlyn grumbled as she stirred the little pile with a finger. "Most of it's been nicked from your room."

A random hair tie, a stylus, an itty-bitty flashlight. Kaitlyn took another look. Hell, there were a few of her own items too. A tiny stone she used to put an edge on her smaller throwing knives, a pair of her medical gloves, and a small square of cotton spotted with a drop of her blood were carefully tucked away.

"Skuld, if you want it back, give me a clipping of your hair."

"What?"

"Look, do you want a moping, depressed ferret or do you want to trade for your toy?"

Silence.

There was a tap at her boot, and Kaitlyn reached back to take the small clipping of gold-streaked brown. It smelled of lavender and Skuld. She held it in front of her so Chester could sniff it, showed him the sex toy, then tapped his nose with it. Then she dropped the bit of Skuld's hair in his cache. After holding the vibrator gingerly between her thumb and forefinger, she passed it back to Skuld.

Chester circled his cache once and then approached her and nuzzled her cheek.

"Yeah, yeah. Don't get too confident, tube rat. This was a special situation."

"Thank you so much, Katy!"

Chester squeaked, his nose twitching as he picked up the scent Kaitlyn already had.

As they stepped into the corridor, Kaitlyn scooped up Chester and handed him to Skuld. "Seal him up."

Still bubbling gratitudes, Skuld did as asked. "Really, I would have died if one of the soldiers had seen it out in the open."

"It's found, we're good." Kaitlyn needed to wrap this session of TMI up in about a minute. "Someone's coming."

But Skuld had too much momentum going. "I really should replace it, but it's such a powerful gadget with five speed settings and it uses a relatively small power source."

And . . . now they were out of time.

"Sounds efficient." Tracer came around the corner with his dog at his heel.

Kaitlyn watched as the big German shepherd dog spent a moment interested in Chester. Again, she placed herself between the dog and Skuld, drawing his attention to her.

"Oh, um. The tool in question is quite efficient, but fairly common." Skuld fumbled her usually easy conversation.

"I'd be interested in learning more about your friend, here, Tracer." Better to change the topic before Skuld died of embarrassment. Luckily, the toy was a discretely concealable kind of thing.

Skuld gave her a smile full of thanks.

Yeah, at the rate they were going, Kaitlyn would never get the sleep she very much wanted to find. The driving need to find Rygard hadn't eased and neither had the imperative to be as fit for duty as possible when the time came.

"Yes. How did you get Max?" Skuld clasped her hands behind her back and took up the line of inquiry.

The pheromones coming from the both of them were going to gag Kaitlyn.

Tracer ran a hand through his close-cropped hair. The gesture suggested he was used to a longer length, and Kaitlyn guessed he'd gone to a barber very recently. "Actually, it wasn't so much me getting Max. He chose me."

"Really?" Skuld was hooked.

"The Kx9 breeds are genetically enhanced." Tracer reached down to rub his dog's ears. He didn't have to reach far. "Breeders could only do so much to increase speed and size. We needed dogs who could understand living in space. They had to be more intelligent than the original breeds, as smart as those were. Max's training isn't limited to a set of learned behaviors based on commands. He understands a lot more."

"Wow." Skuld was suitably impressed. Chester squeaked in response. She gave him a pat of reassurance. "Don't worry, Chester, you're supersmart too."

Kaitlyn didn't miss the way Tracer's eyes fell to Skuld's generous bosom. Considering Chester was tucked into the front of Skuld's ship suit, Kaitlyn decided to give the man a break. It was damned hard not to look—either because of the ferret or because of Skuld's charms.

"Katy works with Chester to train him to recognize objects, retrieve things, and remember short button combinations on simple control boards."

Tracer's eyebrows rose. "Not easy to train ferrets."

"Chester's a fast learner." Skuld was incredibly loyal, not just to her pet. "Katy's published scientific articles on how quickly he learns behaviors."

Ah well, mercenaries specialized in earning creds. Kaitlyn had completed her basic and graduate degrees remotely and set up her own research to keep creds trickling in between missions. Working with Chester had actually gained her quite a bit of attention in certain audiences, especially once Boggle had taken over promoting her articles in the correct academic and animal-lover circles.

"Would you be interested in seeing how Chester works with Max?" Tracer made the offer sound simple. As far as Kaitlyn was concerned, it'd have to involve a crowd. "It looks like we'll be working together planetside anyway."

Normally Kaitlyn worked solo, and she liked it that way. Alone, she had the freedom to shift to panther form if needed, based on the terrain and the nature of any adversaries she encountered. For this mission, she was going to have to be especially sneaky about it. She wouldn't shift directly in front of a soldier if she could help it.

If it couldn't be helped, well, she'd worry about that when the time came. Rygard deserved her best.

"What do you think, Katy?" Skuld's question brought her back to the proposal at hand.

Studying Max, she got the distinct impression he was waiting for her answer too. Head skewed to the side, the dog let the tip of his tongue show, and the end of his tail brushed the corridor floor once.

Cocky pooch.

"Fine." She spoke directly to Max since she hadn't decided if she more than tolerated the handler. "We'll give it a try but you have to promise Chester is safe."

"Of cou—" Tracer began.

But it was Max who rose to walk the few steps separating them, then sat directly in front of Kaitlyn and offered up a paw.

Okay. She'd admit it. She was dying to know what else this dog could do.

For the time being, she shook on their bargain and wondered if she should have set any other prerequisites.

CHAPTER 9

EVEN A FULL SLEEP cycle didn't improve her mood. Normally if a solid "night" of sleep didn't clear things up, Kaitlyn shifted to panther form and went for a run. She went outside if they were planetside or did laps in the cargo bay if they weren't.

When she was in panther form, the world around her became simpler. Her mind processed thoughts without the annoying clutter of worries and suspicions. Or drama. Mercs lived for drama.

Humans live for drama, Kitten.

Katzer's voice still came to her, warm with humor. She sighed and her eyes grew moist; yes, she still needed her memories of him, needed to bounce thoughts off him the way she used to. He'd been key to her survival and her sanity.

"I didn't understand the draw even when I was completely human." Her whisper went out into nowhere with no audible response in return. And it wouldn't come, no matter how long she listened. What came instead was the restless desire to pace, to run, and to feel dirt beneath her paws.

While she lived most of her life as a human, and Dev had worked with her hours every day to help her achieve that, she found she needed a little time as the cat to stay balanced.

Dev didn't agree. *You lived seventeen years of life as a human. The cat is a recent evolution and one that could be reversed once you get the science stuff working.*

Moot point for the morning. With the soldiers on board, she wouldn't shift anyway; just the thought triggered a low growl. She swallowed it and threw on a sports bra and pants. Since a run in panther form wasn't available to her, she'd work off her temper in the ship's gym.

When she saw the soldiers working out, she almost aborted and headed back to her own personal territory. But they were on her ship, and though she shared it with the rest of her crew, she didn't need to cede to them.

She gave a nod each to Durn and Nibs—the two of them were getting in their own strength training. The head of Dev's strike team and their weapons specialist paused as she passed, acknowledging her with a grunt and a chin lift.

After striding past the visiting soldiers working with free weights, she stepped up onto the elliptical pads and pressed the disk-shaped sensors to the insides of her wrists. Slow and steady, at human speed, she didn't let on what she could do with strangers around, but she did up the resistance far above normal levels to at least get her heart rate up. No one would see the resistance setting or think she was anything but a short female running on suspended pads.

To keep the intervals truly random, she amused herself by changing settings every time one of the interlopers tried to lift something too heavy for them and dropped the weights with a loud crash.

Didn't matter how much some people knew about the right way to do things, pride always pushed them to try to impress the general air around them.

Skuld entered after a moment, and Kaitlyn almost stepped off the elliptical disks as she saw every man in the room watch the buxom ship's engineer scamper across the gym to the cardio system. If a single one of them made a wrong move . . .

Only Meathead did more than look, but one of his own men gave him a *thwack* across the shoulder before the man opened his mouth and said something Skuld would notice. As it was, the lewd gesture he'd made caused Kaitlyn's blood to boil and the panther aspect of her to flex its mental claws. She closed her hands in tight fists to hide her fingers in case her claws did come out, the telltale pain of prickling starting under her fingertips.

"Mind if I join you?" Skuld fitted her feet onto another set of pads and set herself up.

Artificial gravity on board wasn't enough to keep up cardiovascular health, and they all kept in good condition, Skuld included.

"Only if you keep your head in your workout and quit trying to catch so much attention," Kaitlyn muttered, but the gym wasn't that big and everyone else could hear them anyway.

Skuld gave her an unrepentant grin. "Cardio is good for the body and attention is good for the ego. I'm being efficient with my time."

"Lovely."

At least Skuld's appearance had triggered additional entertainment from the soldiers. They'd decided to start sparring with each other. Always interesting to see how a professional practiced. It gave clues as to their weaknesses in real combat, hints as to what they might do when there wasn't time to think.

"Who do you think is the best fighter?" Skuld kept her voice to a quiet murmur.

"They're all good, best of the best." She'd give them the compliment without a grudge. "They were wasting their time earlier with the weight lifting, but they're taking the sparring seriously."

"You learning anything?" Skuld's combat skills were limited to the very minimal self-defense Kaitlyn had managed to get her to practice.

"Always." Kaitlyn dialed up the resistance. Watching the sparring matches had made her more aggressive than she'd been when she'd walked in to work out. "Never pass up the opportunity to study a fighting style. Never know what we might have to face someday."

"But they're Terran military. Dev always says we play nice with them."

Kaitlyn shrugged. "A person doesn't always stay a marine for life."

A lot of mercenaries had military in their background, and not all of them were as honorable as Dev's crew.

Each sparring match lasted three minutes, with a third person calling the time. They rotated, taking turns and challenging each other. A few friendly bets were made. They only paused when the military police entered. Bharguest's presence filled the room, pressing all the other egos to the side of Kaitlyn's awareness.

"Our . . . consultant needs his daily exercise," one of the guards explained. "Would you ladies mind stepping away from the cardio equipment and continuing your workouts later?"

Skuld disconnected herself and stepped aside with wide eyes, giving Bharguest a respectable berth. Kaitlyn stood a moment longer, then looked the man directly in the eyes as she stepped off the disks and made way for him without ceding ground.

His answering grin came slow. As Kaitlyn let him pass, she kept herself between him and Skuld.

"Don't worry, little girl, your sweet friend is not my type." Bharguest allowed the guards to get him up on one set of elliptical pads and adjust the apparatus to his size and weight. They didn't bother to change the resistance, but Bharguest didn't have any trouble with Kaitlyn's settings. Any human, even one his size, should have.

It unsettled her when he raised an eyebrow at her. He'd learned something new about her, and knowledge, however small, in his hands left her very wary.

The soldiers had resumed sparring. In fact, one of them had entered a friendly match with Durn. The dark-skinned strike team lead held his own just fine against the marine, one of their field specialists. It ended with both men standing, but to Kaitlyn's eye, Durn had controlled the match. Friendly insults were traded back and forth, and Skuld's laugh tinkled across the room.

The sound released the tension inside Kaitlyn for a moment, and she breathed a silent sigh. Skuld's little bits of joy were just as much a relief for Kaitlyn's mood as the workout.

Tracer entered with Max as Dev's weapons specialist, Nibs, squared off against Specs, Dev's sniper. Kaitlyn was trying to decide which to watch, a dog get on a flat treadmill or two of her fellow crew members try to wrestle blindfolded. The challenge was almost an affectionate one, since Nibs and Specs shared each other's bunks more often than not. They knew each other's bodies well, and that made for a more challenging match in some ways.

"How about you, babes?" Meathead lifted his chin in her direction. The men around him fell silent. "You got the balls to spar with the men?"

Meathead might have tossed the challenge in the general direction of both Kaitlyn and Skuld, but he really spoke to Kaitlyn. Nibs and Durn shook their heads. Both of them had seen this scenario roll out in the past. It was like a bad holo vid.

"Leave the ladies alone, Zec." Specs attempted to reroute the idiot.

"Nah." Zec—she preferred thinking of him as Meathead—wouldn't be deterred. What was with the single-syllable names in these units? "Their captain says this little bit can track as good as our man, better'n most of us. Says she's as good as the mutt over there. I wanna see what the bitch can do."

Bitch? Oh, hell no he didn't just call her a canine.

"You're outta line, Zec." Specs gave the man a shove.

But Zec watched Kaitlyn with a lazy grin, taking a minute to eye her from the ground up. Bad boy thought he was the alpha dog. She'd have laughed if she hadn't had an intense desire to skin him alive. A handful of years wasn't enough time to erase the memory of captors looking at her just the way he did or what they did to her when they opened the cell door. Then, she'd been chained up and scared, her body betraying her with agonizing pain as the virus raged through and rewrote her DNA. Then, her captors did to her as they pleased, and she hadn't had the power to struggle.

Here and now, Meathead had pissed all over her territory. Silent, she stepped onto the sparring mats.

Maybe she should have kept a low profile, and maybe she should have walked away, but she'd done enough of what she ought to do for the day.

Meathead sneered as he stepped onto the mats and stood toe-to-toe with her.

Sour musk and grease filled her nose. His scent hung heavy with testosterone and sweat. Even if she hadn't had a heightened sense of smell, the man would have been an affront. She bared her teeth at him as the others decided who would call the time. "You stink."

"Fucking bitch." He shoved her backward a fraction of a second before Nibs called the bout to a start.

Kaitlyn ignored the general noises of disapproval as she brought her arms up, hands in loose fists. Based on his earlier sparring matches, Meathead liked to start in a stand up and then tended to try to take a smaller opponent to the ground. Now his first strikes were slow and came in wide. She covered easily and returned with lightning-fast striking combinations to his face and exposed torso. Then she danced clear of him quickly. A couple of his fellow marines grunted in approval. She kept her eyes on him, watched his face turn progressively redder with anger.

But he didn't get stupid, not yet. Cautious, he led with a couple of jabs; she batted them away from her face easily. Deciding she was bored with the boxing, she threw a couple of low kicks in with her punches, not intended to take his feet out from under him but to shift his footing and keep him off balance. His brows drew together, and he huffed with the effort to stay on his feet.

Anger and frustration spiced the air. Not long now, and she'd have him.

He changed elevation, crouching down and diving for her a couple of times, trying to take her down where his bulk would squash her, but he was too slow and she danced out of his way, zoning to the left or right and landing a hit or two to the kidneys or back of the head. A grin threatened to stretch her lips, and she consciously kept a straight face. Damn, this was fun.

Though she pulled most of her hits, every one of them landed solid, and the grunts of pain from her opponent gave her guilt-free satisfaction.

The three minutes were winding down, and he had yet to land a single hit. As a last ditch, he hopped up into a clumsy superman punch. She slipped to the outside and tagged his exposed side with a hook to the kidneys. With a howl of rage, Meathead snapped and really came after her.

"Zec!"

Oblivious to the warning shouts of his colleagues, the man went berserk. His added speed, fueled by resentment, crashed through her guard as his fist connected with the side of her head.

Time to get serious because no one would stop him in time.

Bob and weave, cover and return strike. She still had speed and agility on him. When she landed a right slant kick on his upper leg, he visibly paused, no doubt unable to shake the way his quads seized up. Panic entered his eyes as the man realized he couldn't win.

The cat in her gathered itself to pounce.

He stumbled to the side, and Kaitlyn thought he would step off the mat and disengage.

Instead, he grabbed Skuld by the front of her ship suit and threw her into Kaitlyn.

Her rage snapped its leash as she caught Skuld and

spun, redirecting Skuld's momentum to land her in the arms of Tracer. Completing the turn, she hammered Zec with a backfist to the face, followed immediately by a left hook.

Bastard.

As he fell to the side under the blows, she brought up her right knee with enough force to send him up and backward. His feet literally left the ground.

How dare he.

She leaped into the air and came down on top of him, driving her feet into his midsection as she landed.

He'd laid hands on her friend. Threw an innocent into danger.

Knees atop his chest, she drew her right hand back for the killing swipe.

"Enough!" Dev's voice cut through the red haze around her.

She looked up at him and lifted her lips in a silent snarl.

Her captain didn't move, didn't say another word. He met her gaze and stared her down, pitting his will against hers. Faced with those dead-calm eyes, Kaitlyn came back to herself.

She stood, then stepped clear of her prey and awaited orders. The men gave her plenty of clearance.

"I suggest you go cool down."

So civilized. Dev hadn't given her an order, hadn't given her a reason to challenge his authority.

The subtle reminder of her humanity brought with it a tiny splash of shame. She'd lost control.

She glanced to the side. Tracer was fussing over Skuld. She'd be okay. Assured of Skuld's safety, Kaitlyn strode out of the gym.

ONCE SHE REACHED the med bay, she didn't bother to shut the door. Dev would be along in a few moments, and she needed to get back under control before he arrived.

If she couldn't, well, that would be why he was going to check in on her. In the first weeks she'd been aboard ship, he'd been the one to help her remember how to return to human when her cat aspect slipped the leash. There'd been a lot of talking, but she didn't remember what he said as much as the tone of his voice and the way he spoke to her like she was human. He'd helped her remember what she'd been, and he hadn't acted as if she'd already died.

It'd been a long time ago, but apparently she'd never forgotten, even at the cellular level. She'd need to try harder. Regression was not in the game plan.

His footsteps sounded in the corridor sooner than she'd expected. Still, when he appeared in her doorway, his shoulders were relaxed, hands loose, and heartbeat steady. Nothing about his body language spoke of anger or alarm or anything to further agitate her beast.

He studied her for a minute as she watched him. When

he spoke, his voice remained light. "While I agree the man is a waste of air, I'd appreciate it if one of my crew weren't responsible for ending him, especially when we're supposed to be comrades in arms and whatnot."

She'd spit, but she thought the practice was gross. Still, thinking of Meathead made her want to get the bad taste out of her mouth. "He proved he'd throw one of us on the line if it gave him any sort of advantage."

"True enough and I won't fault you for handing him his ass." Dev dismissed the point with a wave of his hand. "I'm more concerned with how close you were to making him a corpse. Your intentions were pretty clear."

A spear of guilt stabbed her. To be honest, it was there and then gone again, burned clean away by the memory of how willing the man had been to toss Skuld into harm's way. And one of Kaitlyn's greatest nightmares was to be responsible for harm to an innocent, especially one who mattered to her the way Skuld did.

No. Skuld was one of hers to protect, and the man meant to hurt her friend. The only regret Kaitlyn suffered was the necessity of sparing the man's life.

"I know you, Kat, so I'm going to promise you he will not be allowed anywhere near Skuld or any of our other shipmates one-on-one." Dev spoke slowly and deliberately, holding his temper in check as much as hers. A part of the reason Kaitlyn looked to him was the way he made crew his family. No doubt he was every bit as angry as she was over what had just happened.

And his anger helped her get hers under control. "Then I'll give you a promise back. If the idiot comes to harm on this ship, it won't be by my hand." She paused. "Or claw."

Dev grinned. "Well now, I think we've had our obligatory talk, as it were."

She hadn't promised not to bite the bastard though. In the past, she'd crushed an attacker's skull in her jaws. Ah well, Dev would hold her to the spirit of the promise, even if she hadn't quite covered the detail.

Besides, he hadn't made her promise to the man's safety once they were all off the ship.

After Dev left, she toyed with the idea for a bit and then discarded it. The man was space flotsam, but he wasn't worth the effort it'd take to plan his demise. Details were a point of pride for her, and if she couldn't do it properly, going undetected, she wouldn't do it at all.

Dev's steps halted in the corridor, then she heard him pace for minute. Inwardly, she cringed.

"Kat." Years of being a merc gave her a hard exterior, but her captain's words could still trigger her anxiety, especially when she knew they were justified.

"You need to get a line on what is bothering you." He gestured back toward the guest quarters. "These men, normally they wouldn't shake your control the way they are, especially not the idiot."

"No." Maybe three years ago it would've been a problem, when she'd struggled harder for control and against trauma in a two-front war inside herself. But not now. "I'm on edge and I can't pin down why. I need to run, clear my head."

"That is not an option and you know it's mostly to keep you safely out of a lab rat's cage."

She nodded. "Aye, Captain."

"You let me know if there's anything I can do to help you get this under control."

This, the talking and his concern, helped. Usually, it was enough to balance her, support her as she worked things through on her own. Impulse took hold of her. "I'm going to talk to the prisoner, Bharguest."

Dev's brows rose almost to his hairline. Obviously not what he was expecting. "You have a reason. I'm sorta blind as to what it might be right now."

"He knows what I am, Dev." Her captain hadn't missed that particular—no, he had been letting a sleeping dog lie. "And he hasn't mentioned a thing to the military men."

"I was of the opinion the less time you spent in his vicinity the better."

Might live longer at least.

Kaitlyn tipped her head sideways. "I'm thinking along different lines, Captain. I'm thinking he's bored and he finds me more interesting than the men guarding him. I've got a hunch he's got useful information, more than he's given them as part of his bargain, and all very valuable to me if I get him to share. Rygard's life could depend on it."

Course getting Bharguest to share would be the tricky part of the game.

Dev remained silent, considering. After a moment, he sighed. "I don't need to warn you the man is dangerous."

Kaitlyn pressed her lips together. "Only reason he's in detainment is because he hasn't gotten bored enough to break out. I get the impression he goes places because he wants to. He toys with the guards because they amuse him. He's playing the military because it pleases him to do so. I don't have all the puzzle pieces yet, but any move he makes is one he does either because it goes in the direction he wants or hell, just because he doesn't have something else to do to amuse him more."

Another hesitation. "You could be right."

Dev had seen more battles, more combat, and more of everything than Kaitlyn had. He could assess a man every bit as well as she could and better. His reluctance wasn't because he didn't believe her.

"You be careful. And you keep in mind our purpose is to work with the military team aboard, not only to rescue your man."

Kaitlyn pressed the tip of her tongue between her teeth. "Aye, Captain."

The corner of Dev's mouth lifted in a shadow of a grin. "You've been saying 'Aye' a bit often of late. I'm starting to get suspicious as to what you'll get up to once you get off this ship."

Kaitlyn blinked wide eyes, once, twice.

"Uh-huh." Dev shook his head. "It's a lucky thing for you I believe you do your best work when you're given a lot of leeway. A man with less nerve would be driven to drink by now."

"You do drink, Captain." And she drank with him occasionally. Who else would have taught her the finer points of Scotch?

Dev threw up his hands. "Drink more, then."

She grinned as he left, for real that time, his steps echoing all the way down the corridor. He wasn't just her captain because he could keep her under control. No, Dev was a man who knew people.

Still, she needed to talk to Bharguest to learn more about others. She glanced at her wrist chrono. She'd log on to find out what Boggle had found for her first, then go talk to the prisoner who wasn't really a prisoner.

"IT'S NOT AS MUCH about how bad it looks. It's how bad it sounds." Boggle's image hovered over her terminal. The resolution was good enough for her to see the sweat bead along his brow. "I'm going to play you the feed I snagged first and then tell you what I found in communications surrounding the transmission."

Kaitlyn nodded.

The three-dimensional hologram flickered. She watched as Rygard's last distress call played before her eyes. He'd already been in direct confrontation from the look of him, and he'd delivered his hurried message in a grim hush. Based on the time stamp of the communication, it couldn't have been long after the last time they'd spoken.

She watched as he shoved the terminal under a tarp to keep it from immediate discovery, understood the reasoning behind leaving it to transmit for as long as possible. It was listening to the struggle, to DeSarto's curse and Rygard's grunt of pain—hearing that did some significant damage to what calm she'd managed to pull together before calling Boggle.

"I need an isolated recording of the sounds made by those biologics, Boggle. Rygard's team was observing a potentially dangerous outpost, but there was no intel to indicate an opposing force capable of taking out their base camp in retaliation. These were supposed to be slavers hunkered down to process in new merchandise and get it off as quickly as possible. All of their firepower should have been invested in defending the outpost. They shouldn't have the . . . resources to launch this kind of attack." She gave herself high points for the rational words, but she subtracted a few for the high-pitched thread of distress straining her vocal cords. Clearing her throat, she tried for a better tone. "You have additional data?"

Boggle's face flashed back on the screen.

"I'll send you the soundtracks right after this call." He

studied her for a moment, brows drawn over close-set eyes. "You're not going to like the communications I intercepted from Captain What's-his-face aboard your ship. He included a recommended course of action along with the Mayday call from Rygard. Reconnaissance only, with utmost caution. He doesn't feel a retrieval will be an effective use of resources because to him, it's obvious the soldiers are dead."

"Listening to the fight, it's obvious they were taken alive." Anger built inside Kaitlyn, burning a hole through her chest. Her cat aspect growled, low and rumbling inside her head. "And What's-his-face's name is Petrico-Calin. The Fourth."

"High chance they didn't stay alive long, according to What's-his-face." Boggle paused, pressing his lips into a thin line.. "Rygard's a heavy hitter, Kaitlyn. It'd be dangerous to take him alive."

Experience told her different. Considering the ferocity of the attack, Rygard might have fought too hard to be worth taking captive, true. But he knew reinforcements were on the way and their general estimated time of arrival. He was also smart enough to play the captive until his team had the support needed to break loose. She'd stick to the evidence they had and find more when she got on the ground.

In spite of her worries, Kaitlyn gave Boggle a rare smile. "You've got good gut instinct. One of these days, you should leave Dysnomia Station and come out on a run with me."

His eyes widened until the whites showed. "Not likely."

She shook her head; there wasn't enough time to coax him while more serious matters were at hand. "If those biologics attacked out of hunger or territory issues, they would have killed Rygard and DeSarto on the spot. It sounded like the entire camp was overwhelmed and you could hear them taken away. Sounds of struggle faded as they left. They were still alive and kicking hard as they went. Normal biologics don't take prisoners."

Any healthy animal on any normal planet only attacked out of defense or out of hunger. Pretty simple. Sentience made things complicated.

Boggle must have had an epiphany because he perked up in his moto-chair, sat forward, and skimmed his fingers so fast over his console that the hologram couldn't display more than a blur. "Original surveys show several structures. Hard to tell how old, but definitely more advanced than the primitive biologics theorized to live on the surface could make. I'll shoot you the images taken from orbit by Rygard's team. They won't be much help on the ground in terms of distance or game trails but they should give you an idea of what direction to begin scouting."

"Any idea what type of biologics those were? Were they native?" They hadn't sounded like any animal she'd ever encountered. Some of those sounds, they had speechlike qualities. If she played the sound tracks back slow, she might learn more.

"Original scans showed primates, but much smaller than these and didn't exhibit anywhere near the level of intelligence the attack suggests. Initial survey team called them simians. The native biologics look like something between a Terran baboon and chimpanzee." Two images flashed side by side for her to study. Boggle's attention was fixed on one of his side monitors, probably on the original reports. Reports he shouldn't have had access to. She'd learned it was better for them all if she didn't ask how he got to the information he dug up. "We didn't get a clear picture of them before he covered the image capture or I'd be able to tell you more."

She chewed on her lower lip. "Something didn't sound right in there, too much of a call-and-response pattern to be random aggression. Those things were communicating, maybe coordinating their attack."

Boggle shrugged. "You would know better than me. I've got the sound tracks all isolated and sending them encrypted now."

"Any chance our friends are watching for transmissions?" Joint mission or not, Petrico-Calin had been drawing the line between his teams and Dev's crew. Those sorts of missions usually resulted in a very detailed division of duties. Dev rolled with those missions, keeping his own team dynamic, ready to handle whatever duties came their way with efficiency. He also taught her a few things about covering their collective asses to be sure any snafu on the part of their partners didn't reflect back on them.

Boggle grinned. "They're trying to monitor. No worries. All of our communications are encrypted and tagged to appear as video game sessions. The data I'm sending now is going to look like a patch to one of the bigger MMORPGs. I'm including the install to the actual game for your terminal in case they decide to check."

Kaitlyn chewed on the concept. "I appreciate the consideration."

Boggle leaned forward, wetting his lips and giving her an unsure-but-game smile, his expression suddenly earnest. "You'll find him. He's tough enough to hold out until you get there."

Despite the situation, she couldn't help the warmth spreading through her chest. One of the best things Dev and Skuld could have ever done had to be dropping her on Dysnomia Station. She'd never admit it—not to them, and not to nerd boy.

"Thank you." Boggle looked up and she gave him a small nod. "I'll check out the info and install the game. Maybe you can do a walk-through with me after this mission."

"No worries." Boggle waved. "I'm not going anywhere."

Kaitlyn took a sharp look at his hologram. He was too flippant, and the undercurrent of wistful resignation wasn't just in her imagination.

"Find Rygard. Hit me up if you have any new data for me to analyze and I'll keep an eye on the transmissions. Signing off."

He terminated the holoprojection, leaving her staring at empty space. If she came out of the next mission alive, she'd have to figure out how to chase the unhappiness out of his voice.

A WHINE SOUNDED outside her door, followed by a soft *woof* and light scratching.

Speaking of unhappy.

Another minute passed and the light scratching came again. Not obnoxious—almost discreet.

She uncurled from her seat, walked across the room, and palmed the door open.

The dog, Max, stood there with his head up, ears forward. He waved his tail in a gentle tock-tock. Still, there was something different about his stance. His balance wasn't distributed evenly over all four paws.

"Where's your human?" A little silly to be talking to a dog, maybe, but the rest of the crew had gotten over any weirdness they experienced when they spoke to her in cat form. It wasn't the same, but this animal was supposed to be smarter than normal canines.

Big ears dipped. He dropped his nose to the threshold and then looked back at her and whined again.

At least he was a polite canine.

"You can come in if you have a real reason to be here. If you're just bored, you can go away."

She watched as he walked into her territory, shoving down her growing aggression. She didn't like letting another large predator into her space, and while this dog couldn't take her, he was still more dangerous than most humans. But as he walked past her, her attention settled on his near hind leg. The coppery scent of blood tinged the air. She looked at the floor and realized he was leaving bloody paw prints behind him.

"Stop where you are." The dog cocked his head sideways. "Either get up on one of the stretchers or lay on your side on the floor where you stand. You can choose, but get your weight off that paw."

She kept one eye on the dog as he stared at her, seeming to consider his choices. She stepped into the doorway to look both ways down the hall. No bloody paw prints. He must have licked up the blood along the way to keep from leaving a trail. Not a bad solution for hiding the blood.

"You're lucky I had a solid dinner." The scent of blood excited her, and the prospect of a wounded animal in her territory piqued her interest, but she had no need to wrestle with her hunger. She always had extra protein bars in her ship suit pockets to keep herself on a full belly in case she ever had to work on crewmates.

While she'd been checking his trail, her new patient had hopped up on one of the stretchers.

She closed the door and approached him, slow and wary. He might have come to her, but wounded was still dangerous, regardless of on man or beast. "You want to show me what happened?"

He laid back his ears.

She raised an eyebrow. "Hey, you came to me. Obviously it means you can't take care of it yourself."

A pause, and the ears drooped. He shifted his weight partially to one side so he could extend the injured hind leg without completely exposing his belly. She couldn't blame him. She had problems presenting herself in a vulnerable position too. As it was, the predator in her couldn't resist eyeing the soft flesh of his underbelly, considering the ease of disembowelment.

Long practice allowed her the self-control to keep her claws in. He'd come to her for healing, and the healer had been a part of her years before the cat aspect had made things complicated. A long, steady breath helped her find the conviction she called on to work on every patient to enter her medical bay. It was stronger than her cat urges, kept the predatory instinct locked away. It was enough for her to take a look at this patient's injury.

Instead of raising the ambient room lights to full, she snagged a standing lamp with her foot to bring it closer and toed the slider to bring up a small area of light for her to get a good look at the paw.

"It's not a constant bleed." She studied his extended leg without touching it first. No blood dripped from his paw, and he hadn't left a bloody trail between each spot he'd put his paw down. He'd only bled when he'd put pressure on it.

None of the claws were broken, which had been her first thought. A broken claw, especially when the break was right above the quick, hurt like hell. She'd done it in cat form once or twice.

"What have you got stuck in there?"

He answered with a soft *woof*.

She took his paw in a gentle hold. Using her fingers to separate his pads, she immediately saw the issue.

"Now where did you pick that up, the holding bay?"

A nasty piece of metal was lodged in the side of one pad, between two toes. It must have gotten wedged in there as he stepped and turned. If he'd placed his paw directly on it, it would have pierced the underside of the pad and he'd have been able to pull it out with his teeth. There was evidence he'd tried anyway. The pad and the skin between his toes appeared irritated.

Straightening, she reached into one of the drawers next to the stretcher. "This is just a surface disinfectant." The astringent scent of the stuff also killed any appetite the scent of blood might have awoken in her. A quick swab to the area and she continued on with her next step. "I'm going to pull this out now. It won't tickle. Promise you won't bite me."

The dog's only answer was a grunt.

She pulled the offending piece of metal out slowly in case it had a jagged edge that might snag the inner flesh. The less damage to the pad and underlying tissue, the better, especially if he had to be ready to run as soon as they hit planetside. As it was, she'd recommend the dog and his handler scout away from her so she wouldn't be tempted to chase him down in his injured state.

"It's out, but stay still. I want to flush it out and get a sealant on it."

He held steady for her, more obedient than even the best of her human patients.

"The sealant will dissolve on its own in about a week." She cleaned up her work space. "No chewing on it, even if your paw itches, or I will put a cone of shame on you."

The dog growled as he hopped off the stretcher. After a moment, he gave her a final whine and a quick lick to her hand and then headed for the door.

She let him out. "You seem to have more sense than most of my patients, so you're welcome. Come back if it starts to swell or feel hot."

A very quiet bark, and he trotted down the corridor.

For a canine, he wasn't half bad. She liked him better than most humans.

CHAPTER 12

"I WAS WONDERING when you'd be back." Bharguest stirred in the recesses of his cell, the only light the one from the energy field keeping him confined. The rest of the room's lights had been turned down to night setting. In the deepest shadows, his eyes had changed to a golden orange and his pupils had become vertical slashes. "You were entertaining earlier today. I wanted to thank you."

"I never fight to entertain others." Kaitlyn hopped onto a counter on the wall opposite his cell, making herself comfortable but still ready to move if need be.

"Oh, 'never' has a finality to it most of us can't afford to honor." He slid closer to the energy field, the light touching his forehead and cheekbones. In the harsh contrast of light and shadows, his face became an inhuman mask.

She was betting the mask was closer to his inner beast than his human facade.

"I came to ask more questions." She didn't bother to try to sound innocent or enticing. They both liked it better when she spoke frankly, and besides, she was feeling neither of those things in the moment.

Bharguest turned his head to the right until his head almost rested on his shoulder. "But you're still not getting to the real questions, Kaitlyn Darah. Ask me. I might answer."

Come closer, my dear, so I can see you better.

Wasn't that from an ancient children's tale?

"Questions limit the answers." Kaitlyn kicked her feet a little, giving in just a bit to the invitation to play. She let her cat out enough to show in her eyes. "In my opinion, any knowledge is worth something eventually. So why don't you share what you feel like sharing?"

He chuckled again. "Very good."

She shrugged.

"The virus, the one they infected you with to change you, how did they introduce it to your system?" His tongue darted out, tasted the air, as he waited.

Ah, at least she hadn't needed to wait long for him to make his first move in this session of chess. "A tattoo gun inked it into my skin."

The machine had been small and sleek, handheld. A thousand tiny needles had plunged into her flesh in unison, injecting the virus into her system as ink buried indelibly into her skin. She'd been left with an instant tattoo of a panther on her left thigh and the virus burning through her cells.

"They branded you."

"Yes." Neutral. She'd shared the same information in her briefings enough times for the retelling to become easy.

He righted his head, his gaze never leaving her. "Tch. No imagination. It doesn't have to be spread across so much surface area to infect a humanoid of your size. You know that right? A single air gun or hypodermic syringe would work just as well."

"Yes." One injection site would have sufficed. Less of

the actual solution carrying the virus would have as well. Her research had provided conclusive results in terms of how much of the virus it would take to infect a fully grown human. They'd given her and her fellow captured classmates more than necessary, and most likely the overdose was why the others had died. Maybe. She still wasn't sure.

"Me, they branded too, but they were disappointed with the results. My scales covered the brand." He tipped his head to the side and rolled one shoulder forward, displaying more of the black and gold scales in their diamond pattern. She thought the pattern might extend down his back, following his spine. "The animal vector they introduced has a strong healing factor, stronger than mammals."

Narrowed down her list of things he could be in addition to human genetic stock. It also added to the unsettling factor. She wasn't a fan of cold-blooded species in general.

"And the shape-shift, it varies from person to person. Doesn't it?"

He grinned, his mouth dropped open somehow without his teeth. "Yes." He drew it out long.

"Have you changed for your military friends yet? Did they ask what you could be?" She was betting he hadn't. They'd be more frightened of him.

"Oh they asked." He turned away from her, rolling his shoulders. Cords of muscle rippled in his neck. She heard his jaw pop. "But I wasn't in the mood. They took blood samples too. I imagine they'll figure it out eventually."

She wouldn't mind a few samples herself. Course, she was betting the samples the Terran military acquired had an associated body count. Now wasn't the time to take such a risk to satisfy her curiosity. Besides, it'd give Dev heartburn.

"Even with cold-blooded animals, the possibilities are numerous." She was running through a list of choices herself. "They'd do better analyzing your saliva."

"Smart, smart girl." He turned back to her, grinning more now, his jaw hanging low and open. "You're getting warmer."

"Doesn't take much to run warmer than you though, does it?" The scientist in her wanted to take some readings on him, get baseline biometrics and run them against his responses to their conversations.

He didn't close his jaw. Instead, he continued to grin with it hanging open and flicked the tip of his tongue against the edges of his upper teeth. "For you? No. For some of the neckless wonders in uniform? We've got a little more in common than I'd prefer."

"I can think of one or two who might've come from under a rock somewhere. Not the type to spark any kind of warm thoughts." She'd commiserate with him on that point.

"None of the people on board this ship do, not really." His tongue flicked across his teeth again. "Oh you're loyal to your captain and fond of him too, but he doesn't generate a real 'spark.' Your little engineer doesn't do it for you either. They're friends, maybe family in the ways that really count. But they don't get you hot and bothered."

"No." And she wasn't going to tell him about her connection to Rygard. Not yet and not based on the current line of conversation.

"That's going to make things all sorts of complicated in the near future."

She waited to see if he'd expand on that.

He only tasted the air again.

"I do fine solo."

He blinked. "Do you? All on your lonesome, with no

one to help you take the edge off? Sure you haven't been feeling a little . . . violent lately?"

"I've got my temper under control." The anger constantly living inside her seethed. It had to be what he was talking about.

"Control isn't what you're going to need." He pushed off the wall and loomed as close to the bars and energy field as possible without setting it off. "You need to embrace your beast, or you will not come out of there alive. Alone, maybe you could, but you're trying to retrieve people. You're going to need the extra help."

She remained silent, too stubborn to argue with him.

"All this time, and such a perfect mutation." He shook his head slowly. "Wasted while you pretend to be just a human."

"I didn't give in to the virus. It didn't take who I am from me."

"Now you're just spouting the lies they told you to save your sanity." He waved the words away. "You came through it—put your big cat claws out and admit you did. Give in. It did change you. You are a full mutation because you let the virus alter every single cell in your body. Every skin cell, every muscle and bone cell, every single neuron firing in that pretty little skull. You are your beast and you're wasting more of your brain than any normal human while you deny it."

The truth of his words rang in the air, struck a chord deep inside her.

"When we land tomorrow, you scout like you're supposed to. Find those soldiers and bring them back if you can." He withdrew, letting the shadows swallow him. "Watch, listen, survive. If you come back, I might tell you more."

IF SHE CAME BACK. Rawr.

Kaitlyn stalked down the corridor. It'd taken all she had to leave the room without saying something she'd regret later. Bharguest had set out to push her buttons, and he'd succeeded. He knew it. She knew it. No sense in confirming the fact.

He'd given her too much to think on and precious little in the way of peace of mind. If she wanted to be honest with herself, she envied him. A prisoner, under confinement and multiple layers of security, stood in more control of his world and his circumstances than she did. Dev had given her a lot of things over the years, skills and tools to grow into a solid mercenary. But she'd never been as completely in control of her mutation, herself, or her life the way Bharguest managed.

How did he do it?

Her footsteps took her toward the galley, by habit for the most part. It'd been several hours since she'd eaten, and whenever she wrestled with frustrating mental puzzles, she headed there. But what she wanted was comfort food, and her favorite synthesizer had malfunctioned. She slowed, pondering the other options. Freeze-dried or reconstituted foodstuffs fulfilled her nutritional requirement but wouldn't satisfy her current craving. Maybe hydroponics? Most of those fruits and vegetables weren't ready for harvesting.

Urk.

"Why are we here again?" It took her a moment to register the male's voice as the dog handler's, Tracer's. His question had been light, but his tone of voice held a warmer note than she'd heard previously. Kaitlyn paused, staying outside the galley and out of line of sight of the door.

"Hand me the laser calibrator? The long-handled one. Yup." Skuld was up to something. Quiet clicks and the high-pitched whine of the calibrator came across crystal clear in the otherwise empty galley. "This synthesizer is Katy's favorite. It's set to make the best cupcakes and brownies we can get outside Terran space."

"So we've spent hours here, trying to fix a dessert maker?"

Tracer must not have had a lot of experience with women. Dev had declared it a necessity in surviving with females on board. Kaitlyn and Skuld emphatically agreed. Lives had been saved because they'd had a reasonable synthesized fudge brownie.

"Katy's been on edge recently and this morning's thing in the gym made her angrier."

How much had Skuld been talking to Tracer? Kaitlyn had been the one to literally toss Skuld into the man's arms, but she hadn't expected Skuld to stay with him.

"Well, I'm happy to help if it'd make your friend a little less threatening." The man wasn't ingratiating himself with Kaitlyn. "She's the most intimidating merc I've met in a long time."

Skuld laughed, and the bright sound mollified Kaitlyn. It always did. "New guys always have one of two reactions. They underestimate her or they're scared of her."

"There's a difference between intimidated and scared."

At least the man had a semblance of a backbone. And, Kaitlyn admitted to herself, he gained a couple of points for not underestimating her.

"She's more than intimidating, then." Skuld's voice took a harder edge. It didn't come out often, but when it did, the conviction was unmistakable. "She's warm and generous and caring. It takes a lot of strength to be as kind as she is.

She just . . . gets embarrassed by it, is all. She doesn't know what to do with thank-yous so she avoids them. It's better to show your thanks instead of stumbling around trying to say it to her."

Silence fell for a moment. "You're a very good friend."

And this wasn't the usual flirty sort of conversation. This one had some depth to it. It was to Tracer's credit that he'd followed along with what seemed like good intentions.

Skuld snorted. "You're missing the point again. She's the kind of friend to be there for you for life. Once you're one of hers, she'll travel galaxies to get to you when you need her. One mission, Cap'n had to empty this ship and set it adrift as a decoy. I stayed aboard to fire the engines back up cold."

"That's not an easy thing to do." Tracer's concern was justified. It wasn't. But Skuld wasn't just any engineer. She could coax life back into any mechanical thing, no matter how cold and rusted it might be.

"Eh. You give the ship the right kind of attention and she'll give you what she needs." Skuld brushed aside her talent. Another set of clicks, and the calibrator hummed again. "But the mission drew out longer than expected, and their shuttle suffered damage. A couple of the men we were laying the trap for managed to board our vessel before the rest of our team could get back. Katy geared up in a deep space suit and hopped from the shuttle back to this ship to get to me."

"Seriously dangerous." Tracer grunted. He must have been lifting the synthesizer for Skuld. "If she misgauged the rotation of the ship, she could've missed and ended up floating in deep space."

Yeah, it hadn't been fun. But she'd have died before letting Skuld face the danger alone, and she'd been the only crew member with the strength and agility to manage it.

"Point is, Katy came for me." Skuld's voice warmed. "Life isn't kind to everyone. And I won't get into details so don't ask. Just believe me when I say Katy has more reason than most not to like people. History has a funny way of taking hold of a person, trapping them. And they walk through the universe mad or angry or scared. Katy? She came through it stronger, yeah, and fierce. But she doesn't use it to strike out at the universe. You just look at her and see a kind and gentle soul, a little jagged around the edges but clear all the same. She deserves good friends. And I want to help her get comfortable with people again. We're working on her people skills, me and Chester and the Cap'n."

Kaitlyn swallowed the lump in her throat and blinked away burning tears. Only Skuld.

"Chester, huh?" Tracer's chuckle was soft, no hint of any mocking. An affirmative squeak triggered another chuckle. Well, at least Chester was with them, chaperoning as it were. The man won more points for not asking probing questions.

"Animals are simpler, honest. Katy likes honest."

True enough. Little tube rat was a pain in the rear and a thief, but he didn't lie or hurt people. Manipulation, torture . . . evil wasn't in his nature.

"Maybe Max can help with her people skills too."

The dog? Seriously? She might've helped him earlier, but she had no intention of dealing with a canine any more than she had to.

"Maybe." Skuld's voice was all melty and sweet. "You don't think badly of Katy?"

"You obviously think a great deal of her." Tracer's

response sounded sincere. "Even if I had any doubts before, I'd think twice based on what you've said. But no, everything I've seen so far points to an intimidating but impressive merc."

"She is good at what she does." Pride. Skuld rarely gave herself enough credit, but she always made it clear how proud she was of Kaitlyn. It made Kaitlyn strive to do better.

"And you brushed it off before, but I'll say it again. You're a good friend." Tracer paused for a moment. Kaitlyn wondered if he'd snuck a kiss. She couldn't see, but heat warmed her cheeks. She didn't mean to be spying on Skuld's intimate moments. "And I'm very glad to have met you."

"Really?" Skuld's breathless voice answered the question of whether he'd kissed her or not. And oh, Skuld had fallen for the dog handler. Kaitlyn stepped away on silent feet and made her way back to her room. Let the two have a few more hours of time to get to know each other. She could get herself a chocolate cupcake later.

"BEGINNING APPROACH. EVERYBODY, GET SOFT."

Kaitlyn relaxed back into her harness as the landing shuttle entered atmosphere and gravity began to set in, pulling her down into her seat. Turbulence had already started to make their entry into the atmosphere a rough ride. Not as bad as it could be, but enough to make her stomach jump.

Katzer had always teased her about the way she took to space flight better than atmosphere. But then he had to go die in space.

Her thoughts were too far in the past. Old flames and echoes had no place in what she had to do here and now. She centered her attention on the dog lying at his handler's feet across the aisle from her.

"Since you're lying there, lemme see that paw."

The handler, Tracer, chuckled. "I figured you must have patched him up when I saw the sealant over the cut."

"Not a cut." Good man to check his dog's health on a regular basis even as distracted as he had been, spending time with Skuld. Max, for his part, looked up at her and laid his ears back in a nervous posture.

"If you chewed on your paw, I wasn't kidding, I'll put a cone of shame on you." She repeated the threat, ignoring the way his lip lifted to bare his teeth. He didn't mean it, yet. "I need to be sure you're good to run out there."

Tracer opened his mouth to speak—a command most likely—but Kaitlyn held up her hand.

"This is between me and Max. He can be a big dog and let me inspect the wound or he can stay on the shuttle once we land."

Meathead sneered. "The mutt is going to get out and do his job."

Meathead was detailed to secure the landing site and clear away underbrush. Fine. Max was out there to help her find Rygard and his team. "If he's got an open wound, he stays on the shuttle, same as any other crew member."

Max's ears swiveled forward, and he looked to Zec. After a moment, the big dog laid his head down and turned on his side, then extended the injured paw as far as he could. She leaned forward, taking a good look.

"Wound is clean, no swelling. Sealant is chewed up a bit, but it'll hold." She raised an eyebrow at Max as he lifted his head. The big dog whined. "No more chewing."

"He won't." Tracer came to his partner's rescue, reaching down to rub between those big ears. "Right, Max?"

Max gave a positive-sounding bark.

Yeah. If she was beginning to hear the nuances in doggy talk, she'd already been around the dog too much.

"He's fine to scout. Just don't send him over any insanely rough terrain without those little bootie things." She paused. "He has those, doesn't he?"

Tracer cleared his throat, hiding what sounded

suspiciously like a chuckle. "Yeah, Max has those as part of his gear."

Well, that was settled then.

After a moment, Tracer made another throat-clearing noise. "Your friend, Skuld . . ."

"She's a good friend." She didn't bother to hide the growl forming in her chest.

Max laid back his ears again.

"No, no. I mean yeah, I noticed how close you two were at the gym." The words literally tumbled out of his mouth. "I was wondering if she was seeing anybody . . ."

Else. If Skuld was seeing anybody else—because her scent was already on Tracer's skin and clothes.

Kaitlyn considered him for a long moment. Not too many of Skuld's lovers ever cared if Skuld was available. Most didn't really care about Skuld's life outside of the moments they wanted her. As picks went, Tracer wasn't a bad sort—definitely a better man than most of the others Kaitlyn had encountered.

"Not currently." Even that bit of data was more than she'd give to any other man.

"Do you know if she . . ."

Oh no, Kaitlyn was not about to get sucked into matchmaking. "Skuld makes her own choices. You'd do best to talk to her directly about whatever is developing between you."

"LANDING PROTOCOLS COMPLETE. Teams are clear to go." Their pilot, Tails, sounded almost bored over the speakers.

Kaitlyn watched the cargo bay doors open and forced

her feet to remain anchored to the floor, all thoughts of intership relationships dismissed. Blue skies, jungle humidity, and a breeze carrying the smell of rich earth called to her. If they'd been on their own, without the add-on military team, she'd have shot out the doors as soon as there was an opening big enough for her body, and Dev wouldn't have said a word in criticism.

But no, they were team players on this mission. And she had to play as part of the human contingent.

An eager whine sounded to her left. Max was ready to get off ship as well.

As soon as the ramp touched dirt, she moved.

The landing site was relatively clear, close to the original campsite but on higher ground with just enough vegetation to set up camouflage. Badger would stay behind and take care of securing the area with a detail of crew members and soldiers, including Zec. It irked Kaitlyn a little to leave her way off the planet, guarded by Meathead, but she trusted her shipmates. That would have to be enough.

Kaitlyn moved forward, listening to the jungle.

The silence in the near vicinity wasn't what surprised her. Natural avian or small biologics would have gone quiet as the shuttle landed. No, it was the sense of something watching and waiting, as out of place in this particular jungle as they all were.

"Kaitlyn, proceed north as planned," Dev's voice whispered from the auditory unit in her ear canal.

Nifty bit of technology from Boggle. Even if she shifted, the communicator piece would remain in her ear canal, allowing Dev or the ship to communicate with her. On missions like this, where they acted in tandem with another team, Dev tended to stay aboard their ship in orbit and direct things from afar. She and the rest of the landing crew were his eyes and ears, hands and feet. Left him free to coordinate with the leadership of the other team. "Tracer and Max will proceed east. Badger and his team will set up a perimeter and venture south to assess terrain."

"Aye, Captain."

"There you go with saying 'Aye' again. It's got me twitchy."

She huffed and set off at an easy jog into the jungle, ducking low to slip through the undergrowth along a game trail she'd spotted. From the wear and tear to the path, she guessed Rygard's team might have used it coming and going. The vegetation showed obvious signs of semirecent clearing. Another few days and the path would be choked with plants again.

It felt good to stretch her legs, fill her lungs with real air. Scents teased her from every direction. This jungle sheltered a wide array of prey. Her cat aspect wanted to run, explore, stalk a target and hunt it down. The urge wasn't simply about hunger, although she'd eaten her prey in the past with a cold practicality.

Rabbits tasted better than protein bars.

It went beyond the need for sustenance. The excitement of the hunt did her soul good too. It freed something inside her, and the tension that built during every long space flight evaporated after a good run and successful hunt.

"Stay on task," she told herself. There was a specific goal this day. Rygard took center stage in her mind, and her cat aspect remembered the scent of him while the human part of her mind recalled the feel of his hands on her skin. She needed to find him.

As soon as she arrived at the camp area, she took in the details of the attack. Tracks entered camp from game trails in every direction. Vines dangled down from the trees, ends torn. Ambushers had caught them all by surprise, coming in from multiple directions, especially above.

The primates on this planet, simians, excelled at tree climbing, according to the survey data Boggle had sent her and her additional research. Many nested in or traveled across treetops. Explained why Rygard's team might not have detected them coming.

Her eyes fell on the communications tent, the canvas walls torn down on one side to expose the table where the equipment had been set up. She crossed the clearing in a few strides, then crouched down to study the area. Every sense expanded wide open, sight and smell, hearing and touch, as she reached out with a fingertip to nudge a tuft of fur still attached to a patch of skin. Not human, it had to belong to one of the attackers. A sniff confirmed her conclusion, and she pulled out a small sample container to collect it for analysis on the ship later.

Rygard's scent was strong inside the tent. Not a surprise. Under duress, he'd surely had adrenaline pumping through his system, and her nose couldn't miss the lingering evidence of violence and anger. Very little blood was to be found anywhere on the ground though. Unfortunately, heavy traffic had packed the dirt into a hard floor, making any sort of useful tracks indiscernible inside the tent.

Circling the perimeter, she located each of the points of initial attack. Several tracks came from the underbrush, but some appeared in the middle of trails. At each of those points, one or several vines hung overhead. The conclusion was obvious.

For a moment, she paused to look up into the trees. Branches spread out in a broad circle from every tree, creating a solid canopy over the camp. Part of the reason

Rygard's team had chosen the site had to have been the natural cover. Yet she doubted any of them had climbed a tree to see how far up the canopy extended. A human might not have been able to make the climb bare-handed. She could.

Just how much canopy was up there?

This jungle had to be very much like the rain forests of Old Terra, with tiers of branches in the canopy supporting life at multiple levels. And the canopy would have been the fastest route to travel, to spy and to approach for attack. Now, it could be her fastest route to go after Rygard.

Still, her captain had given her an order: no shifting, not even a partial. If someone were to see her climbing one of the towering giants, there would be no explaining away the ability. The urge to take the fastest route possible warred with her need to follow orders. Dev's orders were always for a reason, and those reasons kept her human. Shit. She'd be going the longer way, which meant no more wasting time collecting evidence.

"I'm coming." She whispered the words, directing them as much to the jungle as to Rygard.

Returning to the likeliest point, she began to follow the trail. Rygard's scent marked the ground and the broken plant life along the way. He'd struggled for a good distance. At one point, a large portion of dirt had been scuffed up, maybe an attempt at escape. From there, the trail appeared to be a streamlined set of drag marks. They must have knocked him unconscious. She didn't think they'd killed him. There wasn't enough blood for him to have bled out, and there was no trace of the urine or other bodily fluids that would have evacuated his body at death.

As intent as she was on the trail, she kept her senses open to her surroundings as well. Too often, a hunter became prey to a sneakier assassin. The sounds of wildlife were in evidence this far from the ship—birds calling and insects chirping, the occasional rustling of leaves as a small mammal scurried away or a reptile slithered through the deadfall. All normal; none of them giving her early warning of danger approaching.

Still, she kept her knives loose in their sheaths and a gun Rygard had given her ready in its holster at her hip. At close range it didn't matter if she hadn't developed a high level of marksmanship yet. Her target would still end up with a hole in it. She'd learned how to quickly slide the safety on and off to have it at the ready when near immediate danger.

She followed the trail north, just as Boggle's satellite images indicated, for quite a ways. Dusk surrounded her by the time she saw the signs she'd been looking for, hints that she was coming close to their stopping point. Dev had checked in with her twice already, so she paused to give one more report.

"I've got buildings." Formal reporting never had stuck in her training.

"Eyes on them?" Dev didn't worry about it either, not from her.

"Not yet. Artificial light and noise. I'm guessing a fairly large compound. Definite signs of regular perimeter patrols. These would've been in Rygard's reports to his command structure."

"Funny how it didn't end up in the briefing."

The comment wasn't meant for her, though she could hear it, so she didn't bother to answer.

"I want you to wait for backup."

She growled.

"Too many, Kat. If it was just you, going in and coming out, it wouldn't be an issue. There's hopefully an unknown number of survivors. Best chance for success is to be team players on this one. Tracer and his partner are en route, we're contacting the other units now."

The urge to find Rygard drove her, but the logic her captain gave her stalled the beast impulse.

A shout rang out to her left, and she flattened her body to the ground, letting the underbrush cover her.

"I heard that." Dev's voice was a murmur in her ear, hushed and patient.

The new disturbance was far enough away that she responded in a low monotone. "New capture."

A string of curses carried across the jungle, accompanied by wild chittering noises. She recognized the latter from the sound clips Boggle had provided her, and the former, she'd heard on the ship when the idiot lost his temper.

"Can I let them kill him, Captain?"

Dev's sigh carried right through the communication line.

"Going silent."

No time to wait for reinforcement and, as much as she hated Zec, the meathead's capture might expose them all.

"Be careful." Dev would keep his end of the communication line open for her call.

Clenching her teeth hard, she depressed the switch in her back molar, turning off the communicator. On her own now, and off to save someone who would definitely not appreciate it. He wasn't supposed to be there in the first place. She crawled on her belly through the underbrush, taking her time to stalk her new prey. The soldier provided the perfect distraction, even if he definitely hadn't intended to get captured. He made enough noise to wake the dead.

"Hands off ya fucking freaks!"

When she got close enough to see the uproar he'd created, she quickly took in other details of the compound. No fence on the perimeter and no sign of lasers, as far as she could see. Her least favorite person at the moment was being dragged by half a dozen primates into a space between the two largest buildings.

They'd netted him—not a synthetic weave, from what she could tell, but more likely a natural fiber. He should have been able to slice himself free. They'd done a good job taunting him and distracting him, but it shouldn't have prevented him from going for his boot knife. On closer look, she realized all his weapons were gone from their holsters and sheaths. A lone primate walked into the clearing, burdened with a number of guns and knives. Well, that answered where they'd left his gear.

Humans, or at least more-human creatures than the primates, stepped out of one building. None of them smelled right; the breeze was carrying their rank odor right to her. Animals, unless they were sick, smelled of musk but were clean. These smelled of refuse, booze, and chemical recreation.

"What do we have here? A lone human?" The primates bowed their heads low to the newcomers, backing away from the speaker as he approached. He retained more of a human form than any of the others. Bigger too. Well, size mattered to determine dominance in any social structure, especially if intelligence was . . . lacking.

"Fuck off!" Zec had a fascinating opening response to a potential interrogation situation. She'd have to remember to try it sometime if she wanted her captors to immediately kill her.

"Oh no, we've got much better in store for you." Ominous, or it would have been, if the speaker hadn't scratched his rounded belly and belched. He made a strange sound at the simians crouched around him. "He can't be alone."

A slow realization dawned on her as she watched each and every one of them. Natural animals moved with a particular grace, having matured from birth with their physical attributes. These all moved in various states of clumsy motion, jerky and awkward. Worse than youths immediately after a growth spurt, unused to the sudden change in limbs grown overnight.

She'd moved awkwardly once upon a time. It'd taken years of martial arts training with Dev and Nibs to figure out how to use her body again with any kind of efficiency, much less grace.

Genetic mutations. Some more functional than others, but all of them had been infected with some form of virus like the one she'd encountered on Triton Moon Base. Her own personal nightmare multiplied in dozens of terrible permutations.

The dominant loosed a kick, sending one of the underlings rolling. "You and your damned sun! Bunch of cowards! Get out there and look for his team."

Apologetic squeaks—still, not a one of those primates budged. Interesting. While he continued to bluster, threaten, and otherwise intimidate the minions, she considered her options.

Chances were they'd take their newest prisoner to where they were holding any others. She needed to go with Meathead, and none of the buildings had any handy entryways aside from the very obvious doors. Not knowing what time they had left before the leader sprung whatever he had in store for Meathead, she went for the least palatable of the options available to her.

Skirting the edge of the clearing, she remained out of sight until she reached a position upwind, then got to her feet. The gentle breeze wafted through her hair.

It took a minute longer than she'd expected, but a cry finally rosefrom the higher-pitched, nervous primates.

"Well, go get 'im then!" The dominant roared profanity at them, driving them in her direction. "There's still light right there. If you can't do nothin' else, so help me . . ."

She squealed as they boiled through the underbrush to get to her. Stumbling to one side, she let herself fall into the clearing before any of them actually had to hit her. Hands grabbed at her, and she quelled the urge to slash at them with exposed claws. A mess of matted, dirty fur and gnarled hands filled her vision. Misshapen heads bent too close. Fetid breath fell hot around her head and shoulders as twisted faces sniffed at her for too long.

"What are you all waiting for?" The leader better be careful or he was going to bust a vein or his vocal cords. Either one could be amusing.

Feigning bewilderment, she allowed them to grab and carry her across the clearing. Her chest tightened. It took every ounce of will to allow those little hands on her person, to seem weak as she struggled against their hold.

Something was off with these mutants. They should have noticed her lack of fear and her building rage. Maybe they were too new to sift through the meaning of the scents they were picking up.

But they didn't secure her. Aside from removing her weapons, they didn't treat her as a threat at all. They didn't bother to tie and net her the way they did the military man. All to the good as far as she was concerned.

"What have we here?"

Body odor choked her as the leader leaned close. Stupid

man. He smelled more of cheap alcohol and sweat than carnivore. He might have enforced his will over the weak simians, but he didn't do more than annoy her.

Hopefully he took the tremors in her arms and shoulders as fear. When he slapped her hip, she bet he took her jerk reaction as a flinch instead of the reality—she'd had to suppress the lightning desire to kick him in the face.

His awful breath reached her nostrils; the smell of arousal clogged her nose and throat. He didn't seem to use his nose properly either, and he definitely wasn't thinking clearly enough to recognize the danger lying meek in front of him.

Good.

"Fucking idiot girl. Knew you were worthless." Meathead had no idea how lucky he was to have her as a teammate right about then.

The dominant wannabe licked chapped lips. "Let's take this inside, shall we."

His stubby fingers dug into her upper arm as he hauled her to her feet. A few additional commands had the primates dragging Meathead into the larger of the two buildings ahead of them.

"You boys check the rest of the perimeter for any others and then go on ahead to the hangar to finish the inventory on the crap the other simians brought in a couple days ago. I can see our new guests to the cages."

The others leered before leaving. Anger simmered beneath her meek surface; tension coiled as she struggled to keep her beast under control long enough.

Steady, easy. Don't give them any reason to come along.

She counted steps as they entered the building to gauge the distance to each turning for escape later and to keep her mind clear. The cat grew more and more restless as they went deeper inside, every brush of her captor's body against her back as he walked behind her, holding her against him, driving her anger into cold rage. Horny bastard.

But it would serve her purpose. After she found Rygard, she promised herself, this pig would squeal.

When they entered the holding room, a dozen unwashed bodies couldn't hide Rygard's scent from her. He was there, in the room somewhere.

"Put the new fucker in with the rest of the males." Her escort barked out orders at more simians inside the holding area. "Then get out, all of you."

Stupid, but then the bastard was working to her advantage.

Those thick fingers grabbed a handful of her hair.

Memories flashed through her mind. A different hand twisted her waist-long hair into a cord, wrapped it around her neck, told her it would do for a collar until he could get her a proper one.

She didn't let her hair grow that long anymore.

"Lookie what we got here, boys." Back to the present. She blinked, trying to hold on to it as her captor taunted the prisoners already in holding cells. "Should I show you what she's worth?"

"No!" The voice, Rygard's. He'd thrown himself against a cage.

A part of her shrank deep inside her chest. He shouldn't see this aspect of her . . .

The others, the cadets captured with her back then, they'd watched. In horror, in fear for themselves, and for her, they'd shed tears, but none of them looked away. They couldn't. They'd watched as her captor tormented her.

"Maybe I'll share her after I'm done." Her captor's voice from years ago melded with the thing holding her now.

"Touch her and I'll kill you!" Rygard. He had to have a plan. He wasn't one to lose it, not even for her. But what would he think of her when he saw what was about to happen?

An old friend looked at her from forever ago, eyes filled with disgust and fear. What had she been worth to her cadet commanding officer, her fellow students, once she'd escaped back on Triton? Once they knew what had been done to her, saw how she'd been changed, hadn't they turned away? Just a broken toy, a little girl playing at soldier.

Her original intent to destroy this would-be captor shattered as she was swept up in the nightmares of her past. She made no noise when the pig slammed her into the wall, ground his hips into her behind, licked her exposed neck.

Assaulted by reality and remembered nightmares, she withdrew inside her own consciousness until everything started playing out as if it was happening to someone else.

Passive. Steady. It ended quicker if she didn't fight. All she needed to do was wait for it to be over. Hide inside herself. Survive.

Her vision filled with Rygard raging as he threw himself at the bars over and over again. Superimposed over him, she saw her fellow cadets beaten and tortured in front of her as she was tied to the side of their captor's chair. Their despair, their fear of him, and of her, shone in glazed eyes. They'd rather be tortured to death than suffer her fate.

They'd been branded anyway and died in agony when their bodies couldn't handle the mutation.

"Get away from her!"

Would Rygard hate her once he saw?

He had to survive first.

The cat inside her screamed, and the present came crashing back. She could see Rygard and his men straining at the bars to their cells, trying to get to her. Trying to save her. But they were caged and she was not.

Her captor turned her abruptly and shoved her back across a table. He fumbled at his belt, not bothering to tie her down. His mistake.

He was all alone, and she was done remembering.

She surged up, slamming into his chest with her knees and bearing him backward and down to the ground. He opened his mouth to cry out, and she darted in with an uppercut, ripping his gurgling scream away as his entire lower jaw disappeared in a rushing spray of blood.

Never again. She would never be as helpless as she'd been back then.

She crouched over the corpse, panting. His features appeared in sharp relief, the blood vivid and every detail of the gory damage standing out against his pale dead flesh. Her hand hadn't been the only thing to shift. She'd lost control of her eyes too.

***

"KAITLYN." Rygard struggled to keep his voice steady, reaching for a gentle tone at odds with the situation. Wherever she was, it wasn't completely in the present.

She turned her head and stared at him with eyes too wide, her mouth dropping open as she continued a shallow pant. The rest of his men hung back, their tension too close to fear. She wouldn't react well to it.

Fearful men did dangerously stupid things.

He gave them the hand signal to stand by. All was well.

They relaxed a fraction—not much, but it was enough.

Her eyes changed from slitted to human. She turned back to the dead man under her. A quick search turned up the swipe card for the locks on the cages. In moments, she had the doors open and returned to her kill to loot the body.

The dead man had a stun rod, not standard Terran issue, and a handgun—not much else. She took the weapons anyway and handed them off to Rygard without looking at him. He took them and gave her space, standing within arm's reach but not coming any closer.

Close would've been a bad thing right about then.

"Where are yours?" Rygard asked her.

She kept her face turned away. "The primates disarmed us when we were discovered."

Us.

The soldier brought in with her was struggling to get out of the cage, trying to shove aside Rygard's own men. Zec, according to his uniform's identity patch. "We need to get out of here. Leave her in one of the cages. The bitch is a beast." Zec looked around at them all with his mouth open as he breathed hard, spittle around his lips. Man was unhinged. "Did you *see* that? What was that? What did she do to . . ."

He needed to shut the fuck up.

Rygard made another hand signal, sharp and decisive. The tirade was silenced by Rygard's men. They still regarded her with trepidation, but she'd freed them. They were smart enough to weigh the benefit over the freak show. And they still followed his orders.

"If we can make the perimeter, the primates won't follow. Suns are set. They're afraid of the dark." Kaitlyn seemed to be steadier. She stood slowly, straightening her back, and squaring her shoulders. "We need to move out now. I'll cover you. Meathead over there knows the way back to the ship."

Rygard frowned but didn't argue. Without sufficient

weapons, she was their best chance of making it out. It meant she would be shifting.

He'd seen her change to panther form to save him once, and he'd watched her in a brief fight, one-on-one, with a man intent on killing her. More than enough to have faith now.

"On my lead. Keurriger, take him with you." Rygard lifted his chin toward Meathead and then headed for the door. His men followed, falling into a tight standard formation for their team. Meathead fell in with the rest. He had some sense after all.

They made it out of the building before the chittering rose up. The mutants came tumbling out of another building.

"Run. Now!" Kaitlyn charged toward the oncoming simians.

Rygard ran a short way forward and dropped to a knee, motioning for Keurriger to take the men to the nearest gap in the underbrush and out into the jungle. He didn't know the range of the small handgun Kaitlyn had tossed him, so he didn't go for kills yet, instead directing his shots to provide her the best cover possible. If he could make some of them duck or slow down, or throw off their aim, she had a better chance.

Kaitlyn met the lead primates in her human form, shocking the first with a direct front kick to the chest and continuing her momentum forward to meet the other with a solid right punch before it could react. Both dropped immediately. The next fell to her right slant kick, which she brought down on the attacker's upper thigh hard enough to snap his femur.

Impossibly fast, she lashed out with low kicks, sweeping their feet out from under them or blowing out their knees, then high kicks to their torsos and heads. All those in complex combinations along with heavy punches broke ribs, sent her attackers staggering to one side or the other, or dropped them in their tracks.

None of her opponents had been trained to fight, and their numbers weren't a good enough advantage. His girl struck with greater force than any normal human being. If he hadn't seen her in combat before, he might have been tempted to stop and stare. She had a deadly grace to her fighting style he'd never encountered in anyone else.

Rygard picked off any primate headed for a position behind her. Not that she couldn't defend her own six—they were just in a hurry, no time for her to take them all out. She'd bought them all a window to escape, but he was not leaving her behind.

His men hit the edge of the clearing and called back for him. Kaitlyn shifted then, sliding low across the ground to knock the feet out from under several attackers as she changed. A girl would have been in the worst position possible, flat on her back in the midst of attackers, but not a panther.

Four sets of claws slashed, catching the nearest attackers across tendons and causing them to topple to the dirt howling in anguish. One final simian jumped on top of her, and she closed her jaws over its face, suffocating it as she held it with her forelegs and racked its abdomen with her hind claws.

Between one moment and the next, she stood solid on all four paws, surrounded by her fallen foes and covered in gore. Ink black, the panther that was Kaitlyn stared at him and then lifted her lips to display an impressive set of teeth as she snarled.

No words needed. He turned as he stood and headed

for the jungle and the rest of his men. She bounded next to him, and they hit the tree line together. He lost sight of her then—all of them must have. Their eyes darted from shadows to darker recesses in the night, unable to see the big cat among them.

Then she roared, directly next to them, still unseen.

Rygard backed up her command. "Move, run!"

CHAPTER 14

"YOU DELIBERATELY DISOBEYED ORDERS. You jeopardized my entire team and directly threatened the life of one of my soldiers. I should have you court-martialed!" Captain Percival Harold Petrico-Calin IV waved his hands in the midst of his tirade.

"Court-martials are for military." Back in human form, Kaitlyn had no issues with pointing out the obvious.

Considering the pointed look Dev gave her, he might have preferred her still in panther form and unable to egg the other man on any further. Plus, he more than likely had choice words to say to her too.

"Court-martials are for humans," Petrico-Calin sneered. "I don't know what abomination you are, but the scientists will find out."

Fear should have lanced through her. It didn't. The bloodletting and subsequent run through the jungle, driving the men toward the safety of the ship, had been close enough to the hunt to fulfill the need inside her. The satisfaction left her calmer, better able to handle the commanding officer's abrasive tone and body language. In fact, the vein popping out on his forehead during his temper tantrum amused her far more than his words caused worry. They were a long way from Terran space. He didn't have enough manpower to take her in against her will.

Bharguest did . . . something. He hadn't moved, hadn't shifted his weight, but suddenly the attention of every being in the room was on him.

"You're all wasting time." Bharguest directed his words to Petrico-Calin, though his eyes were on Rygard.

Kaitlyn's amusement vanished. Everything inside her went hunter still. Waiting.

"You're useless. The information you gave us got one of my men captured. I sent one of my most loyal in to ensure success of the mission." Petrico-Calin continued his pacing, oblivious to the danger. "I wanted someone I could trust out there, my eyes and ears. You almost got him killed."

Meathead, loyal? Laughable.

"Your man wasn't enough for the threat down there. Not my call to send him in without reinforcement." Bharguest leaned back against the wall behind him, relaxed even in his chains. "Besides, he's back, alive thanks to the lady."

He inclined his head toward Kaitlyn.

Wary, Kaitlyn returned the nod and wondered whether his guards had checked his manacles recently.

"More importantly, I'm wondering where the rest of the men are."

That was the question hanging in the air, the reason Rygard stood at attention, ready to burst, waiting for permission to speak. The commanding officer had gone directly into his tirade instead of the debrief. Rygard had requested permission to speak, twice, and been denied as the captain burned off words.

Rygard and his men stood waiting, in obvious need of medical care. The fact that they were on their feet at all spoke to the sheer quality of each and every one of them. The only reason Kaitlyn had bothered to remain in the room had been for them.

She'd retrieved them. They were hers.

Petrico-Calin turned to Rygard, finally. "Where are the rest of your men, Lieutenant?"

"Gone." Rygard gave his report as quickly as possible, every word punctuated with urgency. "They were shipped out yesterday by our attackers after being prepped with some sort of injection. The rest of us were slated to ship out tomorrow. Permission requested to go after my men, Sir."

Injection? Kaitlyn studied Rygard's face. Did he know what it could be?

"With what ship?" Petrico-Calin waved off Rygard's response. "This ship has orders to return my team and you survivors for immediate debrief and medical evaluation. If others had obeyed my orders, things would not be this out of control."

Tracer and Max had followed orders. They'd still be out in the night if Dev hadn't recalled them. Petrico-Calin had sent them on a completely different trajectory after they'd reported finding Rygard's base camp, far off and away from the outpost. The same might have happened to her if she had been reporting in to Petrico-Calin instead of Dev.

"With all due respect, based on the orders given, your team would have been too late to rescue us." Rygard put the truth out there.

If the military captain had an aneurysm, would Rygard be next in command as the next highest ranking military officer? Kaitlyn debated whether she should offer the man a sedative before her theoretical became an actual.

"What do you know about the orders issued, Lieutenant?"

"Standard procedure to review the communications recordings after a mission, Sir."

Rygard had done his homework with the men on board in the very short time between the moment they'd lifted off planet to when they'd escaped the planet's gravity. Neither he nor any of his men had washed up prior to the briefing, making it obvious what they'd been through. In fact, Kaitlyn was pretty sure he hadn't taken any time to rest at all.

"My first priority is my men, Sir," Rygard continued, his tone carefully neutral. Kaitlyn could smell the anger and frustration in the air from all the men in the room. "Orders could be interpreted as telling us to workwith Captain Rishkillian's team to retrieve my entire team."

"I will interpret the spirit of the orders, Lieutenant." Petrico-Calin ground out the words. "I was the one who found all of you in the first place."

Well, Kaitlyn had to give him a little bit of credit. Meathead wouldn't have been captured if he hadn't been close to the base where they'd been held. It was entirely possible Petrico-Calin had extrapolated the location of the base and sent the brute there. No need to point out she'd found it at the same time, scouting.

At the moment, it seemed prudent for the commanding officer to forget about her.

"Whether we return to base to get you and your men under much-needed medical examination or embark on a wild goose chase is my call, Lieutenant. We have more solid results here, with what's left of your team and the finding of another shape-shifter to turn in to the authorities." Wow but Petrico-Calin was stirring tempers up throughout the room with his choice of words. Besides, there were two shape-shifters on board, and neither of them could be forced to go anywhere without some serious reinforcements. "The rest of your team is likely dead and I will not put any of my team at further risk going after their corpses."

"*Some* of them are likely dead, not all." Bharguest tossed his opinion out there as if it were a matter of fact. "If they were injected, some of them might not have survived the change. These men here haven't been infected. They could all be ready for action with some sleep and a couple of bandages."

She was liking Bharguest more and more, if only because he was willing to say what she really shouldn't—not with the commanding officer thinking of her as a specimen to be collected. None of the men displayed signs of fever, convulsions, or change in body odor—the first stages of the Triton Experiment virus. No one could miss the later stages.

Hard to pin down exactly how long she'd writhed and screamed. Closest she could figure, it had been several days.

"Excuse me?" Petrico-Calin turned toward Bharguest, proving he really wasn't the wisest man in the universe as he gave Rygard his back. Not with Rygard so close to the end of his control.

Tension and unrest hung thick in the air. A tiny tic indicated how hard Rygard was grinding his jaw, and larger muscle groups jumped under his shirt at the shoulders.

"Injection, Captain." Bharguest made a man's rank sound like an insult, or maybe just the man in question's. Kaitlyn figured Bharguest had a problem with authority in general, unless he was the one in charge. "Sounds pretty obvious to everyone in this room, so why pretend? You worry that every one of these men has been infected."

Silence.

"You want them confined until a Terran military medical team can clear them. Because the only medical personnel aboard this ship qualified to conduct the tests is infected." Bharguest shook his head. "It can't be transferred from individual to individual once it has run its course. You should have read the briefing on it. In fact, if you had, you'd note in the references that most of those findings were determined by the only subject known to have survived long enough to conduct the studies."

There went the idea of staying under the radar in this conversation, ejected right out an air lock. Every eye turned to her, even without Bharguest lifting his chin in her direction. She debated tossing the ball back to him. He was obviously a survivor.

"I've seen a lot of victims, gentlemen, changed into some form of lycanthropy or another by the virus." Bharguest's voice took on a hypnotic quality. "It first appeared to your people in Terran space on Triton Moon Base a few years ago, brought by an occupying force—forgotten colonists—exposed to the virus by the very organization you've all stumbled upon, and smart enough to take the science and run with it."

Evil deeds. Memories of the dead rose up in her mind.

Bharguest continued, "Those colonists, where did they go? Oh they didn't set a straight course for the well-defended Mother Earth. No, they made a stop at Triton Moon Base first to set up a preliminary base from which to launch their attack. Sound strategy. And they ran experiments on original Terran stock, the Triton Experiments. They took young, healthy teenagers in good physical condition, well-fed and soft from easy living, and injected them."

Branded them, tattooed. Every brand had been a

different stylization, a different combination of the virus and a chosen animal species. Her captor, the leader, had wanted a pet cat leashed to his command chair. She had the black panther tattooed on her left thigh to remind her.

"Every one of them died an agonizing death . . . except the perfect survivor." Bharguest finished telling everyone the story she still couldn't articulate outside of an official debrief.

Silence again. Kaitlyn wouldn't fill it.

Petrico-Calin stared at her. He had read the briefing. She was sure of it. Just as sure as she was that he didn't feel a drop of empathy for what she'd been through.

"If anyone on this ship would recognize a person exposed to the Triton Experiment virus, it'd be the one human who lived through it." Bharguest seemed to have the entire room under thrall.

Kaitlyn looked him straight in the eye and raised an eyebrow. One? Really?

Bharguest chuckled. "Ah well, I suppose we could say two. Sometimes it's an effort for me to care that I started out human. But the girl there, she still cares. You should thank your stars she does or your men would be dead."

His words broke the strange spell over the assembled men. Dev's crew made small changes in position, moving to stand around her. A division formed between crew and military, but Petrico-Calin stood virtually alone with only Meathead at his shoulder. Whatever the divide, it wasn't crew *against* military, yet.

"Whether she thinks she's human or no, I have my orders." Petrico-Calin reached for firm ground again, holding to the only clear source of authority he had. "We return to Terran space to ensure these men are medically examined by an unbiased medical professional and she is turned in for testing."

"Speaking of orders, we've had a new communication from Terran Command." Dev pushed away from the main entry to the mess hall. He'd slipped out a few minutes prior and returned before most of the room noticed. "They're marked urgent for immediate dissemination to all personnel including you, Captain Petrico-Calin the Fourth, so I'll expedite by reading these aloud for everyone to hear. For immediate dissemination and all that."

Dev did have the best timing she'd ever encountered.

He looked down at the data pad in his hand. "Lots of background red tape here, we'll skip those discussions. Ah here we go. 'Captain Petrico-Calin the Fourth, your orders are hereby altered to include the retrieval of remaining military crew and the investigation of both the whereabouts and identities of those responsible for their capture and treatment.'" Dev nodded. "Well, I think that's clear enough."

"I'll have a look at that." Petrico-Calin strode toward Dev, reaching for the data pad.

"Of course, Captain." Dev moved it slightly out of range of Petrico-Calin's first grab. "I've already ensured a copy of the communication is waiting in the personal data cube of all personnel. You're more than welcome to access it at your convenience from your own terminal. Seeing as you're all guests aboard my ship, consider it a courtesy. It's the least I can do since it looks as if our contract is extended. Now then, I can't have anyone thinking I'm an irresponsible host. I'd recommend our new arrivals report to the medical bay. Virus or no, these boys need to be seen to."

Dev smiled, his face open and projecting a perfectly genial facade. Kaitlyn knew better. Despite the relaxed exterior, her captain was ready to act if Petrico-Calin continued to attempt to take them all back. Whatever rank or position his military partners were, it was still Dev's ship, and he was still captain.

Petrico-Calin looked ready to argue for a long minute, his jaw working and his hands balled into fists. With a visible effort, he too relaxed. "Well, Captain, aren't these orders opportune? We'll go after our men, then, with your crew's help. And then we'll return to Terra with all of them."

There was no doubt about who was included in Petrico-Calin's interpretation of "all."

Still, Kaitlyn would put her faith in her captain and focus on seeing to Rygard and his men. Getting the others back presented a new challenge.

She'd need another conversation with Bharguest. Hell, she'd need several.

"WHAT'S THE PLAN, CAPTAIN RISHKILLIAN?"

Rygard sat on a stretcher in Kaitlyn's medical bay. Kaitlyn had released his men to get some sleep bunked down with the rest of the military contingent. He'd insisted she see all of them first, so he still had an IV attached to his arm as she tended to the multitude of small cuts and taser burns he'd taken during his captivity.

"My pilot, Tails, is running a scan for the emissions trail." Dev leaned in the doorway, arms crossed as he watched Kaitlyn fuss with slide preparation.

"Pardon, Captain." Badger's voice came from the hallway.

Dev straightened and stepped back, revealing the

grizzled noncommissioned officer with Bharguest a short distance behind him in the corridor, flanked by his usual guards.

"I thought your medic should take a closer look at our prisoner." Badger turned to the military escort and motioned them away. "You are dismissed. Lieutenant Rygard and I will escort the prisoner back to his holding cell after we're through here."

Rygard watched the two military police leave. Too complacent.

Dev's features were still arranged in a pleasant expression. "That so?"

"Aye." Badger gave him a short nod. "Seems to me, our prisoner here has an interesting reaction to exposure to certain places on board, maybe people too."

"And you want to test this exposure why?" Rygard asked the NCO.

Rygard tensed. If Petrico-Calin had ordered for the prisoner to be left alone with Kaitlyn . . .

Badger looked at each of them in turn, his eyes lingering on Kaitlyn for only a moment before returning to Rygard. "What did you say to your men before you sent them to their bunks?"

Rygard narrowed his eyes but gave him the answer. "We don't leave our own behind. No matter how long it takes, we'll go back after them."

"Well, and you see, we've both been in the Service a while, seen a lot of missions." Badger scratched at his chin. "Longer it takes, the less likely we're bringing back friends and more chance we're bringing back bodies."

True.

Badger continued. "Information is what we need, and extensive planning. Seeing as you lot are the only people left awake and talking to each other, you're the ones putting together plans." He paused, stepped inside the medical bay, and came to a stop in front of Rygard. "You're an officer who looks out for his men. I mean to help you bring them back."

Rygard gave the man a nod. No thanks between soldiers —not until they all came back. Instead, he watched Bharguest step into the medical bay and take a long, deep breath.

"Stand over there." Kaitlyn's tone of voice was unconcerned, but Rygard could tell she was struggling to hide the hint of steel at the edge of her words. "I'd like you where I can see you."

Bharguest chuckled, a deep, almost-coughing sound, but he moved to the center of the room. He stood with relaxed shoulders, arms loose despite the heavy manacles at his wrists.

"Looks like we found the right place." Tracer stood in the corridor, his big dog at his side.

"This isn't a party." Kaitlyn tapped a fingertip against her desktop. The sound was sharp—too loud for a human nail to be tapping at the plexiglass surface.

"Well, Max is favoring his leg, so I hoped you might take a look." Tracer stepped in with a nod to the captain. "And considering the way we were sent on a wild goose chase down on the surface, I'd like to get a better idea of what we're hunting in the next mission."

"There'll be a briefing." Rygard glared at Tracer.

Tracer spread his hands wide. "There was a briefing last time too. This time, we're tracking down further intel."

Sensible. Rygard looked at Dev. He'd leave it to the captain to decide.

"Barring additional interruptions, let's get to the sharing

of further intel, then." Dev took up his position back at the door, eyes on the big prisoner. "Hassle is at the comm terminal seeing if he can intercept transmissions from the planet. We're figuring they've got to report the escape to somebody. The intel will help give us a target."

"All well and good." Bharguest shrugged. "But if they were deliberately injected, there's only one place they'd be headed."

Rygard began to reply, but Dev beat him to it. "Feel free to share."

"I can take you back to the holding cell," Badger added with a growl.

The prisoner only smiled, his lips parting but not showing any teeth. The effect was particularly disturbing.

"If you want to play games, at least make them quick ones," Kaitlyn called from her seat at her lab desk where she loaded slides into a scanner. "Making us track down the info you already know is a waste of time and you'll just be stuck on the ship staring at a pair of boring military guards."

Bharguest tilted his head, considering. "They are less than entertaining lately."

Kaitlyn only shrugged without looking up from her work. "Share more, talk more. It's a win-win."

Rygard didn't like the way the other man paid so much attention to his girl. Still, for the time being, he was their most complete source of intel, and Bharguest responded best to her. Dev had warned Rygard about the prisoner and that Kaitlyn had been going to Bharguest to learn what he knew. Neither of them had expected Badger to bring the prisoner right into Kaitlyn's room. But then, maybe the salty old NCO hadn't realized Kaitlyn bunked in here.

"Outposts like the one you just infiltrated serve as

supply sources for a bigger market." Bharguest spoke directly to Kaitlyn.

At the mention of a market, she did look up from her analysis. "What kind?"

"It's tailored to a specific clientele, the intergalactic high rollers with too many creds and not enough to occupy their time. It deals in fighters of every size, shape, and species." Bharguest glanced at Rygard and then returned his attention to Kaitlyn. "Normal humans don't stand a chance, not against the other aliens they've collected, so the virus is used to make them a little more . . . interesting in the arenas."

Rygard caught the warning look from Dev and kept his mouth shut instead of cutting in to ask Bharguest directly what he wanted to know. He'd have to follow Kaitlyn's lead here, and the lives of his men depended on her questions.

Kaitlyn rose from her work and came around to check his IV. Quietly, she said, "Another five minutes. I want to be sure we've hydrated you sufficiently to counteract the effects of several days' dehydration. Your blood tests aren't showing the presence of any toxins or virus, so you should be ready for active duty when it comes time to retrieve your men." Then she turned her attention back to Bharguest. "So they're collecting gladiators?"

"Exactly."

"Seems inefficient. Any being fights harder when they want to fight. Slaves generally don't by definition." Kaitlyn continued to fuss over Rygard's bandages, her fingertips fluttering over his skin.

Heat built inside him, not simply a side effect of his near-death experience. It'd been a long time since he'd seen her face-to-face, and he'd missed her in more ways than he cared to analyze with a being like Bharguest standing in the room. No more talk of gladiators. Instead, the prisoner stared steadily at Kaitlyn in that creepy way of his.

The huge man chuckled. "Perfect. A perfect combination."

"That so?" Dev interjected this time, redirecting the prisoner's attention.

"Look at her." Bharguest inclined his head toward Kaitlyn.

Rygard noticed the man never pointed, though he could have. The manacles shackling his wrists didn't confine his fingers.

"Whoever branded her probably took credit, figured she was his work of art." Bharguest shook his head. "But it's a game of chance, the virus."

"Why?" Rygard straightened. He suppressed the intense desire to reach out and try to shake what he wanted to know from the other man.

Bharguest only shook his head.

"The lycanthropy virus is a carrier for the genetic template of a specific species. Once the virus infects every cell, it has no way to replicate. It dies." Kaitlyn picked up the explanation. "What's left behind are mutated cells, the actual genetic code altered to become a combination of the original host and the invading species."

"How well the change takes and how complete the mutation is, there's no way to predict." Bharguest joined in again. "Me, I'm a changed man and I embrace the change. In others, what you see is what you get. They're frozen in a single state. Static. But her, she can change at will from human to panther to any stage in between. She has control at the cellular level. She's singular, a beautiful piece of chance."

Tracer cleared his throat. "And the other men, what are their odds?"

Bharguest shrugged. "They're made of tough stock. Soldiers are hardy. Most will survive the virus, but not like her. Nah. More likely they'll be caught in a static state, some more beast and some more human. How well they use the altered physicality is up to them. Most go crazy without guidance."

"Did you have guidance?" Dev seemed to know the answer, though he'd asked the question.

Bharguest only smiled.

"It's gonna be tricky, infiltrating a place designed to house fighters." Kaitlyn mulled over the challenge aloud as she cleaned up the remains of the medical supplies she'd used. "Fighters with animal senses are near impossible to get past undetected."

She would know.

In the dark of the evening, he and his men could barely see to put one foot in front of the other. But she'd been able to see them all, herd them. Rygard remembered the run through the jungle, hearing her snarl coming from the shadows at intervals. She'd shoved more than one man away from natural deadfalls or dangerous quicksand, keeping them all on solid trails. None of them had been able to keep an accurate tag on her location, and she'd managed every single one of them at a run.

As grateful as Rygard was to her for getting his men to the ship, he couldn't miss the fear in their eyes when they'd broken through the dense cover at the loading ramp. Not many would want to be alone with her.

No doubt, she'd been a far scarier predator than their attackers.

He redirected his thoughts. "Those things back on the planet, you saw them?"

Badger answered. "We were all watching footage retrieved from the surveillance cameras by their man, Hassle, and the feed on the camera attached to her harness."

Tracer nodded confirmation. Rygard glanced at Kaitlyn. No surprise on her face. She must have agreed to the visual feed. It explained why Bharguest knew so much about her shape change. She hadn't lost the harness until she'd shifted completely. Her change completed faster than the last time Rygard had seen her do it. He wondered how much practice she'd been putting in to fine tune her control.

"None of those shifted beyond their mutated form." Kaitlyn came to stand next to Rygard where he sat, close but not quite shoulder to shoulder. "Intelligence seemed stunted too. Normal, unmutated primates would have been smarter."

"Low-level grunts. There's a lot of them in the arenas and they're not expected to last long. In numbers, they're a challenge for most, but other than that, they're fodder for anything bigger and badder," Bharguest confirmed.

"Submissive, every one of them." Kaitlyn added the observation in a quiet murmur, as if thinking more to herself. "The idiot in charge wasn't very dominant to begin with, but he still held position over all of them."

"Could have been weak willed to begin with, before they were ever infected with the virus." Rygard offered her his theory. "I don't think dominance or submissiveness is something to be programmed into genetic code. It's more than simple size, strength, or speed."

"You're right, there." Bharguest spoke directly to Rygard for the first time. "Dominance, and beyond that, being an alpha, is more than physical attributes. The virus can't give it to you."

"So those were infected and likely intended for the purpose they were used for, jumping potential new captives and bringing them into the compound."

"Yes." Bharguest drew out the word. "Exactly. Most of the mutations are meant for a low- or midlevel purpose. The arenas would be too dangerous if too many elite fighters surfaced at once."

"So most of what we'd be facing in the arenas would be like those mutated simians." She might not have found them a challenge, but Rygard's men had. The simians were stupid, but still capable of overwhelming a man in hand-to-hand combat.

"The midlevels are more of a challenge and on par with the majority of aliens brought in to fight." Scratching his chin, Bharguest seemed to consider the numbers. "The elite fighters are usually a surprise, either a lucky find or a rogue mutation. The handlers are always looking to acquire more to replace the low- to midlevels, hope for a good find."

"Doesn't seem to be a good business model to have a constantly high death count." Dev made the point in a light tone. Funny how he always seemed to be in a good mood, but his questions always flushed out more information than Rygard thought was possible.

"Not so many dead. A lot of them are maimed or mutilated, too broken to go on being of any use but to train up newcomers." Bharguest flicked a bit of imaginary dust off his shoulder, then lowered his hands in front of him again. "They need a constant influx of new fighters to replace them, and to keep the crowds interested. Fresh entertainment."

"That's our way in then." Dev nodded.

"Getting in won't be a problem." Kaitlyn didn't bother to state the rest of the thought.

"My men would go in, despite the risk of being infected." Rygard frowned as Kaitlyn shook her head.

"Save your men, Lieutenant." Bharguest didn't make the rank as much of an insult as he'd done earlier with Petrico-Calin. "They would just die in there without the aid of the virus. No. If we go in, it will be those of us already changed and a team ready to work with us."

Kaitlyn remained silent, only looking to her captain.

"Volunteer basis only. There might be another way if we can intercept the ship before it arrives," Dev answered her.

Not likely. The transport had too much of a head start, despite the speed Dev's ship was capable of and the advantage of Bharguest's knowledge. Rygard couldn't ask any of his men to walk into a death trap either.

"We try to intercept and we'll never know the location of the arenas." Kaitlyn pointed out the bigger objective, Rygard's original mission. "This will go on, with other human military teams, civilian colonies, and who knows what other bystanders."

"I escaped." Bharguest rolled his shoulders. "But the location changed since. It was the first bit of intel I gave the powers that be when I tried to cut a deal for my freedom. They went in, found the place abandoned, said I needed to provide different information of value to go free. Wherever the arenas are now, they've only been there for a year, maybe two. I can help you get in and I can get out, but I can't tell you exactly where to find them."

No promise to help any of them get out either. Rygard had to give a certain grudging respect to Bharguest. The man was a survivor of the truest kind, with no loyalties to anyone but himself.

Rygard studied Kaitlyn standing next to him.

She'd come to find him, and she hadn't left a single man behind, even Zec, who would have left her to rape and torture.

Bharguest had at least one thing right. She was beautiful.

"I'm in." Badger stepped forward and gave a nod first to Rygard, then to Dev, and finally to Kaitlyn. "CO tasked me with planning the incursion anyway. I bring it to him, and he'll buy into it. Especially when I plan to be involved personally."

"So are we," Tracer piped up. Rygard eyed them dubiously. A tracking team wouldn't have been his first choice to round out this group. "They want interesting for the arenas. We can give them some variety. We go in and put on a good show, we locate your men, we get out. Take the intel we gather about the inside with us to plan a larger incursion later. Keep it simple."

Kaitlyn nodded. "Fine, we plan with this team. Everyone keep brainstorming." She lifted her chin at Max. "You, up on a stretcher so I can get a look at your paw."

The dog obeyed without hesitation. The rest of them exchanged looks. She was the hub, the reason every one of them was willing to work together, including Bharguest. The knowledge of it passed between them all, and they continued to plan.

ALONE, the space between them was an awkward, tangible thing. The others had left, taking Bharguest back to his holding cell before finding their bunks.

Rygard didn't blame the captain for wanting to personally see the dangerous man back into a secure holding cell. He'd planned to have a word with the commanding officer about the complacent attitude of the military police escorting the prisoner, but having met Petrico-Calin, the Fourth, Rygard wasn't sure it would do any good. Bharguest's cooperation seemed to hinge on his interest in Kaitlyn more than his incarceration.

Not a comfortable situation.

Rygard looked over to where Kaitlyn stood, all the way on the other side of the med bay. "We have a plan."

"There should be a plan B developed sometime between now and when we execute plan A," Kaitlyn commented.

With everyone else gone, her manner had turned shy.

He'd missed it about her, this special facet of her she

never showed her crew—not her captain, not anyone. For the moment, she was his girl.

When he slid off the stretcher and started to walk toward her, she pushed away from the wall and met him halfway across the room. As he pulled her into his arms, she slid her own under his to encircle his waist.

"I missed you." Her whisper in his ear made his heart expand painfully inside his chest, and he crushed her close.

Damn, he couldn't stand the thought of how close he'd come to watching her be violated. He wanted to search her body for every bruise, kiss every hurt, erase the ghost of the scumbag's touch from her skin. He couldn't make himself let her go even the arm's length he'd need to see her.

And she hugged him back, breathing deep and letting the warm air out slowly against his chest. Did she know what she was waking in him? It had been too long, and he wanted to claim her in a way that had nothing to do with civilized behavior.

"Are you all right?" He asked the question instead because it needed to be asked. She'd hold off on thinking about her fight with the jailer for as long as she could, but she needed to admit to him and to herself what had happened back on the planet.

She stilled in his arms for a long moment and then nodded against his shoulder. "I remembered, while I was down there. It distracted me."

More than distracted her. He'd seen the glazed look in her eyes. Torture victims sometimes withdrew so far within themselves, they essentially became vegetables, their minds forever hiding from the pain and suffering of the body. He'd watched, tried to get to her, but he'd seen her disappear into herself before she'd somehow recovered.

He crushed her against him again. "You scared me,

sweetness. Not gonna lie. I think I almost lost you down there."

She didn't argue with him, didn't give him false reassurance. "I'm here now."

He nodded, rubbing his face in her silky hair. "And so am I."

"You're safe."

"And so are you."

She stilled in his arms again. The only reason he didn't worry was because she had pressed herself to him, holding him close in her embrace. After a long time, she whispered against his shirt, "I missed your heartbeat."

Emotion welled up in his throat, and the discomfort in his chest from moments earlier tightened, warmed. Not a feeling he was used to and not something he wanted to examine too closely. Instead, he decided to just savor and enjoy. He was happy.

A question floated to the surface of his thoughts. She might not be able to bear someone too close after what happened back there. Sleep might be impossible.

Shit, it was selfish. Still, he'd ask her and let her decide.

"Can I stay here with you tonight?" He tried to keep the question light, didn't want to pressure her.

She lifted her face from his chest, looked up at him with those deep brown eyes. "Yes."

No fear. Was that what they meant when they said fathomless? He couldn't read anything in her gaze. A tremor ran through her body—faint maybe, but still there. And that, he could understand.

"It's okay, sweetness. We don't need to do anything." He kissed her forehead. When she didn't stiffen or pull away, he pressed another kiss to her temple. "Just let me hold you. Hell, if you don't feel comfortable with that, I can sleep over on one of the patient beds. I just . . . need to be nearby."

He needed to be able to protect her. Not that he could.

"I couldn't get to you. I tried, but I wasn't strong enough to get past those bars, pull that bastard off of you." Suddenly, his jaw was clenched too tight, and he sucked in a ragged breath of air. "And tonight, you're going to have your nightmares. Old ones. New ones. You're bound to and I can't keep you safe from them."

"Rygard . . ."

He tightened his arms carefully around her, tucked her head under his chin. "But I can wake you up. I can be here to hold you while you put them behind you."

Her arms loosened, and she placed her hands at his hips and pressed. He released her, stepped back. He'd leave, though she'd said yes earlier. He didn't want to force himself on her in any way.

"Rygard." His name whispered from her lips, a soft and sweet sound. No darkness there.

Kaitlyn took his hands in hers and stepped backward, tugged him with her. Didn't take much strength. He followed her readily.

"I do want you there. I want to wake up beside you." Her full lips twisted and then she caught her lower lip between her teeth. He wanted to kiss her so bad. "First, I want you to be with me. I want you to run your hands over every part of me until I forget his touch."

He did kiss her then. Couldn't help himself.

Her lips softened under his immediately, opened for him. Her tongue met his in a tentative touch. Struggling for control, trying to remember she needed gentleness, he backed off and sucked gently at her plump lower lip.

A growl rose up from her, and her hands tightened on his as she captured his mouth with her own.

His Kaitlyn was hungry. And she was making it clear. If he was a smart man, he'd give her what she hungered for, soon.

Yes, ma'am.

He lifted her hands and pressed them against his chest, still kissing her, reveling in the taste of her. She responded by caressing him, sliding her fingertips over his collarbone. Her touch sent shivers through him.

Time to return the favor.

He ran his hands over her, down past her shoulder blades, the curve of her back, and lower, until he cupped the tight cheeks of her ass and squeezed. Her hands balled into fists around the fabric of his shirt. He chuckled against her lips and did it all again. She nipped at his mouth this time. When he repeated the caress a third time, he dipped his head, set his mouth against her shoulder, and bit, just hard enough to make her gasp. As she tossed back her head, he lifted her.

She squeaked and clutched at his shoulders for balance before she wrapped her legs around his waist.

Gods, he enjoyed how cute she was, and hot, and sexy, all at the same time.

"You know I'm too heavy for this."

He captured her mouth again, drowned out the rest of her protest. Sure, her tight body weighed more than a normal human her size and build. But those butterflies bruised too easily. His Kaitlyn, she could take him.

"Put me down." She panted, breathless. Good.

"Where?" He dragged his lips down her neck, buried his face in the front of her ship suit.

Her thighs tightened at his waist. "Um . . . over . . . my bunk. Over there."

Their mouths met in a clash of lips, teeth and tongues dancing. When the toes of his boots hit the edge of her bunk, he still didn't let her down right away. He liked having her wrapped around him.

"Too many clothes."

She was right. He gave her rump one more squeeze and then dumped her on the mattress.

"Hey!"

He grinned at her, undoing his shirt. "Hey, what?"

Wide brown eyes stared at his chest as he revealed skin. Her gaze tracked the familiar scars across his chest.

"It's not like you haven't seen me recently."

Her voice came quiet, her eyes never wavering from watching him undress. "It's different, seeing you in person. Doesn't matter how good the resolution is in the hologram, the real you is so much better."

Warmth spread through his core.

When she reached for the seal to her ship suit, he protested. "I want to do the unwrapping. You stay right where you are."

No more wasted time. He had his boots off and dropped his pants. There was no way she was going to doubt how much he'd missed her.

"I'm not staying here for much longer." She had the very tip of her tongue pressed to the edge of her upper teeth.

All he could think of was what he wanted to do with that tongue of hers.

"No worries. I'm not keeping you waiting anymore." He caught her mouth, nipped the corners as he pressed her back on her bunk.

This time, he ran his hands over her front, along her side, and down her long thighs. Slow, soothing motions made her relax under him and clutch at his biceps at the same time. He dragged his mouth down her neck and pressed kisses across her collarbone. Her eyes closed and her head tipped back when he unsealed her ship suit.

She'd come a long way since their first time together. Still sweet, but now she trusted him.

He opened her ship suit and admired her breasts, caught up in the sexiest black lace. His girl did love her lingerie, and he heartily approved. Cupping each breast in turn, he squeezed and molded them in his hands, making her squirm under him. Her nipples were already taut nubs, and it only took a little more pressure for them to pop over the edge of her lace bra. No way he could resist. He closed his lips over one, circled it with his tongue, and then sucked.

"Ah!" Her sweet voice sounded surprised. Her hand slid from his bicep to grasp the back of his head, and her thighs squeezed his hips.

A wave of lust rushed through him, and he ground his hips into hers. Control? What control?

He had her ship suit off her as fast as he could without hurting her, glad she'd kicked off her grav boots sometime during the desperate struggle with fabric. And just like that, he had silken, soft skin under his hands.

His hands weren't the only ones busy. She ran hers over his chest and sides. Then her fingertips coasted over the length of his cock, drawing a groan from deep inside him.

"I love your hands," she whispered.

His? "Yours are going to end me before I get inside you, sweetness."

He caught her hands and pressed them to his shoulders

as he knelt. She shuddered as he coaxed her knees up, pressed his palms just under her cheeks, and squeezed.

"Like that?"

She mumbled something. Her hands gripped his shoulders. He'd take that for a yes.

EVERY INCH of Kaitlyn's skin tingled. The shadows of the past burned to ashes under Rygard's touch, and her entire being focused on what his hands were doing to her . . . and how open she was to what he was about to do next.

His hands gripped the backs of her thighs, sending another wave of excitement through her, then they were pressing her legs farther open. As she became aware of cool air on her exposed mound, he brushed his lips against her most sensitive flesh.

No claws! Still, he was going to have nail marks in the skin across his shoulders.

A pause? Her eyes flew open, and she looked down to see what had caused him to stop.

He was watching her, the look in his eyes full of decadent promises. "Hold on to something."

Not trusting her control over her claws, she moved her hands to the mattress on either side of her and took a good grip. He lifted an eyebrow at her and didn't break eye contact as he extended his tongue and ran it along the length of her slit.

Sensation shot through her, and she threw back her head, then bucked hard in his grip. He didn't give her time to recover. He closed his mouth over her and began to alternate between sucking and nipping at her clit. His hands kept a hold of her legs, running up and down the outsides of her thighs one moment and then gripping the backs again.

She writhed in his hold, tearing holes in the mattress under her hands. When she thought she couldn't take any more of the torturous pleasure, he spread one hand over her lower abdomen. Holding her with gentle pressure, he continued to circle and tease her clit with his tongue while he used his free hand to run a finger around her entrance.

She ached to have him inside her. Needed him to touch the places she couldn't reach. "Rygard, please . . ."

His finger slid inside her as his mouth closed over her clit and sucked. He pumped in and out, sending wave after wave of pleasure through her until it all pooled in her lower belly.

She cried out as her orgasm ripped through her, and still, he didn't stop. He stroked her and licked her, prolonged her shuddering release until she gasped for air.

Then he rose up between her legs. She opened her eyes again, reached into a compartment at the side of her bed, and brought out a compact canister. He took it from her and sprayed on a condom, then tossed the canister toward the end of the bed. Anticipation had pulled the tension inside her taut again as she watched him position himself with one hand and brace his other hand on the mattress beside her.

"Do you want this?" The tip of his penis nudged at her entrance, but he held back, waited for her permission.

She swallowed hard, surprised at the deep ache she still had inside her. Needed him to fill her. "Yes."

He entered her, a long and slow slide. His girth stretched her muscles, and she angled her hips to take more of him. When he was buried to the hilt inside of her, she felt so completely taken, so right. He ran a hand over the length of her body again, from her collarbone to her chest, down her belly, and over her hip to take a hold of her ass. He rolled his hips, drawing a moan from her.

"Ready?" His voice had gone hoarse, his jaw tightened.

"Yes." Please.

Only then did he begin moving inside her, slow at first and then picking up the pace. She reached for him, setting her hands on either side of his hips, urging him faster and deeper. He bent over her, slid his arms under her back until he could grip her shoulders. The movement gave him more leverage, allowed him deeper inside her, and she shuddered with the wonderful feeling of it. She bent her head to his shoulder, muffled her cries in his strength. Then he tangled a hand in her hair and tugged just enough to make her take a breath, then took her mouth with his in a kiss that sent her drowning as they came together.

This moment was theirs. Here and now. They'd deal with tomorrow when it arrived.

FIGHTING KAT

BOOK 3

CHAPTER 1

"STATE YOUR NAME, planet of origin, and business."

"Rishkill. Terra. Trainer."

Rygard kept his eyes lowered, watching Devron Rishkillian—captain of the mercenary ship currently in orbit and their mission lead—from the corner of his eye as Dev held his counterfeit wrist ident out for scanning.

The best deceptions were crafted from as much truth as possible.

Instead of turning his wrist over for the scan, exposing the vulnerable underside, Dev held his arm out with his hand in a loose fist. To a casual onlooker, it'd seem Dev's arm was extended to its fullest length, but his elbow was soft, and the captain had enough slack to pop a jab if need be. After a momentary clash of glares, the Sketz'es guard was forced to hold the scanner under Dev's wrist to get the data.

This entire facility was owned and run by the reptilian race known as the Sketz'es. From the guards to the overseers on the upper walls surrounding the facility, all of them were watching the incoming "stock" and ready for outbursts or last, desperate attempts to escape. As an unmodified human, Rygard was considered weak compared to the specimens being brought in and the least of their worries.

That was for the best because he wanted to get inside. His entire team was focused on three simple objectives. Step one: insertion. Step two: locate the abducted soldiers. Step three: extraction.

"Be assertive from the very beginning," Bharguest had warned Dev before they'd arrived. "No one will believe you could train all of us otherwise. Every move, every gesture is a pissing contest."

Dev was playing out the game exactly as their guide instructed, and the guard responded with a stiff posture, dropped gaze, and reptilian tail curled low between his legs. Rygard wasn't fooled though and kept an eye on that tail. Bharguest had spent time briefing them on the fighting habits of the more common aliens they'd be pitted against. Sketz'es weren't above putting their own kind in the arenas, and the lizard-like aliens could do a lot of damage with those tails in a fight.

Even with the majority of his service career spent on secret ops missions outside the Terran solar system, Rygard hadn't encountered as many alien species as he'd seen come and go through the main gates of what Bharguest called the Colosseum. Based on the stylized signage alongside the gates, it had different names in every alien language.

"You intend to enter your property in the games, Trainer Rishkill?" The guard tapped a sequence on his data pad with a wicked curved claw. "How many and in what configuration?"

"Two pairs, one lone gladiator." Dev tossed out the data with brisk efficiency.

The guard's cold gaze swept over Rygard. At his side,

Kaitlyn's fur lifted along her shoulders and spine as she arched her back and bared her teeth to hiss. She was in her panther form, and a large one, for that particular species of big cat. Sleek and muscled under her almost perfectly black fur, she was an impressive sight. Several other trainers had paused in passing to admire her.

Both Kaitlyn and Max emanated enough dominance and aggression to set off other animals in cages as they were wheeled past. The fact that she and Max—the black-and-tan canine—stood close, neither animal molesting the other, demonstrated enough training and "obedience" to have trainers approach Dev with offers for the dog too.

It wasn't Kaitlyn and Max who were the subject of skeptical regard from the Sketz'es in this moment.

"Unaltered humans do not do well in the games." The guard's crest lifted along the back of his neck in a weak attempt at a challenge.

Rygard gritted his teeth but remained silent. He was in top physical shape for a human—one of Terran military's finest. Sure, he wasn't a giant like some of the other fighters around them. He was wide through the shoulders and chest, but still agile enough to use speed to his advantage. His dark hair complemented his white skin, tanned to an olive tone from months planetside on the previous assignment that had led him to this mission. As humans went, he was a brawler and looked the part, but he was a good-looking brawler.

Maybe as compared to the other beings in this place, he wasn't quite as impressive as he was used to being.

Dev shrugged, not giving any ground to the Sketz'es. "They are trained to work with their counterparts. Levels the playing field. The human males can hold their own." He grinned. "But by all means, enter them in the lower brackets. It's more creds in my pocket when they win."

Bharguest rolled his shoulders and popped a vertebra in his neck. The big man was significantly taller than either Rygard or Tracer, the other human in their party. Heavy muscles bulged under pale skin, accented by black and gold scales in a diamond pattern over his neck and across his shoulders.

Fine. Rygard could admit to himself that he wasn't personally the most impressive figure in their group.

The Sketze's studied them each individually, probably doing an additional assessment in response to Dev's taunt. After a moment, he spoke, slowly, thoughtfully. "The group is an unusual configuration. It's not often we see mixed sentient and non-sentient combinations, but we do have them."

Rygard kept his expression neutral. Kaitlyn only blinked slowly in her panther form, not giving away her nature yet. Even Bharguest was on his best behavior, remaining silent. Rygard had half expected the big man to chuckle at the Sketz'es comment or make some kind of infuriatingly vague statement to drive up everyone's stress levels.

Bharguest's silence only unnerved Rygard instead.

"Two pairs, and the big one." Apparently, Dev had decided there was a need to clarify. Dev met the Sketz'es gaze with calm and a raised eyebrow. "He's the solo fighter."

Silence. The guard lashed his tail, tapped at his screen, and then passed a card under the reader. Placing it on the small counter of his station, he bobbed his head. "They'll be entered in the fourteenth-level brackets. The card gives access to the holding area and provides a holographic display to lead you to their assigned pens. You are granted access to the trainer's box for viewing the arenas. Check in a half cycle prior to each fight. You are responsible for any damages if your property engages in any altercations outside of the arenas."

Rygard snorted, not bothering to hold in his amusement. The guard scowled, obviously annoyed with Rygard's confidence. Rygard met him, stare for stare, until the other's gaze slid sideways.

They might be slaves, or passing as them, but they were warriors. Broken slaves didn't last in the kind of hell they were walking into.

"That's enough now, move on." A blunt rod prodded Rygard's shoulder, just hard enough to look rough but not enough to leave a bruise that might impede any much-needed range of motion later.

Badger, the NCO from the military portion of the team, knew how to play a role every bit as much as Dev. The old soldier was posing as a "handler" for this operation and would accompany Dev wherever he went. The rest of them would be in the pens waiting for their fights and looking for Rygard's abducted personnel.

This mission was a joint effort between Terran military and Dev's mercenary team. Normally, Rygard would have felt more comfortable with military in the lead and mercenaries supplementing the effort. This time, though, he didn't trust his chain of command, and he refused to leave half of his team still in captivity. So here they were, a joint team, about to walk into hell to bring his people out.

Rygard glared a moment longer, enough to make the reptilian guard lash his tail again. Satisfied, he followed after Kaitlyn's captain as he strode toward the big elevators where other trainers were loading their property.

Kaitlyn padded alongside him and behind Dev, silent.

When some other humanoid strayed too close, she lifted her upper lip to display gleaming fangs. The errant slave prudently altered his course to rejoin his line and give her more space, tripping over chains to get away.

Tracer and Max were given similar consideration, and everyone, slaves and trainers alike, gave Bharguest a wide berth.

Something twisted inside Rygard's gut. He trusted Kaitlyn and Dev. Tracer was a good man, or the Kx9 wouldn't have chosen him as a handler. But Bharguest. Everything about the man pushed buttons, brought out the ugly inside him.

It might have been a pissing contest, but they weren't there to prove who was the biggest and baddest. If Bharguest got them in and helped rescue Rygard's men, then Rygard could swallow his pride.

Another well-placed prod from Badger got them all onto an elevator. Rygard got the sense they were dropping several levels below ground before they came to a stop. When the safety gate opened, they stepped out into another time period.

The Colosseum was built atop a complex cave structure. Dim lighting had been installed in recesses along the walls, illuminating the passageways enough for them to walk but leaving the ceiling above them shrouded in darkness. Side tunnels branched off from the main corridor, leading off into a maze. The ident card in Dev's hand served as their guide—a tiny holographic map projected before him. Without it, they'd have been lost. When they turned down a secondary tunnel, they started to see the holding cells lining either side.

Beings moved inside those pocket caves, slaves plucked from every race Rygard had ever encountered and some new to him. Some stood right at the force field, watching them walk by, and others were nothing but shadows in the recesses of the cells.

Max growled, and Tracer dropped a hand on the big dog's head. The Kx9 ceased and moved ahead of Tracer a pace or two. Rygard had seen one or two of the teams in action before, enough to know the dog was positioning himself to defend his handler if necessary.

Rygard didn't blame the dog for feeling defensive. The level of animosity in the caves, combined with the claustrophobia of the tunnels, had him consciously flexing his hands to keep from clenching them into fists. Kaitlyn moved beside him, a deathly silent shadow lost in the dim lighting save for a tiny metallic node piercing her left ear.

The little device wasn't simply jewelry. She'd refused to wear a collar, and Dev had told them all to come up with another idea to make the owners of the Colosseum believe she was under control. It had needed to be visible, give the impression of being a method to restrain or deter a potentially dangerous asset. Skuld had designed a solution, a small device that flashed in response to a compact control mechanism on Dev's wrist with the added bonus of some communicator functionality for Rygard and Tracer, who didn't have the sleek tech Kaitlyn had installed in the back of her jaw. Both Kaitlyn and Max wore one.

Knowing some of the nightmares haunting Kaitlyn's nights, Rygard hadn't dug further, and he'd helped redirect Petrico-Calin's snide commentary about making the mission more difficult. Petrico-Calin might have been the ranking officer present for this mission, but he was exactly why Rygard was glad this was a joint operation.

The innovation meant Kaitlyn, and Max, could hear any communication from Dev, and so could Rygard or

Tracer if they leaned close enough to their partner. It was also small enough to stay in place when Kaitlyn had to shift from panther to human form.

It was brilliant. So convincing that guards had believed it controlled her and Max effectively enough to ask after the cost of the design.

It hadn't been the first time Rygard had mentally thanked the stars Dev and his team were mercs with a sense of honor and a code of their own. Other, less savory types with the kind of ingenuity and skills Dev had aboard his ship would have redefined the black market.

Rygard's thoughts were interrupted as they reached an empty cave, indicated in Dev's guiding hologram by a blinking sphere.

Dev motioned inside. "In you go. Wait here until showtime and follow the guards when they come for you. Stay alive, every one of you."

Simple commands. And again, the best deception held truth at its core. His instructions were in line with the role he played, and Dev sincerely meant every word.

Badger gave each of them a prod to herd them into the cave. Dev thumbed the ident card and the holding shield activated, locking them inside. Without another word, Dev and Badger headed back the way they came.

KAITLYN PACED the length of the cavern. She would allow Max to do his doggy thing and sniff at the perimeter. The Kx9 was smart enough to avoid setting off the force fields at the opening of the cave and along one wall blocking an archway to the next cave over.

Voluntary or not, confinement bothered her. It made it harder for her to hold on to the more complex human thought process. She'd been practicing, but this would be the longest she'd remained in panther form, ever. Plus, she didn't like pretending to be a belonging. It ran too close to being a slave. She'd been there, done that, killed the people who'd done unspeakable things to her.

The scents of misery and fear filled the hallways of this place. They should accomplish the mission and get out. This cavern was a death trap.

Only minutes into the mission, she already had to quell the urge to throw herself against the force fields, make an escape. The walls were too close, brought memories of another time when she'd been held prisoner. Though her captivity on Triton Moon Base had been spent in a square room, not a cavern.

A prison was a prison. It didn't matter what the walls were made of.

Her restless gaze swept across the rest of the beings in the room, her team for this mission. It was Rygard who made eye contact with her first and held it. A corner of his mouth turned upward in the faintest hint of his usual lopsided grin. The anxious, edgy feelings churning inside her eased just a little. She'd come for him because he was a leader who wouldn't abandon his team. And because he meant too much to her to let him do this without her help.

Admitting that probably wasn't wise. His commanding officer for this mission wanted nothing more than to wrap her up like a gift and send her to Terran Command back on Earth as a lab specimen. She would have been safer leaving the ship and disappearing until the Terran military teams had gone back. Dev would've let her rejoin his crew when the coast was clear.

But it was Rygard whose team had been attacked during a remote planetary surveillance mission. It was for his sake that she'd exposed herself as a mutated human, a shape-shifter, while rescuing him and half his team. Now they were in pursuit of the other half, and this mission would not succeed without her. So here she was again. For Rygard.

She should probably think through exactly what he meant to her. Later. After this mission was completed. If they survived.

From the other cells, random sounds of growling and clicking, groaning and cursing merged in an ugly version of white noise. Her memory added to it a cacophony of frightened shouts and tortured screams as her classmates suffered with her. How many of them had been captured back then, a dozen or more? It took less than a week for all of them to die. All except Kaitlyn.

Footsteps sounded in the passageway, and the ambient suffering reduced to a fearful simmer. It had been the same way back then: all of them quieted, hoping the guards hadn't come for them, even if it meant somebody else would be taken.

Defiant, Kaitlyn moved to the mouth of the cave and watched the Sketz'es guards walk past. They barely spared a look for her, overconfident in the security of the force fields. Or maybe they considered the two-footed fighters more dangerous than the four-footed.

Stupid of them, and to her advantage.

Satisfied she could take the guards if need be, her mental ghosts quieted. She turned to consider their cave again.

There was enough room for all of them to lie down with little space to spare. If any of them intended to limber up or prepare for a fight, the others would have to stay back against the walls. There were no nooks or crannies in which to hide from the surveillance sensors.

Speaking was going to be a problem.

There was no place to shift without being seen. Someone would realize she was more than a tamed panther.

Stepping away from the main opening, she approached the archway, curious.

Years ago, when she'd been taken during the attack on Triton Moon Base, she'd been a prisoner of war. The circumstances and the setting were different. She needed to keep that in mind as memories kept coming back to her. She could handle this.

She'd never been able to see her classmates unless they'd been taken out to watch each other suffer for the amusement of their keepers. In contrast, these caverns seemed to be a network, some with pockets divided by force fields and others naturally separated. Theirs adjoined only one other and it wasn't empty.

Shadows shifted in the darkness beyond the pale glow of the force field. Bipedal and somewhat humanoid, she judged. They were much quieter than humans or Sketz'es. The force field filtered any clues scent might have given her. A low growl emerged from the other side, tweaking a fairly new memory and bringing it to the forefront in contrast to the older.

The growl was feline, and not any Terran big cat like her. No. She'd heard a threat like it not too long ago on Dysnomia Station, and the maker had been a completely different kind of alien. Considering the trouble that had been, she really wondered what kind of universal god Murphy must be. Murphy's Law seemed to touch every living thing, even at the edges of the galaxy.

"Everything okay?" Rygard stepped to her side, close enough to touch, though he didn't.

She'd noticed his hesitation a few times since she'd shifted form. He'd had no trouble touching her as a human; as a panther, he seemed unsure. She wondered if he was repulsed by her in this shape.

A snarl interrupted her thoughts this time, and she bared her teeth in response. A face emerged from the darkness, level with hers. The alien feline was a starved version of the race she and Rygard had encountered on Dysnomia Station. Gaunt, its cheekbones and eye sockets stood out in stark relief. Skin stretched too taut over the frame of its face. Starved or not, it still had a set of fangs to rival her own.

Ugh, and its drool made her happy she couldn't smell its breath. The thing hadn't eaten clean in some time, and its mouth seemed to be rotting along with whatever it'd managed to subsist on down here.

Rygard stood his ground, no sign of fear despite the surprise she could scent in his reaction. He'd barely flinched.

"*Ganna kei al.*" A deep voice came from out of her line of sight, and the thing in front of her *did* flinch. She'd heard the words before and she was guessing they meant to stand down, or something along those lines.

Since the felid withdrew, she'd count that as an affirmation of her assumption. She could see him now, past the glow of the force field, crouching low on all fours despite having evolved to walk upright.

The speaker stepped closer, enough for her to see he stood tall on two legs. Equally emaciated, the remains of what must have once been ornate robes hung off his frame. Despite his weakened condition, the male held himself erect and his musculature rippled beneath his hide. A dominant male, this one, perhaps more of an alpha than the big felid she and Rygard had encountered back on Dysnomia Station.

And his golden eyes were fastened on her neck.

She didn't know why she'd decided to wear the pendant. It'd been around her neck since the day she'd received it as a gift. A necklace, given in thanks, was different to her from a collar. The cord was hidden in her fur, the pendant all that was visible.

Wear it.

The felid had given her a command back then. She

didn't have to obey; she'd worn it because it'd resonated with her. Something about the polished blue amber stone against her skin comforted her, especially because she could feel it whether her skin was bare or protected by fur.

"You are human." The male addressed Rygard, never taking his eyes from the pendant around her neck. At least, she was going to assume the male was talking to Rygard because she sure as hell couldn't answer him.

"Yes." Rygard gave the affirmative with caution. Either he'd assumed the male was talking to him too or he'd decided to cover for her. Whichever, it was a good idea.

"Where did you come across that?" The felid didn't point. Instead, he lifted his chin in her general direction, and he did not sound pleased.

"It was a gift."

Yup. And considering what she'd gone through, she planned to keep it.

"You are not lying."

Interesting—she couldn't catch scents coming across the force field, so neither could they. The male had to be relying on Rygard's voice inflection and body language to detect a lie. Much harder to do without the aid of smell to confirm. Seeing these aliens in this dungeon only proved how much of a melting pot this place was.

Out of the corner of her eye, she caught the sharp movement of Rygard's shrug. His growing agitation was no surprise since the last time they'd met this species, he'd been branded a murderer. The damning part of it was that it had been rightfully so in his mind. He might have been under orders, but he'd wrestled with the right and wrong of what he and his men had done. Making it right had mattered to him. Not dying had sort of been a side benefit there.

Rygard was good at not dying.

Kaitlyn liked him fine that way, but she worried about his priorities.

"How did you come by the gift?" The alien cat stepped closer to the force field, and with him came the other. Still crouching on all fours, it crowded the bigger male's leg and glared at Kaitlyn.

She twitched an ear and then deliberately lay down. The smaller male wasn't a threat.

"We met one of your kind, not too long ago." Rygard cut the explanation short there. "The gift and the story are hers."

Oh and that explained everything.

Kaitlyn huffed. Then again, this wasn't the place to go into any kind of detail.

The silence stretched out into a long wait as the big male stared at Kaitlyn. She raised her eyes to his and blinked once, twice. He wasn't a threat to her either, force field or no.

The others had gone still behind her. Even Tracer was doing a good job, for a human, at being a statue. She flipped the end of her tail. The big male could stare at her all he wanted, but he wouldn't get the answers he sought simply by looking at her.

"She is not kindred."

She twitched her ear again. Another plus one to the big guy.

Rygard didn't bother to answer. They both had an idea of what kindred were. They'd pulled two cubs out of an illegal shadow market on Dysnomia Station. As far as Kaitlyn was concerned, the cubs were pure cat, not a sentient species per se. Considering how clearly the cubs had made their emotions known, they might have had enhanced intelligence, something along the lines of the tinkering in Max's genetics. She hadn't spent enough time with the cubs to know for sure.

There was another long silence before the big alien spoke again. "You will not wait long to fight. Keep away from the cage walls. Control the center."

Interesting. The tips were an offering of good faith. She hadn't been expecting any of those. None of them had. The question was, How could it be of benefit to them?

"Thank you." Rygard nodded once and then backed away from the force field.

Kaitlyn rose, holding her head high. Both of the aliens watched her, their eyes fastened on the pendant under her throat. She really didn't like the attention near the soft tissue of her neck. Still, the cool amber grounded her, gave her a calm she used to have to work for.

"If you survive, we would talk more with you." The dominant male was still looking at her, not Rygard. "Live, little one."

Pfft. *Little.*

She flicked an ear in his direction. Size wasn't the only advantage she had over prey. Speed, strength, and agility were hers, as well as the natural weapons she had in feline form. Leopards could overwhelm prey many times their size, drag the carcass long distances, and climb with the added weight. Being a panther, not just a leopard, added to her advantage in these dark caverns. Her melanistic variation of a normal leopard's coat allowed her to blend better into darkness and shadows, a nightmare with teeth and claws.

In any case, what was it with so many people telling her to live? She planned on it. The more people hoping for her survival, the better, she supposed, but everyone telling her to felt almost like a jinx.

She turned and padded over to the far wall, which was deepest in shadow. Lying down again, she positioned herself to see all of the entryways into the cavern, knowing what little light there was would reflect in her eyes. It might not bother the felids still watching her, but it would creep the hell out of the guards when they came.

It didn't take much time for Rygard to come and sit next to her, then draw up his knees so he could rest his elbows on them.

"Seems like every chance I get to be with you in person, we end up on a mission where all the males are only interested in you."

She curled her lip to flash long white fangs at him. It wasn't limited to heterosexual males, and it definitely wasn't like she did it on purpose.

Bharguest snorted. "You think this is bad. Give it a day."

"And what, she turns into a prime rib platter?" Rygard's tone bordered on aggressive. The hint of humor sounded forced, but it kept his words from inciting the predator instinct in their dubious ally.

Kaitlyn watched Bharguest carefully anyway. He was too unpredictable. The man only smiled, nostrils flaring as he breathed in through his nose.

"Her scent is changing. Your girl is coming into heat."

Oh hell no.

Suddenly, her irritability made sense. Her tight skin and fevers. She'd experienced similar symptoms in the past, but never this acute and never all the symptoms at the same time. It meant she might have experienced heats in the past without realizing what they were, but she wondered how long Bharguest had known. Another question, for later, was whether this would be an isolated occurrence due to her surroundings or was she going to experience increasingly intense heats as she aged?

"Relax." Bharguest chuckled. "There's nothing more interesting than watching a fighter try to kill what they want to fuck."

Charming.

"MOST HUMANOIDS DON'T WANT a big cat." Rygard's words came out choked.

Kaitlyn heartily agreed, both with what he said and what he sounded like he felt.

That . . . would have been more than awkward. She might be her beast aspect in a lot of ways, but the imagery Bharguest had called up sent awful shivers through her. No, no, and *no*. Thank freaking goodness Rygard seemed to feel the same.

Bharguest shrugged. "If the two of you are going to survive this place, she's going to have to use every advantage she's got. Anything that confuses her opponent or provides any kind of distraction is an opening for both of you to win and survive. You also shouldn't rely on her remaining a big cat. Staying in one form is a death sentence for you both."

Changing shape during a fight was risky. Sure, she'd done it, but those had been extenuating circumstances. Once engaged, she usually committed to one form or the other until it was over.

You are your beast and you're wasting more of your brain than any normal human while you deny it.

Bharguest had made the statement back on the ship during one of their conversations when he sat in the ship's containment area. He might have been brought on board Dev's ship as a consultant to the Terran military, but the military unit led by Petrico-Calin treated him like a prisoner.

Technically, Bharguest was a prisoner offering his knowledge of these galactic fighting arenas in exchange for his freedom. If anyone was being honest, Bharguest could slip away and be free any time he got bored enough. And he'd leave a body count in his wake. She wasn't entirely sure why he chose to be here with them for this specific mission now. But it was definitely by his choice.

She shook her head and twitched her tail in annoyance. She would chew on the thought for a while because the words tasted of truth.

"How will it affect her, going into a heat cycle?" Tracer watched her, not wary but curious. Next to him, Max sat relaxed and watchful. "Others reacting to her could be an advantage but is she going to be handicapped physically or mentally?"

All the males were looking at her by the end of the question. Annoyance burned hotter, turning to anger. She bared her teeth at them all.

Bharguest grinned. "I wouldn't say it'll be debilitating for her, but she might be more likely to give someone else a handicap. Say, a maiming or a few new holes in their hide."

Kaitlyn resisted the urge to flex her claws.

Boots sounded in the hallway again. Two humanoids approached, different from the earlier guards. These were heavier and walked with more purpose, approaching fairly quickly.

Max's head turned, his big ears swiveling toward the sound. The dog's hearing was as good as her own. Tracer stopped whatever question he'd been about to ask. Looked for whatever had his partner's attention. Good handler.

For Skuld's sake, Kaitlyn hoped Tracer would make it through this mission unscathed. He was leaner than Rygard, with a medium height and build for a human. He had a charming smile and an easy-going demeanor that helped him get along with just about anybody. Among humans, he could probably hold his own in a fight, but now that they'd gotten a few glimpses of what they were up against, she felt Tracer's greatest strength would be his partnership with his Kx9, Max. She wasn't sure it would be enough.

Skuld wanted him to come back to her alive, so Kaitlyn would do what she could to make certain he returned to her best friend. But this was a mission, and he was a soldier; they both knew he needed to carry his own weight.

Still, Kaitlyn hoped he wouldn't have to fight right away.

"That was quick." Bharguest sounded pleased. "I guess we'll find out which of us gets to play first."

Rygard rose to his feet and moved forward to stand at the force field. Kaitlyn hesitated a moment before joining him. Seemed like a bad idea to be out in the open, but she wouldn't leave him to stand alone.

These two humanoids were heavily armed. One aimed some sort of plasma rifle at the other occupants in their cave while his partner fixed a reptilian gaze on Rygard.

"That man and the panther." The slight hiss as the reptilian pronounced the *th* sound tickled Kaitlyn's ears. "All others stay back or be shot."

Thank you, Captain Obvious.

Then again, looking at the strange aggression burning in the eyes of some of the other beings standing right at the force fields in other crevices, Kaitlyn wondered if it might not be so obvious after a prolonged period down here.

"Come."

The force field deactivated. Rygard didn't hesitate, but he didn't move quickly either. He stepped forward because it was prudent to do so. He wasn't particularly obedient. Kaitlyn remained at his side, allowing him to take the lead.

Part of her wanted to zone to one side, keep the two reptiles from flanking them, but that wasn't the purpose of tonight's situation. No, they had to play along for the time being.

The guards led them back through the corridors, taking a different route than Dev's hologram had led them. It looked the same to the eye, but Kaitlyn's nose told her more. Even with the aid of her enhanced senses, she had to pay careful attention to their path. Too many scents confused the trails, some of them astringent, and she was betting they kept the corridors clean for more than simple sanitary purposes. It'd be a challenge to find their way out when the time came.

They stepped onto a new set of elevators. Faint traces of blood streaked the floor, and as they rose through the levels, the sounds of cheers and shouts grew louder. When they stopped and were told to step off the platform, they were still underground.

Ventilation on this level was better, yet it stank of sweat and drink, excitement and violence. Everywhere, the tang of fear tainted the air. The only light fell in columns clustered ahead of them, and Rygard slowed his pace in the reduced visibility.

As they drew closer, it became clear that each pool of light was a cage. In some, matches were already going on, combatants performing for the cheering crowd watching from above. In others, the fighters waited in the shadows outside the cage walls for their turn. She and Rygard were led to one cage and herded into a small holding pen attached to the side of an octagonal arena. On the other side, she could make out a big humanoid shape and another animal.

Badger was suddenly there, handing Rygard his weapons through a small slot. Wordlessly, Rygard shrugged into his gear, clipping the harness across his chest and waist. His hands passed swiftly over the various sheaths, and Kaitlyn took a visual inventory. All blades, no firearms—the configuration was as much for her as for him. At least two of the blades were attached to the back of his harness where he wasn't likely to reach for them.

The fight would be a well-matched one, as far as the organizers were concerned.

An announcer's voice projected over the shouts of the crowds. Kaitlyn didn't bother to absorb the words. No doubt most of the onlookers had their own personal translators in earbuds or headsets. Instead, she studied the walls of the octagon. Thick strands of plasteel, woven to look like a net, stretched across the frame of the cage, allowing onlookers to see while the combatants were effectively contained. She couldn't even slip a paw through any of the holes. And unlike netting made of cord or rope, these walls wouldn't give on impact. Considering the felid's earlier warning, she decided it'd be a bad idea to be caught up against the honeycomb-patterned walls.

Glancing up into the light, she saw fists pumping beyond the glare. She could make out the same netted pattern, confirming the cage was fully enclosed overhead too. She wouldn't be able to leap up out of the cage if necessary. At least the onlookers couldn't throw anything too harmful down on their heads. Liquids were a different story.

She'd borrow one worry at a time.

The gates to the holding pens opened simultaneously, and the guards used shock rods to prod them from their niches into the main cage.

Growling, Kaitlyn stalked to one side, truly annoyed and glad to have avoided the rods. Such a shock, right before a fight, could have caused seized muscles she didn't care to overcome.

Rygard had stepped forward and was sizing up the other humanoid. The other man, if she wanted to call him one, was huge. Towering over Rygard by close to two feet, the opponent was at least as wide and wearing dented armor across his chest and shoulders.

Circling the cage opposite her, the beast of the pair let out a hiss.

The good news? It was focused on her and not Rygard.

That was the bad news too.

The thing had to outweigh her by almost a hundred pounds. A triangular head swung to and fro as its tongue flicked out to taste the air. Tiny eyes peered across the way, blinking in the garish light shining down on them. Each of its four feet ended in wicked hooked claws, nonretractable based on the way they clicked on the hard floor. As it dropped its jaw to hiss at her again, she caught sight of a solid row of nasty curved teeth, made to rip and tear.

Damned biggest lizard she had ever seen, and she wondered briefly if someone had nabbed one from Old Terra and tinkered with genetics to make the monster. She vaguely remembered images from her student days, something called a Komodo dragon.

Obviously a predator, the thing was built low to the ground with powerful legs and a thick tail. She was going to have a hard time rendering the thing harmless. Likely, there'd be no halfway about it. She'd have to kill it, or it would try its hardest to kill her and her partner.

The big humanoid let out a cry, a strangled sound of aggression no natural beast would make. It lunged at Rygard, and her partner sidestepped the first attack.

She didn't have much time to watch because the Komodo dragon charged. It came at her in a dark blur and she, too, dodged to one side, barely avoiding the struggling males. It lashed out with a powerful tail, knocking the feet out from under both Rygard and his opponent as Kaitlyn barely hopped over.

Frustration twisted inside her. She wouldn't be able to put this thing on its back quickly. She moved around the cage as it hissed at her again and bobbed its head in jerking movements. It was too fast, and it didn't care about its humanoid as much as she cared about Rygard. It whipped its tail around, heedless of the battling humanoids. If their fight brought them too close, damned thing might turn and take a chunk out of one of them.

Not something her partner could survive.

The cage didn't give them enough room to properly maneuver. She'd have to get in close range in order to draw blood, before it could get tired chasing her. Fear shivered across her pelt, and she shook it off. No time. No doubt.

Kill it.

She lashed her own tail, deliberately mirroring its body language. The thing hissed again, dropping its tiny head low and hunching its heavy shoulders. Dropping her own head, she bared her teeth and hissed back.

Come get me.

Sure enough, it charged her again, a dark streak across the width of the cage.

Shouts and screams of the watching crowd rose in a crescendo as she waited, waited to the last possible second before leaping straight up into the air and rotating 180 degrees to land on the thing's back. Latching in with her front claws, she bit deep into the tough leather just behind its skull. Holding on for dear life, she raked it as best she could with her hind claws, leaning all of her weight forward over its head.

As she'd expected, the thing thrashed side to side, trying to turn and take a bite out of her. As long as she kept her hindquarters mobile, it couldn't catch her. Her front paws were gouging into its shoulders from the strain of carrying all her weight, and the muscles of her back stretched cruelly as it whipped her to and fro.

The pounds of pressure she could apply with her jaw gave her a firm hold on its neck. She bit deeper despite the foul taste of its hide. It reared up on the cage wall and slammed them both down on the hard surface with a massive jolt, dislodging her claws. Still, she bit deeper, sinking one front set of claws and then another back into its shoulders as she regained her hold. She blinked her eyes, struggling to clear her vision as the crowd around them pounded a beat into the ceiling.

Its sides were slick with blood now, and it began smacking sideways into the hard plasteel net of the octagon. Each impact was punctuated by cheers.

Their struggle had carried them around the octagon. Every blow jarred her entire body, flung her hindquarters into the wall. Still, she hung on, even though her jaw felt ready to dislocate. At the edge of her peripheral vision, she could see the males struggling at the other side of the cage. Rygard still lived.

Finally, Kaitlyn's teeth hit the solid resistance of bone. She'd found the damned thing's spine. The lizard hissed again, a desperate note in the fierce sound. It picked up speed, trying to dislodge her against the wall. She needed to end it before the monster succeeded.

She found the rhythm of its panicked thrashing, then waited for it to throw itself into the side of the cage. As it lunged to the side, she threw all her body weight in the other direction, wrenching its neck in her jaws.

A sickening snap could be heard despite the cries of the crowd, and the Komodo dragon lay still.

Triumph washed through her, and she stood with both front paws planted on her kill. Staring up into the bright lights, she bared her teeth at the wildly gesticulating shadows and roared her defiance.

She turned her attention to Rygard's fight as it raged on the other side of the cage. Her partner held his own, barely, but he'd lost control of the center of the ring. Had to, while she'd been grappling with her prey. His opponent had him with his back to the cage wall, defending more than landing any telling blows.

Rygard was a stand-up striker, not really a grappler if he could help it, and if the bigger male overwhelmed him and took the fight to the ground, her partner would be in trouble. Luckily, the other humanoid looked to be a stand-up brawler too.

She'd been willing to let Rygard find his own way to a win, but his opponent had gotten through his guard, landing a hammer-fisted blow to the side of his head. Taking advantage of Rygard's disorientation, the big humanoid wrapped both arms around her lover's upper body and hoisted him up in a bear hug, trapping his arms against his sides.

Rygard tried for a headbutt, bucking and searching to find some weak point to win his way free. He attempted hammer blows to his opponent's torso while hooking his feet on the inside of the male's knees to break his stance. As the air was slowly being crushed out of him, Kaitlyn darted into the fray and landed on the big male's shoulders.

Armor protected the back of his neck and shoulders. Her claws could only find purchase to hold and not to gouge flesh. The big male stumbled backward a few steps with the weight of her on his back; still, he refused to let Rygard go.

Desperately, Kaitlyn yowled. Her lover was turning red in the face, and his fierce eyes were beginning to lose focus.

She darted her gaze from his face to his harness and the combat knife strapped over his shoulder. Their opponent's hold on Rygard had shifted the harness just enough to put the sheath out of reach, if she stayed where she was.

No way to reach it with her mouth. No way to grasp the handle with her claws.

Only one other choice remained.

Pain and agony screamed through her in a burning moment as her claws turned to hands. Her spine shortened and curved, and her toes scrabbled for purchase against the big male's armor without the aid of claws.

Gritting her teeth against the protest of every muscle, she reached over her opponent's shoulder and yanked the combat knife free of Rygard's harness. Swiftly, and with all the strength she could muster, she brought it around and inward, finding the gap under their opponent's arm, stabbing once, twice. The thing screamed and dropped

Rygard, then reached back for her with its good arm as blood streamed down from the deep gashes under its other.

She dropped off its back before it could grab hold and toss her, then crouched naked in the center of the octagon. Fear chilled her skin as she tried to hide her vulnerability. Quickly, she reversed the combat knife in her right hand and prepared to take the oncoming attack.

But Rygard wasn't out of the fight. From where he'd fallen, he'd recovered, and he took the big male's feet out from under him with a powerful leg sweep. When it hit the ground, Rygard grabbed its bad arm and caught it in an arm bar hold, then used all his strength to bend its arm beyond natural range of motion until something gave with a sickening pop.

The humanoid screamed.

Rygard yanked another combat knife free of his harness, then buried it to the hilt in the side of the thing's neck.

The horrible scream cut off in a gurgling sputter as blood fountained from a major artery.

Kaitlyn watched, ready, as the life left the big male. After the first fountain of blood, the crimson spurted out in time with its failing heart, waning and weakening.

Flat eyes stared at them, and a thick tongue lolled out of its mouth.

It might have started out human, but whatever it had been mutated into had been cold-blooded and as reptilian as the Komodo dragon–like thing she'd killed.

Rygard stood, his own knife at the ready, and sidestepped toward her until the both of them stood back-to-back in the center of the ring. If another battle was about to start, they were ready for it.

CHAPTER 4

"THIS IS DEFINITELY POSING AN ISSUE." Dev's voice came across the communication node still nestled in Kaitlyn's earlobe.

Rygard knelt next to where she crouched in the back of the cave, leaning close to listen. Her proximity always drew him, heated his blood. Something about her at this moment, fresh from their time in the cage, set him on fire. One by one, he extended his fingers, stretching open his hand before closing it into a tight fist again. Repeating the motions with his other hand, he found himself steady enough to listen back in on Dev's commentary.

"Part of the reason we sent you in panther form was to avoid the issues inherent with sending a female of any kind into what basically amounts to a prison." A tapping noise began to punctuate Dev's words. Rygard remembered seeing the captain tap his comm when he was thinking. "I've had to turn down several offers from interested buyers."

"That's a lot of bodies to hide on this rock." Her shoulders were relaxed, hands loose, and face serene, but

Rygard noticed the way the German Shepherd Dog was watching her. Alert.

Dev chuckled. "For the time being, we think you're safe from idiots because I've said I'm saving you for possible mating."

Kaitlyn snorted, or blew a raspberry. "Max is fully loaded. And the rest of our boys are intact. But most of those males? Gotta be shooting blanks."

Rygard swallowed a bark of laughter and ignored the odd flutter in his stomach. None of his soldiers ever used banter the way Kaitlyn did with her captain. Must have been a merc thing.

Dev's voice took on a bored tone. "I've also said I won't pay damages for any males stupid enough to attempt forcing themselves on you. There's a lot of agreement among the bigger sponsors that your value lies in both your fighting prowess and your viability as a breeder so they've made it clear they'd be displeased to see you damaged outside the fighting cages. Your potential value has gone up significantly and they've raised all of you several rankings in the brackets because of it."

While Rygard didn't feel better about the situation, at least it seemed as if Kaitlyn's surprise shape-shift had accelerated their progress through the tournament brackets. It significantly increased their chances of survival if they had to fight their way through fewer levels. And while they were surviving, Dev and Badger would be their eyes.

"Badger and I have been taking turns watching the matches." Dev continued to keep his voice low. He might have been in a secluded location somewhere above, but it wouldn't necessarily be secure. "We haven't seen what we're looking for yet, but there's a couple groups coming up in the next hour that look promising. Once we find them, we'll update you. In the meantime, don't die."

Easier said than done. Rygard leaned back against the cavern wall, seated next to Kaitlyn. If it hadn't been for her, he'd have lost consciousness in the death grip of their opponent. Yeah, he'd killed the bastard, but she'd broken the hold and drawn first blood.

Once both their enemies lay dead and it became obvious no more were coming, Badger had been there, ordering Rygard to hand his weapons and harness back over. It'd taken a lot to hand over the combat knives. For Kaitlyn, it had been a nastier internal struggle. Naked and exposed, beautiful even streaked in blood, he'd seen the death in her eyes as she snarled at the crowd in her human form. She'd have killed anyone else who'd have tried to disarm her.

Once Rygard had removed his harness, though, he'd yanked off his shirt and given it to her. The gesture had seemed to snap her out of her rage.

"How're you feeling?" The question seemed way less than adequate.

Her eyes had gone cold, blank. He wondered if she saw him at all or if she was trapped inside a nightmare. "I could be warmer."

Not too much they could do about that. His shirt hit her at midthigh and covered most of her, but they had all come in with minimal clothing.

"I could . . ."

She shook her head. "Keep your pants." Then the corners of her mouth turned up in a faint smile. "I appreciate the offer but they'd mess with my range of motion in the next fight. Besides, if I have to shift again, we'll both be without pants."

"You going to shift back to panther?" She'd be warmer that way. And safer.

"Dev doesn't seem too worried currently." She glanced at the entrance to their cave. "I'll shift back to panther in a bit, after we're sure we've done all the talking we need to do."

He didn't agree, but it wasn't like he could force her to shift. He'd seen the way the guards looked at her, the way their nostrils flared and their tongues flicked out to taste the air near her. They hadn't done it when she'd been a panther. His body hadn't responded to her either, but now, he knew she could smell his arousal, and his proximity was probably keeping her on edge.

Heat seeped into his skin as her hand came to rest on his forearm. "Hey you."

He met her gaze, the warmer brown he'd come to know. "I'm here."

"It's twisted, what I am." Her words came in a whisper, her brows drawn together as she dropped her gaze to where her hand lay on his arm. "And you still want me for me. It means a lot to me."

He cleared his throat. "Now's a suck time to mention it, but looking at you as a big cat was kind of weird."

She tilted her head to one side. "I'd be a little freaked if you weren't weirded out by me in that shape. We never talked about it before."

"The first couple of times you did it, it was quick. I barely spent time near you." He shook his head. "It didn't have time to sink in."

"And later?"

He knew what she meant: their conversations and holo calls when she'd been in human form. "I was talking to you, seeing you." It was easy to forget she turned furry.

"You can't ignore it on this mission."

Maybe he should think on it harder, what it might mean for a future with her. To him, at this moment, she was still his Kaitlyn. He could only see so far ahead and still keep an eye on what they had at hand.

"True." He paused, searching for the words he wanted. "All the times you've made the shift for me? Fighting for me or at my side, I'd be a complete-ass idiot to be weirded out over it."

"I wouldn't blame you for your body's reaction if you didn't want me anymore."

He covered her hand with his, the silken smoothness of her skin making him wish he could run his hand over other parts of her. "It doesn't seem to be an issue, does it? We'll meet that obstacle if it comes up. Let's not borrow more trouble. We've got enough to survive as it is."

"Not to interrupt an obvious moment, but I had a couple of questions." Tracer stepped closer, his big dog moving to give Kaitlyn a gentle nudge at the shoulder. "I'm sure he has a couple of his own comments too."

No need to ask who. Bharguest stood in the darkest shadows of the cavern, his eyes catching just enough of the light to show orange in the darkness. Human eyes didn't do that.

Tracer didn't bother him, and they needed to do a team debrief. Rygard still had an issue calling Bharguest a part of the team regardless of the information the prisoner had been providing.

"You don't have to like me, soldier boy." Bharguest's words floated out of the shadows. "But you need me. She needs me. And I came in here to play your game."

The sick part was that it *was* a game to the man, not a mission and not loyalty to anyone. The prisoner would leave them all there if he took the notion to go find a different game to play.

Kaitlyn shook her head. "Having fun, are you?"

"It twists you inside, doesn't it?" The tip of his tongue flicked out and wet his lower lip. "Because somewhere, in a little corner of your heart, you're having fun too."

Kaitlyn didn't answer. Alarmed, Rygard looked at her long and hard and wondered about the truth of Bharguest's insight. Rygard had worked with mercenaries before, but those people did what they did in the pursuit of creds. Bharguest's actions had nothing to do with currency. Kaitlyn was better. He was sure of it.

"I survived." Kaitlyn threw the words down. "We both did. And thank you for the tip. You want us to sing your praises?"

Bharguest chuckled. "Funny girl." When Bharguest stopped smiling, the vertical slits that were his pupils widened briefly. Rygard wondered what Kaitlyn could see in the cover the shadows provided Bharguest. After a moment, Bharguest spoke again. "I want to hear what the dog lover wants to know."

Tracer cleared his throat, obviously unsettled. Max moved to stand between him and Bharguest, the fur across his back relaxed but his pose still watchful. "This fight, is this what we're going to expect when it's our turn?"

Rygard wanted to give encouragement, but he'd come back from his own bout looking like hell.

"No way to know who you're going against unless Dev can give us a heads up on the way. You'll have time to size them up while you're waiting to get into the cages." Kaitlyn gave a brief description of the layout and the octagon in which they'd been placed.

Rygard recalled most of what she shared, but he

marveled at the level of detail she remembered and how she parsed what was important to tell up front and then provided the additional supporting information.

"You think there are different places to hold the fights though." Tracer hunkered down close but kept enough of a space open for Bharguest to join if he wanted to.

"There are different floors for the various brackets in the tournaments," Bharguest interjected.

Kaitlyn only raised an eyebrow.

"As you progress to higher levels, you're matched against better fighters in different arenas. To keep things interesting, they might change from the generic octagon to a pit or a cage with water features. Fire is popular, so is sand. You might be given weapons aside from the ones your handler gives you before entering the arena." Bharguest held his hands out to the side and spread his fingers wide. "Anything to keep it entertaining."

"Oh, joyful." Her tone was anything but.

Rygard felt about the same way. If she hadn't been sitting next to him, he'd have spit into the sand covering the cavern floor.

"You." Bharguest stuck his chin out at Tracer. "You need to worry since we've been boosted in the brackets. The next fight will be a harder challenge. The dog's smart, but smarts will only get you so far in the cages."

"You think we're not as strong a pair as Rygard and Kaitlyn?" No pride in Tracer's voice—no fear either. "Don't waste our time undermining our confidence. Give us something constructive."

"I like you." Funny how none of them seemed overly happy when Bharguest said that. "You and the dog move as a unit. You've trained together, seen combat together."

"Yeah." Tracer stood, and Max moved into a position at

his handler's left. The big dog stood so his right hip brushed Tracer's leg.

"You two are a better-matched pair." Bharguest stirred, and the darkness around him seemed to swirl. "You'll last longer than most expect, make some gamblers good creds."

Tracer didn't reply, but his surprise was obvious in his raised eyebrows and wide eyes. Any more shock and his mouth might have dropped open.

Disgruntled, Rygard had to admit he and Kaitlyn hadn't fought as a pair. They'd divided to conquer.

"It's as much my fault as yours." Kaitlyn nudged him. "We've been in scuffles side by side before, but we're going to have to think to make coordinated attacks."

Stopping to think usually got a person killed.

From the small frown hovering around her lips, she knew it as well as he did. "We've got no choice. We're going to have to learn or bleed."

"Or die." Bharguest sounded far too amused.

Predictable response. When Bharguest stepped out of his niche, the light caught his skin. More scales covered his body, the black and gold diamond pattern covering the majority of his shoulders and extending down his arms. The scales over his abdomen were larger and wider, like armor plates protecting his softest parts.

Shape-shifter.

Having seen Kaitlyn shift when dealing with the primates back on the other planet, and knowing the man had been infected with the virus, Rygard still wasn't prepared for the otherworldly aspect of Bharguest. He hadn't completed a full shape-shift, not even close, but he wasn't static either. His shift took him far enough away from human to shake Rygard to the core.

The change didn't make him look like the reptilians

guarding them. Instead, Bharguest appeared mostly human, only increasing the unsettling effect of his reptilian skin and more prominent facial structures. Brow ridges and cheekbones had risen, stretching the skin of his face tight. His nose had receded until the nostrils were slits. He dropped his jaw again in a weird grin, his tongue pressed to the back of his top teeth to reveal an odd nodule.

Kaitlyn shuddered.

"Snakes have a scent receptor in their mouths to analyze airborne chemicals. You haven't had a weird tongue habit, you're literally tasting the air. Why haven't we seen others like you? All the rest have been mammalian."

"I don't play well with others." Bharguest paused, a forked tongue slipping out. "I've killed too many of my partners in . . . cold blood."

Had Bharguest been the first? Rygard wondered how long the virus experiments had been going on. Not that it mattered. It was more curiosity than anything else.

"Jeezus." Tracer continued a streak of stronger curses under his breath. Standing next to him, Max didn't make a sound, but the big dog's ears went back and the fur across his shoulders began to stand on end.

It was Kaitlyn who headed off the charge before any of them realized Bharguest had moved.

She met him straight on before he managed to reach Tracer, before Max could jerk free of his handler's hold. The two of them crashed to one side, Kaitlyn twisting just enough to turn the bigger shifter's back into the force field separating them from the adjoining area. The field flared, blinding them all for a fraction of a second as the acrid smell of burning flesh filled the cramped space.

Bharguest only laughed.

Rygard lunged toward them. She couldn't hold off the

psycho for more than a minute, he was sure. But Bharguest was falling. Kaitlyn disengaged and leaped backward to land directly in front of him, still facing Bharguest. She had one arm out, signaling for the rest of them to stay back.

Farther back, Tracer had his arms wrapped around Max. The big dog raged but stayed within the restraining hold of his handler.

"Excellent." Bharguest continued laughing. The bastard lay on the ground where he'd fallen, clutching his belly, writhing with amusement.

"Do it again and I'm going to forget you can help us." A snarl rose up from Kaitlyn.

Rygard couldn't see her face, but her fingers were curled and ended in claws. She'd partially shifted, faster than in the cage earlier.

What did it take out of her to shift so often, so fast?

He wouldn't risk asking her in front of Bharguest, but there had to be a reason why the other man didn't shift until now, and Rygard doubted it had to do with dramatic effect.

"But the looks on their faces." Bharguest sat up, his back brushing the force field as he did. He reached over his shoulder, and when he withdrew his fingers, they were slick with dark fluid. Touching them to his forked tongue, Bharguest took his time cleaning the blood away. "Thanks for this. A little pain keeps my reflexes sharp."

Bloodthirsty didn't cover it.

Rygard sent a prayer then, to whatever powers on high, that Bharguest was the next to go into the fights on the levels above them. It just seemed like a hell of a good idea to direct the man's attention at someone else, anyone besides their own team.

"You're fun, I have to admit." Bharguest shook his head. "More fun than I thought you'd be back on the ship. Others died before they ever knew I was coming at them. But you all, you're even leaving me alive."

Others. Teammates.

"You didn't escape this place before. You always planned to come back." Kaitlyn made the statement, rising up out of her crouch to slowly circle the other man. "You went looking for more gladiators to play with, here, in this hellhole."

"The fights here got boring. I like to play more complex games." Bharguest shrugged. "But no, I didn't bring you all here to be a part of the livestock."

"There's an obvious question hanging, then." Rygard kept his eyes on Bharguest, trying to track Kaitlyn at the edge of his peripheral vision. "Why did you bring us all here? I'm doubting you had a sudden charitable desire to help me save my unit."

The other man seemed to be watching only Kaitlyn.

"What I was doing doesn't matter anymore." Bharguest deliberately leaned back into the force field. This time, Rygard heard the sizzle. "What I found is more interesting."

No need to ask what. It wasn't likely they'd find out the more important answer yet.

Apparently, Kaitlyn had decided the same. She brushed dirt from her skin and rolled her shoulders. Her eyes never dropped though, never strayed from Bharguest. "While I'd love to go dramatic and wordy here, maybe start a speech on how we're not going to play your game anymore, it's not reality. We're here. We're playing."

"And you're learning." Bharguest drew the words out, left them hanging in the air. "You'll have to do better, though."

"She's good enough to stop you." As soon as the words left Tracer's mouth, Rygard knew they weren't true. Saw it in the way Bharguest's thin brow rose a millimeter and in the slow blink from Kaitlyn.

"As long as you keep improving, I'll let them all live." Bharguest spread his hands out. "Not just winning, not just surviving. Get better at being what you are and I'll respect your charming loyalty to your team."

Kaitlyn didn't move, didn't answer. Only blinked again, her lids falling over her eyes in a slow drop. When they rose, they revealed slitted pupils.

CHAPTER 5

"YOUR TEAM IS TOO DAMAGED to continue in the current configuration."

Kaitlyn stood in what passed for a triage-and-treatment center. Far as she could tell, it was designed to prolong a slave's torment in this hellhole just by keeping them alive longer. Medical equipment and supplies were beyond primitive, enough to stop immediately life-threatening issues but without the sophistication to truly repair tissues or broken bones.

"Well, I've made plenty credits on this first trip. Might be wise to stop here, take my team back and patch 'em up." Dev gave the smaller reptilian a closed-mouth smile. Kaitlyn wouldn't have had the self-control to forgo showing teeth. "I do plan to come back another time."

After swishing his tail, the overseer darted a glance past each of them, his gaze lingering a moment longer on Bharguest and then on her.

"You have the option to reconfigure your team," the Sketz'es allowed.

"Of course." Dev nodded. "I had several

recommendations from my fellow trainers. I'll take it into consideration for the next time I make an entry. You've been gracious hosts."

The reptilian's tongue flicked out. Kaitlyn wondered if he could taste his own anxiety.

The overseer was obviously discomfited over the entire team standing in the triage area. Most trainers might have returned the uninjured, or at least less damaged, back to the caverns below. But Dev had stated his training included making sure his team saw the suffering of fellow teammates. Team building for the cold and heartless.

"You have other options." A nictitating membrane slid over each eye.

That was new. She made a mental note to research the characteristic.

Dev scratched his growing scruff. "Options? That I might. But a man has to judge when the best time would be to step back. I like to keep my creds on the positive side, make a good impression."

The tail swished again, stirring up dust in a puff. "You could reconfigure your group, submit them all as a single entry."

Tracer moved where he lay on a gurney, his midsection wrapped in makeshift bandaging. It'd been sufficient to stabilize his broken ribs for the time being, but Kaitlyn didn't trust their medic. If Tracer went into another fight, one of those broken ribs could puncture a lung.

It'd been his injuries that brought them all to triage in the first place. Several of the slash wounds he'd suffered needed sealing or suturing. He might not have survived the blood loss.

"All the same, I'd rather come back with a solid team, especially for the sort of big to-do you all've got planned in the next day or two. I'm told these happen on a fairly regular basis." As Dev shrugged, he motioned to Badger. The older soldier began to nudge Tracer off the gurney, and Max sniffed eagerly at his handler. "Besides, I see no reason to keep my team here just for a standby position."

"We are prepared to advance your team, provided you present the recommended grouping." The answer came too quick. The reptilian's desperation bothered Kaitlyn, made the fine hairs on the back of her neck stand on end.

If she'd been in panther form, the fur all along her spine would have raised.

Dev stepped closer to the overseer, within claw's reach. "That's a sudden change of heart. Is there something you want to tell me? Maybe I'd be smarter to take my team and reconsider."

Kaitlyn could cover the distance between herself and the reptilian in a heartbeat. He might get a claw on Dev, maybe, but her captain did a good job of defending himself. So she held her ground when the overseer raised a clawed hand and opened it in a slow, deliberate gesture of peace. "Of course, you are welcome to do as you wish. It is merely my job to ensure you are aware of all the opportunities open to you."

Liar. She smelled the deceit in the air, tasted it. He'd grown too used to speaking to humanoid pirates and slave owners. He had his body language and tone under control, but his stinking pheromones gave him away to an enhanced mutation with heightened senses like herself.

"However, your team performed in a most impressive manner over the last few fights. The human-and-canine team are damaged, but unexpectedly survived more than once. The human-and-mutated human team has further exceeded expectations. The large mutated human has proven successful against our better solo fighters. As a whole, they're . . . interesting."

"They've been projected as the underdogs in every match they've been given." Dev's voice had gone flat, hard. "As an owner, I do understand the need to test the new and unproven. I'm only willing to risk so much in fights, putting my assets at significant disadvantage."

"Precisely why entering your newly configured team would be recommended." The reptilian wasn't good at dissembling. The sweeter tone required came across as whining from him. "In the free-for-all format, all entries are projected to be entering with equal chances of survival. To win would more than triple the gains you've made on this trip thus far, whether your team emerges victorious or not."

Or not. As in, they all died.

Kaitlyn considered Tracer and Max. The big dog returned her gaze with a somber look of his own. She honestly wondered how much of all this the Kx9 understood. He couldn't talk, but hell, he responded as if he had a higher comprehension of conversation than most of the roughnecks they had signed on to new missions.

Max leaned into his handler's thigh. The low whine was almost inaudible.

He should be worried. Tracer was currently the most vulnerable, with Rygard coming in a close second. She'd have to work to patch the both of them up more before the coming fight, considering the direction the conversation was going.

"Yeah, about that." Dev's smile turned tight, his lips pressed together. "Interesting the way betting isn't limited to just who wins. I'm not so new to this game that I don't have concerns. There's wagers going based on how long a particular team, or individual, manages to survive. A person with as much invested as I have would want to know more about the safeguards you all have in place to prevent any . . . favoritism."

"Oh no, no. The main purpose behind these events isn't the wagering."

Dev crossed his arms. "Really? Enlighten me, if you'd be so kind."

"Well, we do have fresh entries every day. Not all of them are as skilled or well equipped as yours."

Most of them were dead meat walking.

Kaitlyn had seen them cowering in their little caverns. Some of them were fighters, perhaps warriors. But not most.

The overseer continued with a shrug. "We do like to keep our audiences entertained with continually refreshed candidates. The occasional extravaganza provides an added level of excitement."

"You mean a higher body count for a bloodthirsty crowd."

The overseer's smile actually managed to send a chill through Kaitlyn, especially when he ran his tongue across his thin lips. She wondered if he personally ate any of the fresh kills from the fight.

The day after the big event, many of those caves would be empty and waiting for fresh blood.

"Regardless, we must ensure a certain number of quality teams," the reptilian admitted.

Ah, the truth finally revealed. Kaitlyn had been expecting something with more significance, but she supposed it might have more impact on him than any of them would know.

The reptilian tapped his data pad. "Those who remain standing at the end of the event will be handsomely rewarded. In this case, there can be more than one winning team as the goal is solely to survive to the end of the set time limit."

"I'll think on it." Dev turned away from the overseer.

Her captain would enter them. He'd make the overseer work a little bit more, but the outcome was decided.

Either way, there was a high likelihood Rygard's soldiers would be entered in the free-for-all too. It might be their only chance to get close to them. The challenging part would be the escape.

Fun.

It came over her slowly, washing across her skin in a cold wave: the awareness of Bharguest's attention fastened on her. She didn't have to look up; she knew he'd appear to be watching something else.

She must have done something interesting to him again. It'd been this way as she'd gone into every fight and burned off the effects of her heat through violence, rather than giving in to any desire for sex. She'd emerged from every match feeling more feral, more elated from the win. But rather than taking her longer to get back to her human mindset, she settled into herself easily. Maybe it was because Rygard and she reviewed their fights, discussed how they could improve. It prompted her back into a human thought pattern.

Either way, Bharguest was focused on her, observing. When his attention sharpened, she felt it and became aware she'd done a new thing. Or maybe repeated a behavior and verified a pattern.

The question wasn't what she'd done, it was what it meant and whether she wanted to admit she knew, even to herself.

"FIGHT WITH MAX ON YOUR RIGHT." Kaitlyn tucked in the end of the bandage to Tracer's midsection. "Anything you can do to discourage hits to your side will give you a better chance to come out of the next skirmish standing."

"Max and I know what we need to do." Tracer's face was pale, a fine sheen of sweat across his forehead. "Funny. Hurt like a bitch when you rewrapped me, but I can breathe easier now you're done."

"Uh-huh." Kaitlyn helped him lean back against the cavern wall. "Your ribs are properly supported now, not just held in around your internal organs. Try not to shift or cause a worse fracture."

She didn't want to talk much more. In the beginning, they'd talked in the evenings. It passed the time between fights and gave them something to focus on besides the sounds of misery from others in the caverns around them. She'd thought it wouldn't be a bad idea to get a better measure of this person Skuld liked. Skuld had liked Tracer enough to ask him to come back to her. Not something Kaitlyn had ever heard Skuld do.

Tracer proved to be a good man. He had a decent sense of humor and a warm heart. He'd joined the service because he'd believed he could do some good out in the galaxy. He was someone Kaitlyn was willing to consider a friend. Now, she wasn't sure Tracer would make it back, and she was struggling to shut those feelings away where conflicting emotions wouldn't risk the lives of their entire team.

"How'll we know if I mess up my ribs more?"

She shrugged. "You'll have trouble asking those questions you're so fond of tossing out there. Or, you might cough up blood. A jagged end will have a good chance of puncturing your lungs. Let's avoid that if at all possible. "

"Let's."

Kaitlyn rose and turned away.

"Hey." Tracer's voice sounded hoarse, maybe from pain, maybe from emotion. None of them would tell.

"Yeah?" She didn't turn around. If she didn't look at Tracer, she'd have to look at Max, and those sad brown eyes would crack her.

"I figure it's a good idea to toss another question over to you while I can."

She didn't answer, but she turned her head to the side so he could tell she was listening.

"No family to ask, I figure you're closest thing to it." Tracer chuckled. "You going to rip holes in my hide if I ask Skuld to spend more time with me, intimate time? You think she'd consider long-term, long-distance with me?"

Her preferred threats ran along the lines of delivering a crushed skull or broken neck. It was less of a biohazard to clean up if she didn't spill blood across the decks. But Tracer had proved himself a good man this mission, and it didn't seem like he was joking. Neither was she, most of the time, and she didn't plan to give him the usual threat, as a lighthearted warning or otherwise.

"If she enjoys your company, you don't have to worry about anything but healing up and keeping her happy." And because she couldn't swallow past the lump in her throat, she did turn then, and fastened her gaze on Max. "You be careful when you play with Chester. The tube rat is bendy but he's fragile. You got it?"

The dog lifted his big head, and his ears swiveled forward.

"I mean it."

She retreated then, too disturbed to pretend to be positive.

You were never the fake-cheerful type, anyway.

How long had it been since she'd heard Katzer's voice?

Well years, in reality, and inside her head it had been a while too. Definitely not since they'd descended into this hellhole.

You make the best of everything, Kitten. Even in the places no one else would, you could find a way.

He'd said those words to her back on Triton Moon Base when he'd dreamed of leaving. He'd wanted a life of adventure, to go beyond the Earth's solar system. He'd have loved being a part of Dev's crew.

Not her. She'd never shared his dream. Hers had been to follow a well-defined path to becoming a commissioned officer in the Terran military. She'd believed it was a sure way to get into the best funded research programs. But had those dreams really been hers? She'd picked them because she'd been assured they were possible. He'd accused her of being too complacent on the moon base back then, willing to place the sure bet and make the best of it.

Then, after the injection, she'd given up even those dreams. It'd been easier to choose what was in front of her, rather than look forward to future possibilities that weren't meant for her.

Had she developed a comfort zone, even here?

"You've got ghosts in your eyes, sweetness."

Rygard's presence hadn't done more than register at the periphery of her awareness when he'd first stepped to her side. Now, warmth bloomed at her core and spread along her extremities. His musk filled her nose, and she wanted to press a kiss at his collarbone, flick her tongue out to taste the salty-sweet of his skin.

"Now you've got a whole lot of something else on your mind." His voice triggered shivers along her spine, a delicious sort of wonderful. How long had it been since he'd run his hands over her body?

Her skin burned and her nipples chafed underneath the light fabric of his shirt. The only reason she could bear wearing the garment was because it was his, carried his scent. She wanted his touch, craved his hands on her.

Breathe. Only breathing didn't help because his scent filled her lungs, made her mouth water for the taste of his skin on her tongue.

He touched her then, slipping a finger under her chin and forcing her gaze from his broad chest up to his face. "Hey. Wherever your mind is, trust me, I wanna be there with you, but the normal you wouldn't want that here."

She didn't nip at the corner of his mouth to shut him up. Instead, she lifted her lip and bared her teeth in a silent snarl. He was right. "Whatever this is, it's getting worse."

"The last fight, I've never seen you that vicious."

There'd been several facing them; Rygard would talk about only one after the fact.

"You heard the things he said he'd do to me if he won against us."

"And I wanted to kill him for it. You beat me to it." A pause. "But you didn't have to slash him from neck to groin."

"I finished the kill."

"Yeah, after you stood over him. After he begged for it." His voice had taken on a different darkness with a bitter edge.

She took a step back, and his hand dropped away from her chin. Her skin felt cool in its absence. "It took a minute, to get past what I wanted to do to him. You know he'd done worse to the others he'd fought, the females they gave him as rewards. That one talked way the hell too much during a fight. It's why he lost."

"You've never been cruel before, Kaitlyn." The use of her full name instead of a term of endearment from him splashed over her like cold water.

She snarled out loud then, stepped up into his personal space. "What was he to the others, the ones too weak to stop him from doing what he wanted? What would he have been to me?"

"You're better than that." Rygard's jaw clenched. He didn't give ground. "If it hadn't been for the other three we needed to eliminate, I'd have put that rabid idiot down before you twisted yourself."

Memories flashed across her eyes of a time when the panther aspect first gained control of her. She parted her lips, dropping her jaw a bit to pant and cool herself.

"I was twisted long before you met me." He lifted a hand to touch her again, but she shook her head, maintaining the tiny gap between them. "Dev helped me play at being human, but this place . . . you can see what I am."

"You're better than this."

She shook her head, then gave him the truth nagging at her. "I can live here, be all of me here. This place challenges every part of what I am."

She'd missed it. Reveled in exercising her abilities instead of using a bit at a time. "Right now, I'm thinking about the fight to come and I'm excited for it."

"You're revved up overall. The heat thing is driving you insane."

"No. The heat is driving me to violence and the combat is the only place I can clear my head."

"Okay. I get that." Rygard studied her. "And I'd help

you in other ways if we were alone in this place, but we're not and neither of us wants it that way. Still, when you get into those rings, you don't have to be cruel. You can enjoy the adrenaline, savor the victory, but let it be a clean victory. When you come back to yourself, you'll like yourself better for it."

When was the last time she'd liked herself?

This time, when he stepped up to her, she didn't fade to the side.

He slipped his hand into her hair, and she leaned into it, rubbing her cheek into his palm. "Trust me, sweetness, you can be this part of you without being someone you won't forgive."

His touch soothed her, calmed the irritation and burning across her skin. In its place, an ache woke low in her belly—a need to be filled.

"This." The bitter taste remained in her mouth, and she twisted her lips in a parody of a smile. "This heat thing is every bit as much a part of me and I don't think I ever recognized it before we got here."

"Never recognized it." A pause. "Never this strong before?"

"Hell, I figured it was premenstrual symptoms and ignored it."

When he chuckled, she let a corner of her mouth turn up. From him, she didn't mind the mirth. Damn, it made it easier to stomach if someone found the humor in the insanity of it all.

"You are maturing, small one."

Kaitlyn lifted her head to see the bigger of the two felid aliens standing in the archway. He watched them, his tailing swinging back and forth behind his legs in an almost-hypnotic sway. Beyond him, his smaller companion crouched. Within her own enclosure, a pair of eyes glowed in the shadows to one side of the archway. She wondered when it had stopped bothering her to have Bharguest constantly staring.

"However you came by your second nature, it is younger than your true form." The dominant felid gestured at her, head to toe.

"I ran tests on a weekly basis." She took a step toward the archway and decided it wasn't cowardly to welcome the change in conversation. "The genetic mutations stabilized weeks after the original viral infection."

The felid cocked his head to the side. "What we are is not the sum of our components. Cells, tissues, structures can be assembled and the whole may yet remain lifeless. It is our thought processes, our experiences, and how we take the gained knowledge forward that make us more."

"I think, therefore, I kill." Well, maybe the old cliché went a little differently.

"A simple thought. The young think in such terms." The felid seemed to smile, or at least the corners of his mouth turned up. No teeth.

Good thing. She already wanted to bare her own.

"I spend plenty of time in panther form. There's a difference in the way I think. I don't waste time worrying about what-ifs or doubts."

"As a child, you did the same." The felid raised a hand, palm outward and fingers splayed. "You think only in terms of one form or the other, no in-between. I will guess you approach combat in the same way."

She held her tongue. After all, she might find herself facing him in the cages before it was all over.

"Push yourself to think. Transition smoothly from shape to shape, keeping the best of each aspect for any given situation, much the way you would switch from fighting style to style."

"Why are you so full of the advice, all of a sudden?" Rygard stepped to her side.

Having him stand shoulder to shoulder with her settled something inside, as if something she hadn't looked for had slid into place.

"Seems to be a lot of you interested in me, lately." She lifted her chin in Bharguest's direction. The only answer was the disappearance and reappearance of his glowing eyes as he slowly blinked. "I'd normally be annoyed, but I'll admit most of the commentary has been constructive."

She lifted her own hand, palm outward. Spreading her fingers, she visualized her change as she bore down, tensing each tendon until her claws slowly emerged. It took more concentration to hold the partial shift, rather than change straight into a panther.

"A pupil who listens, absorbs knowledge, and applies it. This is a rarity." The felid closed his hand, let it fall to his side. "And I would like to see you survive long enough to become a friend."

She raised an eyebrow. In a place like this, friendships were dangerous. Tracer would already be leaving a hole in her if he didn't pull through. She wouldn't dare consider the possibility of Rygard going down.

The felid tipped its head to one side in a brief concession. "Perhaps friend enough to share how you came to be the way you are."

Friend enough? She'd never actually shared her story with a friend. Dev had been there and so had Boggle. The only other iterations of her story had been in impersonal debriefs. Rygard, well, at the time, he'd been somewhere between an enemy and a one-night stand. She hadn't trusted him to be a friend.

"We've seen many from your solar system brought through these caverns. Many have been infected by a virus to make them better warriors. If it does not kill them, it makes them physically stronger but not better. They might survive longer, provide more sport, but they are still meat walking."

How long had these felids been here?

Kaitlyn glanced again to the smaller felid alien. How long had it taken for that one to lose it?

Would she need to worry about it within her group?

"We have learned some things about this virus." The felid offered his hand again. "Share your story of how you came to such a complete melding of aspects and we will add to your research."

How much of his species' culture involved body language? She watched him more carefully: his ears and nose, his posture. Stupid of her to allow the conversation to progress as if he was just another human.

"You're not mutants. How much can you know about it?" Rygard folded his arms across his chest.

The smaller alien's ears swiveled back, but the larger's remained forward. His nostrils flared, and she thought she caught a twitch of his upper lip. Yeah, Rygard's stance was aggressive enough to push buttons.

"Bioengineering and cellular manipulation are developed sciences within our culture. Genetic alteration would not be ethical but we recognize the application." The felid gestured to the smaller. "My companion was a scientist."

And would never be again. Even if they continued to survive, nothing about the smaller male's behavior indicated he'd be doing any critical thinking anytime soon. The only small blessing was that the scientist didn't seem to be bothered by her heat at all. Even the bigger felid showed signs of restraining himself from reaching for her.

She spared a breath of relief on the scientist's behalf. He didn't need proximity to her heat making his suffering worse, scrambling his hormones more.

"You've taken samples or done analysis? I think not." Perhaps she should have left the doubt to Rygard, but she'd never been great at tag team interrogation. Simpler to ask her own questions.

"The prisoners talk of when the injection was done. There is a specific sponsor."

Kaitlyn perked up at the new information. All their intel had come from Bharguest, and Rygard's people had been injected prior to shipment to the Colosseum, but they'd never heard about who'd given the order.

"Incubation time for the virus has been fairly short, only a day or two." She offered a bit of her findings, fishing.

The felid nodded. "Many prisoners are injected on arrival. After a day, they begin to sweat and within two they are writhing, screaming. Some do not survive. Those that do are changed. The guards here watch, provide water, but otherwise do not make the transition any easier. If the prisoners can nurse each other, some do. Others are overcome by the new animal aspect."

Grim silence fell.

It wasn't hard to imagine what might happen to a person, driven by an unfamiliar animal instinct. Kaitlyn remembered the fear, the urge to attack and win her way free. She hadn't been thinking the first time she'd taken a life.

"What do you mean?" Rygard asked. He didn't know

that about her, about the cost of the shifting from human to animal to human again.

"He's talking about the hunger." She didn't take her eyes off the felid, watching as one ear twitched and taking note of the slow blink of his eyes. He'd been fishing for information too. "Every shift and shape change takes energy. Metabolic rate increases and the calories burned need to be replaced."

Because the BioDome on Triton Moon Base had plenty of harmless small game and fish seeded in the terraformed lakes, she'd been able to satisfy the intense hunger that followed the initial changes to her body in those first days.

"You've never had an issue." The alarm was mostly kept out of his voice, but Rygard's concern was still palpable.

"We've always been awarded a victory meal after our battles. No danger for us and my control has gotten very good over the years. Besides, I came into this in good condition, well-fed and with plenty of supplements. The captives here might not have been in the best of condition when they arrived. Add that to the hardship of the infection and the trauma to their bodies, and the need to heal would burn up any reserves they might have. They'd be voracious and confined with only the other beings in their cavern."

She'd watched Bharguest all the same. Victory meal or no, the preference for live prey might override his already-questionable loyalties to teammates. He'd eat a person if it would mess with another person's mind. It was becoming clear his loyalty only went as far as his use of a person for entertainment purposes.

"How were the injections given?" Was there a different mode of delivery from the method used on her years ago?

"Hypoinjection in the meaty portion of the arm or leg. Sometimes whatever large muscle group is accessible if the victim was conscious and struggling." The smaller alien approached while the big one gave the answer. There might still be someone home behind the vacant mask after all. "The injection site is obvious, a large circular mark."

Ah, well, her captors must have decided to stylize the hypoinjection tools after stealing the technology after all. Most of those types liked to put a personal twist on the intellectual property to make it their own. Besides, hadn't Bharguest told her a single injection site was all it took? The branding had been a cosmetic change in mode of delivery.

"Your mark, it is the cat on your thigh." It might have been a question, but it lacked the proper inflection.

She treated it as a question anyway. "The original was a black panther, like a brand of what they intended to make me. The claw marks across it are my doing."

She'd attempted to stop the spread of the virus, bleed it out at the point of injection before the changes took hold. It hadn't worked, but the gouges scarred. Since the full change, she tended to heal clean and scar free. Those might be the last she'd ever have.

Course, several opponents had tried to give her new ones in this place. There might be a chance to test the theory yet.

"Many races hold the faith that the mind can guide the body." The big felid's words had turned thoughtful, and she wasn't sure he was talking directly to her anymore. "Many of those who don't survive are weak, driven mad by the change and they fail to comprehend what has happened to them. You, and your large companion, remained stable. The mental fortitude is admirable."

She almost laughed. Bharguest was there with them, but she wasn't sure she'd refer to him as her companion.

"Apparently, I've still a lot to learn." She twisted her

mouth into a wry grin. No harm in admitting that what Bharguest had been nagging her about was beginning to make sense, at least to her. "Comprehending what I am and accepting are two different things. In order to make the most of anything, there's a distinct need to quit swimming against the current of reality."

"Denial ain't just a river. Smart girl." Bharguest's voice sounded rusty. He must have been in a partial shift. "I can't wait to see how you do in the coming free-for-all."

She wasn't sure which was creepier, the idea of his commentary making sense to her, or that both of them knew the ancient pun.

"We will be entered in the event as well."

"Gather 'round boys and girls." Dev's voice whispered in Kaitlyn's ear.

Whatever else she'd wanted to say, it was no longer the time. Motioning to Rygard to follow, she moved to Tracer's side.

Rygard leaned in close to her, and Tracer threw his arm around Max's shoulders. They all got comfortable and waited for Dev's next communication.

The next few minutes dragged out in a strained silence.

"Hopefully, you've all had sufficient time to assemble."

Maybe Kaitlyn would talk to Skuld about creating an acknowledgement signal. Not any sort of audible to give away a two-way conversation, but at least a button to reply. The old one for "yes" and two for "no" could prove an elegant solution.

"There's an extraction plan in place."

Well good. Perhaps there'd be no need to go through the free-for-all.

"Our esteemed friend, Petrico-Calin the Fourth, devised it."

They were all doomed.

"Now Kat, before you go thinking along the lines of gloom and doom, his plan has potential." Dev hesitated, and she heard his telltale finger tap against the communication unit. "It's going to require a lot of work on your part to survive, but you've always shown a strong knack for it. I'll tell you his plan first, and then what I want you all to do. If we're lucky, we'll still get all of you out."

Even when her captain proved his genius, it was a good idea to keep an eye out for miracles.

CHAPTER 6

THE CHAIN HUNG down Rygard's hips, its heavy iron band fitted around his waist loose enough to sit low but too tight for him to shove down over his hip bones and off. It was annoying, at the very minimum. At least it didn't impede his range of motion for his arms or legs. Still, if the weight of the chain bothered him, he wondered how much it'd hinder Kaitlyn, similarly chained at the waist and connected to the rest of them by a heavy center hub.

"You okay with this?" He kept his voice low as they walked down the corridor.

Kaitlyn shrugged. "The guards seem to want me in humanoid form."

Rygard raised an eyebrow. Sounded too passive for her. "They couldn't make you change, not without causing physical damage. Why not go in there on your own terms?"

He did prefer fighting at her side when she was in human form. He was getting better at reading her intent during a fight, coordinating with her. In panther form, he couldn't anticipate her next moves.

But then, neither could their opponents.

"They'd have pushed Dev to put a collar on me so they could chain me to the hub the way Max is. Dev got away without it when we first came in, but the way they want the teams connected for this party? No way."

Rygard eyed the handler and Kx9. The big dog walked behind them as easily as if the chain hanging from his collar had been a leash. No big deal, apparently, but from what he knew of Kaitlyn, a very serious issue for her. Having listened to the debriefs Boggle had made available to him, he still didn't think he could understand the true extent of what she'd suffered. Her captain might, having been there with her for part of it, but what Rygard could understand on an intellectual level wasn't enough. Someday his girl would tell him more about the time she'd spent in captivity. Otherwise, he couldn't help her face her demons.

"Chained to one partner would have been enough of a challenge." Kaitlyn eyed the links between them. "It's the freaking five-way hub that makes this a clusterfuck."

Yeah.

The overseer hadn't been kidding when he'd told Dev he would be entering them as a single unit. Each of them was chained at the waist, Max at the collar, to a central point. They'd taken a few moments coming out of their cavern simply to figure out how much distance each of them needed to walk comfortably without the links or hub dragging on the ground. Rygard had been subtly moving to and fro as they walked, getting used to Kaitlyn on his right and Tracer following behind him. What truly worried him was Bharguest on the other side of Kaitlyn.

"Clusterfuck? Nah. This'll be fun." Bharguest stalked along diagonally behind Kaitlyn. "You have me at your back, after all."

She didn't glance over her shoulder at him as she

continued down the corridor at an easy walk. "Last I checked, you don't play well with others. And you tend to kill your playmates."

"Aw, I have played a little rough at times." Bharguest chuckled. "None of them could hold their own. You, at least, have a chance in what's to come."

"So you say." Rygard couldn't keep from biting off the words, even if he knew it only amused the other man. "You've had all sorts of hints for her, but I don't hear any constructive commentary."

"She's a sharp girl. I don't need to spell too much out for her. Where would the fun be?"

How Bharguest could find this hellhole fun was beyond Rygard, but then, the truth of it was that the man had come back, willing and eager too. Partially because Kaitlyn was interesting to him, and mainly because this place was his playground.

"They put some thought into the bindings." Tracer's voice floated over Rygard's shoulder. "The thing around Kaitlyn's waist is tight enough, I don't think she'd slip out of it whether she made a full shift to panther form or not."

"It's a snug fit." Kaitlyn shrugged. She still wore his shirt. The rules allowed combatants to fight naked, but she preferred not. She'd also found some extra strips of fabric early on to fashion underpants and bind her breasts. She didn't want to leave her most private parts exposed when she was fighting, both for the emotional and physical vulnerability she'd experience going without.

It's damned annoying, she'd said. *I'd knock myself out with these flying free.*

Rygard hadn't been able to hide his grin despite her snarl. She was well-endowed when it came to her breasts.

"Human, panther, so far you've mostly been one or the

other." The humor had gone out of Bharguest's voice, and it sounded creepier toneless. "Get more creative. We talked about it earlier."

"It's not like she can change into some other animal." Rygard couldn't stop himself from snapping at the other man.

Bharguest chuckled, probably to get a rise out of him. "With her control at the cellular level, she could do so much more than just be one or the other. She already does it all the time. All that's left is application in an even deadlier kind of way."

"Trying to make another serial killer?"

"Looking to see something amusing become a thing of violent beauty."

A shiver ran down Rygard's spine at the reverent tone. Tracer cleared his throat, looking every bit as weirded out. Kaitlyn just kept on walking.

"You all have been a pleasant surprise." The chain jerked at Rygard's waist, and he darted a look back at Bharguest. The man had his chain wrapped around one fist.

"You going along with the game plan then?" Kaitlyn sounded bored, but Rygard was pretty sure they all wanted to know the answer.

There was a pause, and Rygard figured they wouldn't get one.

A dull roar began to echo through the corridors, and light brightened the far end. They were getting close. The noise of the crowd, cheering and screaming, rose with every step.

Rygard almost missed Bharguest's answer.

"Sure. Until the time to play nice comes to an end."

"WE SEE YOU."

Normally, that'd indicate a serious failure on her part; however, Kaitlyn wasn't scouting or playing hide and seek.

From the moment she and the others emerged from the tunnel, the cheering had escalated until she couldn't sort out the voices or process anything but the deafening roar.

Anticipation rose in a wave and rushed through her. Her heartbeat quickened.

Skuld's tech matched the challenge of the crowds, and Dev's voice still came through clearly at her ear.

Unfortunately, only she and Max could hear him as they all stood spread out on the sands as far as their chains would allow them. The dog might be sharp, but how much would he act on based off what he heard?

"Spotted two humanoid groups. One is about fifty yards to your left, Kaitlyn. Eight survivors." Dev delivered the information in a quick, terse undertone. Then his voice picked up to normal speaking volume. He must not have been standing in a secure location. "Interesting group over there, way on the other end of the arena from mine. Badger, what're the odds on that group of humans? Close to a dozen of them, and they look not too worn out. Think they have a chance?"

She drew in deep breaths. Anger, desperation, and the metallic tang of fear filled the air directly around them. Closing her eyes and parting her lips, she tasted sand and sweat on the air.

It was humid on the floor of the huge stadium. The sand beneath her feet shifted. It was deep, more than a mere inch or so of covering. She could dig in, gain traction on it. An unwary opponent could twist and lose their footing on it.

Good.

"Well now, it'll be interesting to see how the human-based mutations do out there." Dev was continuing his conversation with Badger and her. "I do like the underdogs. Mine surprised everyone. But those other teams, their trainers act like they dropped their property in there as fodder. I'd be interested to see how they hold up as units. Some of 'em look to be trained to at least move in formations, especially the one nearer my group. Not sure how effective they'll be though. They're looking pretty ragged."

Kaitlyn nodded. She opened her eyes and scanned the area around her. A strange calm settled over her. Combat was coming, and she savored the anticipation.

First, she needed to identify allies and enemies. Her captain was relying on her.

"To our left." She didn't gesture, but Rygard's head turned. "Do you recognize any of them?"

He straightened, hands clenched. "Barely."

But they'd found them.

"Well then, the question is whether they'll recognize you." She stood her ground when he would have moved toward them. "Not until the signal to start goes off. We're going to have to hope their training holds and they follow your lead in the middle of everything."

Bharguest clicked his tongue. "No need to give away the game just yet. Got to kill a few first. Then see if you all survive."

Kaitlyn suppressed a shudder. And then she set her jaw. It hadn't been a shudder of revulsion. Bharguest's excitement had resonated.

Flex fingers. Keep claws retracted, for now. But be ready. Watch for the soft spots, points of vulnerability.

She swallowed hard. Quick kills, for all of them. If she

was going to embrace becoming a monster, she wouldn't be the kind of monster who enjoyed cruelty.

The announcements had started—hard to comprehend over the ongoing shouts of the crowd. All the poor souls standing on the sands waited for the bells, the signal to start. Anything else meant less than nothing.

"Ready." Tracer might have said the word to assure himself as much as the rest of the team.

She'd have to trust the dog to cover his master's weak side. But she'd keep an eye on him if possible. She could tell herself it was only for Skuld, but it wasn't.

The bells rang. Different from the ones she'd heard below ground in the pits and cages. These were bigger, and the deep sound drowned out the screaming of the onlookers. Vibrated in her sternum.

A half dozen scrawny reptilian slaves ran screaming toward them in a desperate charge, too frightened to stand and wait for death to come to them. A moment of pity squeezed in her belly.

Kaitlyn pivoted slowly, keeping the rest of the stadium in her peripherals as she watched them come. Half-stumbling, they ran toward her team, each of them focused on a different member.

Shame. If they'd all targeted her, they might have had a longer life span. Hey, a minute or two counted.

Two engaged her as the rest went for Rygard or one of the others. Laughable. She crouched low and knocked their feet out from under them with a leg sweep. She got to her feet, taking care to keep clear of her own chain while they floundered in theirs. Their panic kept her attention as they thrashed. Her teammates yanked the chains to either side as they met their own aggressors. Bharguest caught his attacker by the throat and lifted the assailant with a single hand.

When the attacker's scream cut off, she figured Bharguest had crushed a windpipe.

A quick kill. Relief washed through her. She didn't want to know how she'd feel watching Bharguest take his time.

Rygard took on his with a flurry of strikes to the face and body. Quick and devastating, the force of his attack sent his opponent reeling back into the mess of slaves. They all became fouled in their chains. One cried out as a chain wrapped around his leg and flipped him on his back.

"Make it clean, if you need to." Bharguest's words snapped across the roar of the crowds. "But don't leave them alive to come at us again."

No blade to make it easy. They'd all been sent in bare-handed.

When one of her attackers found his footing and charged her again, she drove him back with a kick to the chest. The crowds in the stadiums screamed in delight. Then she darted in, closing the space before he could regain his balance.

Clean, merciful.

Some of the onlookers were throwing pieces of fabric and flowers down on them. A tribute to the violence.

She landed a left jab, then a right hook, then let the momentum carry her into a turn, dancing for the audience. Her spinning kick caught him in the side of the head with crushing force. He fell to the ground as she turned back, unwinding the chain at her waist.

She couldn't spin more—not enough give in the chain. And the binding around her waist remained too tight to slide. She growled in frustration.

The other fool to engage her stared at his fallen companion. If he ran, she couldn't go after him until her team finished dispatching their opponents. But she wanted him to run. The panther in her loved a chase. Craved it.

Instead, she feinted back and gave the men on her team slack in the chains.

Desperation flared in the reptilian's face. His mouth twisted into a horrible grimace. He lifted his lip and bared what few teeth he had left.

Anger crashed through her. How dare he? As if she was a herd beast, easily tempted into charging? A growl rumbled from deep within her chest. She crouched but didn't move. If he wanted death, he could come to her.

He gave in first. Fear drove him forward as his teammates were dying around him. He ran toward Kaitlyn screaming, arms up, hands in a sad parody of claws.

Real claws flashed from her hands. She grinned as her fingertips burned with the pain of the shift. A fierce glee bloomed inside her. She darted in low as he charged her and then faded to the left at the last moment. Her uppercut caught him in the gut. The power of it drove her hand into soft tissue and up into his thoracic cavity.

With practice, she'd be able to close her hand around an opponent's heart someday.

Not this time.

She yanked back her hand, and the man fell to his knees clutching his abdomen. By the time he toppled to the sand, he was dead.

Not clean, that. But it'd been quick.

The chains were proving to be a pain in the ass. Not a surprise.

Even if she'd been careful not to become fouled in her own, the dead man's chain caught on Bharguest's. Her teammate reached down with a hiss, picked up the dead body, yanked it to clear his bindings, and then threw it at what remained of the attackers.

At least the first group.

Another group rushed them from Kaitlyn's right. Several attacked Tracer, but Max did a good job of guarding his injured side. Relief cooled her temper a fraction. She paused a precious moment to eye the hub and chains before taking a quick step forward and grabbing up the slack of hers. As one attacker struggled to fend off Max with upraised arms, he gave her his back. Mistake. She wrapped her chain around his neck and gave it a decisive jerk. His neck snapped and his stinking body fell to the ground.

Ugh. Had he smelled of piss and rot before he'd died?

"Back up." She barked out the command to the others. "Too many bodies underfoot."

The others inched toward the edge of the arena, each of them involved in fending off idiots, none of them having trouble holding their own, yet. Once she had them all on clear footing again, she risked a look beyond their immediate range of influence.

The likeliest group was close. A few more steps and they'd be within earshot, for humans too.

"Bharguest."

The big man turned to her, teeth bared. "You going to tell me something soft? Like disable and not kill?"

He had two by their chains, and the scrawny slaves pummeled useless fists against his arm and shoulder. One sank teeth into his wrist. Spittle flew from their mouths, no sense left in their eyes.

Her gut twisted. Bile rose up to the back of her throat, burning. She saw a reflection of what she was becoming in the monster standing next to her.

Survive first. Find peace with what we've done after.

"Make neat piles." She turned away a quarter turn. In this kind of chaos, giving him her back wasn't wise.

These were easy kills. Her panther aspect growled and snapped. Some of these died smiling. Death could be a sweet release, maybe? She wondered.

More important issues nagged her. Where were the real warriors?

"DeSarto!"

That was a name she recognized. The chain at her waist jerked as Rygard lunged for his friend. He didn't get too distracted though, taking out an attacker on his right as he went.

"Who the fuck?" DeSarto had blood on his hands. Well, paws. Maybe they were still hands—hard to tell under the white tufts of fur growing from his black skin. Some sense still lurked in his dark eyes. "What the hell are you doing here, Rygard?"

"Forget that. Get with us. We're here for all of you." Rygard's gesture swept to include Kaitlyn and the rest of the team.

As DeSarto opened his mouth to respond, a batch of aliens rushed Kaitlyn. She drove the first back with a front kick as Bharguest snagged another right off his feet. Rygard took a third down with a crushing kick to the knees. Max hamstringed a fourth.

Kaitlyn wasn't sure how. Someone's chain had caught her behind the legs. The world tilted backward. She tried to bring her knees to her chest, turn her backward fall into a complete flip to land on her feet. But the chain caught her left foot, fouled her balance, and she landed flat on her back.

Air left her chest in a whoosh. Her vision went black and then returned in a burst of sparks.

Too vulnerable.

She reached above her shoulders, planted her hands in the sand behind her head, and shoved. As she did a kip-up to regain her feet, the heavy chain wrapped around her ankle yanked her foot out from under her. Shit. Dropping into a crouch to keep from losing her footing again, she saw the aliens. Two insectoids held the chain, mandibles gnashing with the effort. Rage seared through her.

She snarled.

They'd caught her by surprise. Still, the two of them on the other end lacked the strength to hold her. Pathetic beings, trembling, smelling of acid and fear. She couldn't immediately make out their gender, but it didn't matter. Not here. The muscles in her left thigh and calf burned in protest as she yanked her leg back. Sharp pain exploded in her ankle and lanced all the way up to her hip. The two insectoids lost their own footing and fell forward.

Mine.

In an instant, she was on them. Never bothering to stand back up on two feet, she extended claws again from her human hands and swiped one alien across the face and the other across the neck. She pounced on the first, grabbed one side of its mandibles, and twisted its head forward. The burn of the shape change in her jaw was there and then gone, and when she bit deep into the insectoid's neck, it was with a leopard's force. Its exoskeleton gave way with a loud *crack.*

Its companion beat at her shoulder and shouted at her in a high-pitched series of squeals. When she lifted her head and bared her teeth, its multifaceted eyes whirled in shades of red and yellow. She kicked back at it hard with both feet. Her clawed toes caught it in its unarmored midsection. Rags shredded, and her hand sank deep into the soft tissue of its abdomen. The whirling in its eyes slowed and faded as its eyes glazed over in shock. The insectoid tipped onto its back, staring as its own entrails spilled out into the sand.

The burn in her jaw and at her toe tips only made her angrier. It took another precious second to disentangle herself from their chain.

Rygard and Bharguest had covered her and were each holding their own. Max had a limp, and Tracer had taken a hit to his weak side. Blood soaked his clothes, and as she slid in beside him, she could hear his wet cough. Not good.

Another moment passed and the field around them was clear of attackers.

"Up." Rygard shouted orders to his newly found men. "We head up into the stands, there."

His unit had a soldier down. Another was tied up in dragging their fallen comrade. They wouldn't leave a soldier behind, but the blasted chains were making things crazy complicated.

Thunder rumbled through the stadium. Tremors ran through the sand beneath her feet. Gates rose at several points around the edge. From each emerged a new threat, all of them armed. One rode in on a chariot; another was mounted on some horned beast. A half a dozen new players entered the field. The real warriors had entered the ring.

"Son of a bitch." The curse came through on the comm in a mutter.

Yup. Dev was probably pissed his team had been dropped out in the arena from the start like the other slave meat. Mostly because they'd all be more tired now.

"Plan doesn't change. Clean up what you can and get clear." .

She nodded. He'd see her acknowledgement.

It was Bharguest who engaged first.

A heavily furred opponent charged them on what looked to be a six-legged horse, if horses were saber-toothed. He swung a huge long-handled sledgehammer, almost catching Tracer in the back of the head. The trainer ducked in time, but barely. The rest of them tightened up back-to-back. Rygard's soldiers did the same, leaving enough space between their groups to give them room to fight.

Chained as they were, and unarmed, they'd all have to get a little more creative.

The rider continued his charge to the end of the arena and wheeled his steed around to come at them again. Several slaves fell under the hooves of the mount; others met with the sledgehammer, landing in the sand bleeding and broken.

On the horse's second pass, Bharguest reached out and caught hold of the sledgehammer. She heard something pop in her teammate's arm with the strain. But the sudden move unseated their attacker, landing him flat on his back in the sand.

She pounced. Dismounted, the opponent wore little armor. It took one slash to the neck to finish him.

"Kaitlyn!"

She turned at the sound of Rygard's voice, but he'd been too slow. She'd been too slow.

Bharguest had the sledgehammer in his hands, raised high in the air. In an arc too fast for human eyes to see, it came down.

She stared for a split second. One link of the chain attaching her to the hub was shattered. One was enough.

"Go." Bharguest laughed then. The sound of it had nothing to do with sanity. "Clear a path and let's see what you can do."

CHAPTER 7

SOMETHING SNAPPED LOOSE INSIDE KAITLYN.

She stared down at the broken chain with wide eyes, then dropped her mouth open slightly as she panted for breath. Hot. The taste of blood and death hit her tongue. She snapped her mouth shut.

Free.

Erratic movement caught her eye. Prey ran everywhere.

"Well, Badger, I'd wager we're going to see some interesting things in the next couple of minutes," Dev's voice whispered in her ear, bringing her back. Again.

Steadied, she looked up, past the chaos on the sands around her. The crowds watching rose up in the stadium seating, brought to their feet by the carnage. There were a dozen tiers of bloodthirsty onlookers shouting and cheering. And above them were the private boxes. She scanned left and right until she saw the blue light wink at her.

A tiny laser light was streaming from a ring on Dev's hand, harmless and easy to miss. Dev was her very own beacon, lighting a path through a sea of not-so-innocent bystanders who had better get out of the way or die. She had a mission to complete.

The deafening noise of the crowd faded to the background. The immediate sounds of fighting around her heightened. Her vision sharpened, becoming crystal clear as she made a controlled shift of her eyes to cat.

She darted ahead of her team. The first slave to bar her path died before he hit the ground, his throat slashed by her clawed hand. Another came at her, his desperation a miasma clogging her nose. She whipped around and caught him along the side of his head in a spin kick strong enough to crack his jaw. A third rushed her with an earsplitting shriek. Kaitlyn sidestepped the woman's outstretched arms and silenced her with a backhanded strike.

The cries of the wounded and shouts of fear came to her, and she passed them by. She catalogued them but ignored anything on the periphery. What mattered was her immediate sphere of influence, and in this battle, her range was limited to her pouncing distance.

One of the real warriors moved to intercept her, swinging a spiky ball on the end of a long chain. She grinned, watching its orbit. It took too long to make a full revolution. He relied on it to keep his victims at a distance until the thing smashed into them.

Fool.

She didn't slow her pace as she neared him. Instead, she leaped into the air, covering several meters. She landed on his shoulders with her knees. Before he could raise his arms to pry her off, she drove her elbows into the top of his skull. She hopped clear as he fell to his knees. Blood trickled down the sides of his forehead and into wide-open unseeing eyes. He toppled over, maybe dead, definitely not a threat any longer.

The weaker slaves stumbled to get out of her way, their eyes wide with fear. Their mouths twisted in panic as they scrambled. A tiny part of her shriveled. Some of those slaves took on the faces of old schoolmates. Half-forgotten expressions of terror and rejection flitted across her vision.

She'd spent a long time pretending this part of her didn't exist.

Shaking her head, she set her jaw and flexed her claws. She had a mission to complete, and she'd use every skill she had to do it. Cry later.

A few more steps carried her to the wall, and she took the height of it at a run. She caught the top edge and pulled herself up in a smooth motion, then crouched on the top for a brief moment.

A guard rushed at her. She leaped into the air and landed back on the wall, behind him. Without coming out of her crouch, she pivoted and landed a spinning kick to the back of his head. He didn't make a sound as he pitched over the side and down to the melee below. Onlookers scrambled to get away from her. Frightened noncombatants, not worth her attention. There were too many opponents to take down first.

"Careful, Kat. Almost dropped a body onto Rygard's head. He might not thank you for it."

Dev must not have had too many listeners nearby anymore.

A different kind of rumble shook the stadium. The stone of the wall beneath her hands and feet trembled. Her claws gave her better purchase, but other beings in the stands lost their footing. Dust and rubble fell from the ceiling high above them.

Dev's curse could've stained the air around him blue. Though when he spoke into the comm, he'd regained his composure. "Well, seems Petrico-Calin is running on a slightly accelerated timeline from the original briefing."

Son of a . . . well, she'd not want to insult any female unfortunate enough to have birthed Petrico-Calin anyway. Air support wasn't supposed to have arrived until they were all clear in the risers, not vulnerable out in the stadium sands.

"Rygard." Maintaining a partial shift, his name came out rough, as almost a cough. Her lover turned anyway. "Get them up. Now. We've got no time. No time."

He didn't respond to her, only turned and barked out orders of his own.

Bharguest still had the damned sledgehammer and was setting the others loose one at a time, in between gleeful killing blows to whatever slave had the misfortune to stumble into his path.

Speaking of which, she needed to finish clearing one.

Many of the guards had turned away, distracted by the mass hysteria. This wouldn't be about fighting them at the moment.

A thought triggered pain that seared its way down her spine and outward to every extremity. Her muscles stretched and snapped into a different configuration. Her bone structure dissolved and reformed. Standing in panther form, she let out a roar.

Onlookers screamed. They'd thought themselves safe up in the stands, and suddenly the carnage had come to them. Aliens fell backward, dropped to fours or sixes, and scuttled out of reach.

She leaped to a higher row of seating and shifted in midair. The pain of it almost blinded her. Half-human, half-cat, she let out a bloodcurdling scream of her own and swiped at a merchant so wrapped in luxury fabrics and furs, he couldn't flee. Gold chains fell to the ground as the male squealed and shambled away.

Another guard finally made his way to her, and she shifted back to full human. Rygard's shirt was in shreds, though the bindings over her breasts held for the time being. Good. As he approached, she dove into a handspring and caught him around the neck with her legs. Her momentum swung him around and snapped his neck.

She'd shifted fully back to panther again by the time she landed on the ground. A bounding leap, and she landed on another guard's back. The reptilian flailed as she bit deep into the back of its skull and crushed its spine. Different enemy, different set of natural weapons to take it out. She had plenty of targets with which to play, experiment.

If she took any hits, they didn't slow her, so she didn't take notice. None of the beings she met directly scored a hit on her. Laser fire burned past her ear at one point. The scent of scorched fur burned her nose. A moment later, she rinsed away the scent in blood as she buried her fangs deep into the side of a reptilian guard's neck.

Shift after shift, from panther to human and combinations in between, she moved up the tiers of seating. Every change gave her the advantage of shock and surprise against her opponents. Merchants, traders, and gamblers struggled to get away from her rampage. Guards came for her, fighting against the tide of those fleeing.

Blood, fear, and anger saturated the air around her. Her predator instinct to chase, run down her prey, was overridden by the continual attacks. The guards were her real enemies. They had to be eliminated to make way for her teammates. It was important to get high up into the stands, then pick a spot and hold her ground until the rest arrived.

"That's good, Kat. You're there."

The comm still worked despite the repeated changes to her form. She let out a panther scream before slashing another opponent with claws.

"They're almost all up on the wall."

Slow humans.

An animal sounded a challenge. The call was like a trumpet, but the thing charging at her had six legs and a horn on its nose. Beady eyes targeted her from a triangular head, armored and made like a battering ram. The beast looked like a Terran rhino. She shifted to panther form but didn't leap out of its path. Instead, she crouched low between the stadium seats.

A rider sat astride but carried no major weapons, only a club. He wasn't the immediate worry.

Stumbling over chairs, the animal swung its head side to side, slamming into the seats and sending them flying in all directions. As it reached her, she darted up, closed her jaws around its muzzle, and wrapped her forearms around its head. With all her strength, she yanked downward.

The sudden addition of her body weight combined with its forward momentum was too much for the animal. The thing flipped over her and landed hard on its back with a loud *crack*. It cried out, the sound of a stricken animal, and only the front pair of legs pawed at the air.

A wiry form landed on her before she released the crippled mount.

The rider.

The club rose and fell. He landed half a dozen hits across the back of her head and shoulders before she got her feet under her. Little bugger was quick. Good thing he wasn't strong. Lying still, she feigned unconsciousness. Her attacker paused. Warm fluid seeped through her fur, and the acrid scent of urine stung her nose.

Bastard was pissing on her.

Too early for a victory celebration like that, but she'd better make her move before he decided to defecate too.

She rolled on her back and shifted as she did. Her legs lengthened as her clawed feet caught the skinny rider in the abdomen. She completed her move and stood as a human again. His intestines spilled out before his face could register surprise. Her right hook knocked him over and he stayed down. It might not have been necessary, but hell, it felt good.

"Tell me he didn't do what I think he did."

Good thing she couldn't answer her captain right then.

Explosions rocked the stadium. She dropped down behind a few seats as the ceiling finally gave way. A shuttle hovered above the new entrance to the Colosseum. Their shuttle. Dozens of tiny projectiles launched from the shuttle's missile bays and landed on the sands with sharp pops followed by ominous hisses.

"Funny how timing seems to be all sorts of fubar."

Yeah, Dev didn't sound overly distressed though. Good thing they were ahead of schedule too. Her chest burned as she sucked in air. Thick clouds of gas were issuing from the cans, but they weren't the correct color for standard crowd control. The screams of the remaining slaves weren't right— they weren't falling unconscious. The sounds were of agony and death. Petrico-Calin must have ordered more permanent measures. Not right. Their own men could've been caught in the gas.

"You smell." Bharguest's gravelly voice didn't make her hair stand on end this time. Maybe she had too much adrenaline coursing through her.

"Let's not talk about what I smell like." She curled her lip and bared her teeth at him.

He chuckled. "Every fight has its sacrifices."

Slaves were clearing the wall now, along with their own teams. They were trying to escape the deadly gas hanging low over the sand.

Bharguest stood with her, back-to-back. He swung his sledgehammer in an almost-casual arc, catching another attacker and sending him tumbling back down the stands.

"Don't slow our soldiers down." She watched Rygard's unit struggle to reach their vantage point.

Some of them were still able-bodied. All of them were in humanoid form. Well, mostly, if you didn't count fur. A few gripped the walls with claws and bared elongated teeth at nearby slaves. Others she watched with a predator's gaze and found more prey than threat. It wasn't just about the injuries and bloodstained rags. It was about the hopeless, glazed look in their eyes and the grim set of their mouths. They were resigned to die here.

She could help the slaves. And not in the way she'd originally come here to. Death was a kind of mercy.

"Are they yours yet, these soldiers? Do you feel responsible for them?" Bharguest swung the sledgehammer up above them both and brought it down on a row of seats. A pack of slaves still chained together changed their direction and headed up and away from them.

A lot to say there for sheer intimidation factor.

"They're Rygard's soldiers."

She watched as Rygard helped his last man over the wall and up the stands. Tracer struggled only a few steps ahead of him, Max at his side. The Kx9 handler moved like a dead man walking, with blood trickling down the corner of his mouth to his jaw. Bad, but maybe not hopeless. As long Tracer managed to stay on his feet, she thought she had a chance of fixing him. For Skuld.

The shuttle descended through the gaping hole in the roof, turning in a slow rotation as if hesitating.

"The team is scrambling to start the extraction." Dev's words were clipped, short. "I'm leaving my position in two minutes."

Another moment of self-inflicted agony burned through her as she shifted to full panther form and bounded down the tiers. Bharguest could hold their ground for a moment. The soldiers needed her help covering their retreat.

The Colosseum might have been in chaos, but it wasn't much different from the madness of the arenas. The danger came in waves, the combatants moving in predictable flows. She watched the patterns, intercepted when Rygard's soldiers were threatened.

Too many responded in fear and anger. They struck out at anything within reach, including her. No matter. None of the blows landed, and her claws found targets in their foes. Flesh and blood tore under her fangs. Bones snapped.

"Annah kai al!"

The words had no meaning for her.

"She has the blood rage."

Those didn't make any sense either.

One of the bigger warriors, an armed gladiator, tossed a net over her. Lightning seared through her hands and arms as she shifted, grabbed the net, and turned with it before it landed. A twist of her wrist kept the thing spinning, and she sent it out low, entangling two Sketz'es guards. Movement flashed at the periphery of her vision, and she launched skyward. Her leap took her in an arc, and she landed hard on the gladiator's shoulders, then rotated as the force of her landing took them both to the ground. His neck broke with a satisfying snap as they hit plascrete, and she rolled clear.

And there it was, an ebb in the flow of battle.

"*Maa ta tomo*. Friend."

Not a word for the killing field.

The speaker repeated the words, hands held before him. Unsafe for him to do so. Risky. But there he stood, with another figure crouched at his side watching the madness around them. She knew the pair. They'd made it off the sands.

"Come, little one. Your friends are gathered above us. Let go the blood rage."

"Kaitlyn!" Rygard's voice.

"Kat, let's go!" Her captain.

She straightened from her crouch but didn't let go of her current shape. She wanted hands with claws, required the greatest flexibility from both her aspects. Debris fell from the ceiling, and random laser fire still shot across the amphitheater from the private boxes. Had to be trainers and slave owners. Guards had better aim. They needed to make themselves scarce before people with real weapons training arrived.

The big felid had already begun climbing the stands, his companion at his heels. She followed suit, leaving room between her and them. Clustered groups caught more attention. The only others left on the stands were straggling slaves and injured bystanders. The rest had fled or were dead.

The shuttle couldn't land on the risers, but Dev had anticipated the issue. A gondola lowered by crane came from the side door. Most of the survivors of Rygard's team had already been lifted along with Badger.

She'd been lost in the fighting too long.

As they arrived, Rygard gave the felids a long look. For a moment, everything stopped.

Dev had a rifle lifted to his shoulder, his head bent to the sight scope. "Whatever it is, we don't have time for it."

He fired once. A man far up in the boxes screamed and fell from the broken viewing window.

"Without them, I'd still be down there. You'd have had to leave me." She motioned for the two felids to board the gondola. Bharguest, Tracer, and Max were holding a perimeter.

"Better than 'they followed me home, can I keep them?' I guess. Get 'em aboard." Dev understood. He always did.

She turned to Rygard. "Go with them. You're the only one who knows everybody. You're going to be needed up on the shuttle."

No arguments—not in combat. Rygard handed her a gun and got on board. She shifted the rest of the way back to human and gingerly held the weapon.

"You did learn how to shoot one, didn't you?"

Well . . . "Trained, yes. Am I good? I'd rate myself as *needs improvement.*"

"Shit!"

The gondola rose and almost reached the shuttle door when the air around them exploded.

Kaitlyn crouched low, covering her head. Rygard's shirt hung by a few threads, and the binding around her breasts wouldn't hold much longer. If she had to engage in hand-to-hand combat again, she'd shift to panther form. Fighting nude in human form was doable, but not preferred. Her breasts, especially her nipples, were too sensitive, and she would make a mistake trying to avoid catching a nipple on something. In some ways, it was damned easier to be a cat.

A moment later, she peered up at the shuttle, watched

the gondola sway wildly. Hands reached out to catch the top, haul the passengers into safety.

"Complication, Captain." Dev didn't look up at her, but crouched low beside her, head still bent to the scope. Another man fell from a nearby balcony.

"Damned idiot was lobbing concussion grenades. Going to bring the whole place down around our heads."

For her part, she got off two shots in the general direction of the oncoming guards. They ducked and took refuge behind some upturned chairs.

"Shuttle might've already done that." She watched as the men above wrestled with the gondola and crane. "Crane's busted. They're going to be throwing down towlines in a minute."

True to her prediction, Specs peered over the edge and shouted something. Too much noise all around to understand, but she figured she already knew what was coming.

Specs tossed a black bundle out.

"Retrieve. I've got you covered." Dev sighted and fired, paused, and did it again.

She darted out into the open and grabbed the package. A quick slash with her claws and she had the bundle loose and was pulling apart the harnesses. One was tagged with a bright orange patch, its configuration obviously not for a man.

"Max!" She called for the dog first because it'd take the longest to get the thing on him. When the big dog ignored her, she left a normal harness next to Dev and tossed another over to Bharguest. "Tracer, get Max's harness on him."

The first towline dropped. Bharguest didn't bother with the harness. Instead, he looped the line over the toe of his boot and took a grip with one hand. As they raised him upward, he shot in all directions.

Who'd been crazy enough to give him a firearm?

She fired off another series of shots in the direction Bharguest had been shooting. Considering how bad she was, the same question could be asked of her.

"You're up next, Kat." Dev shrugged into his harness.

She slipped into her own. Tracer and Max were backing their way toward where she and Dev crouched. Their perimeter of safety was already crumbling.

Slaves and guards alike converged on their position. The shuttle was like a beacon. For some of them, a wild chance of safety. For others, a really big target.

The towline came down and fell across her shoulders. Stars exploded across her sight with the impact of the heavy rope. A growl sounded, then a shout. Dev cursed.

She blinked furiously to clear her vision and fumbled around trying to get the hook fastened on her harness. Suddenly Tracer was there, batting her hands away. He not only got her hook set in the steel loop, but he hooked a second to it as well.

Squinting, she got a good look at his face. Blood ran down one side, and what skin showed through was a ghastly gray under a thin film of grit and sand. More blood trickled from the corner of his mouth, and a wet wheezing accompanied each breath he took.

Shit.

"Take Max. Take care of him for me." The plea in his voice made her heart stop.

No. Skuld . . .

"He won't . . ." The protest died, but she was certain the dog wouldn't come with her.

Tracer coughed, spit more globs of blood. "Go, buddy. Go with Kaitlyn."

Oh no . . .

Max lunged against the harness, almost yanking her off her feet. The towline tightened and lifted them both. Not knowing what else to do, the big dog hanging heavy from the hook at her waist, she got a grip on the back of his harness and steadied him as they rose.

Tracer stood for a moment, watching them both.

"Stay with her, Max. Stay with her."

A pack of Sketz'es charged their position down below. She tried to shoot into the group of them. At least one fell with a scream. She couldn't keep firing though, not as they got closer to Dev and Tracer. She cursed and stopped. Her shots were going too wild, would do more harm than good.

Max barked again, struggled. She flipped the safety back on the gun and held on to his harness as best she could with both hands. Another towline went sailing down past her.

Tracer shouted something, a challenge. He rushed out of cover and into the oncoming group of Sketz'es. Her heart seized. Max uttered a tortured sound, part howl, part desperate bark.

"No!"

Dev fired another shot and another. Then he hooked the towline to his harness and raised his rifle to his shoulder again. Hands grabbed Kaitlyn, hauled her and Max inside the shuttle, and shoved them to the side. Specs tossed her line back out the side of the shuttle, just in case there was a miracle for Tracer.

"Keep that thing under control!"

She didn't know who issued the command, didn't know if he referred to her or to Max, but she wrapped her arms around the German Shepherd Dog's chest and held him back. Otherwise, Max would've jumped right back out the shuttle side door and fallen to his death. Max lunged, fought her hold, but he didn't bite her. She held strong, tried her best not to break anything on either of them as she did.

Tracer's face rose up in her vision: the blood at the corner of his mouth, the whistling sound as he breathed. She hugged Max closer to her, heedless of the dog's growling and struggling. He might still bite her, but she wouldn't let him go after his master—not when Tracer had asked her to take care of him.

They had a hold of Dev, pulled him inside to safety, and at a grim nod from him, they closed the shuttle door.

CHAPTER 8

"WOW, you guys look like you need a good cup of coffee."

Kaitlyn narrowed her eyes at the hologram of Boggle. He had a talent for understatement. She and Rygard had taken time to shower and pull on ship suits, but Rygard hadn't shaved and the both of them were covered in scrapes and bruises.

She healed fast and clean, but not that fast.

"It was an intense mission, man." Rygard spoke over her shoulder from where he sat on her bunk. Close enough to be touching, but he wasn't.

Another twist added to the knot inside her that'd been growing since the free-for-all in the Colosseum.

"Data transfer incoming." She hit the send command on the control board.

"Receiving." Boggle's nimble fingers flew across his console. After a moment, he reached off-screen and lifted a handful of popcorn to his mouth. "So. Whatcha sending me?"

"In-depth reports," Rygard answered. "My entire team made individual reports to be included in the package to

Terran headquarters. The most detailed is DeSarto's. The rest, might not be as coherent. Consider this a . . . backup."

"Gotcha." Boggle's eyes darted back and forth. The rapid eye motion had been slightly unnerving the first time Kaitlyn had spoken to him via holo, but she'd come to learn it was just Boggle reading multiple displays. "Yeah no. Only a few communications coming through from Dev's ship. The military coding and security flags make the one you all care about kind of obvious. It's a little too small to contain all that data. The report the Terran military is getting is going to be light on the details."

"You're not hacking that communication are you?" Rygard's question came sharp, his concern evident.

Boggle coughed popcorn bits over his console. Hastily brushing them away, he shook his head. "N-no. Course not."

Kaitlyn twisted her lips to keep from smiling. "Your tip is plenty of help, Boggle. No need to dig anywhere dangerous."

Unless it was absolutely necessary.

"Okay, your reports are downloaded to my servers for safekeeping." He grabbed a bottle and took a swig from the strange nozzle.

"Is that a filter bottle?" Kaitlyn peered at the holo. "For water?"

"What? A man can't be properly hydrated?" Too defensive. Boggle might have been breaking into a fresh sweat. Hard to tell because he sweated a lot.

"Hydration is good." She cocked her head to the side, curious. "But you practically mainline coffee most of the day. I don't remember you having any taste for plain water."

Had she ever seen a blush start at the ears and spread across the face?

"A man can look to his health." Rygard's voice was full of amusement. "Things come up in life and little changes turn out to be pretty good."

A pause. Then Rygard's voice hardened. "Little changes. Nothing major, right?"

There was a guy thing passing between them, and Kaitlyn bubbled with questions. She kept a lid on them because Rygard gently tugged her ponytail.

"What? Nah. Just a friend made a suggestion and it couldn't hurt to give it a try. Water once in a while isn't bad and I figure it cuts down the creds I spend shipping in coffee. I mean, I only cut back a couple of cups a day. It's not like I gave it up or anything."

Good. Otherwise, Kaitlyn might not have any place to go for a good cup of brew the next time she stopped at Dysnomia Station.

"Seriously though, Rygard, it's good to see you safe and with all your body parts intact." Boggle shoved another batch of popcorn in his mouth. "Well, the parts that I can see. I'm assuming Kaitlyn checked over the rest."

She wasn't going to take the bait.

Rygard snorted. "It was a near thing too many times to count. You're welcome to view my report for the details, man."

Kaitlyn blinked once, slowly. Rygard's offer was unexpected.

Boggle swallowed hard and then took a big swig of water. When he looked back at them, his expression was somber. "I appreciate the trust."

"Last time I was on Dysnomia Station, we couldn't have made things right without you and this time, I'm guessing you had a few things to do with my rescue. Every time I've worked with you, you've proven yourself to be good people."

"You too."

Things were sounding awkward now. In a minute, one or both of them was going to clear his throat or use some other distraction tactic.

"Of note," she interrupted, before things got too maudlin. "We ran into more of those alien felids, Boggle. We got a name for the species yet? Any info on their home system or form of government?"

"Funny you ask." Boggle made a sliding motion across the bottom of his image. "I ran a search on them after your encounter here. They're not in the station logs. They didn't register a system of origin or species."

"So how did they circumvent the regulations requiring they log that data?"

Boggle shrugged. "Station officials are still looking into that. But then, they're investigating how an illegal shadow market the size of the one you shut down managed to establish itself in the first place."

"A good hacker would have a theory about our felid friends." Kaitlyn raised an eyebrow.

"Oh and I'm not just good." Boggle wiggled his thin eyebrows at her in return, catching her by surprise. He'd never returned such a sally in the past.

"You've got something, then." The amusement colored Rygard's voice. It was good to hear again.

"Duh." Several images superimposed themselves over Boggle's hologram. "The ship they registered was the same make and model as a standard Terran mercantile ship. And there was an ambassador clearance associated with the ownership identification. Enough of one that full credentials for captain or crew weren't required. Since their purpose for docking was logged as recreational and not commercial, there was minimal initial investigation."

Well, it might have been considered recreational if one considered a revenge hunt of Rygard and his unit a game. It was all in the point of view.

When the hell did her sense of humor start sounding like Bharguest's?

Boggle was still going on, lost in the data, his voice hushed as he studied his own displays. "They knew the station regs and used the approach that would provide them the fewest obstacles. These guys were good too. The security feed was tampered with so there's never a clear look at the crew. There's not even footage of you and Rygard and I know the two of you visited that ship." He cursed. "It's damned hard to tell where the splices are in the footage. I'm impressed."

And so was she. It'd take a lot to impress Boggle. She was betting he was going to spend the near future trying to either replicate what they'd done or manage to do better.

"We're going to need to get information on them soon though, whether we do it through technology or face-to-face." She chewed on her lower lip.

"Face-to-face?"

"Yeah. It's in Rygard's report. Not only did we come out of the thing with all his personnel more or less whole, but we came up heavy with a pair of the felids too."

She owed them for pulling her out of the lust for violence. The memory of it hung in her mind as a red haze flavored with the taste of blood and death.

"They're in guest quarters for now." Rygard shifted behind her, as if he'd jerked his head toward the door. "One was pretty civil on the shuttle and Captain Rishkillian agreed to allow them to send communication. We're guessing they're going to contact wherever home is and arrange for retrieval now that they've been rescued."

"Got to keep a close eye on the second one though." Kaitlyn sighed. "He suffered major trauma and I'm not so sure he'll come all the way back to the 'normal' way of thinking, at least for his species."

Could prove to be problematic, but hopefully not their problem. After all, it'd been the Colosseum and the Sketz'es that'd done it to him. If they could keep things peaceful aboard Dev's ship, the damaged felid might feel safe enough to remain passive until he could receive proper treatment from his own kind. She was walking proof that post-traumatic stress disorder could be mostly overcome, but she wasn't the best candidate to treat it.

"What're the odds you'd run into them again?" Boggle asked.

"Run a calculation algorithm on it." She shrugged. "Either way, they're calling home and will soon be gone. We've got to get Rygard and the rest of his unit back to the Terran solar system. I took blood samples from all the soldiers, including the ones infected. All have stabilized for now, and will survive, but they're in different stages of assimilating their mutations. I figured any research would need samples as early as possible to start trending the progression of the changes."

She reached forward to her own terminal and shot that file off to Boggle.

"Receiving."

She'd spoken briefly to each of the infected, an awkward pep talk as it were. Rygard had been with her, encouraging her, helping her tear open old scars to let out the pain beneath.

Of them all, Rygard's friend DeSarto seemed to have

the most control over his mutation. He was able to bring his form almost completely back to human, with only a few tufts of fur left on the backs of his hands. Interestingly enough, his fur wasn't white. Each hair was hollow and clear, giving the appearance of white, especially contrasted against his black skin. Kaitlyn had recommended he access databases for an animal from Old Earth called a polar bear.

DeSarto had recognized her and acknowledged what she'd done out there on the sands for them. The others were in various phases of shock, anger at what had happened to them, and relief at being rescued. It hadn't mattered what she'd said, only that they saw she'd already been through it, survived, and managed to remain sane.

Sort of.

"You need to get some rest, Kaitlyn." Boggle had stopped snacking, wasn't even looking at his various displays. Instead, his close-set eyes were fixed directly on her. "Rygard too, but you, you've still got thoughts running through your mind faster than lines of code running through my compiler."

It was then that Rygard really touched her. His hand settled on her shoulder, heavy and warm. "I'll see if I can get her to sleep, man. We'll try to get in touch with you again in the next few days."

"I'll keep an eye on communications traffic for you."

"Thanks."

"YOU HEARD THE GEEK." Rygard forced himself to get up from Kaitlyn's bunk when all he really wanted to do was wrap his arms around her. He settled for standing close enough for his thigh to brush her leg where she'd let it hang off the side. "You've been on the move since we got back. It's time for you to get some rest."

She stared at him for a long moment, those somber eyes of hers unreadable. Then she wrinkled her nose and rubbed the heel of her palm over one eye.

Did she realize how she could turn incredibly cute in the space between one second and the next?

"I swear I was too wound up to sleep before now." Raising her arms above her head, she reached for the ceiling in a long stretch.

And damn but she'd know what she was doing to him in a couple of seconds. Her sense of smell wouldn't miss it.

Right on cue, she let her arms fall into her lap and settled her gaze on him, the intensity of her regard searing straight through him. Whatever she was looking for, she wasn't finding it, because doubt clouded her gaze and her lashes dropped over her eyes.

Concern hit his chest harder than a physical strike, but he forced himself to wait. Let her come to him. She'd been cornered too many times this last mission.

She hesitated for a moment and then asked her question. "What are you going to do now?"

He'd meant to tell her one thing but changed his mind. "Depends on what you want me to do."

A slight crease appeared in her forehead. She was probably overthinking things. She wasn't good at telling him what she wanted yet. Not quite sure enough in knowing herself, his lady.

"I know what I want to do, but I want to give you space to decide." He held up a hand, wanting to get the next part in before she jumped to a conclusion. "Given the choice, I want to stay here with you, for the night. If you feel safer on your own, feel uncomfortable in any way, I can go bunk with my unit. It's okay. But if you want me to stay, don't go saying anything to try to prevent me from feeling obligated either. This isn't about that."

She blinked. It took her a minute to work through what he'd said, and well, he hadn't made much sense. But there it was, what was on his mind.

"You saw me down there."

Not what he expected her to say. He answered slow, cautious. "Yes."

"The shifting I did, I wasn't always panther."

"No."

"I wasn't always completely human either."

"No." Where was this going?

She took a deep breath, then let it out in a controlled sigh. "Somewhere in there, the line between human and panther blurred inside my head. Before, Dev helped me be human and I didn't think of being a panther unless I needed the skills and tools, like putting on a uniform with a specific set of gear. It was something I could tuck away and only bring out once in a while. But now . . ."

She looked down at her hands and he followed her gaze. Her human fingertips morphed before his eyes to claws and then back to fingertips. Her upturned hand showed the soft pink flesh of her palm change over, becoming darker and tougher—the beginning of the pad on the underside of a paw.

When he studied her face, she was biting her lip, her canines lengthened.

"Careful." He kept his tone gentle. She jerked anyway, possibly too sensitive and expecting censure from him. "Don't cut your lip or I'm going to have to kiss it better."

"You're not disgusted with me?" From the sound of her words, she was. "Not horrified by the animal I've become?"

"We're all animals, when you boil it down to the basic biologics. The one thing that place did was show me the kind of melting pot the universe is. The truth is, neither of us would've survived if you'd stuck with being human."

And hell if he enjoyed admitting Bharguest had been right.

"We're not in a life-and-death situation anymore." Her hands closed into fists. "And I don't think I can go back to being just human."

"You weren't when I met you anyway." He rested a knee on her bunk, placed his hands over hers. From what he'd been learning watching her and Max, he needed to stay on level with her. Even when what he wanted to do was settle down on his knees in front of her so he could look into her down-turned face. "We haven't seen the last of life-threatening situations either. It's what we do, darlin'."

There it was—the small upturn at the corners of her mouth as she tried not to smile in response to his playful tone. He reached around her and tugged at her ponytail holder until her hair fell loose.

"So as far as I'm concerned, you becoming a better killer is all to the good. Just keep that heart of yours too."

The deadly killer sitting on the bunk beside him wrinkled her nose again. Did she realize it was becoming a habit? "Wasn't quite where I was going with that."

"Maybe." He couldn't resist brushing a lock of dark hair to the side so he could see more of her face.

"You're okay with me being like this. I'm still working on it." She paused, her features going still. "You still want me?"

Those last words forced their way out in a whisper.

"You've reminded me and Boggle in the past, you can

smell arousal. You know I do." Gods, he wanted to kiss her. But he wouldn't—not until she was ready to believe him.

"That's physical." She turned her head to the side, her shoulders hunched. "Plus, I'm still in heat. You can't help pheromones."

"No." He reached for her, slipped a finger under her chin, and gently turned her to face him. "I can't. But I do have a brain and I'm attracted to a lot more than your body."

"You've seen me change, over and over again." Her voice came in a strained whisper. Tears welled up, threatened to break his heart. "You saw me kill, told me I was bordering on cruel."

"You stood back from it in the next fight. I saw. You decided not to be." He shook his head. "Every decision you make causes me to fall for you even harder. Doesn't matter what you change into or what uniform you wear. You are so beautiful, with so much heart, I can't get you out of my system. Don't want to."

She surged up into his arms before he could go on. He wrapped his arms around her and held her tight as shuddering sobs wracked her frame. She'd taken fistfuls of his shirt and was holding on with a fierce need.

As soon as it started, it was over. She pressed her face into his shoulder, taking in deep, measured breaths.

"Stay with me tonight?" She kept her face buried in his shirt as she asked.

Even with his encouragement, it must've taken a lot of courage for her to ask him. He'd guess he'd barely scratched the surface of how much she'd kept bottled up inside her.

"Kaitlyn."

When she looked up, doubt still darkened her gaze. He was done with words.

He bent his head, gave her plenty of time to pull away.

She didn't. When their lips met, he simply enjoyed the press of his mouth on hers. The way her lips softened under his and then parted tempted him more than anything else he could imagine.

Taking his time, he lifted his hand to the nape of her neck and encouraged her to tilt her head farther back as he teased her and let his tongue dance with hers. Tentative at first, she met him with shy strokes of her tongue. After a few moments, she grew more eager and her hands changed grip on his shirt, encouraging him to press his body along the length of hers.

He used his other hand to enjoy the curve of her, then grasp her tight behind. She nipped the corner of his mouth in response, and he deepened their kiss, careful not to crush her, not to push too far, too fast.

He'd missed her. Her scent was a heady combination of sweet and spicy, her lips soft, the taste of her mouth honeyed. He wanted to taste other parts of her.

A low growl rumbled up from Kaitlyn's chest, a strange vibration against his sternum where she pressed up against him. He paused, she froze, but then he only held her close and kissed her again.

"Frustrated, sweetness?"

She pulled away enough to look up at his face. Opened her mouth to say something, but no words came out.

"The growl is sexy. I don't think I want you going furry on me, but the growl is sexy." He watched her weigh his words, test for the truth with all her senses. Impatient, he raised an eyebrow. "What does it take to make you purr?"

Deep rose stained her cheeks. His breath caught in his throat. Beautiful.

She stepped away and he let her go. Before he could worry, she stopped, only a few inches away. Her hands rose up slow, hesitant, and unsealed her ship suit. Her eyes remained fixed low, her long lashes casting shadows over her cheeks. Her clothes fell around her ankles, caught by her ship boots.

He dropped to his knees, then placed his hands on her hips and gazed up the length of her. "I want to taste you."

She bit her lip. He loved the way she did that. When she placed her hands on his shoulders, he took that as permission.

Slow. Savor.

He pressed a kiss on the waistband of her lace panties, then another on the seam at her hip. When he hovered over the juncture between her thighs, her hands tightened on his shoulders. He took it as a sign she wanted more and pressed another kiss against her, then nipped at the delicate fabric. She jumped, and a tiny bit of moisture tinged her panties.

Grinning then, he hooked his fingers into her waistband and slid her underwear down her long legs. He helped her out of her boots and the legs of her ship suit, then finally out of the fragile undergarment. Then he decided to kiss his way up one long leg, taking his time to enjoy her soft skin.

When he looked up at her, she was looking down at him with wide eyes, her breath coming in shallow pants. He could make her pant harder.

He drew a finger along her inner thigh, ran his fingertip over the crease of her sex. Her grip on his shoulders flexed. He used his other hand at the inside of her knee to encourage her to widen her stance. And then he kissed her again, this time brushing his lips over her labia. She trembled, clutched at him.

He traced her crease with two fingertips and gently parted her folds. She let out a whimper. Oh, he wasn't nearly done yet.

He tasted her then—ran his tongue over her and explored her delicate folds. She swayed, and he slid his free hand up the back of her leg to grip her behind and steady her. He feasted.

So good. She tasted so good.

Her hands had clasped his head and ran through his short hair, encouraging him. He licked and nibbled, found her little nub hidden in the delicate folds of skin and pressed it hard with the tip of his tongue.

She called out. Might have been his name; he wasn't sure.

He fastened his mouth over her clit and moved his two fingers, exploring her opening. Her butt flexed under his other hand, and he gripped her tighter. She was so wet, ready for him. But he wasn't done with her yet.

He suckled her clit, nipped, and suckled again, luring her in a rhythm. As she drew a deep breath, he slid his fingers inside her, and her entire body tensed as she called out.

He held her, enjoying the feel of her inner muscles clenching around his fingers. He pumped her a few times, helped lengthen her orgasm.

"Rygard." His name left her lips in a breathless whisper, and he smiled.

FINE TREMORS RAN through her from the orgasm. Oh and the satisfied, smug look on his face. No fair.

She was still hungry, and she wanted him wrung out and spent alongside her. It didn't take too much to urge him to stand. He helped her get him naked. She ran her hands over the flat muscles of his chest, his broad shoulders, and his well-defined arms. By the time her exploration traveled down his torso to his hips, his cock was hard and waiting for her.

She wrapped one hand around the length of him, marveling at the softness of his skin. His eyes almost rolled up into the back of his head, and he lifted his hands to grasp her shoulders.

Good. It was his turn to be off-balance.

She played then, teasing the underside of his balls with her fingertips as she continued to caress his shaft with her other hand. She leaned forward enough for her breasts to brush his front, pleased when he reached around her back to undo the clasp to her bra and let it fall down her arms and around her wrists.

She giggled at the sight of her bra draped over his penis.

"Having fun?"

"Mmm."

He took her by the wrists, gently, and pulled her hands away from him. "I've been wanting you a long, long time. Too much of that and we'll need to wait longer."

She raised her gaze to his. "I want you now."

He met her halfway in a kiss—this one anything but gentle and every bit as hungry as she felt. The taste of her in his mouth gave her pause, but his tongue played with hers and teased her. She moved her hands from his loose grip and took hold of his shoulders. Leaning into him, she found his stance solid, and before he could grip her, she hopped up and wrapped her legs around his waist.

He grunted in surprise, and for a moment, she worried she'd be too heavy. But this was Rygard.

He laughed. "You are so incredibly sexy."

His hands curved under her bottom, supporting her.

They kissed, and she nipped at the corners of his mouth as he walked in the general direction of her bunk.

It couldn't have been more than a step or two, but they stumbled into the privacy divider and the wall on the other side. They eventually made it. Laughter mingled with deep kisses and little groans.

He laid her down gently on her bunk with one hand curved over her head, protecting her from knocking it on the lower ceiling in the alcove. Flat on her back, she reached for him.

He slid into her suddenly, taking her in a firm move of possession. The rock-hard length of him stretched her, filled her until she arched her back with the pleasure of it.

"Ah!"

And he held there, inside her, both of them panting hard.

"Good?" He held her hips, wouldn't let her move.

Finally, she answered, "Yes, yes! Rygard, please!"

He drew back then and plunged into her at a frantic pace. She could only lift her hips for him, accept him as he drove into her, each hard stroke bringing her closer and closer to the edge again. Her pleasure grew until every muscle in her body clenched.

"That's it." Rygard slammed into her harder, faster. "Come with me, sweetness. Come. With. Me."

She lost control. Ecstasy shuddered through her entire body as he came inside her in a hot rush. He collapsed on top of her, and they held each other through the storm of their climaxes.

CHAPTER 9

THE SOUND of tiny paws scampering across the floor woke Kaitlyn.

She peered through the darkness and ignored the sharp stab of pain in her eyes as she made the minute shift to panther vision. Rygard slept at her back, spooned around her, the heavy weight of his arm on her waist a comfort and a reminder that they were safe in her territory. As she studied their little visitor, she kept her breathing steady and refrained from moving to avoid waking Rygard. He needed the rest, to heal.

Chester poked around in the pile of discarded rags from their captivity. His long back arched as he dug headfirst in the garments. A couple of pieces flew a few centimeters away as he tossed them, in search of something.

Nothing there a tube rat would want—not a stitch of lace or silk.

Kaitlyn had planned to incinerate the rags, but cleaning everyone up and tending to injuries had taken precedence.

Apparently, Chester found something to his liking: he emerged with a soft cloth clenched in his mouth. Little eyes glittered, and he chattered in excitement before quieting as if he realized he might wake someone.

Too late.

Rygard was awake too. His breathing paused, and his hand pressed flat against her belly. It was too dark for him to be able to see Skuld's pet, but he must have heard him.

Kaitlyn spread her hand over Rygard's—a reassurance. His arm tightened around her just a bit.

Chester dragged his prize free of the pile and turned his head toward where she and Rygard lay. Then the little thief headed for the door, dragging his loot with him.

Okay, curiosity and all that.

Kaitlyn twisted her upper body toward Rygard and rubbed her head under his chin. The scent of him, hale and whole, filled her with contentment. She pressed a soft kiss against the line of his jaw and then gently tugged his arm off her waist.

He let her go with a kiss to the forehead and a naughtier caress of her behind. Sliding out from under the light blanket covering them both, she stood and stepped into one of her ship suits.

The fabric hugged her limbs, and she figured she'd have to get familiar with the restriction of being fully clothed again. A welcome necessity, though she experienced an awkward hesitation at present. Weird what things a person had to get accustomed to on the return to "normal" living.

Even weirder than Chester stealing cotton instead of silk.

She padded silently out of the medical bay and down the corridor on bare feet. No need to keep the ferret in sight—his scent trail was warm and his musk stronger than she remembered. He must have been agitated. She didn't want to distract him from his intent, so she gave him a head start. Better chance to find out whatever he was up to that way.

He didn't head back to Skuld's room in the engineering bay.

Instead, he scampered from corridor to corridor until he reached the weapons storage room. Well, he'd had a cache in there. It seemed as if years had passed since the day she'd found it and regained the purloined toy Skuld had been freaking out over. It was also the spot where Tracer and Skuld had first had a chance to interact at length.

A pang hit her in the chest. She hadn't taken time yet to deal with Tracer's absence personally.

She stepped into the storage room just in time to see Chester's tail and a trailing bit of cloth turn the corner and disappear behind one of the racks. She followed close at that point, not worried about giving him more of a lead.

As she turned the corner, her chest tightened in sad sympathy. Lying on the floor in a corner was Max, his nose between his front paws. Chester dragged the cloth to him and came to a stop right in front of the big dog's muzzle.

Not to personify a tube rat, but hell, she could hear the concern in the little squeaks Chester made.

Using his nose and his forepaws, Chester tucked the cloth under Max's muzzle until the German Shepherd Dog lifted his head. Big ears swiveled forward, and the sound of one long sniff broke the silence. Sad brown eyes looked up at her, through her, and then Max dropped his head down on the cloth with a heavy sigh.

"What are we going to do with you?" She didn't have to whisper. The room was far enough away from the crew quarters. Still, the space around them pressed in close, full of silence and . . . waiting. Waiting for a man they'd left behind.

"He's not coming." They hadn't been able to recover Tracer's body. Captain Petrico-Calin IV wouldn't risk sending a recovery team.

Max didn't move his head, only turned those dark eyes up toward her.

"I'm sorry." Damn it, she'd already held Skuld as she cried for what could have been. It'd been awkward as hell, and Kaitlyn would have bled straight from the heart if she could have found a way to bring Tracer back alive. Anything to spare Skuld the loss.

Irony, that. She was pretty sure she could manage to overcome a heart wound, given the acceleration to her healing ability.

Lying in front of her was another broken heart. This one had a hole in it no instrument in her medical bay could detect or stitch up. She ached for him, even if he was a canine.

Tracer's face swam up in her mind's eye again: the grim line of his mouth, the blood dribbling from the corner and down his jaw. He'd known he was dead. He had to have sustained internal bleeding from his injuries.

A growl rose in her throat. She might have been able to stop the bleeding, repair the internal damage, or at least stabilize Tracer and drop him into cryo for transport back to a decent medical facility. But no, the idiot had to literally drop a dog on her and run off in an act of kamikaze heroics.

Chester let out another concerned squeak and scampered over to her. He placed a paw on her big toe for a half a second and then returned to Max. After climbing up onto the canine's broad shoulders, Chester curled into a sad ball between Max's shoulder blades.

Her feet moved without her conscious thought. A few steps, and she was folding down to sit beside the furry pair.

Up close, she could identify the stolen rag now. Chester had nabbed a scrap from what was left of Rygard's shirt, the one she'd worn for most of her time spent in the hellhole. It barely carried his scent anymore, but hers permeated every fiber.

They hadn't been able to bring anything back of Tracer's. Her scent must've been the next best thing. Hard to say for certain what was going on in Chester's furry little mind.

Hesitant, not sure what good she could do here, she extended her hand and placed it on Max's head. Those big ears drooped. His coat felt rough under her palm—too many days of bad nutrition and rough living in the caves. She ran her hand over the rest of him, ignoring Chester's disgruntled squeak when she dislodged him from his perch. Too thin, bones were prominent under the German Shepherd Dog's skin. When she touched his nose, it felt dry and warm to the touch.

"We need to get an IV in you." His brown eyes remained dull—no acknowledgement and none of the comprehension she'd seen in them in the past. "And you need to eat."

It was hardly possible, as he was already lying on the floor, but Max flattened himself even further. He closed his eyes and covered his face with one paw.

If Chester hadn't taken notice of the big dog, Max might have lain here and pined away before anyone noticed. They'd have another dead body on their hands. She rose to her feet.

No more deaths; not tonight anyway.

"Up. On your feet." She didn't raise her voice. It hadn't been a request either.

Eyes remained closed, but ears swiveled forward.

Chester uttered an excited chatter and scrambled up her pants leg and torso until he reached her shoulder. From his perch, the little ferret gave an imperious squeak of his own.

Max didn't move further.

Her temper heated her blood. He'd survived. Tracer had sacrificed himself in order for all of them to live, especially Max. She be damned if she'd let the dog waste it. Stupid male.

"Up, Max." She snapped out the words. No room for disobedience this time.

The big dog's ears swiveled toward her again slowly. He weighed her words, looking out at her from eyes clouded in pain. His gaze cleared, and for a moment, she caught a glimpse of the sharp intelligence she'd seen when she'd first met him. She swallowed against the lump in her throat as she watched him struggle to stand. It took far too long, and when he made it up, he swayed. Three shaky steps later, he leaned his chin on her shoulder. He'd done it, for her.

"Let's go."

RYGARD SAT up and pulled on the pants of his uniform as soon as Kaitlyn left. Wherever she was going, he figured she'd be awake and not ready to immediately snuggle up again. Her heat might have been wearing off, but it still hit her in waves of restlessness whether she noticed or not.

Footsteps sounded in the corridor, and Rygard hustled to get the rest of his uniform together. When Captain Petrico-Calin IV entered the medical bay, his mouth was twisted in a frown.

Could he be more obvious?

Rygard snapped to attention and gave the captain the

salute his rank required. A return salute didn't come until after a long, unnecessary pause. Inwardly, Rygard seethed, but he didn't give the other man the satisfaction of seeing it show on his face.

"At ease." Petrico-Calin walked a few steps forward, glancing around the room. "I noticed you weren't bunking with your soldiers, Lieutenant Rygard. Were your injuries more serious then reported?"

"No Sir." Rygard kept his gaze forward. As far as he was concerned, this was an interrogation. No way was he ever going to let his guard down around this man after the debacle of the rescue mission.

"Then why are you still in the medical bay?"

The answer was obvious, and every other man on board knew it. They also had enough respect not to say a word about it. Anger boiled inside Rygard. He was off duty. There was no reason for Petrico-Calin to stick his dirty nose into the affairs of tired soldiers.

"Rygard, thank you for staying to lend a hand." Kaitlyn walked in then, her arms full of German Shepherd Dog.

He swallowed whatever he'd been about to say, and good thing. He hadn't slapped a filter on his brain. Instead, he strode forward and helped Kaitlyn settle Max onto one of the patient beds. "What happened?"

"He's pining for his handler." Her hands moved quickly as she reached into drawers for the supplies she needed. "He needs fluids stat. And he hasn't been eating. If we can't get him to swallow sustenance, I'm going to have to put a direct tap on his stomach. Not an easy thing for his breed."

"That's a valuable animal, woman." Petrico-Calin walked up, immediately getting in Kaitlyn's way as she turned back to Max with an IV needle in hand. "What did you do to him?"

"I found him." Kaitlyn growled. When she bared her teeth, her canines lengthened. Petrico-Calin paled and backed up a step.

Bad move. A smart man never gave ground to a challenge like that.

Her growl ceased and she moved into action. "Hold this." She shoved the ready IV needle toward Rygard. He took it carefully from her, making sure to only touch it where she had. He didn't want to mess with the sterile needle point.

Swift and efficient, she retrieved a set of clippers from another drawer and shaved a patch from Max's foreleg. She disinfected the area with a swab and took the IV needle back. Within moments, she had it in a vein and was taping it to the dog's leg to keep it in place.

"Stay." Her command voice stopped Rygard in his tracks. He'd never heard her use the tone before and it demanded obedience, even if she was talking to Max and not to him. The dog heaved a big sigh and closed his eyes. Had the dog ever truly listened to anyone but Tracer?

Sure, he'd heard her talk at the dog before. Back then it'd seemed like a contest of wills.

"Be sure you give that animal the utmost care." Petrico-Calin really didn't know when to keep his mouth shut. "He'll need to go back to the Kx9 division until another handler can be assigned to him."

"He's mourning." Kaitlyn didn't spare a glance in Petrico-Calin's direction, but she angled herself so as not to give him her back either. Max seemed to be watching the captain through half-lidded eyes. "I need to get this line established and then I'm going to have to pull some real chicken from the galley."

Petrico-Calin made a sound of disgust. "All Kx9 units

come with their own special feed. Everyone knows they only eat that. If you poison military property . . ."

"The feed is for when he's in top condition and eating properly. He's been through trauma and hasn't eaten decent food since before we all got out of that hellhole." Kaitlyn's voice had gone flat. The fine hair on the back of Rygard's arm stood on end. She had almost no control left. "His stomach won't handle regular feed at this point and he needs the most easily digestible protein I can provide him. You don't want me to put a tube in his stomach."

"Why not? Sounds like the most efficient solution to ensure he consumes exactly what he should. Couldn't he just spit it out if you fed him by mouth?"

Kaitlyn growled. Did she see how the captain stiffened? "I looked it up on my portable on the way here. Their stomachs are prone to torsion because they aren't anchored to the inside of the thoracic cavity by connective tissue. Having the stomach loose makes putting a tube in him harder and keeping it in place seriously prone to complications. I don't have the facilities here to monitor him properly and it'd be better if we could get him to eat normally, regardless. He needs to want to live."

Did any of them realize the brilliance of the mind inside her head? Too busy dealing with the physical, it was easy to forget how incredibly smart she was.

"What he wants is irrelevant. He is military property. Once you have that Kx9 stabilized, get him in his crate and ready for transportation. He must be returned to the Kx9 division."

Rygard almost stepped forward then, sure Kaitlyn would spring over the patient table and at Petrico-Calin's throat. Instead, she ran a gentle hand over the big dog's head, paused, and then fondled his ears.

"There was no enlistment. He never swore an oath." Her words came quiet. "He chose a master, gave him unquestioning loyalty. That kind of heart deserves better than a number designation and a crate."

"Such sympathy. You deserve to be in a crate right alongside that mutt."

Anger hazed Rygard's vision.

"You have something to say, Lieutenant?" Petrico-Calin faced him, his chin lifted. The officer was hoping for a fight, wanted a reason to court-martial his ass.

"You've been making a lot of threats tonight, Captain Petrico-Calin the Fourth." Kaitlyn broke the tension between them. "For now, I have work to do and luckily for all of us, it's in line with your orders. Let me get to it."

Petrico-Calin didn't take his eyes off Rygard, but his shoulders relaxed and an arrogant smirk spread across his face. "You have no idea. Get some rest. You never know what can happen on the long trip back to Terra."

Foreboding ran through Rygard's veins, ice-cold and lightning fast. It was all he could do to let Petrico-Calin leave without grabbing two handfuls of the front of the man's shirt and shaking the information out of him.

"Whatever knowledge he's savoring, it won't be exclusively his for long." Kaitlyn wasn't looking at Rygard though; her attention was still directed at Max. She fixed a nutrient-solution bag on a hook above the dog. "Max, stay."

The dog heaved another big sigh, but he didn't move as she stepped away from him and toward Rygard.

"I won't let him take you." He pulled her to him, held her tight.

"No."

He thought she'd said it as a statement of faith in him.

But she'd buried her face into his shoulder, and a faint tremble came with her next breath.

"No, Rygard, you will let him."

"Like hell . . ."

Lithe arms circled his waist, crushed him close with a strength greater than most men, cutting off his air and what he'd been about to say. "Don't say anything you can't take back. As long as we're here, on Dev's ship, we have options."

She loosened her hold, and he savored a taste of air. Before they'd gone into the Colosseum, shit, not too long ago, her show of strength might have left him uneasy and withdrawing. Now . . .

"You're incredibly sexy when you're assertive. You know that?"

Her eyes widened and a surprised laugh popped out of her. "You're incorrigible."

"Doesn't mean I'm wrong."

Dusky rose spread across her cheeks. "I'm going down to the galley. Would you watch Max and make sure he doesn't pull his IV loose?"

He kissed her then, for asking him rather than telling him what to do. "I've seen an IV or two. Shouldn't be a problem."

KAITLYN HEADED FOR THE CORRIDOR, a small smile playing on her lips. Despite Petrico-Calin's threat hanging in the air, the warmth of Rygard's mouth on hers had sent tingles through her body.

They'd come through hell and back. She was in her home territory now with not only her captain and crew at her back but also Rygard at her side.

"Kat."

Speaking of her captain, his voice issued from the comm system. She halted by the door and spoke to the air. "Aye, Captain."

"What?" No surprise that Rygard sounded puzzled.

On night setting, she had the volume in the medical bay turned down low to avoid disturbing any patients. Any communications broadcast across the comm would be audible to her and Max tonight, not a normal human.

She held up a hand to forestall any further questions from Rygard and tapped her ear to give him an idea of what was going on.

"We've got a situation." Dev's words were carefully measured. "I need you on point but you're going to need backup."

"Where?"

"Holding cells. Start tracking. Do not engage without reinforcement."

Bharguest.

She was out the door and down the hallway, tossing a few words over her shoulder to Rygard as she went. "Remember, that IV stays in."

Best to give him a job to do; otherwise, he'd never stay put. Rygard was still too damaged from the last adventure to handle a close quarters altercation with Bharguest. Hell, all of them were.

The corridors were empty. They were still in the middle of the ship's night cycle, and in the aftermath of the escape from the Colosseum, she hadn't paid attention to who had been put on watch.

Despite her haste, she came to a solid halt at the junction approaching the holding cells. Caution came to the forefront, and she opened up all her senses as best she could.

The scent of fresh blood came to her first. The metallic tang was becoming too familiar. Was it a bad thing her mouth began to water at the smell of it? Probably. But the fetid smell of bowels erased any taste she might have for human flesh.

Ugh.

Well, gross, but she'd be thankful for blessings coming in unexpected ways.

No sounds from the holding cell, and no movement in the darkness of the corridor. Dev must have seen the bodies from the security visuals feeding up to the ship's bridge.

After touching the wall console, she keyed up the bridge.

"Report." Dev didn't sound happy.

"Two men down, the military police."

"You have a trail."

"That's a yes."

"I'm dancing with our Captain the Fourth over who has jurisdiction. My ship, his men. Track as best you can. I don't want this bastard loose on my ship while we're digging into bureaucratic bullshit."

As she crouched low, she shifted to panther form. No sense in leaving her fragile human back and neck open to attack when she could track better on four paws. Bharguest hadn't bothered to hide his scent, which made her more cautious.

His trail took her down the less-traveled corridors, ones he'd have gone through only maybe once or twice during his time on board. No mystery as to what he was up to. His path was leading directly to the cargo hold.

If she remained on his scent trail, she'd come face-to-face with either him or whatever trap he'd left as a present. Any trap he could cobble together wouldn't be sophisticated. Still, she had no doubt it'd be fatal. From the quick visual she'd taken of the dead guards' bodies, Bharguest had looted them for their weapons and gear.

Time to take the path less traveled.

It took moments to pop the nearest access to the ventilation shafts. Her training experiments with Chester included runs throughout every part of the ship using the shafts, so they were almost as clean as the corridors. No dust to stir up, no worries about having her sight impaired if crud got into her eyes.

Once inside, she headed toward the cargo hold with a brief stop at each grate to catch Bharguest's scent and reassure herself he was indeed moving along the anticipated route. Dark as it was, the nighttime lights in the corridors provided just enough for her to see by in the enclosed space.

Funny how they didn't bother her as much as cages or caverns did.

Learn to move silent in these and they'll never know how we got from point A to point B.

Katzer had been right, years ago. The occupying force on Triton Moon Base had never discovered how the cadets had been moving around domes and escaping detection. Knowing those routes had been her salvation when she had finally escaped captivity.

Of course, back then, it'd been harder for her to pass through the tight spaces without making noise. A leopard's paw pads gave her an advantage over magnetic ship boots, and she'd left her clothes back at the entrance point.

A sound came from below, barely audible: the soft brush of fabric against a hard surface. She froze. Bharguest's scent came to her from the nearest grate, his strange musk heady as she crouched at the ready. The hunt, it was over too soon.

A minute stretched out into several. No further sound. She crept forward, headed for the next grate and the nearest console to signal Dev.

Shots rang out in two short bursts. The panel gave way beneath her and she was falling. Stretching out her paws to catch herself, she kept herself soft for impact. But she never hit the ground.

A hand caught her by the throat, snapping her out of the air and slamming her against a wall. Legs wrapped around her waist. An arm slid around her neck and under her jaw in a guillotine choke.

"Shift and I break your neck," Bharguest whispered in her ear.

A growl rumbled deep in her chest. Fine. She had more to hurt him with in this form anyway.

He chuckled. His hold didn't loosen. "You were doing so good, little one. You forgot how vipers hunt their prey."

Well, now she remembered.

As ambush predators, some snakes lay next to a log or other game trail with their chin resting on the surface. The vibrations warned them when their target approached.

"You almost fooled me. If you'd waited another minute, I might've moved on."

Almost only counted with children's games . . . and hand grenades.

His arm tightened around her neck until her jaw threatened to pop and her vertebrae strained. "What will I do with you now?"

Laying limp, passive, went against every instinct she had, whether it be human or animal. But she had to wait for the right moment, the right leverage point. Only he wasn't giving her any openings.

Stars began to burst across her vision, and darkness crept along the periphery. Air started to burn in her lungs, and her own pulse beat hard against the pressure he applied to her throat.

Too much. Her mind stopped logical thought. Panic washed through her, and she bucked in his grasp. His legs tightened around her, iron coiled around her hips. She lashed out blindly with all four sets of claws. Caught nothing but air. Her lungs screamed for it, couldn't find any. Her lips were drawn back. She would've snarled if she could.

"You've come far." His words came from a long way away, low and gravelly. "Down there, in the Colosseum. You had it, the killing rage. And you came back from it."

Black crawled across her sight. Her focus narrowed to the console on the wall.

Dev.

Call for Dev, Kitten. Call him.

Katzer had known back then. Wanted Dev near her before he said his goodbyes. Dev could call her back to being human.

But not from being dead.

Darkness closed over her vision. Bharguest spoke in her ear again, "You learn fast, little one. You're not just human anymore. Don't go back to pretending. There's more than the Colosseum out there and there's bigger, badder monsters than you. I'm out there and I'm the better killer. I'll expect more from you next time."

CHAPTER 10

"KAT. REPORT. KAITLYN."

Maybe her captain *could* call her back from the dead.

Precious seconds passed—too many—as she gathered her thoughts enough to shift to human form. As she dragged herself to the wall and slammed the comm with her palm, the shuttle's air lock sealed and the locks began cycling their releases.

"He's getting away." No need to say who.

"We see that. He's overridden bridge control and bypassed securities. Damn, the man is fast. A military detail is one minute from you. Badger and one of the grunts. You have a uniform nearby?"

She released the comm and forced her body to obey as she darted farther into the cargo hold and up a series of stacked containers to one of the support beams stretching across the room. She nabbed a stashed ship suit, then yanked it on without bothering to worry about undergarments. By the time the military detail arrived at the cargo bay, she had the ship suit sealed and her feet shoved into a spare pair of boots.

Signaling to the younger man to remain a few paces back, Badger watched her leap down the containers. The old soldier looked her up and down and gave her a nod. "You okay?"

"I'm alive."

He shouldered his firearm and scratched his chin. He hadn't shaved yet, and his scruff showed like salt and pepper against his brown skin. "That's a surprise."

"Yeah." She nodded and walked back over to the comm unit. "Are we chasing him down, Captain?"

"Well, it looks like we've got a lot of surprises going on tonight. All sorts of people seem to be coming and going."

Bharguest was gone, getting away.

She opened her mouth to protest, but loud clangs sounded across the cargo bay and the entire ship shuddered. A tractor beam must have taken hold.

There weren't too many ships large enough to take Dev's ship into tow, much less attach docking clamps big enough to make that kind of noise.

"Do we have friendlies or am I preparing for another fight?" She strode toward the big cargo bay doors. A forced entry was most likely to come through those.

Badger and his man followed her, readying their weapons. Convenient the way they came along without questioning. But then, Badger had been down there with Dev, seen her in action.

"Friendlies. Stand down." Dev's voice didn't sound alarmed over the comm, but it didn't sound pleased either. "I'm en route."

Well then, waiting seemed like the plan. Running her hands through her hair, she tried to pull herself into a semblance of a presentable appearance. Luckily, the ship suit provided enough coverage that the lack of anything else wouldn't be detectable. Skuld did it all the time.

"Your bruises, they're fading." Badger stared at her. Or rather, his gaze fastened on her neck.

Not a surprise. Well, not surprising that Bharguest had left nasty bruising around her neck. "I heal fast. It's a perk of being a genetic aberration."

"The men aren't healing as fast as that." No accusation in Badger's tone. No, he made the statement a question.

She shrugged. "I've had the virus longer and my mutation is more complete. I'll know once I have a chance to analyze the blood samples I took more. So far none of them have a full mutation to their genetic code. They're mostly human." Well, one stood out. "DeSarto's mutation is looking to be the most advanced, but he's also got better control than the others. It helps balance things out."

"Hard to tell." Badger glanced up the corridor and then to his man. "They're having a hard time staying calm in the bunks now that some of them are recovering from the sedatives you gave them. Couple of scuffles have broken out. Think maybe they're trying to see who's top dog?"

Not a good sign but not going to lead to the bloodshed he was worried about either. "They were together long enough in the caves to figure that part out." She would put her creds on DeSarto. Rygard's big friend had size and confidence over the others. "It's not usually the alpha or the contention for alpha that causes the issues. It's all the rest figuring out the pecking order below. There's constant jockeying for position. It'd help if they were allowed to get out of the room, get a little distance to let them calm down."

Badger shook his head. "Captain Petrico-Calin gave orders to confine them to quarters. Keep 'em from infecting the rest of us."

She frowned. "It's not transmissible from humanoid to humanoid. Once the mutation is complete, the viral agent used to introduce the genetic code dies. This far into their change, they aren't contagious anymore."

Silence. Badger, at least, seemed conflicted. The other only wore a blank look. Damn, she was used to Rygard. He always seemed to follow or at least ask enough clarifying questions to eventually catch up.

"They can't give it to the rest of you. Neither can I."

She'd be willing to bet the two of them had orders to confine her as well as Bharguest. Regret weighed heavily in her gut. She did not want to scuffle with Badger. If she had to hurt the old soldier, she'd feel bad.

He was a good person—helped them on the mission. But he could only remain flexible with orders to a certain extent. Judging from the grim set of his mouth, he had no wiggle room. Where was Dev?

"Just so we're clear, your military commanding officer does not have jurisdiction over my captain's crew, not any of us."

Badger's expression didn't change, but his younger companion gave it away.

"We have our orders."

Obviously.

Kaitlyn didn't blink. The room came into sharper focus as her pupils changed. "I like you well enough, Badger, and I've got nothing against him either, but neither of you is going to take me."

A muscle jumped in Badger's cheek as he tightened his jaw.

"To be honest, Petrico-Calin had a death wish for the two of you if he sent you after Bharguest, much less the both of us."

No way was she going to be confined in a room full of not-so-shiny new shape-shifters. Hell, her control stabilized only recently as it was. Rygard might not forgive her for having to hurt them all.

Badger's fingers tightened on his firearm. His muscles bunched in his arm as he readied to draw his weapon to his shoulder.

Too slow. She'd be faster.

"Everyone play nice." Dev appeared in the aperture leading from the ship's main corridor. Specs and Tails stood behind him along with a good half dozen of their ground crew.

"You took your time." Of course, she'd heard them coming, but poor Badger might have gotten hurt if they'd arrived a minute later.

Ignoring the nervous enlisted man, Kaitlyn kept her attention on Badger. His brows quirked up in surprise, and the deep creases across his forehead smoothed away. The scent of his aggression faded.

Good. Just as she'd hoped—following orders.

"Ah well, I had to get a bit spiffed up." Dev's tone was light, but his brows were drawn close and the set of his jaw also grim. "And I swung around the long way to invite a couple more to the party."

As they all stepped through to the cargo bay area, her crewmates spread out on either side. Rygard walked down to stand by Badger, and the older soldier relaxed further.

"What is Max doing off his IV?" She speared first the big dog with a look and then Rygard.

Rygard held up one hand. "He wasn't going to stay behind. I figured disconnecting his line was better than letting him rip it out on his own."

Max whined as he moved to stand at her side, his broad

shoulder brushing her hip. When he looked up at her, his big ears drooped and pinned down to his skull.

"Don't give me sad eyes. You were supposed to stay." Eyeing him warily, she watched for signs of tremors or fatigue. He'd improved. Still, he needed rest and food.

"Why is that animal not in a crate and ready for shipping?"

Captain Petrico-Calin IV strode into the cargo bay with the rest of his team. Rygard's men, even the uninfected, were notably missing.

Kaitlyn snapped her mouth shut and swallowed her order for Max to head back to the medical bay where he could rest. Hell if she was going to send him anywhere she couldn't keep him out of a crate. Then again, Petrico-Calin glared at her as if he might have been referring to her.

He could suck on freeze-dried space rations.

More footsteps in the corridor, a heavier tread than hers yet quieter than humans. The more dominant felid had to duck through the aperture to step into the cargo hold. Someone had given him a wrap of some sort—Skuld maybe. He'd arranged it around his hips in an interesting drape and held it in place with a belt. His companion followed him on all fours, still wearing nothing but his fur.

Seeing them, Petrico-Calin's eyes bugged out. Maybe the taste in his mouth was worse than space rations.

"Thank you, Captain Rishkillian, for inviting us to join you." The bigger male nodded to Dev.

The cargo bay doors signaled completion of the air lock cycle.

"Oh good, we've got the welcome party all settled." Dev moved to stand on Kaitlyn's other side. Specs and Tails stepped in to flank them both.

Since when had she rated second in command? Even if

Dev called her his first mate, Specs and Tails had always stood shoulder to shoulder with her in the past. The three of them had been of equal rank in so far as mercs had rank. Besides, it'd always helped her blend.

"No chance of you standing in the background for this one, Kat." Dev knew her too well because she was certain she hadn't betrayed her disgruntlement on her face. "We might as well have you standing where you'll do the most good."

Best to keep her mouth shut, especially since the huge cargo bay doors were opening.

Good thing Dev had assembled a solid complement of crew too. Their "friendlies" were Terran military and all formal in pristine white uniforms. Only a half dozen of the soldiers making their entrance had stripes on their arms. All the rest carried shoulder ranks and a colorful plaque of ribbons fastened to their chests. High-ranking wasn't the word for it.

"Captain Rishkillian, permission to come aboard." The general, by the polished stars on her uniform, greeted Dev with a perfunctory nod.

Dev only nodded in return. "Permission granted."

No witty commentary. Her captain was walking a line and not ready to test his footing yet. As Dev made introductions, she kept her nods respectful and her eye contact brief.

"General, I'm certain you received my reports." Petrico-Calin wasted no time once salutes were exchanged.

Hard to tell since the general and her party had to step past Kaitlyn to fully board the ship, but if at all possible, the general's back got stiffer. It wasn't just the starch in her uniform.

"Indeed, Captain. Interesting reading."

Oh that did not sound encouraging, especially considering the smirk crossing Petrico-Calin's face.

"Then . . ."

The general held up a hand. "A moment, please." She turned back to Dev. "Captain Rishkillian, my officers tell me a shuttle took off from your ship a few minutes ago."

"The monster escaped—"

Dev smoothly spoke over Petrico-Calin's blurted beginning. "Escaped prisoner, General. We were intending to pursue. My communications officer notified your bridge as soon as you locked onto us."

"I'm afraid our intercept made that impossible. My apologies. We can send a scout out after your lost shuttle if you prefer."

"At this point, your scout is better equipped to track and apprehend, General, if it isn't a draw on your resources."

The general raised her hand, and one of the enlisted soldiers headed back to the military ship at double time. "Not at all, Captain Rishkillian. The escapee is a military prisoner in any case and our responsibility. I'm told the two military police assigned to guard the prisoner died."

"An unfortunate loss." Dev wasn't lying; his voice was heavy with regret.

"Have you completed your investigation? I'd like to get the bodies aboard and would appreciate a copy of your report."

Dev dropped his composure then, running a hand through his hair. "About that . . ."

"I assigned a detail to guard the area for an official military investigation, of course." Petrico-Calin seemed pleased to interrupt Dev in turn. "It's ready whenever your men can come aboard."

The general made a quarter turn in order to address

Petrico-Calin while remaining open to Dev. Silver-gray eyebrows drew together. "It would have been more expedient for Captain Rishkillian's crew to conduct the investigation."

"Well, it's not as if they have a dedicated forensics team." Petrico-Calin waved away his own comment. "We can't place our trust in their team's findings."

As much as she disliked the man, he had a point about the forensics team. As the ship's medic, she usually conducted whatever forensics investigation they needed. Generally though, they knew how a person died. In this case, Bharguest had done the damage with his bare hands. Not much in the way of interesting lab work to conduct there.

"We'd be happy to turn over copies of the security feed, General." Dev made the offer with aplomb.

"Appreciated, Captain." The general studied Petrico-Calin for a moment. "And Captain Petrico-Calin . . ."

"The Fourth, Sir."

"If you could place a detail to secure the scene of death, why did you not supplement the security set to guard the prisoner in the first place? An additional two soldiers might have made the difference."

The smirk fell from Petrico-Calin's face. Nice to see. Kaitlyn decided it would be more prudent not to voice her own opinion, and Dev didn't say anything either.

Aw, they were both maturing.

Two or four, Bharguest still would have left the ship when he no longer felt like playing his game. He'd finished with his toys. The additional security detail would have simply meant more bodies in the prisoner's wake.

She should have been one of them. Why he hadn't killed her was a worry for later.

One of the officers was watching her. He'd been ignoring the conversation, and the weight of his gaze began to raise the fine hairs across her skin. She set her teeth against the urge to snarl.

Next to her, Max leaned into her hip, his big shoulder a warm pressure. She dropped her hand into his fur and steadied herself. If she didn't, the dog was going to knock her over.

"We've also received communication from the Baihunen government."

Who the hell were the Baihunens?

The general must have moved on to a different topic, and she'd missed Petrico-Calin's response. Damn.

"It is a pleasure to meet you, General." The larger male felid nodded.

Might have been good for them to share the name of their race earlier. It would have saved Boggle some research time. But then, she supposed they'd all been a little distracted.

"Our governments are in talks for a proposed alliance at this time." The general's tone was respectful, perhaps tinged with deference. Her back wasn't as stiff, and she made minute shifts of her weight from one foot to the other. Nervous. "While Terrans and Baihunens have had chance encounters in the past, this incident has convinced high-level officials on both sides that an alliance might be mutually beneficial."

"My"—the alien seemed to be groping for a word—"pride brother and I are grateful for the aid of those present for our rescue from the Colosseum. We were a family group, traveling when we were captured. He and I are the only survivors, the last remaining of our blood line."

"Please accept my condolences. Fortuitous that our people could be of help."

And completely not in the plan as far as the military had been concerned. Petrico-Calin had chewed her and Dev out when they'd all arrived back on the ship. He'd wanted to toss them into confinement along with Bharguest.

"I'm not sure I understand, General. How does this take priority over my mission?" For once, Petrico-Calin asked a question she had on her mind too.

Although alien relations did seem fairly important in the big scheme of things, there were soldiers who needed to get back to Terra for treatment and rehabilitation. Virus or no, they'd suffered serious trauma down in the caves. They hadn't had a "trainer" like Dev to protect them.

"Our primary orders are to see the council member here safely back to his home system." There was the deference again. "As soon as the Baihunens received the transmission from the council member, they reached out to Terran authority to ensure he and his . . . pride brother returned home. The Terran government has promised our full cooperation."

Dev nodded. "Of course."

Good for them. They'd been a great help in the caves.

The big male caught her attention. He had that trick of Bharguest's. With no overt movement, one minute he was standing there and the next minute he was standing there and everyone in the room was paying attention to him. Now that was command presence.

"We appreciate your help, General." He twitched an ear. "I am hoping our other requests were also communicated."

"Absolutely." The general turned to Dev. "I'm told you have a crew member specifically suited to interactions with a feline-like species. Something about having the innate ability to read the necessary body language and signals inherent in the Baihunen culture."

"Ah." Dev rubbed his chin. He might fool everyone else, but the bastard was hiding a grin behind his hand. "I believe you're looking for my second, Kaitlyn Darah."

"We've been authorized to give Kaitlyn Darah ambassador status and appoint her liaison to the Baihunens on contract for the term of one year as we enter alliance negotiations, subject to renewal as necessary."

Ambassador? Political immunity and freedom from military jurisdiction. Bonus. Wait, didn't that require diplomatic skills? Were they crazy?

No way could Dev have manipulated that into happening. No way.

"As her captain, holding her current contract, I'd be happy to sit down with your staff and negotiate a subcontract agreement." Of course Dev was going to turn a profit off of all this.

"We'd be most grateful if you would work out the details, Captain Rishkillian." She had the distinct impression the big Baihunen was suppressing laughter. Hard to tell.

"You must be joking." Petrico-Calin spit the words out. For once, she agreed with him. "That . . . that thing belongs in a cage before she infects the rest of my men."

Okay, no. She didn't.

Petrico-Calin was still going, though. "And I want that man over there, Lieutenant Rygard, taken into custody and quarantined too."

Now she was going to break Petrico-Calin's neck and rip out his spine.

"Those measures are unnecessary." Every head turned

in her direction. She kept her words directed at the general. Petrico-Calin had the mouth, but she knew who had the rank. "I submitted the results of all blood work. The tests provide conclusive evidence of which soldiers have been infected by the lycanthropy virus and to what degree. Lieutenant Rygard is clear and completely human."

"He spent the entire night with you." There was no mistaking the implication there.

No point in acknowledging it and giving it any power in the discussion.

"None of the people aboard this ship is capable of passing on the virus by physical contact or exchange of bodily fluids."

However, if somebody had a vial of the live virus squirreled away somewhere, there could be issues. Daydreams of jabbing an injection gun up Petrico-Calin's ass were inappropriate.

The general studied her for a few long moments, her face perfectly neutral. Kaitlyn made a mental note never to play poker or chess with the woman, at least not until she got to know her better. Jury was still out as to whether she wanted to.

"While your report was not included in the original transmission, Ambassador Darah, it was received. I haven't read it in its entirety but my science officers provided me with the abstract." The general might have smiled. Maybe. The quirk at the corner of her mouth might have been an odd tic. "Your work comes with very high recommendation from my science officer along with an invitation to join him over a meal while we get the details worked out regarding next steps in this highly unusual situation."

All right, the heat at her cheeks might have been in response to the praise. A girl didn't receive a compliment from an officer wearing that many stars on their collar very often.

Petrico-Calin's eyes bugged out of his head, and a very prominent vein began popping across his forehead.

The general turned back to him. "Captain, your work in rescuing the captured team is commended as well. Your next set of orders is to take command of the smaller ship we have in tow and return to Terran solar system with the infected soldiers in order to get them the treatment they need. We'll see to it that you are fully supplied and in command with your original team."

All but Tracer. And what about Max?

"Fine." Petrico-Calin shot her an evil look, and his mouth twisted. "The dog is to be put in a crate and loaded for transport back to Terra."

If she said no, she'd be taking the bait. "He still requires medical attention."

Petrico-Calin gathered breath to bellow at her, but the other officer standing with the general spoke up. "What medical attention are you recommending?"

He'd never stopped staring at her. She tightened her hand in the fur of Max's ruff. Kaitlyn hadn't realized how much she'd steadied the both of them.

"He needs to finish a course of IV fluids and I was headed to the galley to get him plain protein, preferably chicken or some other mild aviary."

"How did you plan to give it to him?"

"Ground and boiled if he'd take it. Otherwise, I'd have to install a stomach tube. He's too active to submit to a feeding tube in his throat, too much danger of choking or airway obstruction. Plus, he'd dislodge it and possibly do himself damage in the process." Maybe she didn't have to grind out the words, but there were a whole lot of eyes on her and at least one pair would have killed if possible. "He's on his feet right now so I'm thinking he'll eat if I can get him to a quiet place to talk some reason into him."

"Why do you think he isn't eating?"

The weight of the other stares faded away. Sadness rose in a wave, tightened her throat, and she let it emerge in her expression as she addressed the man asking the questions. "Years ago, one of my best friends signed off in combat. He blinked out of existence in a silent explosion in space. I didn't eat for days. My guess is Max is doing the same."

She looked down at the German Shepherd Dog to find him watching her, his eyes so incredibly sad.

"Given the choice, he might never eat again." She hadn't wanted to.

Would she have if Dev hadn't come to her? Told her to eat? Threatened to shove it down her throat? Then guilted her?

"Max will eat if someone gives him the right reason." She returned her attention to the man, the officer so interested in the dog. "I'm not sure it'd be doing him any favors though, not if Petrico-Calin is going to take him away."

Her fingers wandered up the back of Max's neck and fondled the silky softness of his ears. The big dog let out a sigh and relaxed his head high against her waist.

"You will address me as Captain Petrico-Calin the Fourth." Petrico-Calin shook a finger in their direction. "And that is very valuable military property. What you think is irrelevant."

"Actually, she's spoken in the best interest of the Kx9." The officer took out a data pad and tapped on the screen. "According to my records, Max is young by German Shepherd Dog standards and he had only one handler in his history. You've managed very well considering this is his first loss. It's nothing short of amazing he's reimprinted so soon."

"Come again?"

Oh hey, she and Dev were back on the same wavelength. Confused.

"The German Shepherd Dog breed was chosen for the Kx9 program for certain innate qualities, loyalty among them." The officer took speaking to them in turns, including the general in his discussion. "Because of the genetic enhancements to the breed, the dogs have proven to be extremely independent in their behavior until they imprint on a specific individual. The Kx9 units aren't assigned a handler, they choose."

He chose me.

That's what Tracer had said. Oh, no. Now wait a minute.

"Normally the dogs are returned to the Kx9 kennels and assessed prior to introducing them to handler candidates. This situation is unusual. Still, I've recorded my report and will let them know Kx9-8775 will not be returning to the kennels."

"He's not staying here." Contrary to her statement, the German Shepherd Dog in question remained leaning heavily against her side.

The officer blinked. "You don't have a choice."

"He's military. He's a working dog. He needs to be out on missions with a soldier who knows how to work him." All true things, and she didn't fit any of those requirements. "He needs somebody who actually likes him."

"If we take him back, he'll either try to find a way back to you"—the potential havoc or associated tragedy was not worth considering—"or he'll pine away again from the separation."

She'd just put a lot of effort into getting him onto his feet.

Time to point out the insanely huge elephant in the room. "I'm a cat. I don't think anyone here doesn't know about it at this point. He's a dog."

Said out loud, her argument sounded incredibly stupid.

The officer shrugged. "Look lady, this is one hell of a complicated situation. My job is simple. I make recommendations based on the best interest of the dog. Kx9-8775 is imprinted on you and here he stays. I let higher ranks figure out the details."

Well, that explained why the man held the position he had. Simple is as simple does. Must be nice.

"This isn't Noah's Ark—" Dev began, at the same time the general said, "Arrangements will be made—"

They both looked at each other.

"I have a great bottle of Scotch to go with those contract negotiations, General."

"I'll have my galley whip up some snacks to go with it."

Wait, they couldn't be serious. She glanced down at Max. He looked back at her.

Denial. She'd never been one to pursue an exercise in futility.

"If you drool on my underwear, you're sleeping with Chester."

CHAPTER 11

"YOU'RE TAKING ALL of this extremely well."

Kaitlyn glanced back as Rygard followed her into the medical bay. "I'm not in chains. Max isn't in a crate. Neither of us is being shipped back to the Terran solar system against our will. I'll call it a win."

"Some people tend to trust the military." Rygard's voice was quiet. Not the dangerously soft tone he took on when he was angry, something new.

She turned to face him, putting some thought into what she wanted to say. "The military is for you. You have a lot invested in it, I get that."

Once upon a time, all she'd ever dreamed of was being a commissioned officer conducting scientific research on a battle cruiser just like the one cradling Dev's ship in her hold.

Her dreams had shattered with the hiss of a hypogun and the virus changing her genetic code.

"I do believe you could be one of the really good officers. The ones who actually uphold the code of honor and integrity they built the corps around. We need you in the service to counteract the negative influences."

Rygard tilted his head toward her with an upraised eyebrow. "Negative influences?"

"Idiots, bullies, and arrogant bastards, to be specific."

A grin spread across his face. "There's my lady."

She rolled her eyes. "I was trying to be sincere here. You really can do some good in the service. You're at home with your people. Seeing you with your team and within your reporting structure gives me a little faith in the service. The general is a good officer too."

"So far as I can tell, yes she is."

"It'd be a completely different story if Petrico-Calin had his way." She frowned. "I'd have had to take some drastic measures and the military would not be as happy with me."

No way would she have allowed the man to take her back to Terra.

"He'd have had you locked in a glass cube for testing"—Rygard ground out the words—"over my dead body."

"Well, the story is different now."

"Thanks to Boggle slipping in the full set of reports. He really is a good friend."

Kaitlyn nodded.

Rygard stepped across the space separating them and slid a hand around her waist. "And you are an ambassador now. A very important personage."

She grimaced. "Headed on a babysitting run to get the . . . Baihunens back home. Who knows how it's going to go?"

"It'll be an interesting run."

"You've only got half your team with you." She searched his face. "Are you really okay with Petrico-Calin taking the rest of your men back to Terra? You sure they won't end up in glass cubes too?"

Rygard's expression darkened, but he set his jaw. "The general agreed the men had been through enough. I trust her to honor her word. Hopefully, the labs can find a way to reverse the changes since it's so new to all of them. If not, they probably won't be allowed to continue in service."

No use giving false hope.

"Virus already had a full progression through each of them. The same reason they're not infectious is the same reason there's little chance to reverse the changes." She paused. "Hope, but don't set them up for a second round of crushing. They've already beat the odds by surviving the mutation. It's been more than a week now. The changes have progressed and will keep evolving for some of them. They're going to want to separate the larger species like DeSarto. He could kill a person before he realized it."

She paused. She'd almost hurt her fellow cadets when she'd first escaped. Later, there'd been a few close calls with Durn and Specs too when she'd first come aboard. The crew could've hated her. Instead, Durn had started sparring with her. The sparring and timing drills had helped her learn her body's limits.

"Your people are going to need friendly faces." She had them. "I'll send on all the data I've got, have Boggle check in on their progress. Maybe I can help with their acclimation."

"No doubt." Rygard dropped a kiss on her forehead. "They owe their lives to you. And you're a pretty incredible example of 'life goes on.'"

"Am I?" Somehow the solid backbone she'd had out in the main cargo bay was turning to jelly. Her chest tightened. "And you're okay with me the way I am? You know I can't go back to being human."

"It's been too long," Rygard agreed.

She shook her head. Then paused. "Well, it has been too long. But that's not what I meant."

They'd all changed down in the Colosseum. The animal she'd become to survive had taken physical form, but it had roots deeper in her psyche.

"You saw combat before I met you. You killed." Rygard hooked his free hand under her chin and turned her face toward his. "They were all controlled missions. In and out. You were never immersed for that long. Dev never signed your crew on for a full-out battle, much less a prolonged war. What you went through, every soldier does eventually."

"You helped keep me from turning into a monster."

At least, figuratively speaking. No saving the physical reality.

"I helped you find your own code, so you could go forward with as little regret possible. It's the only way to live with yourself."

How many memories did he have? The Colosseum hadn't changed him as much. What kind of wars had he fought to live through that hell and come out steady?

"There's still a lot I don't know about you."

He chuckled and caressed the line of her jaw until she leaned into his palm. "There hasn't been a lot of time up 'til now. Should be a pretty quiet trip out to the Baihunens. What did you want to know first?"

She lifted her hands, rested them on either side of his waist. "I had questions. I swear I did."

"Yeah?" He breathed his question across her lips.

So close, his eyes filled with heat and darkness. Not the scary kind of darkness, no—the good kind.

"I forget."

"You'll remember later." His hands stroked the length of her body.

"Max still needs . . ."

"He does. He's being looked over by the Kx9 specialist. He won't need you for a little while."

Well, then. "I need you."

He kissed her, unhurried and undeniable.

She let herself melt into him until her entire body pressed against his. His arms wrapped around her, secure and strong. For a moment, she was lost in his kiss, in the taste of him, the musk of his scent filling her with every gasped breath.

When he released her, she undressed in a flurry—unsealed her ship suit and tossed her boots. He did the same. When their bodies met again, skin against skin, his kisses became fiercer, more possessive. And she met his with the strength of her own desire, hungrily devouring his mouth.

His strong hands gripped her behind, lifted her. She wrapped her legs around his waist and let her head fall back as he buried his face in her breasts. He drew hot kisses across the underside of each breast and then ran his tongue around first one nipple and then the other. When the heat of his mouth closed over a nipple, she cried out.

He suckled, each soft tug drawing pleasure out of her. As he continued, he gripped her bottom with his hands, massaged, and pinched a little.

She was growing wet, aching with need.

"I can't wait." Her words came out in little pants.

He released her nipple and nuzzled between her breasts. "No?"

She swallowed hard. "Not a second longer."

His hands tightened on her, tilting her hips. The tip of

his penis nudged at her entrance, and she gasped. He caught and held her with his gaze intensely focused as he slowly pushed inside her.

She let out a noise, something. Might have been a word. Really, not.

"You are so tight, feel so good." He groaned. "Hold on, sweetness."

She held on with everything she had, too taken by the pleasure of him filling her to find words. He must have bent his knees. Somehow, he withdrew almost completely and then slid back inside her. He did it again, and again. Every stroke brought him deeper.

He picked up the pace, driving into her harder, until her breasts bounced. He caught one nipple in his mouth, and she dug her fingertips into his shoulders and curled over him as her inner muscles clenched. His mouth let go of her nipple, and he buried his head into the side of her neck as he plunged deeper and deeper inside her, his hands gripping her hips hard.

"Rygard!" She was coming, desperately needed him to come with her.

Her orgasm ripped through her as a coarse cry exploded from him.

A moment later, his hands eased their grip on her. "I need to let you down. Don't think we're going to make it to your bunk."

She could feel the muscles of his torso quivering, could only imagine how he was still standing, much less holding her up too. She unhooked her ankles and tested her own legs as he lowered her.

Trembly, but they'd hold her.

She stumbled with him to her bunk. Took a moment to nab a few wipes to clean themselves up until they had the energy to make it into a shower. He lay down and drew her with him, tucking her in against his side with her head pillowed on his chest. He even reached above their heads and grabbed her light blanket from one of her cubbies, then pulled it over the both of them.

"Rygard?" She whispered his name against his chest, barely able to hear her own voice over the pounding of their heartbeats.

"Hmm?"

"I remembered one of my questions."

Chuckling, he rolled to one side and pulled her in against his chest again. "Ask."

"This thing between us. It's not temporary."

"That's not a question."

"I still need to ask."

The smile faded from his face. She didn't look down, wouldn't turn away from the truth of his answer. Her heart trembled.

He cupped her face with his free hand, his eyes dark and somber. "I'm here, sweetness, with you. Doesn't matter how much distance the next mission puts between us. We're going to make this work."

Relief swept through her, and she wrapped her arms around him, held him tight.

He murmured soft words into her hair. "I know. We don't have to say it out loud. I know."

ACKNOWLEDGMENTS

Thank you to Diana M. Pho and Tara Rayers for your editorial expertise. Your insight and suggestions were invaluable as I revised this series for re-release.

Writing a series is a heck of a project all on its own, re-releasing it is a whole new endeavor, with fresh challenges and lessons to learn. I would have been lost without Katee Robert, Asa Maria Bradley, and Gail Carriger. Thank you so much.

My thanks as well to K Tempest Bradford for the encouragement and support. I've also got to give a shout out here to the Gaming Excuses: Foodie Edition group on Discord for keeping up my morale when I thought I didn't have enough energy to survive this project.

And always, thank you to Matthew for your patience and support.

Finally, thank you to my readers. I hope you enjoy these stories!

Bestselling author Piper J. Drake is best known for her romantic suspense series, the True Heroes, of which the fourth book is acknowledged as a RWA Trailblazer as the first own voices Thai American (Southeast Asian) romance in the USA. Piper is also the author of the Safeguard series (romantic suspense), the Triton Experiment series (science fiction romance), and the London Shifters series (paranormal romance), as well as several standalone novels, short stories, and rpgs. Her new contemporary fantasy series, Mythwoven, launches in April 2023 with Wings Once Cursed & Bound.

Piper is the cohost of the 20 Minute Delay podcast with Gail Carriger, a gamer, foodie, and wanderer. Usually not lost.

You can read more about her work on her website by using the QR code or going to: piperjdrake.com

www.ingramcontent.com/pod-product-compliance
Lightning Source LLC
Chambersburg PA
CBHW050953210726
48287CB00004B/1210